WITH
GENTLY SMILING
JAWS

Terry White

IndePenPress

First published in Great Britain by Indepenpress

All paper used in the printing of this book has been made from
wood grown in managed, sustainable forests.

ISBN13: 978-1905621-91-0

Printed and bound in the UK
Indepenpress is an imprint of Indepenpress Publishing Limited
25 Eastern Place
Brighton
BN2 1GJ

A catalogue record of this book is available from
the British Library

Cover design Juliet White
Jacqueline Abromeit

To Juliet

With thanks to Diana, Corinna, Maureen,
Lyn, Jane and Joanna; and to Terry Darlow
for his support.

How doth the little Crocodile
Improve his shining tail,
And pour the waters of the Nile
On every golden scale

How cheerfully he seems to grin
How neatly spreads his claws,
And welcomes little fishes in
With gently smiling jaws!

Lewis Carroll

CHAPTER ONE

It was nice to be successful - OK maybe that's pushing it a bit but at least I felt successful. Not in the 'multi mega pound' class of the big city you understand but at least in the 'able to carry the mortgage and eat fillet steak now and then category' - and now seemed as good a time as any.

I re-read the fax for the umpteenth time that morning but there it was in black and white, or rather greyish jerky letters on the smooth creamy paper, the Minister had signed the commissioning acceptance and the responsibility had passed from us to them. For a brief moment it felt good to have the load lifted but of course life is not as simple as that. What it did mean, and this was more significant to us, to our wives, families, offspring, ox, ass and stranger within our gates - if that is how you see the bank manager - was that our remaining 20% payment would be released. We would be paid for our labours at last. The Egyptian Ministry of Industry had clutched this money tightly to its collective bosom, like its first suckling child, for the last three years and as a result our relationship with 'The Bank That Likes To Listen' had become a strained monologue. Strained on our part, and a monologue from them asking when they could expect the money 'to restore', as they sarcastically put it, 'the normal banking relationship' whereby we deposited funds with them and not vice versa! Our sub-contract design engineers on the plant equipment and services sides were also feeling the pinch, because on the old established principle of 'when we get paid you get paid', we hadn't, so they hadn't - and their bank managers were putting on the squeeze as well.

The fax sent from Cairo not two hours ago, was signed by our agent Mazin Al Jabril, he of the sharp suits and a mind to match. One thing you could be sure about was that if anybody had done well out of this contract Mazin had, ripping a few percent off here and a few percent off there. Still that was the Middle East and he had oiled wheels and lubricated stiff situations to help the progress of the job on many occasions - so he told us. These days he was the only man we had in Egypt, pushing our paperwork through the vast bureaucracy of the Ministries of Planning, Industry, Finance and Economics with full power of attorney to act on the firm's behalf. The days of the big design office and 50 site staff supervising the construction had long gone once the job was complete. Still, leaving him out there had eventually paid off and now we had the final signature on the final document. I flicked the fax back on to the cluttered desk, Hugo had already seen it, and phoned the bank to forestall the daily inquiring call. Jesus, for the bank that 'likes to listen' you had a job to get a word in when Jenkins started rabbiting on about his 'exposed position'. We were peanuts compared to the bank's South American debt but I bet the sod didn't phone the president of Argentina every day and moan about his exposure. I don't know what the Spanish is for 'stick it up your arse' but I bet Jenkins would have found out soon enough.

Now though the boot was on the other foot, with $2 million winging its way across the world to tap the old debit column like a fairy's wand and transform it to a modest credit, we were in the pound seats. With all the extortionate interest Jenkins had made in the past three years, and his capital back safely tucked up in his strong room, he would be the bank's blue-eyed boy eager to repeat the experience and lend to us again - but next time it would be on much better terms. Oh yes, when any new borrowing was required we had the muscle now to screw down the rate substantially. It would be 'yes Mr Moon, yes Mr Elmes, no Mr Moon, no Mr Elmes, three bags full Mr Moon, three bags full Mr Elmes' and not the snotty 'Look here, Moon, you keep telling me this money is safe - well where is it?' to which I had had no effective reply and he knew it.

I contemplated the concept a moment or two longer rolling the sonorous phrases of my future dealings with him round my mind. Expressions like "Perhaps we should deal with your Chairman, Jenkins - deal with the engine driver not the oily rag" and "We'll give you just one more chance at this Jenkins, and if your rate is not competitive, well..."

I was just savouring the situation when the phone interrupted my thoughts. "Marcus, it's Dan Herlihan for you."

"OK, put him through, Belinda," I said. I was looking forward to this conversation. Dan's firm had had a tough time on the electrical engineering and services design without complaining and had done a top professional job. It was going to be nice to give him the good news - eventually.

"Hi Dan, how goes it?"

"Hi, Marcus, fine thanks, we sent off the last of the operating manuals last week by airmail to Cairo, and Shamsi has confirmed their arrival."

"Yes, well I wanted to have a word with you, Dan, about your firm's performance on this job - particularly on the commissioning side."

I paused whilst he readjusted his thoughts and the initial buoyant tone became wary.

"What's the problem?"

"I have in my hand a piece of paper..." I started to smile - Moon returns triumphant from Munich and the cheering crowds of relieved people at Croydon carry him shoulder high - peace in our time... With some asperity in his voice he interrupted my reverie.

"Marcus, most people have a piece of paper in their hand at some time or other during the day. What they do with it is their affair but if you are going to regale me with your revolting physiological functions I must point out that I do not see what that has to do with our performance."

He had a point, I conceded that, but I continued, unruffled.

"As I was saying, I have in my hand a piece of paper, a fax from the Minister himself about the commissioning." I paused, a little white lie perhaps, just to sharpen his anxieties.

"For Christ's sake do get on with it," cried Dan, "if there's yet something else wrong we will just have to get out there and sort it out."

"It's too late for that," I intoned. "I'll read it to you," which I did:

04/3/97 TO CONDES GROUP

GREETINGS IN ALLAH
HIS EXCELLENCY THE MINISTER OF INDUSTRY SIGNED FINAL
COMMISSIONING CERTIFICATE THIS MORNING AUTHORISING RELEASE
OF FUNDS AND ACCEPTING RESPONSIBILITY FOR OPERATION OF JEBEL
AKHDAR STEELPLANT,
MAZIN AL JABRIL

There was a puzzled silence.

"I don't understand," queried Dan. "What does that mean - or does it mean what I think it means?"

I laughed. "It does indeed, Daniel, we are finished, at long last after five long years of design, construction and commissioning we are finished – clean, clear and complete. And when Mazin presents the commissioning certificate to the bank in Cairo, they will release the money and drinks all round."

"Bloody marvellous, absolutely fantastic," he cried, "but you had me going for a moment there. I thought 'Oh God, yet another problem, yet another visit, yet more expenditure.' It seemed it would never end. When will the funds get here?"

"Well you know banks, because it is a dollar payment they have to transfer the money to Citibank in New York and after they have hung on to it for a few days to accumulate a bit of interest they pass it to London. Ten days to a fortnight I would say."

"Great," he enthused, "I'll phone our bank now, what will you do, transfer our share direct on an inter-bank transfer?"

"I'll give written instructions to the bank that as soon as the funds arrive they are to be distributed that way and that should satisfy everyone."

We agreed to meet for lunch and a little celebration the following week and closed the call.

The euphoria persisted, I still fancied a steak, in that sort of mood it was either a poke or a meal - preferably both - or all three with a meal in the middle, but as it was midday in the office and Belinda had just got engaged to some junior barrister 7 ft tall with a chin that could smash through arctic pack-ice, it would have to be lunch. I wondered what Hugo was doing because he was a bit of a knife and fork artist on his day and we could celebrate.

I slipped on my jacket and, before departing to seek my co-director, looked wistfully round my office. Only the drawing stand and the computer terminal looked new, everything else was tatty. The large veneered chipboard bookcase, stained to look like oak and stuffed with engineering text books, Institution journals, old reports, maps and site investigation logs gave it a cosy feeling - at least to me - but feelings couldn't conceal the worn carpet under the desk where anxious feet had scuffled a hole, or the re-stained desk itself with side table and scuffed plastic chairs. We could not afford to waste money on frivolities - but now...

I set aside thoughts of gleaming Danish stainless steel and leather, or English polished rosewood and hide and passed purposefully through into Belinda's outer sanctum. Her office was much more modern - white units, efficient and businesslike with computer, dictaphone and intercom. I eyed her up speculatively, a slim dark girl, athletic figure but enough in the right places; she was feeding some data into the processor.

"Not wearing the engagement ring today, Bel, I see?" It was an old line but I liked to tease. She gave me a sweet smile - she knew what was coming.

"Yes I am, Marcus - look." She proffered the ring finger of her left hand on which was perched a rather small diamond heavily built up with chips and white gold.

"Just a tick, hang on a moment, I thought I caught a glimpse of a sparkle in there somewhere - yes there we are, if you hold it at that angle to the light you can actually..."

"Marcus - piss off."

"You're worth better than that, Belinda, make the cheapskate buy you a proper ring..."

"Well at least he has bought me a ring," she retorted with an emphasis on the 'he'. I felt a pang of envy then, and maybe a touch of guilt. Belinda and I had had a nice thing going until a few months ago but I didn't want anything permanent at that time and she felt that she was getting left on the shelf at 24 - 24 for heaven's sake, so when the litigious chin had made her an offer she couldn't refuse, she didn't! I was not pleased about that I can tell you, and I didn't regard it as my role in life to strew his path to the altar with rose petals either. I deliberately ignored the implication of her reply and continued. "I should get him down to Hatton Garden smartly to fork out for a diamond that reflects both the extent of his undying passion for you and considerably more light than that one."

"Bye Marcus." She continued smiling but I could see the slight doubt creep into her eyes.

Well, she was worth more. As a PA - excellent, but as a bonking secretary - out of this world - and I knew what fees those barristers charged, so balls to him, he could fork out for some more substantial tangible evidence of his evil desires.

I grinned to myself and walked through the always-open door of my co-director's office. Hugo Elmes was standing, back to the door, gazing out of his window at the winter sunshine reflected in the brown waters of the tidal Thames. A short spare scholarly figure, at fifty, some 20 years older than me, but still filled with youthful enthusiasm for all that he did. He turned when he heard my polite tap on the door as I passed through, his face tanned from his recent skiing trip creased into a smile that stemmed naturally from his dark brown eyes.

"Something of a relief, eh Marcus."

I raised my eyes heavenwards. "You can say that again, I've already had Dan Herlihan on the phone and given him the glad tidings." I slumped my 6 ft 2 into a comfortable armchair in front of the desk. Unlike my rabbit hole, Hugo's office was nicely furnished in polished teak and green leather. We used it for all important client meetings - mine was used for dumping coats - but then he had had it for a long time ever since the days when he was the senior partner of the old partnership and I a mere junior engineer hireling.

The last ten years had seen some great changes in the firm, however I had progressed steadily upwards as some of the older partners retired and other younger ones left to do their own thing. By the time we changed our method of operation from that of a partnership to a more complicated Limited company structure, I had made it to number two. Our old partnership now practiced as the CONDES Group, a name that neatly covered what we did in civil engineering consultancy design. The CONDES Group for all its grandiose title embraced only two companies. A parent company, Bridge Holdings Limited, which held our meagre assets, rented our offices, owned our battered furniture and which, for tax reasons, accumulated our profits or losses; and its subsidiary company, Consultant Design Group, which entered into all the contracts by which we were retained, employed all the staff, including Hugo and I (thank God!) paid all the bills and received all the fees. The whole thing was lumped together and generally referred to as CONDES. Our tax advisers had also recommended that to avoid some future capital gains tax, the parent company should be registered in Jersey and the majority of its shares held by an offshore trust. Accordingly we had arranged for a Jersey advocate to set this up in St Helier, so that it was all legal and above board. However Hugo held 15% personally as I did a 10% share.

I looked at him fondly. "Are you free for lunch? If so I thought I'd treat us to a bottle of champagne and a nice steak down at Luigi's."

He laughed, "Well I was just going to suggest the same to you."

I waited - well I am a Yorkshireman - and so did he - it was his tight-fisted Scottish blood, and then we both burst out laughing. "OK, he grinned, "I'll do the champers and you do the lunch?"

"Right," I responded, "deal done."

Cursing his driver soundly and telling him to wait, Mazin Al Jabril slid out of the cool air-conditioned interior of the Mercedes 500SEL past his bodyguard holding open the door and headed for the main entrance of the National Bank of Egypt 100 metres away. Even though it was February it was still 30° in the shade in the centre of Cairo. The driver had not been able to park right outside the entrance and to have to walk even that short distance irritated him.

"Take me to the manager immediately," he snapped at the young receptionist seated at the desk on the right of the hallway. The bank was hot and teeming with people, messengers shouting, people waving pieces of paper over their heads and everybody else's heads, grubby notes being counted and recounted by grubbier fingers and crowds at every cashier point. There was no way Mazin Al Jabril was going to get involved in that lot.

"Do you have an appointment, sir?" The question was very tentative.

The receptionist was overawed as were most people by Mazin. Nobody knew his early background, but he had arrived in Egypt some 20 years ago and secured a minor post in the Customs department. That had been his making and from there he had progressed to more senior positions in states up and down the gulf, each time pocketing very small percentages of the increasing revenue that passed through his sticky fingers until he was set to launch out on his own as a bona fide businessman. He was tall and well built with a smooth brown arrogant face, a hawkish nose permanently cocked at a supercilious angle, thick salt and pepper hair perfectly coiffured, but the most striking thing about him was his light grey suit. It was immaculate. A perfect fit. Not a crease showed across the shoulders or on the arms, the lapels were pressed flat and the jacket tapered to his slim waist. The trousers were beautifully cut with sharp creases resting neatly on shining

9

Gucci shoes. A cream silk shirt and striped English club silk tie set off the whole ensemble. He looked very important - he also looked even more irritated, he didn't make appointments with bank managers and riff-raff like that unless it suited him.

"Just tell the manager Mazin Al Jabril is here - now," he snapped. His foot tapped angrily on the cracked tiles.

The call was duly made and instantly with profuse apologies for the unfortunate delay and a savage look at the unhappy girl the manager ushered him into his air-conditioned office suite. Respectfully seated personally by the manager in a deep leather armchair round the mother of pearl inlaid coffee table he was offered coffee or tea. He chose the coffee. "Medium," he requested. The manager nodded to the hovering servant. "The same." Whilst they waited for the grounds in the thick black steaming liquid to settle to the bottom of the small cup, idle talk was exchanged as customary. Only during the sipping of the bittersweet mud was it polite to move on to business matters. Mazin Al Jabril moved on to them swiftly, he didn't want there to be any delays that might cause him a problem.

"You have received certified authority from the Ministry of Finance to make a $2 million transfer to one of the companies I represent here - The CONDES Group." It was not a question it was a statement of fact. The manager nodded.

"You will be transferring this to CONDES in the usual way via Citibank New York, I presume?" Again the manager nodded.

"Right," said Mazin decisively. "This is my authority, and written on this paper are my precise instructions. Read them and tell me if there are any problems." He handed the manager a legal document bristling with seals, stamps and signatures, and a plain unheaded piece of paper typed in Arabic. The manager put on his spectacles and examined the documents carefully. Mazin waited.

10

"No, no there do not seem to be any problems," he murmured after a while. "Do you have your passport with you?" Mazin produced a green and gold booklet from his pocket and placed it on the table.

The manager examined it comparing the photograph with the bearer and giving a satisfied grunt.

"You see," explained the manager, "we have to be careful because there is nothing on these two documents," he indicated the two pieces of paper, "to confirm that the Mazin Al Jabril mentioned here is you."

"Don't be a donkey, man," snapped Mazin, "you've known me for 20 years."

The manager gave a weak smile, "Yes that is so but..."

"By Allah, don't waste time, have we finished now?" He reached for the passport to replace it in his pocket but the manager forestalled him. "I must fax the details of your passport to New York - for the same reason, you understand." He was nettled by being called a donkey, so added waspishly, "The Americans have not had the pleasure of your acquaintance for 20 years." He pressed a bell and handed the passport to the eager assistant.

"Photocopy this, Jassim, and bring the lot back to me." Mazin shifted uneasily as his passport was whisked out of sight and remained silent until it reappeared three minutes later. Sliding it away in his pocket with a feeling of relief he briefly shook hands, exchanged final greetings and allowed himself to be ushered down to the front door where his bodyguard was waiting.

Swiss Air flight SR110 from Geneva touched down ten minutes early at Kennedy International Airport. Mazin Al Jabril with two burly companions passed quickly through Immigration and

Customs to the waiting limo. The car drove straight to Citibank, where following a phone call from a Swiss lawyer, an appointment had been arranged with the Executive Vice President Middle East.

The business was transacted quickly, American fashion, not leisurely Middle East fashion. Mazin handed over his passport, the VP checked it against the attested telex and the faxed details from the National Bank of Egypt. He seemed satisfied and held down a button on his intercom whilst cocking an eyebrow at Mazin. "OK, Al, to whom do you want the draft payable?"

Mazin winced at the mutilation of his name. "Just leave it blank and I will deal with that later."

The VP shook his head and grunted. "No can do, Al, we gotta have a name - those are the rules."

This threw Mazin, he hadn't expected that, the VP was waiting impatiently, pen poised.

"Investment and Resource Holdings SA," he blurted out hastily and then cursed silently under his breath. Investment and Resource Holdings was the name of his main holding company, the company that owned and controlled all his other activities, the keystone of what he liked to think was his empire. It was a closely-guarded secret that IRH SA belonged to him, only one person knew that for certain, and that was Mazin; one other person, his Swiss lawyer, believed it to be so but could never swear to it - and now this American had been given a clue. He sucked in a sharp breath of annoyance. By the Holy book he should have given the name of one of the subsidiaries, IRH Panama or Caymans. He cursed to himself again, to change it now would only draw attention to it and the VP was already giving instructions through his intercom. He thought this through very quickly; who would know? Only the VP and the clerk filling in the bank draft. He shrugged to himself - it was of no importance or significance to them, why should it be. The bank would not reveal anything, why should they, it was all perfectly above board as far as they were concerned. The VP confirmed the instructions and three minutes later Mazin Al Jabril was back in his limo with a bank draft for $2 million made payable to Investment and Resource Holdings SA of Geneva in his wallet. Within the bank the transaction was recorded on hard disk of the IBM data storage facility as a small electrical charge hidden amongst billions of other similar miniscule vibrating electrons where it was expected that it would remain un-remarked for evermore.

"Don't forget you're taking Dan Herlihan out to lunch today Marcus, do you want me to book somewhere and what time?"

I clapped my hand to my forehead, "I'd forgotten about that, Bel - yes, book us in at Le Suquet for 1 o'clock and let Dan know - and can you get me Jenkins at the bank on the phone."

My phone rang, I switched it to the loudspeaker.

"Hello Mr Jenkins, how are things in the money markets this morning, booming I trust?"

"Good morning Mr Moon, nicely thank you." The voice was very prim and pursed as though he was being force-fed half a lemon. "What can I do for you?"

"Has our money arrived yet - the $2 million?" There was a short pause presumably whilst he consulted his VDU.

"I regret to say, Mr Moon, that it has not."

I felt disappointed, it was ten days now since Mazin Al Jabril's fax message but money transfers from the Middle East, particularly via American banks, always took time so I thanked him and pressed the button that severed the connection. I sat back tapping my teeth with a pencil. Dan would not be too pleased either, I would have liked to have been the bearer of glad tidings. Still, lunch at Le Suquet was always a treat and Herlihan good company. I would try the bank again on Monday after all the weekend transactions had filtered through.

Nothing had arrived by Monday either and I cursed Citibank. I asked Jenkins if he would chase it up with them in New York but he suggested that a better approach was for me to contact the originator of the transfer, the National Bank of Egypt, and get some dates and reference numbers. He would then be able to pursue it. I got Belinda to type a fax to the National Bank asking for confirmation that the certificate of authority had been received, the money transferred to Citibank for onward transfer to London and for the time, date and reference number of the transaction. It was Thursday before they replied and the message was brief:

$2,000,000 (US dollars two million) transferred to Citibank
New York 08/2/97 Ref INI/2011436/623/14

So at least it was on its way, it was just bloody US bankers holding it up to clock up some interest at our expense. I asked Belinda to get me Mr Jenkins again and gave him the details. He said he would have to go through proper channels and I refrained from comment.

It was 3.30 on Friday afternoon when I got the word. I was never at my best on Friday afternoons but this particular afternoon was a humdinger. Belinda was clearly suffering from PMT and had bitten my head off for pointing out that PMT always made her irritable, and my prospective lunch companion had cancelled at the last minute with some feeble excuse about his workload but I reckoned the swine was off to the golf course because it was a fine day. This had left me with an appetite like a horse and nowhere to go. I had to settle for the travelling sandwich basket brigade at the office who, by the time they got to me had only cheese and pickle or corned beef left. I didn't like either, bought both, ate them hurriedly and now they lay, an indigestible lump, right in the solar plexus.

Then Jenkins phoned.

Hugo had gone home early. He was going to some City Livery function or other and claimed he needed two hours to get into his best bib and tucker to confront the City Fathers over boiled fish and a loving cup. I thought the loving cup would taste bitter to him tonight. There wouldn't be much loving involved after he learned the news I was about to give him. Impatiently I waited until I thought he had had sufficient time to make it to his house in Putney and I dialled his number. I didn't want this going through the switchboard. He answered the phone almost immediately and there was a touch of asperity in his voice.

"Elmes."

"Hugo, it's Marcus."

"Oh hi Marcus, can you make it quick, I have got to be at the Goldsmith's Hall by 6.30." I'd known Hugo many years and one of the things he couldn't abide was flannelling and beating around the bush, so I gave it to him straight.

"Jenkins from the bank has just telephoned..."

"Oh good," said Hugo, "so the money has arrived at last."

"That's just it, Hugo, the money hasn't arrived, in fact it has disappeared from the bank in New York."

"Disappeared, what do you mean disappeared, it can't just disappear."

"Well, according to Jenkins it has done exactly that. Apparently the money was sent from the National Bank of Egypt on the 8th by telex transfer, and was withdrawn from the Citibank account at commencement of business on the following day. You will recall there is a seven-hour time difference between Cairo and New York."

15

"But who withdrew it, Marcus, where has it gone?" The alarm in his voice only reflected the trepidation in my mind.

"That I don't know, Jenkins is looking into it but you will also appreciate that that was over ten days ago and the one thing that is certain is that it has not arrived in our account here."

"Jesus H Christ. I do not like the sound of this one little bit, what else did Jenkins say?"

I cleared my throat. "He wants to see us at the bank at 10.30 on Monday."

There was a pause. "Well I suppose there is nothing we can do between now and then, let us just hope it is some ghastly mistake and by Monday, Jenkins has got to the bottom of it."

"Yeah let's hope so," I murmured. "Have a nice weekend."

I put down the phone. There was no point in panicking yet or creating alarm amongst the people to whom we owed money. I asked Belinda to bring me in the finance file and all the CONDES bank files and set out to prepare a schedule of exactly where we stood financially at this present time. She could obviously sense there was something wrong, fortunately put it down to her earlier irritation with me over the PMT episode and therefore did not question me. I worked late into the night that Friday and when I finally tossed the pen to one side and looked at the credits and debits, the situation - like the policeman's lot - was not a happy one. We owed our co-consultants the best part of £400,000 and the bank just over £700,000, against that I had drawn up a list of our somewhat dubious assets. If you threw in my battered 1952 MG and Hugo's Audi Quattro, a load of second-hand drawing office furniture and the new computer on which we had spent £80,000, the whole lot added up to £180,000. But it would be lucky to fetch £40,000 at a knock down and sell off sale. The only bright side was our 'work in progress' figure, which, excluding the Egyptian Steel work contract, totalled £620,000. That had been written down to the lowest acceptable level for tax purposes, but again it contained two Middle East contracts, which if they suffered the same fate as the Egyptian steelworks contract, would wipe out any benefit there. I sat back in my chair, hands behind my head. There was nothing else I could do at this time and therefore there was not much point in worrying about it. We could start our worrying programme on Monday morning if the news was still bad. I gave a grim smile. The guy who would be doing the most worrying this weekend would be Jenkins. All we stood to lose was everything we'd got and everything we had built up whereas he might lose seniority and suffer a reduced pension. It was not much of a consolation but it was all I had. I looked at my watch, there was just time for a quick pint down at the Frog and Nightgown and there was bound to be one or two friends there who could cheer me up although there was no way I could tell them what the problem was. That had to be a tightly kept secret until we had either a solution or there was no option but to put the company into receivership. I shuddered at the thought, then pulled myself up. Be realistic Marcus, I told myself, it must be a mistake at the bank, the money has obviously been sent somewhere in error, and by now Citibank will have chased it and recovered it and it could well be winging its way across the Atlantic to London - $2 million just doesn't disappear - or does it? And even if it had, the bank had no authority to pay it anywhere else, so, as it was their mistake, they would have to recompense us fully for it.

The Frog was packed to the doors as was usual on a Friday night, but I eased myself through the crowd to our customary corner. Sure enough, there was half a dozen friends and acquaintances wedged in and it was a sure bet what the topics of conversation would be: sex, business in the City, sex, Saturday's Rugby International against Wales and sex again. There were two girls there - a very striking tall blonde girl with quick intelligent eyes whom I had never seen before and a cheerful brunette who was attached to one of the guys who worked in the City. I said "Hi" all round, checked whose glasses were empty which, when they realised what I was doing, amounted to all of them, and squeezed up to the bar laying in the next round of drinks. The blonde girl drank dry Martini. I joined in the conversation in a half-hearted way but I could not put the Citibank problem out of my mind. I suddenly remembered that the guy with the cheerful brunette worked for Citibank in the Aldwych, so I thought I would do a little probing to reassure myself. I waited until an opportune moment and then said, "James, by the way, do banks ever make mistakes?"

"Sure," he said, "why, are you having problems?"

I kept a straight face. These guys are sharp.

"No, not specifically," I replied, "it was just out of general interest, but as an example can the bank take money from your account without your express instructions?"

He frowned a little. "You mean things like bank charges?" I was getting into deep water here, I could see this becoming embarrassing so decided not to pursue it any further.

"Yes, I suppose so," I muttered, then listened whilst he rambled on about whereas the bank didn't have to have specific instructions to levy bank charges, that was part of the standard contract between the depositor and the bank etc etc. I ended up none the wiser except for an acknowledgement that banks do make mistakes, but then so do we all and I knew that anyway. I declined the offer of another drink, said my farewells, noticing as I did so that the blonde girl's eyes held mine for a split second or two - they really were big green intelligent eyes - and made for the door.

Hugo and I took a taxi to the bank on Monday morning, we were both dressed in our best suits, striped shirts, Hugo with his Old Carthusian tie and me with a discreet blue and purple striped tie which looked as though it might be a Guards Regiment, or a distinguished public school, but was in fact Mary Quant. We arrived on the dot at 10.30 and were ushered swiftly through to Jenkins' secretary's office. There we sat for half an hour with nothing to do except twiddle our thumbs or read umpteen pamphlets on what miraculous services the bank could provide which would enrich all our lives. They did not have a pamphlet on bailing out consultant civil engineers who had got themselves stuffed right up a creek. The bank's annual report and accounts were also there and clearly they were making enough money, in spite of their South American debt, not to bat an eyelid at our problems, at least that was how it seemed to me but I did not like this long wait. Hugo was very quiet and kept smoothing down his hair, a sure sign that he was nervous. The door of Jenkins' office opened, and the little stone-faced man beckoned us within. He indicated to two chairs and closed the door gently before taking his place on the other side of his large desk. Good manners prevailed.

"Would you like some coffee or tea?" he asked.

"No thank you," said Hugo.

"Yes please," said I. We both looked at each other.

"OK," said Hugo, "if you're having coffee, I'll have coffee."

"Oh I don't mind," I replied, "I don't mind having tea." We realised that we were displaying our nervousness, not a good thing to do in front of bankers. I turned to Jenkins. "Make it two teas please, Mr Jenkins." He gave the necessary instructions over his intercom and then turned to us spreading both his hands out on the desk, fingers downwards, the banking equivalent of donning the black cap. We braced ourselves.

"I am afraid, gentlemen, that we have had final and irrevocable confirmation that the $2 million was withdrawn legitimately from the Citibank account ten days ago."

"But that can't be," gasped Hugo, "nobody had any authority to withdraw that money. Instructions were given that it should be transferred directly here."

Jenkins looked down examining his fingernails. "Citibank have assured us that they are quite satisfied that the instructions they received were fully authorised, that they did precisely as they were directed to by the National Bank of Egypt, who, in turn were instructed by their client." He looked up at us now with an expression of suspicious distaste on his face. Hell's teeth, I thought, he thinks that we have nicked it. I looked across at Hugo, but he too was looking at me rather strangely.

"Now hang on a minute," I said, "this is as much a mystery to me as it is to you," embracing both of them. I looked at Jenkins. "Did you find out where the money went?" It was the only constructive question I could think of.

He shrugged, "All Citibank would tell us was that they complied with the instructions they were given and they were not at liberty to disclose any more." Whilst we were grappling with this astonishing, interesting but totally non-revealing piece of information, he continued in a nastier tone, "I must also tell you that as a result of this, this bank has felt it incumbent to review your facility with us."

"Look," said Hugo, turning to Jenkins with a pleading note in his voice. "Just give us another 48 hours and let us see if we can get to the bottom of this. We will contact our agent in Cairo and the National Bank of Egypt and see what we can turn up."

Jenkins hesitated, looking at us through narrowed eyes, you could see he was weighing up the alternative of calling in his loan immediately, which would probably leave him with egg all over his face as far as his superiors were concerned, and waiting 48 hours in which case the problem may be resolved.

"Right," he said slowly, "I will give you 48 hours, we meet here at 10.30 on Wednesday morning."

At that moment there was a knock on the door and our tea arrived, so we had to sit there making uncomfortable small talk for a precious five minutes whilst we sipped the scalding brew. It was like asking your executioner how his mother was keeping these days, before he kicked the block into position and hefted the axe.

As soon as we were clear of the bank's environs I turned to Hugo and said, "Look Hugo, I know nothing about this whatsoever. I know that I have been handling the Egyptian steel contract, and that it is my responsibility, but what has happened to this money is much a mystery to me as it is to you."

He gave me a long steady look and then said decisively, "OK, Marcus, let us both get stuck into this and find out what has happened."

Arriving back at the office and ignoring all messages and other calls on our time we both went into Hugo's office to use his two private lines.

"I'll do Mazin Al Jabril," said Hugo, "you do the National Bank."

After some delay I got through to the National Bank of Egypt just before they closed. The manager was too busy to speak to me, which got right up my nose, but I managed to get hold of one of his assistants and sweet-talked him into looking into it. I held on for five minutes until he returned. He confirmed that the money had indeed been sent to Citibank on the date they had advised us. He added that the other instructions were also contained within the same telex.

I frowned. "What other instructions?" I asked.

"The instructions to Citibank to prepare the bank draft for collection by Mr Al Jabril," he replied.

"What?" I gasped. "But the bank had no authority to give any such instruction."

"I'm am sorry, Mr Moon," he said, "but I understand that the instruction came personally from Mr Al Jabril."

"But he had no authority to give any instruction," I shouted, "he is only our agent, he doesn't operate the bank account."

"Mr Moon, Mr Al Jabril produced full power of attorney to act for your firm, which quite clearly covered operation of the bank account."

I went cold all over. "Fucking hell," I muttered to myself and anybody else who was around, I began to see the awful reality of it now. Things began to slot into place with a dreadful certainty.

There was no point in carrying on the conversation further with the National Bank of Egypt. So I thanked the assistant manager for his help and turned to Hugo who was sitting there holding a dead telephone in his hand looking at me. He had obviously, from the half conversation he had overheard, picked up the gist.

"So Al Jabril's got it," he summarised. "I have just spoken to his office or what was his office, to be told that he moved out of there ten days ago." He turned to me with a sad anger in his eyes, I knew what was coming but I didn't really have a complete answer. "How could you be so sodding stupid as to give him full power of attorney to operate our bank account?" he burst out.

"I didn't," I said, trying to inject the calmness into my voice that I certainly didn't feel. "I gave him full power of attorney to act as our agent because that is demanded by the Egyptian Department of Commerce and Industry in order to register and trade in Egypt."

"But didn't you read the power of attorney before you issued it?"

"Yes, of course I did," I cried, "but requirements are that all documentation shall be in Arabic and so the document was drawn up in Arabic and an English translation done." Light dawned and the final piece of the jigsaw fell into position with a determining thud. I said slowly, as if to myself, "And who did the translation... Mazin Al Jabril."

"My God," said Hugo quietly, "we have been well and truly stuffed. The bastard could be anywhere now, we have no chance of getting this money back."

"We could sue him," I ventured.

"Sue? Sue him where, in what court? Egyptian courts? US courts? Even if we managed to get him into court he would claim that he was acting with full authority."

"It doesn't say he has full authority to take 20% of our fee," I ground out savagely. "Two per cent was all he was entitled to under his contract. I'll get out his agency agreement." I slipped into my office and brought back the file containing all our agency agreements. I flicked through it quickly and failed to turn up Mazin Al Jabril's. I went through it again more slowly and again failed to turn it up. Finally I went through it page by page and there was no copy of the agreement there.

"Somebody has taken it out of the file," I said quietly. "Al Jabril was alone in my office for a few minutes when he came to London six months ago, he must have extracted it then."

The final nail in our coffin came next morning with the delivery of an airmail letter from the People's Democratic Republic of South Yemen. It contained two things: a photocopy of our missing agency agreement with Mazin Al Jabril in which the 2% had been changed by the addition of a zero to 20%, and a receipted account from Al Jabril confirming receipt of his 20% commission for the Egyptian steelworks contract in full and final settlement of all outstanding debts.

"That's it," said Hugo with dismal finality. "He's stitched us up well and truly. There is now not a snowflake in hell's chance of getting our money back. No court in the world would give a decision in our favour even if we could get him into court."

I nodded, I had to agree. This was no spur of the moment swindle, he'd planned this all along, right from when he did the translation of the power of attorney. And it had been he who did the Arabic draft in the first place to comply, as he claimed, with the complicated requirements of the Ministry of Commerce.

We sat there looking at each other, neither of us knowing what to do. There was a prolonged silence, the stillness of defeat. Hugo put his head in his hands. "I don't think we can survive this Marcus, I think it'll wipe us out and some of our friends with us. We've had it."

CHAPTER TWO

There was a clunk as Syrian Air's night flight from Damascus locked its undercarriage as it prepared to touch down in the early morning light at London Gatwick.

I eased one foot out of the magazine rack and one elbow from the ashtray and tried to stretch the stiffness out of my bones. The flight up from Abu Dhabi to Damascus had been half empty and so I had been able to extend over two seats, but this flight was packed in 'peasant' class where I was travelling, so sleep had been difficult.

After an hour's wait I collected my battered bag, slung it over my shoulder and passed unhindered through Customs to the Gatwick Express. A quick shave and clean shirt in my flat and I was sliding the MG into my car space at the office by 10.30.

The receptionist greeted me with a smile but when I got to my office Belinda's first words were, "My God, Marcus, you look like shit! Let me get you a strong coffee."

"Thanks, Bel. Two sugars today please."

"Oh! By the way, Mr Elmes is out at a meeting but he left a message to say can you join him and Brian in the Frog and Nightgown at 12.30?"

That was a bit odd, I thought, normally Hugo and Brian wanted a rundown of my overseas visits, but the meeting was usually held in Hugo's office.

"Yeah, OK, I'll be there," I told her. "Do you know what it's about?"

"No, but Brian and Mr Elmes have gone to the bank for their meeting."

Christ, I thought, not more bloody trouble. I thought we were doing well under the circumstances.

"They seemed quite cheerful," she added.

"Well that was something, I always had a feeling of foreboding when meetings were called at the bank.

I emptied my briefcase on to the desk and surveyed its contents: mainly contract documents full of 'hereinafters' and 'wherein-befores' and silver foil packets of pills. I felt more like a medical lawyer than an engineer. Belinda brought in my sweet coffee and asked, "So how was the trip?"

I grinned ruefully. "From a business point of view - excellent, all the projects are on time and on cost. There's some new design work for us and fees are being paid - late, but at least we're getting them."

I picked at a mosquito bite on my wrist. "From a health and safety point of view - my health and safety - the usual!"

She smiled sympathetically and drifted back to her domain. I finished drafting out my report for Belinda to print and at 12.20 wandered out in the direction of the pub. My timing was good because as I arrived at the door Hugo and Brian arrived simultaneously from the opposite direction.

"God, you look like shit," said Hugo as he ushered me through the door, "what is it this time, the dreaded Rashid's revenge?"

This was getting a bit wearing. I was starting to get a complex about my looks. Perhaps I was metamorphosing into some alien creature.

I studied them back and they both looked perky enough. So the meeting at the bank can't have been too bad. In fact they appeared positively chirpy, even Brian not noted for his excitable nature seemed to be having difficulty containing himself.

I said nothing until we were tucked in our regular corner of the bar with a pint glass of Ruddles real ale apiece standing three quarters full in front of us.

"OK you two, what are you up to?"

Hugo looked at Brian expectantly. "Go on, tell him Brian, to some extent it is your baby."

I looked at Brian's serious pale face, flanked by lank dark hair. It was very easy to misjudge Brian Mason, he appeared a rather drab, slightly stooped insignificant figure in his Burton suits and quiet dull ties, but those belied a very determined nature and clothed a man with a strong sense of loyalty. Over the past two long dreadful years, I had grown to like and respect Brian Mason, after a somewhat traumatic start. Brian was the man put in by the bank to oversee and control all our financial activities. Not a cheque could be signed, a payment made, a contract entered into, fee rendered or salary increased without Brian's say so. He had been an absolute bastard to start with, even querying such small items of expenditure as 25p for a mop to wash the inside of the tea mugs in the staff kitchen. It had been a bloody hard unremitting grind for the last two years, but there is no doubt that we were definitely pulling the business round and only last week, we had secured our second decent sized World Bank project to design as principal project engineers, a new aluminium smelter in the Middle East.

I still recalled with horror our Wednesday meeting two years ago with Jenkins of the bank at his office. Was it as long ago as that? Jenkins had been flanked by two of his business development director colleagues when Hugo and I turned up besuited and betied as before. It was just like a court martial. Jenkins still clearly believed that somehow we had spirited the money away and had begun the meeting by stating that the bank was instantly cancelling all our facilities, they were immediately calling in the outstanding loan which amounted to...and one of his colleagues passed him a piece of paper - £827,364.95 which was attracting interest at the rate of...again another bit of paper was passed, 9.5% and what were we going to do about it. Before we could say, "Nothing", he said: "And if the answer is nothing, we shall immediately put in the receivers and liquidate the business."

Hugo is the tactful one in our company and so I left it to Hugo to do the pleadings and I must say, he was good. He told them the full story from beginning to end, he presented them with the schedules I had prepared showing the value of our assets, together with the value of our work in progress, this he confirmed by referring them to our annual accounts and he pleaded that if the bank only gave us time, continued to support our business, we should be able to pay off our debt to the bank within five years.

Jenkins was totally unmoved, and in fact hinted that as there was a strong suspicion of fraud in this case, then the bank was considering going after all our personal assets as well as the company's. Although this would be serious for me, it was devastating for Hugo. He had a wife, a home, three children - all being educated at private schools - and the firm was his whole life. It would have killed him. I stood there watching his face go white and his shoulders slump like a beaten man. It really pissed me off no end that the bloody bank could do this to a man who had never done a dishonest thing in his whole life. A man who was a fine and clever engineer, who always put his clients and staff first and did the very best he could for them, and I decided that I was not going to stand for it. One thing about being right down on the floor is that there is nowhere lower to go, so you can say what you like and do what you like and they can't do any more to you. We had always played it straight with the bank, not asked for or been offered any favours, and over the years they had made a lot of money out of our business. Now, when the relationship was being put to the test, they were bolting for cover down the first funk hole. Bloody typical!

I felt a cold rage building up inside me as I listened to Jenkins disdainfully brush Hugo's reasonable explanation aside. I stood up slowly and leant over the table so that my nose was about 20cm from his. He recoiled in alarm, it was the first time I had seen a flicker of fear on his stone face. That encouraged me to continue.

"Let me spell it out to you quite clearly, Mr Jenkins. Mr Elmes is far too much of a gentleman to lay it precisely on the line so let me do that so that there is no misunderstanding.

"You put this company into receivership and you will get nothing. Not a bean. And do you know why? No, of course you don't, so I'll tell you why. Because the assets people like you only consider and put a value on are the tangible ones; the bits you can seize and sell. However in our case these consist of a load of second-hand furniture and a few computers and printers. The real assets of the business are here in front of you and in the people whom we employ. The name Hugo Elmes is worth 50 times as much to the business as the figures in the balance sheet assets column for a load of junk that wouldn't fetch £500 in the knackers yard!"

I just hoped that Hugo would take this as a compliment, it was meant as such but I hadn't time to consider the niceties.

I continued whilst I had Jenkins on the back foot. "And as soon as any of our clients hear that we have been put into receivership, and Hugo is no longer in charge, they will withdraw or cancel their work as they are entitled to do under the contracts. The overseas clients will not even pay for the work in hand - work that has been done - and will challenge you to sue them for it in their courts - and you know how far you'll get with that!"

Jenkins blinked and the other two shuffled uncomfortably in their seats. Obviously they hadn't thought this through. I pressed on.

"So to summarise: put us into receivership and you will get fuck all but a load of trouble. Continue to support us and we will pay off any overdraft within five years." I leant over closer to Jenkins. "Have I made myself clear?"

From the expression of alarm that flickered across his face I obviously had. He hastily slid his chair back further out of reach, anticipating the next phase of this frank and free discussion might well come up as a fat nose.

I eased back a little and continued. "However, this company has a first-class reputation with governments, private clients and the World Bank which, provided the senior people can be motivated, will continue to produce an increasing amount of work and an increasing amount of profit. You have seen our accounts for the past five years and seen how the company has grown. OK, so we have had a major setback here, because of the dishonesty of one corrupt gentleman, but that does not mean that the rest of our clients and associates in the Middle East barrel are rotten, in fact far from it. If you continue to support this company both Hugo and I guarantee to put our every waking hour into building it up and repaying you."

I sat down and looked round at the three of them and then said quietly, "On the other hand, if you will not support it, then you can go and screw yourselves, because we will wash our hands of the entire business leaving you to sort out the whole mess and the consequent litigation that will follow!"

They hadn't thought of that, and in truth, neither had I before, but it was a good line to throw in because banks hate the idea of being sued; bad publicity, and this would be an area outside their normal expertise.

So, before they could respond, I stood up and took Hugo's arm. "Good afternoon gentlemen," I bade them, and dragged him out of the door still bemused and silent.

We had called at the nearest pub and sank a double brandy each, which restored some of the colour to his cheeks and tightened up my bowels.

"Well Marcus, you certainly seem to have a way with words," he had said, "I'm not sure that telling our bankers to go forth and multiply is a way through to their hearts and minds though."

He was right really; I could have blown it well and truly. But there again there was no point messing about, we had put all the cards on the table, they now knew the score so there would be no misunderstandings - at least not on our part - and the two business development directors should be sufficient realists to carry the message up to the higher echelons of the bank whatever Jenkins thought. Hugo still looked very depressed.

"I suppose we must wait and see what happens, although I don't hold out much hope."

"Hugo," I responded, "we are not going to wait and see anything, you are going to take your Old Carthusian tie and your masonic handshake, go into the City and get around all your banking friends and other contacts and plead our case. Two directors of this bank are OC's so make a start with them, but contact the other friends as well because it may well be another bank will support us, so get cracking. I'll keep the firm running."

He did and I did.

Ten days later we were summoned back to the bank again, this time there were four people from the bank. The three previous attendees and Brian Mason. The unrelenting Jenkins had obviously had his arm twisted because through gritted teeth he told us that the bank had reluctantly agreed to support us, but that they would lay down very strict conditions for so doing. Brian Mason was to be put into our company, we to bear all his salary and costs and he would have complete and sole financial discretion about every single aspect of our activities.

We agreed. We would have agreed to almost anything at that time to save the consultancy, and by the time the lawyers had finished with us we had been trussed up financially like a Christmas turkey with Brian Mason as the stuffing. I had disliked him. At times I hated his guts. He cut salaries, there was no business entertaining, every single item of expenditure was examined and pruned if unnecessary, and for six months we lived in hell. But Brian also proved himself constructive as well as destructive and provided us with excellent advice in the drafting of the financial terms of contracts which enabled us to both make money out of exchange rates as well as the contract itself. It also enabled us to insure ourselves against any unforeseen losses and consequently borrow against the contracts. This in turn helped our cash flow and the expansion of the business. Notwithstanding that however, it had been a painful and salutary experience. Hugo and I had flown the world in bucket shop seats on antiquated aircraft to pestilential places. We had stayed in cockroach-infested cheap hotels, eaten revolting food and sweated in numerous un-airconditioned waiting rooms. But we had dug out the business. My insides had had so much Lomotil blocker and my anatomy so many jabs for typhus, tetanus, yellow fever, cholera, hepatitis, malaria, bubonic plague and every other virus, bacterial infection, contagion and miasma going that I was permanently constipated, sore and fevered. Every single item of expenditure had to be accounted for and any that could not came out of our own pockets. The rows were frequent and furious but the bank had us by the balls so there was no way we could win. It was a tough unremitting miserable grind.

In all that time, most of it spent in the Middle East, I had not once come across Mazin Al Jabril. I heard of him. Rumour had it that he had bought himself pads in New York or London or Monaco or Paris or any of the other fleshpots of the Western world, but he was never where I happened to be - or if he was he was keeping well out of sight.

I wanted to meet him, I really did. I don't know what I would have done if I had - not much probably in the event - but at least I would have had the satisfaction of telling him just what I thought about him, and I may have been able to get in one good punch before they threw me in the slammer! I jest; well half jest, it was a comforting thought even if unrealistic. Having him laid out in the road and slowly flattened by a road roller from the feet up was more comforting. But the best I could come up with as I lay scratching my bites, sweating and sleepless in my non-airconditioned flea pit in Mahmoud's Golden Palace Hotel, was having him staked out over a fire ants' nest, naked and covered in honey!

Brian Mason might be a bastard but he was doing his job, Mazin Al Jabril was just a bastard.

Time is a great healer and my rancour had gradually been replaced over the past two years by an increasing satisfaction that our efforts, and that included our dedicated and loyal staff plus Brian, had slowly pulled us up by our boot laces from seriously deep shit. Last year's accounts had shown a reasonable profit compared with the thumping loss of the previous year, and indeed if one ignored that loss, then over the last five years we had an impressive rate of growth. This year's draft accounts were due anytime now. Was this what the suppressed excitement was about? I studied Brian carefully, he was not a man who displayed his emotions at all except in the most extreme circumstances when he either cleared his throat disapprovingly or nodded. Excitement could be injurious to his health, I thought. Then for one moment it looked as if it had been, he seemed to be having some kind of seizure. I shot a startled glace at Hugo but he was smiling still - and then I got it, Brian Mason was laughing.

"Strewth Brian, you gave me quite a turn then. What's so funny that it's provoked even you into venturing into new territory?"

He spluttered along for a few more seconds and then coughed out, "It's not funny Marcus, it's a miracle. I'm laughing because I'm happy."

It wasn't the accounts then, the constant strain of the daily grind struggling to make ends meet, robbing Peter to pay Paul and watching every penny had finally broken him, still better him than me although it had been touch and go at one point.

"Happy, Brian? Happy?" I looked at Hugo, "Can you remember what happiness was, Hugo. Happy? I seem to have a vague recollection in the dim distant past beyond the aeons of time what..."

"Shut up Marcus and just listen," cut in Hugo. "Go on, tell him Brian."

Brian paused. "We have wiped out our overdraft," he proclaimed. "This last fee payment from the EU has put us into credit."

It took time to sink in, we had been aiming to pay off the bank in four to five years, to have done it in two was indeed a miracle. I couldn't believe it. A favourable set of draft accounts showing a continued improvement in the business would have been one thing - and that alone would have merited rejoicing, but to wipe out our OD - that was unbelievable.

"What about working capital etc etc?" I ventured questioningly.

Brian shook his head. "I have allowed for that, with our guaranteed insured future fee income we shall fluctuate into and out of the red for the next two to three months and after that we will operate in the black."

"And new work?" I queried.

"That can be handled on a contract to contract basis, the bank will give us the facility."

"Hmm," I murmured more to myself than anyone, still in shock.

Now there were three things about this conversation that I liked including the obvious one that we were out of hock. I liked Brian's use of the word 'we' instead of 'you', and I liked the idea that Brian must have negotiated with Jenkins, with his own bank in fact, to obtain us a new facility. Brian could well have his career prospects enhanced by a permanent move as a result of this, I thought. I looked at Hugo and smiled. We were both thinking along the same lines.

"Right," said Hugo, "I think that the firm can now run to a bottle of champagne for a double celebration!"

Brian looked puzzled. "I can understand celebrating getting the bank off our backs but what is the other occasion?"

"The other occasion, my dear Brian, is to offer you the position as finance director of CONDES with a profit share. The detail we can sort out later."

He gulped and blushed. "But I thought you didn't like me very much!"

I cut in. "Brian, it is you, as much as anybody, who has pulled this firm up from the pit. Alright, you're a tough, miserable bastard but we want you as our tough, miserable bastard." I grinned at him. "So what do you say?"

"Well, if you put it like that how can I refuse?"

CHAPTER THREE

The brief for the new Sharjah steel plant ran to over 400 pages in three separate sections, it was a typical World Bank project document put together by bureaucrats using ten words where one would suffice trying to tie up tightly every nut, bolt and nail and leaving holes right in the kernel you could drive a team of lawyers through - if you wished to. It had taken me the best part of the week to read the first two sections on 'Demography, Transport and Infrastructure' followed by 'Buildings'. I was just starting on 'Plant and Equipment' with red eyes and stultified brain when I became aware of Hugo standing in front of my desk. He had that ability to shimmer into and out of rooms without disturbance and it was always, as now, disconcerting. What was even more disconcerting was the look on his face. It was a cross between the look of a father about to deliver judgement on the boyfriend caught with his hand inside his daughter's knickers and the look on the boyfriend's face having been so caught. His mouth gasped and he was swallowing hard.

"Let me guess, Hugo," I murmured, "it's a codfish."

This seemed to restore some balance and he closed his mouth momentarily.

"What is?"

"Your impression," I said, "and it's very good, should go down well at the Worshipful Company of Fishmongers' annual smoker."

He ignored my observation but it had at least enabled him to gather himself together to say whatever it was he was going to say. I put down my marker pen and waited. Hugo began to lower himself into one of my battered chairs but changed his mind and commenced wandering about. I hoped that whatever was coming wouldn't take too long, I doubted if the carpet could stand much strolling, it was held together by drafting tape in more than a few places. Hugo cleared his throat. "Now look here, Marcus, I know you, and you mustn't go off the deep end at what I have to tell you - discuss with you rather. You have got to take a business-like view, think professionally, and if you - we, decided certain things then any decisions we take must purely be on the basis of rational logical argument. I don't think we should just say no - or yes, on entirely emotional grounds without weighing up the advantages and disadvantages of what is, has been, could be, proposed to us. Do you understand?"

"No," I said.

He looked disappointed. "Is that a no saying that you will go off the deep end or a no that you don't think we should evaluate logical argument?"

I smiled; Hugo trying to be tactful and soften me up was always worth a few minutes of entertainment. I glanced at the carpet; it seemed to be holding together reasonably well so maybe I could run this a little further.

"That no is a no which means I don't understand," I replied.

He looked at me again nervously. "I thought I'd made it perfectly clear," he complained.

I leaned back in my chair. "Hugo, if you could get to the point then it would be even clearer and even a dimwit like me may be able to grasp what you are trying to put over."

He frowned. "I'm not sure that I am too happy about your selection of words there," he said. "I'm not trying to put anything over anybody, I just want to discuss something that has come up this afternoon and it's a bit tricky."

"What's it about, Hugo?"

I thought that if I could get him to approach the matter indirectly it may make it easier. He didn't seem upset or distressed, it obviously wasn't too serious, maybe he had been caught with his hand somewhere it shouldn't have been. I reviewed the possibilities. Not his wife - unless of course it was in Tesco - a grope in the grocers. But so what, that wasn't exactly a crime like shoplifting. Janet, his secretary? He'd asked me if he could give her a rise - perhaps that is what he meant. Anyhow that was fine by me provided it kept the company's wage bill down. Maybe we could get Hugo to go round all the girls. Ms Herring in accounts would be a real test. To get past her hairy chin and Harris tweeds for the sake of £500 per year would be dedication to the Brian Mason creed indeed. I heard him clear his throat again and found he was looking at me with a puzzled expression on his face.

"Are you alright?" he enquired solicitously. "You seem a bit vacant."

"No, no fine." I said, "but carry on. You were about to tell me what it is that has brought you to my humble office this fine autumn morn," I prompted.

"That," he said, gesturing towards the World Bank's massive brief for the Sharjah Steel plant.

"What about it? I've nearly finished the first analysis, it's one hell of a big job. Do you know that if they do phases two and three it could cost up to half a billion dollars? That's $20 million in design fees alone."

Hugo scratched his chin, "What do you think our chances are?" he enquired.

"I think they are excellent," I replied, "we have already got our systems set up for the aluminium smelter which the

World Bank has approved, so we should have an edge over our competitors."

Hugo leant over the desk, his knuckles pressing hard on the surface. "But what if we could have an even sharper edge," he asked, looking me straight in the eye.

I began to have a funny feeling. "Go on Hugo," I said, grimly returning his look and fixing his gaze. He couldn't back off now, it had to come and it did.

"I've had a phone call from an old, er, contact of ours who is in a position to do a lot for us. He is very well connected with..."

I interrupted, "Who Hugo?"

"Let me finish Marcus..."

"Who Hugo?" I held his eyes.

"Mazin Al Jabril."

"No!" I said forcefully.

"There you are Marcus," he burst out, "I knew you'd go off the deep end without considering the position, I just knew it."

"What is there to consider?" I exploded, "the man's a bloody crook. He's ripped us off to the tune of $2 million, he damn near ruined us, he has ruined three other consultants, friends and colleagues of ours and thanks to that bastard we've had two years of hell, sweat and tears to get this firm back on its feet and you want to give him another shot at the title?"

"No I don't," cried Hugo making calming motions, flapping his hands up and down. If this was his chicken impression I didn't think it a patch on his codfish. It would not result in a standing acclamation at the Poulterer's Dinner and I told him so. He ignored that as well.

"Just listen, Marcus, that's all I ask, and then when you've heard what I have to say, you decide."

"I can decide?" I stressed the 'I'.

"Yes, you can decide," he agreed.

"OK, shoot."

I sat back with anger rising but prepared to listen to Hugo's tale for in spite of my teasing Hugo was not a devious man, neither was he short of common sense, and if he felt there was some mileage in an idea there usually was - but not always!

"As you know to get a World Bank job you have to be registered with the World Bank." I nodded and he continued.

"If a country wishes to develop an industry it puts up its feasibility study to the WB and applies for the funds to execute it. If the World Bank approves the project after carrying out its own studies, it will put to the recipient country a list of suitably qualified and experienced consultants who can design such a project. Then, once the list has been approved or modified by the recipient country, the World Bank, acting as agent for the country, invites bids from the final list for the design of the project, analyses these and recommends to the government of the country which bid to accept."

I knew all this, it was standard stuff. "So?" I said.

"So," said Hugo, "Mazin Al Jabril has seen our name on the list of five consultants put to the Sharjah government by the World Bank."

I began to have a nasty suspicion - if Al Jabril had seen the list, which was very confidential, he must have some pretty highly placed contact in the Ministry of Industrial Development in Sharjah. He could be in a position to get us crossed off. Hugo continued.

"He phoned me this afternoon to tell me this and to suggest that were we to employ him as our agent in Sharjah he could virtually guarantee that we got the project."

"Oh yes," I scoffed, "and how much up front does he want for this 'guarantee'. Two million dollars? You know as well as I do, Hugo, that nobody can guarantee a World Bank project.

The man's got a bloody nerve I'll grant you that. Thanks but no thanks!"

Hugo held up his hand. "There's more, don't be too hasty. He doesn't want anything up front and don't forget for World Bank jobs they pay us direct - there's no way he can get his hands on our money at any time. He wants to negotiate an agency agreement as soon as possible, the percentage was not discussed, and in return he will guarantee to have the number of bidders reduced from five to three, knocking out the Germans and the Japanese who would be our keenest competitors. Also, as long as our bid is near the other two he guarantees that we will get the job."

"I can't possibly see how he can guarantee that," I retorted.

"His brother is the Minister of Industrial Development in Sharjah," said Hugo quietly.

"God help us," was all I could say.

I was still not sold on this at all. Once bitten, particularly by a very venomous snake, twice or three times shy. It was all very well for Hugo to say that we would be paid direct by World Bank but Mazin Al Jabril was a very smart cookie and I would not now trust him one inch. Besides he had taken us very severely once, why the hell should we help him make another fortune on our backs, because that was what it was about really. Mazin was not proposing this for our benefit, it was not a retarded attack of conscience trying to set previous wrongs to rights. No way, he was in it for one thing only - him! And he would climb aboard the most likely gravy train that would ultimately benefit him. Why had he come to us and not to the Americans or the Germans or the Indians? He must either think we stood the best chance, or the others were already fixed up with agents. I knew that at least

41

three of the companies including the Japs and the Germans had already done work in Sharjah so they must have agents. It still seemed strange, Mazin Al Jabril never did anything without a good reason and, with his brother the Minister, he was in the front row stalls. Not 100% guarantee, there would be other powerful local influences lobbying for this job but the Minister held the advantage because everything had to pass through him and he could block it, change it, distort it or whatever. From our point of view that could be either good news or bad news. My inclination was to kick the bastard into touch forthwith but, to mollify Hugo a little, I told him I would go home and sleep on it. He seemed satisfied with that and shimmered back to his office - perhaps to give Janet her rise?

Tonight, as most Monday nights, was my squash night with Jamie Swallow and it was whilst coaxing the ancient MG through the rush hour traffic towards Hammersmith using half the brain to keep the car moving that the other half, turning over the afternoon's events, threw up the vague glimmerings of an idea.

Jamie was already at the club when I strode into the changing room. There he was stripped off ready in sparkling white kit doing his warming up exercises. Big thighs and biceps pumping up and down as he did his push-ups, cheerful face gleaming with health under a shock of dark hair. He even had creases down the front of his shorts.

"Hi Marcus, feeling fit as a ferret tonight, you're really going to get a game you'll know you've been in."

I nodded and tipped my Adidas bag onto the bench. The smell was awful. There was something green and malodorous filming the sweatshirt, shorts and towel, now lying in a pulsating pile like some vast culture dish, I really must remember to take my kit down to the launderette sometime. I didn't actually fancy putting any of the gear on but there was no option, it was all I had and I cursed my forgetfulness for leaving it in the bag all week. Jamie poked it contemptuously with the end of his racket.

"Having to resort to chemical warfare then?" he sniffed.

I grinned. "It's OK for you, Swally, your plump little box of fun turns you out like an advert for New Dazzling Persil, folks like me have other responsibilities carrying British industry on our shoulders." I noticed the Citibank logo on his sweatshirt and it reminded me of what I wanted to ask him.

"James, does the bank keep records of all your transactions worldwide?"

"We do," he replied. "Why do you want to know?"

"How far back would these records stretch?" I continued.

He scratched his head. "I dunno, ten, twenty years, maybe longer."

"Do all the branches of Citibank do the same?"

"As far as I know, at least all the branches I've worked in did. Why, what's this about Marcus, are you having problems again?" He looked concerned. The circumstances of our encounter and defeat at the hands of Mazin Al Jabril were widely known now amongst friends and the financial world. The initial distancing from failure that occurred when we looked to be about to go under had been replaced by sympathy and cautious support when we demonstrated that we had no intention of doing so.

"No James, it's really to tie up the previous problem that I wanted to ask your help."

He looked wary, bankers always do when you ask them for something nebulous outright. A sort of bland blankness passes over their faces, a look that is trying both at the same time to be totally non-committal and intelligently interested in case it could be a good deal. They don't want to put you off too early.

"What can I do, I thought you were over that now and it was water under the bridge?"

I managed to struggle into my algae-coated shirt and rubbed off some of the worst patches with the equally mildew covered towel. I would solve the towel problem when it came to having a shower after the match. Ugh, when wearing it the smell was worse - the thing to do was to keep moving to keep a constant current of fresh air passing over the revolting garments. I jogged up and down pretending that I was warming up whilst I decided how to put my request.

"Yes we are," I said, "and as I mentioned before, it is really just to tie up a loose end that has been nagging me." I continued. "When Citibank New York gave this guy the bank draft then presumably they kept a record of the transaction?"

Jamie nodded. "Yeah, I would think so."

"Do you think you could find out for me to whom the draft was made payable?"

I stopped jogging and waited while he thought this one out. When he replied it was more as if he was talking to himself.

"We wouldn't have a record in London, and New York might think it peculiar if I asked for it through Communications. I don't think I could call it up direct on my screen because I do not have the access code." My heart began to sink but then he brightened. "I know what, I'm going to New York next week Marcus, I'll see what I can do there. I don't see this as a problem for the bank, it was your account so morally we wouldn't be breaking confidentiality."

I liked that; I liked it when bankers started talking about morals. It was unfamiliar ground to most of them and they usually ended up floundering helplessly in a bog of their own ignorance. I smiled nicely, which was difficult with the stench that had gathered during my brief period of immobility, thanked him and looked forward to hearing from him, and then stuffed him 15-4, 15-3.

After we had showered and changed, I had had to use my mouldy towel with whatever pestilence it might have contained, we nipped out for a quick pint at the Frog and Nightgown. Jamie's chubby cheerful girlfriend was waiting there with three of four other people we knew. As we came into the bar they waved us across. I paused to order Jamie a pint of lager and myself a bitter. There was one other girl in the group standing with her back to me that I didn't recognise. She was wearing tight fitting cream corduroys and a black jacket. The trousers showed a very nicely rounded bottom and long legs. Her hair hung down her back and was tied with a black ribbon at the nape of the neck. From the back at any rate she looked interesting - mind you that often happens and a full frontal results in disappointment. I brought our drinks across and greeted them. "Evening all."

Andy King-Knight said, "I don't thing you've met Kate before."

I turned to face the blonde girl as she turned to me. My heart leaped - good although the back was, the front was something special.

"No I don't think I have," I said as we shook hands, and then something about her face stirred my memory. I had a long careful look to see if I could remember what it was. This provoked a coarse laugh from Jamie Swallow and King-Knight moved hastily forward in a proprietorial sort of way. The girl flushed slightly under my scrutiny and I drew back hurriedly.

"I'm sorry," I stammered, "I didn't mean to be rude, but I'm sure we have met somewhere before." It was an old and corny line and I expected a standard put down, but she smiled showing white even teeth.

"We have," she said. "Here - about two years ago."

I pounded my fist on the bar. "That's right, you drink dry Martinis, I remember your eyes. They've stayed with me ever since like the Cheshire cat's smile."

"Oh, so you're an 'Alice' fan, are you?" she enquired, ignoring my feeble attempt at a compliment.

I was even more surprised - it was only cognoscenti that referred to Lewis Carroll's books and poems under the all-embracing title 'Alice'.

"I am indeed. 'Alice' was standard reading for all mathematicians at my school and I've never forgotten it."

She nodded slowly in mutual agreement. "Me too," she said, "and where did you go to school?"

"York, I spent my formative years in York."

She looked slightly disappointed. "Well, we do not have that in common, my parents travelled a lot so I was educated in many odd places but York was not amongst them."

"'The sun was shining on the sea, shining with all his might, and this was odd, because it was, the middle of the night'," I quoted.

She laughed again. "*The Walrus and the Carpenter*," she said, "but you missed out the middle two lines."

I laughed as well. "OK," I replied.

"'Di dum di dum di dum, di dum di dum di dum.'"

"No I think there's a di dum extra," she chuckled, tapping her fingers on the bar, long slim fingers - without anything around the third one on her left hand I noticed - as she repeated the cadence of the verse.

Now you will appreciate that all this sounds like just so much drivel, it clearly does nothing to push forward the frontiers of science or further the eradication of human suffering but I have to tell you that it was making me happy.

Since our Al Jabril experience all my waking hours had been spent restoring the fortunes of CONDES. As a result my personal life had suffered severely and my love life was all but extinct. The two or three girlfriends I had had, had soon quit when they realised that they were relegated to second place in my affairs after work and I suppose one couldn't blame them. Four months was the longest anyone had lasted and she left when I appeared covered in mosquito bites, sand fly bites and prickly heat rashes. She had recoiled saying how could she tell if herpes or worse was not concealed somewhere amongst the scaly purple patches and fiery red lumps. Belinda had married her lawyer but had been good for a friendly bonk or two in passing when the mood took her. The 'brief' had put paid to that by making her pregnant - at least I hoped it was him. Still we were both tall, brown-haired and blue-eyed so maybe it didn't matter that much. I couldn't wait to see what the baby would look like though, due any time now. I became conscious of Andy King-Knight slowly inserting himself between Kate and me, a determined look forming on his well-scrubbed pink face as he tried to ease a wide enough gap between us for him to be comfortable in. He had a problem though, he was only 5 ft 4 and as I was 6 ft 2 and Kate about 6 ft and as neither of us moved back he ended up with his nose pressed firmly into my chest and his back against Kate. From this position he could neither speak nor drink and we carried on our conversation over the top of his head.

"So where have you been the last two years," I enquired. "I've not seen you in here since or I would have most certainly remembered."

She raised an eyebrow. "Would you? Well I got a job in Switzerland for six months and since I got back I haven't been out that much." She wrinkled her nose and gave a couple of tentative sniffs as if scenting the air.

"And now?" I asked, wondering if King-Knight had just dropped a crafty one to try to separate us.

"And now I work for him." She pointed downwards at the top of King-Knight's head. "I'm a property negotiator with Andrew." Again she sniffed.

"Have you noticed," I murmured, "how when men are going bald their parting gets lower and lower and the strands of hair plastered across their balding pate get thinner and thinner." King-Knight stirred.

"Take Andy for instance," and I began to pick strands of hair from his head, which did actually show signs of thinning. "Now it is said in some circles that baldness is a sign of virility but that is not always true you know."

"Is that so," she smiled.

"Yes indeed it is. I can tell you on the best authority that Andrew here has great difficulty getting it up these days, don't you, son?" I gave him a hug which effectively stopped him from moving.

"What do you think of sex between a man and a woman?" I asked her conversationally. Her eyes widened slightly at this seemingly rather sudden jump from the frivolities to direct involvement in one of life's most essential but more discreet activities. But before she could respond I continued. "That's how Andrew likes his, as you can tell." I patted him paternally on the top of his head. "But he's very particular which man and woman he's between."

"Whatever turns him on," she responded with a grin. I squeezed him more tightly to me as he began to struggle and a smothered gasp of indignation emerged from around my thorax area.

"Estate agents are particularly prone to this," I continued. "It stems from their disgusting habits of playing with themselves instead of getting involved in team games when at school."

"I'm an estate agent," she reminded me with a frown.

"Present company excepted," I nodded graciously, relaxing my grip for a second which allowed Andy to wriggle out and escape my embrace. His face was now bright red and he was highly indignant.

"God strewth, Marcus, what are you wearing, you smell like something at the bottom of a very old compost heap."

The others in my vicinity were also beginning to test the air as well and it didn't take me long to realise that all this olfactory radar was slowly zeroing in on the source of emission - me. Under the pretext of reaching for my drink I discreetly had a sniff at my shirt. Oh Lord, there was no doubt, the noxious odour of decomposition and decay wafted from the open neck. I risked an apprehensive glance at Kate, the distance between us had definitely increased. She returned my glance with a faint frown. Jamie, still sore from his stuffing at squash and a friend not noted for his discretion, at least not now, burst out laughing.

"It's his squash kit," he spluttered, "you should see it, straight from the primeval swamp. The only way he can win is to asphyxiate you first." He began to elaborate enthusiastically, and without any defence, coupled with the warmth of the pub beginning to heat up those nasty little cultures that still obviously lurked in the recesses of my person, I felt that the only way to even preserve a modicum of face was to beat a strategic retreat. Also, I was worried now that some awful infection could result, and a disinfectant shower at the earliest opportunity seemed a very good idea. The one thing I hadn't been inoculated, vaccinated, pasteurised, sterilised or impregnated against was algae attack. The thought of being slowly consumed by some voracious spores did not fill me with joy. I made a few hasty feeble excuses aimed generally into the middle of the group, not daring to meet Kate's eyes again, finished my drink and pushed off rapidly towards the glass door.

I squeezed the MG into a vacant slot on a yellow line outside Palmerston Mansions - one of the long row of refurbished Victorian apartment blocks which front Prince of Wales Drive, Battersea. The Moon residence, a one bed flat, was up on the second floor but I headed straight down to the basement boiler room - and headed straight back up again, you can't burn rotting squash kit in an oil fired boiler. But it was not going to escape its fate that easily, it was definitely and irrevocably for the chop. A little matter like oil firing was not going to reprieve the offensive garments that had been the direct cause of my early departure from those big green eyes.

"Out damned spots and death to all infidels," I cried as I rammed them into the plastic waste bin liner and hurled it and its foul contents far down the rubbish chute. I stood there wild-eyed and panting, glaring after the unmourned gear.

"Been for a jog then, Mr Moon? That's what I like to see, a man who takes care of himself."

I spun round embarrassed, wondering how much she'd heard. My neighbour, the widow who lived opposite, was standing in her doorway watching me with puzzled interest.

"Yes Mrs Aberdeen, or rather no Mrs Aberdeen - er just run up the stairs," I explained, holding my stomach and miming puffing.

She sniffed. "There's a funny smell out here, Mr Moon, can you smell it? It must be the cats again." She tutted indignantly. I nodded, flashed her a weak smile and pushed hastily through my door into quiet seclusion. I didn't feel like another half hour of Mrs Aberdeen and the cats saga again this evening. She had this thing about cats in the building and was convinced that all the residents, me included I supposed, secreted hordes of cats in their apartments hiding them deliberately from her. "I know they're there, Mr Moon, I can sense their wicked yellow eyes on me all the time - but they hide them you know." She was a kind old stick really, but a renegade husband had removed her marbles with the efficiency of Elgin. Having observed my performance with the foetid squash kit, she probably thought the same of me.

My flat was a mess, a cosy mess but still a mess. It had never bothered me till now but tonight for some reason, I saw it as it really was. Mrs Jolly 'did for me' twice a week, changing the sheets and towels and cleaning as best she could, but even her efforts could not prevail against the kind of hand to mouth existence I had been living. Piles of books, papers and reports littered the floor of the sitting/dining-room. Carved wooden idols, silver spouted coffee pots, cast brass Buddhas, orange water shakers, batik wall hangings and lacquered Chinese bowls were pushed onto various shelves and ledges, all treasured mementos of hurried visits to souks at points south and east of Cairo where I had been routinely taken to the cleaners by the local strolling merchants.

I stripped off my clothes, they didn't smell too badly in themselves, it was me that the odour was coming from. Turning the shower on full and running it hot, with the long handled brush and the Lifebuoy I scrubbed every single bit of me. Every nook and every cranny where that damned mould could have lodged, every lump and projection got the treatment, some of it was painful and some quite exciting, but nothing deflected me from my task. After I had dried off and donned a white towelling robe I scanned the contents of the fridge for something to eat. There was a packet of bacon, half a dozen eggs and an opened can of beans. I ate bacon, egg and beans - what the catering trade euphemistically refer to as 'the chef's special'. Having washed up - I didn't used to do that previously until the sink was overflowing with crockery - and stacked the dishes to dry, I put Dvorak's Symphony No 9 from the New World, the slow movement, on the CD player and slumped into my worn leather armchair to think.

It had certainly been one hell of a day and it had left me with two very simple problems: how to stuff Mazin Al Jabril even more thoroughly than he had stuffed us, and how to get Kate into bed. The two problems were simple enough to identify, finding the solutions would be a different kettle of fish altogether. It was hard to concentrate on the one without being distracted by the other. The overall priority was Kate, but the immediate priority, for Hugo wanted my answer quickly, was Mazin. I had to think that we had a chance at least to get even before I would bring myself to deal with that man again. But Hugo was right when he warned me cautiously that Mazin may be able to do us major harm. It was a tricky situation.

I took an A4 pad and a Pentel and wrote down all the things I knew about Mazin Al Jabril. There were factual things and emotional things; the facts I dealt with first, they were straightforward. He was tall, good looking, I had to admit that, and when he wanted to be, charming with it. He was always immaculately dressed, in his middle 40s and rich - very rich I assumed, from his lavish style of living. How rich was difficult to assess. The appearance of wealth could be a front, it often was with Middle Eastern entrepreneurs and fixers, but I doubted that in Mazin's case. Originally from Egypt some said, he claimed to be a citizen of the United Emirates although I had seen a Syrian passport in his possession on one occasion when I caught a glimpse inside his open briefcase. But wherever he came from and whatever else he was, the one thing I was certain about, he was clever. Streetwise clever and sophisticated clever. Mazin knew all the angles, all the tricks. He had pulled most of them himself at one time or another so he was certainly no mug. That was fine, I thought somewhat ruefully, whilst we believed he was on our side but we should have realised that the only side Mazin could ever be on was his own. He had houses or villas in Monte Carlo, Cairo, Beirut - until ironically the Syrians lobbed a shell into his swimming pool and blew the foundations from under the building - and almost certainly elsewhere. At one time he had his own jet - a Cessna Citation it used to be when we last had dealings with him - and numerous expensive cars. His boat was a 60 ft Riva, or so he once told me.

I looked round my flat after I'd written this. How on earth could I, the proud owner or rather co-owner with the building society, of this tiny but desirable, nay bijou residence, as the estate agent described it when selling it to me, plus an ancient car, a £400 overdraft, and sod all else, compete with him. I shook my head slowly then carried on writing. 'Emotional side' I wrote, and then compiled a list of appropriate adjectives: ruthless, greedy, deceitful, unreliable, dangerous, cunning, sharp. I stopped. It was pointless to continue, all the misanthropic adjectives I could think of applied to him in one form or another and none of them gave me any inspiration whatsoever. In fact all in all it seemed to me that to even try to sort out Mazin Al Jabril would not be only a futile waste of time, but was likely to provoke a backlash from his displeasure that could do us irreparable damage.

I threw the pen down and went to put in a new disc. Bugger Mazin Al Jabril, Kate was a much more pleasurable avenue to pursue. I could either ring her at Andy King-Knight's office, or chance that we would meet up in the Frog and Nightgown again. The former seemed the best bet and then I realised I didn't know her other name. I smiled to myself, there couldn't be many Kates in Andy's firm, he only had offices in the Kensington and Chelsea areas, maybe four or five in all and to ring round those was no problem. But then I was stuck. What to say? I hadn't exactly got off to a flying start. Malodorous Moon, I could see them falling about in hysterics. On second thoughts, maybe I'd try the pub next Monday after I'd turned over Jamie Swallow at squash again. Damn - I'd have to buy some new kit, at least some socks and shorts. My 'Smile you're in Barbados' tee shirt would do to play in. I rooted about in the cupboard in the bedroom and eventually turned it up. A bit creased but it smelt clean, thank God.

I'd forgotten that Jamie Swallow was going to the States.

It was late afternoon before I saw Hugo, he'd obviously put a good lunch away somewhere, from his flushed cheeks and over-enthusiastic greeting.

"Marcus, my good chap, how goes it in the world of heavy civil engineering today - so far - that is?" He frowned slightly as he stumbled over the words and then brightened. "And what news about, you know?" He gave me a conspiratorial wink.

"Let's go into your office," I said, taking his arm and guiding him through the door into the privacy of his office. Trying to talk rationally to a wellied-up Elmes out in the reception area was not to be recommended. I wanted all his concentration if we were going to get anywhere with the Al Jabril factor. Janet slid in behind us with a cup of strong black coffee and put in on the desk in front of him.

"Tea, Marcus?" she asked, turning to me.

"Please."

She gave Hugo a sympathetic smile and went out. Hugo sat down heavily behind his desk and blinked ponderously until both his eyes focussed on approximately the same point. He carefully planted his elbows on the blotter and leaned forward, a sure sign that although the larger part of a bottle of good claret and a few brandies reposed within him he was going to be businesslike. At least I hoped they reposed, apart from the spots of colour on his cheeks, he looked dangerously pale and sweaty. I eased my chair back out of technicolour yawn range and waited face fixed in rapt concentration for him to open the batting. He sensed my seriousness and made a visible effort to gather himself together. He began tentatively.

"Did you give any thought to, er, the little problem about an agent for the, er, Sharjah job?"

He put his fingertips together and tried to focus his eyes on me over the top of his spectacles. I gave it him straight - no dilution with bullshit.

"The answer is yes, I gave it a lot of thought, and no, I wouldn't touch the bastard with a barge pole."

I looked straight at him. Hugo frowned and wrinkled up his face distastefully. He breathed heavily down his nose as though clearing a fall of soot. "I don't think we should be too hasty about this, Marcus, let us consider all the pros and cons before we reject his offer."

"Cons is the right word," I said savagely. "Do you really want to give him chance to turn us over again?"

Hugo heaved a heavy sigh - the sort a saint full of arrows would emit, and made a big effort to gather himself together. I could see I was going to get the full Elmes convincing argument treatment. He was brilliant at this. I sat back and waited, quite prepared to appreciate a master of his craft at work. Sometimes he could go on for hours, and at the end of it I have seen the recipients so confused that they have had to ask Hugo which choice he thought they should make. I hoped this was going to be short.

"Look at it this way, Marcus. The guy may be able to do us some good, and if he benefits almost certainly we can benefit. Likewise he can do us a lot of harm with his family connections."

"If he is what he says he is," I interjected.

"Oh he is, I assure you. I checked with the UAE Embassy and got a full list of their state Ministers. An Al Jabril is definitely the Minister of Industry in Sharjah. And don't forget," he added, "that he stuck his neck out for us in Iraq..."

"And himself," I interjected bitterly.

"OK, and himself, but if he had been caught he could have been shot."

I gave a short laugh. "Yes, but we didn't ask him to go round bribing government officials, you went bananas when you found out - and I might add, it was not for our benefit he was doing it, he was the one that got the equipment agencies, and we knew nothing about it till it was too late. Acting both for us and doing that was illegal." I paused as a very satisfying idea came into my head. "Anyway, why don't we report him to the Iraqi authorities and let them shoot him when they find him!"

Janet came in with my tea and I took the moment to savour Al Jabril stuck in front of a firing squad - I could not rustle up one drop of sympathy. Hugo sipped his coffee slowly. "Much as I agree with your sentiments, being realistic this guy would be no good to us with bullet holes in him, that would not get our money back."

I sat up at this. "Does that mean you have an idea, Hugo?"

He shook his head sadly. "No, not yet, but just remember the old Confucian saying: 'If a man does you harm, go fishing - and sooner or later he will come floating past you in the river'."

I sat silently looking at him - he'd done it again. It was a very good argument. I could see the force of it clearly.

"He who wishes to sup with the devil should use a long spoon," I misquoted back, but Hugo knew he had me won over. He smiled in his dignified way, slowly stood up, walked round the desk and honked all over my shoes!

Hugo had faxed Mazin saying that in principle we were interested in his proposal but would require to discuss the matter thoroughly before we would be prepared to enter into any form of agreement. The fax was sufficiently cool to indicate that we had not forgotten our previous experience at his hands but businesslike to show that we were 'men of the world' and a new deal is a new deal. It was suggested that a meeting be held in London to explore the arrangement within the next two weeks. "He won't like that," I told Hugo. "Putting himself within the reach of the long arm of British justice will not appeal to him at all."

"But he'll come," smiled Hugo.

"Oh yes, he'll come," I said.

CHAPTER FOUR

I was sitting in my office the following Monday wondering who I could phone to try out my brand new squash kit on when the phone rang. It was Jamie Swallow calling from New York.

"Oh hi James, I was just thinking who I could thrash in your stead, what can I do for you?"

He laughed. "It's what I can do for you, Marcus. You remember you asked me if I could find out something about a bank draft?"

"Shit," I said, "of course. Did you manage it?"

"No problem," he replied cheerfully, "we just ran it through the computer. The draft was made payable to..." I could hear him rustling some papers... "Investment and Resource Holdings SA, and handed to a Mazin Al Jabril, Syrian passport number..."

I cut him short there. "Yes, I know about Al Jabril but can you tell me where this Investment and Resource Holdings is registered?"

"Hmm," he murmured, "that we don't know but as it's a Société Anonyme then it must be in a French company law area. I would try Switzerland - Geneva first if I were you. This guy Al Jabril's appointment with the bank here was made by a Swiss lawyer from Geneva."

We made some small talk and after thanking him I put the phone down. I looked at the details I had scribbled on my pad, they meant nothing at present but at least it was a start - a small triumph. We knew something that Mazin wouldn't think we knew. On the strength of my luck running today I scrapped the idea of squash this evening, abandoned visiting the Frog and Nightgown and seized the London business telephone directory. There were four King-Knight offices and I phoned each in turn. She was at the last one - the one in Kensington Church Street.

"Kate?" the telephonist echoed, "Oh you must mean Kate Tennant, I'll put you through." Tennant eh! - a good name for an estate agent. I was thinking about this when she suddenly spoke, catching me unprepared.

"Kate here, can I help you?"

"Oh, ah, yes, well it's me, Marcus."

"Marcus?" she repeated. "Marcus who?"

And then I remembered that when we had met in the pub that stupid prat King-Knight didn't tell her my name and she hadn't asked. I put that right immediately.

"Marcus Moon - we met in the Frog and Nightgown last Monday." I was waiting anxiously for some acknowledgement of recognition.

"Oh, Malodorous Marcus," she laughed.

Well, at least she laughed. I forced a laugh in reply. "Ha ha ha, yes I'm afraid so, but malodorous no longer." I gritted my teeth. I could kill that sod Jamie Swallow, that really got me off to a good start that did. I continued hoping I sounded more confident than I felt, not easy when the label of 'stinky' has already been affixed.

"The offending kit has been disposed of - permanently," I added.

"The whole world can breathe again then," she observed. "I heard all about it after you had gone - you obviously need someone to look after you better."

My heart leaped, was it merely a light-hearted observation on my pathetic state or was it a tentative offer? Maybe it was, maybe it wasn't, let's find out.

"Well there is a vacancy you know," I ventured, holding my breath. She paused for a moment.

"So you have lots of spare time then?"

I couldn't see quite where this was leading so I ploughed on.

"Some, but there is an empty void in my heart."

"Well I hope you fill it," she replied.

"No offers?" I enquired hopefully, not willing to be put off as easily as that.

Her voice became more serious. "No offers, I already have that job." I saw hope vanishing hot foot over the horizon with its arse aflame.

"Ah, so you're married," I couldn't keep the disappointment out of my voice.

"No, she replied, "but I've got a guy."

It couldn't be Andy King-Knight, could it? - well could it?

"Andy?" I ventured.

"Christ no!" she chuckled again and then abruptly changed the subject. "But enough about me, what did you want?"

"Want?"

"Well you phoned remember?"

What did I want, I knew exactly what I wanted, I wanted to take her out to dinner, I wanted to talk to her, I wanted to make her laugh, I wanted to look into those green bright eyes, I wanted to find out all about her, to kiss her, caress her, take her to bed, that's what I bloody well wanted. But what I wanted and what it sounded like I was going to get were clearly not going to coincide.

"Are you still there?" she enquired.

I brought myself back to earth.

"Yes, oh yes I was just thinking," I murmured. I pulled my thoughts together. "You remember when we talked in the pub you told me you had worked in Switzerland for six months on European property?"

"Yes?" she said enquiringly.

"Do you by any chance have a contact or friend in Geneva who would get some information from the Registrar of Commerce there about a Swiss Company?"

I paused anxiously, it was a bit blunt. I would have much preferred to ask the favour over dinner.

She hesitated and then said hurriedly, "Look Marcus, I've got to go, there are people waiting to see me. Why don't we meet for a drink in the pub and discuss it then?"

I thought quickly. "Not the pub," I said, "too many flapping ears. Let's make it Corks wine bar in Oakley Street at say 6 o'clock. Is that OK?"

"Fine," she said, "see you there."

I exhaled a slow whistle. Well that was a foot in the door for starters, let the battle commence with my unknown adversary whose feet were currently well established under her table by the sound of it.

I had just put down the phone when it rang again. It was Brian Mason wanting to know when we could have a meeting to discuss our fee proposals for the Sharjah Steel job. We arranged to meet the following day in my office. There was still just over two weeks to go before our bid had to be in but there was a lot of work to do in that time. Rather than risking the post I was going to deliver it in Washington personally. I thumped the desk - that reminded me I must ask the formidable Margaret Braithwaite to book my flights.

Ms Margaret J Braithwaite had come to me as my secretary following Belinda's departure to her prospective confinement and future entry into motherhood. She had been working for me for a couple of months now and we were almost finished with the initial clashing of horns to decide who would be the leader of the herd - whether it was to be me or her that ran the show! This 12 round catch weight competition was currently approaching the last round with both contestants still on their feet slugging it out toe to toe.

Brian Mason, as head of administration had done all the advertising and interviewing for the post of 'Secretary and personal assistant wanted. To work for a director of an international firm of consultant civil engineers. Good salary and working conditions. Apply etc etc!'

This was done whilst I was away from the office in some pestilential part of the globe trying to get business.

"By God, Brian," I had commented on my return, "you really have a way with words. That should pull 'em in in their thousands. How could they resist such purple prose?"

"Sarcasm is the lowest form of wit, Moon," he had countered, adding: "You should realise that these days all advertisements for staff have to be so non-committal to avoid being hung, drawn, quartered, castrated, pilloried and neutered under the Equal Opportunities Act, the Sex Discrimination Bill, The Race Relations Act, The Handicapped Persons Bill, Save the Whale, Stuff the Pope and Scotland the Brave that we have no option but to be dull and boring." My basic specification, which I had carefully left with him, had been totally ignored.

"I didn't think slender, blonde and with big tits would satisfy all the legislative criteria," he had explained patiently when he told me that he thought he had found the ideal person for the job. "I have fulfilled two of your three requirements however; he is a slim fair-haired young man and very well qualified apart from the fact that he wears perfume and rather tight trousers."

Now Brian is not noted for a sense of humour, so when he tells me that my new secretary is a limp lily of dubious sexuality I am inclined to believe him. I am also inclined to fall down in a foaming fit knowing what all my friends of both sexes are going to start thinking when they learned about this - as assuredly they would because some sneak would tell them within 24 hours. After fulminating for a full five minutes until I ran out of steam, I noticed the flicker of a smirk across his pale face.

"Oh Christ, Brian, you're not having me on?" I exclaimed. "Tell me it's a joke!" I pleaded. "Please tell me it's a joke?"

He actually laughed out loud. That was now twice in six months he had done that. It was slightly disturbing. Leaving the bank to work for us was causing serious personality changes to young Mason, I thought. He'd be coming to work without his waistcoat next.

"It's a joke, Marcus, just a joke. Your new sec/PA is a charming middle-aged lady. A Miss Margaret Braithwaite, very well qualified - she ran a large admin office in her last job and I think you will find her most efficient and reliable."

I was so relieved I didn't enquire any further.

Belinda had left on the Friday before with her eyes full of tears, her arms full of chocolates and her car full of things for the baby. It had been kisses all round and, for me, a quick squeeze of the balls. I winced at the thought, there had been a touch of malevolence in her vice-like grip rather than any erotic stimulation. However, off she had gone promising to bring the baby in for us to coo over after she had ejected it and polished it up a bit. It slipped my mind over the weekend that the new girl was due to start Monday so when I strolled through Belinda's old office at 9.15 on the Monday morning I was nonplussed to put it mildly to see, sitting at Belinda's desk, on Belinda's chair, hammering away at Belinda's word processor, a formidable grand dame. What was even less plussing was to notice that on Belinda's old desk lying facing the door was a stained triangular length of oak with the words 'Major Margaret J Braithwaite' painted boldly on it in black lettering. She was so engrossed in her hammering that she had not heard my entry. I slid quietly out backwards and beat it rapidly down to Brian Mason's office.

"Brian," I said with a warning note in my voice, "who the fuck is that in Belinda's office?"

Unfazed he replied blandly, "That, Marcus, is your new secretary/PA - Major Margaret Braithwaite, ex British Army. Fit and rarin' to go."

He smiled again. At this rate our Brian could be turning into a barrel of laughs if he wasn't careful - but not today he wouldn't, not after I had finished with him.

"And what am I supposed to do?" I enquired sarcastically, "click my heels and salute every time I want to go for a crap! It's my office, Brian," I stressed, "and she's in there at the moment, like Horatius guarding the bridge, beating the shit out of your word processor. She seems to think that it's one of the old-fashioned Imperials and really giving it some hammer. It won't stand that sort of treatment for long I can tell you."

That straightened him up a bit, he was aggressively proud of our computers and word processors, regarding them as his 'babies' and the system had cost an arm and a leg to install. The thought of it being mutilated by some ham-fisted harridan did not appeal to his possessive accountant's mind. Equipment could be written off over three years on the books, but ignorantly beating it to death over six months - that made losses. He decided to appeal to my better nature - not necessarily a good thing at any time and almost certainly not under the present circumstances, but he gave it a shot.

"Look Marcus, don't be too hasty about her, let me give you a bit of her background to put you in the picture and then I am sure you will get on famously. You with your kind heart, she with her drill boots..."

"Brian!..." I growled warningly.

"Yes, yes OK. She is 49 years old, unmarried, been in the Army for 25 years and recently retired. She was a senior admin officer. At her interview I found her a bit formal but that was probably nerves, I thought that she was a genuinely nice person as well as competent and that was why I took her on. You need somebody to organise you a bit, Marcus, we've always thought so, she'll be good for you," he finished off.

Oh, so that's what this was all about, was it? There'd been some internal discussions about this, had there, discussions to which I was not privy? A little plotting had been done. Both Hugo and Brian kept telling me I was too laid back and easy going, so now I had been given a minder. OK, well let us see, I thought. Let the reed bend with the wind and when the storm was over...

"Fine, Brian, thank you very much." I was politeness itself, gave him a nod and went back up the corridor to tackle the 4th Tank Regiment single-handed.

Adopting a brisk businesslike approach I strode into her office on my way through to mine.

"Good morning," I breezed. "Fine start to the week, and how are we today?"

She spun round immediately and riveted me with the sort of glare through her spectacles that could punch a hole through armour plate. Spectacles, I noticed, which were secured by a thin piece of cord hanging round her neck. She raked me from head to toe, taking in the slacks, open-necked shirt and sweater. "I didn't hear you knock," she barked.

It's amazing how the brain still manages to work quite well when you're standing there poised in mid stride with the vocal chords paralysed and your mouth opening and closing silently.

How do I handle this, I was thinking. Do I bark back 'Atten-shun, Lieutenant Colonel Moon here! Right at ease,' or do I retreat, tail between legs, turn round and knock timidly, seeking admission to the orderly office.

"Well?" she barked again even more fiercely.

This shook me from my momentary paralysis. There was a serious danger here that if I didn't handle this right she'd have me running every which way but loose, which was not my scene, definitely not my scene at all. Right, I thought, blow this for a game of soldiers, it was my office and if there were going to be rules on how it was to be run then they were going to be my rules. That's what I thought and that was how it was going to start.

"I am Marcus Moon, Margaret." None of that 'Major' crap, I wasn't even prepared to ask her what she preferred to be called, it was going to be Margaret. Marge or Maggie would be pushing it a bit too far for openers although to be borne in mind. The response was gratifying - slightly puzzling but gratifying.

"Oh I'm terribly sorry, Mr Moon, it's just that I didn't want people taking the liberty of walking through to your office when you're not there, it wouldn't be right. How do you do. I'm Margaret Braithwaite." She stood up and proffered a hand. I eyed it cautiously, recalling that it was one of those hands that had been hammering the bejesus out of the keyboard so enthusiastically, but it appeared normal enough suspended there. I took it warily and received a warm crushing vigorous handshake in return. She could have held down a job in the Wigmore wankery any time - dealing with the masochists. As I discreetly massaged my crushed knuckles, with the formalities over, she became all brisk and businesslike.

"I've put all your mail on your desk in what seemed to me to be the order of importance, but of course being new here I've a lot to learn. Now would you like coffee or tea and how do you like it? I brought a few chocolate oatmeals in today just in case you would like a bicky with your drink. There have been two telephone calls, I have put notes on your desk. We should get proper message pads printed but I'll get to that later.

"And one other thing, Mr Elmes said could you pop in and see him when you have a moment to spare."

"I..."

"I looked in our diary - not much in there, is there?" She gave me a look as if to suggest I had been holding out on her... "and have booked that down for 10 o'clock."

"I..."

"It is now 9.32 so that gives us time to change out of our site clothes and have our coffee - or tea."

I waited. This was all a bit much for me at 9.32 and ten seconds. Belinda usually just gave me my coffee hot, strong, sweet, black and then quietly left me alone to emerge from my chrysalis into the real world about 10 o'clock. I definitely was not at my best in the early part of the morning. First things first, as my mother always used to say.

"Coffee please Margaret, coffee in the morning, tea in the afternoons. And the coffee hot, strong, sweet and black."

"And a bicky!" she added.

Oh God, a bicky! I nodded speechless. I remembered something, "I think Belinda has left you an 'aide memoire' somewhere - top left-hand drawer of her desk - she said she would. It may be of help."

Her lips pursed primly, she reached over and handed me a sheet of paper from the top of the pile in her 'out' tray without comment. It was headed 'Marcus Moon' and closely typed. I scanned the first sentence. It read 'Marcus is a randy long streak of pump water who is definitely not the marrying kind.' I glanced up, she was watching me expressionlessly. I read on, 'He is self-centred, untidy, disorganised, over-sexed, unreliable and will make some unfortunate girl a very bad husband.'

The wicked little bitch! I didn't read any more but crumpled the sheet into a ball and tossed it into the waste basket saying, with a forced smile, "I'm actually quite well organised." It was very weak but it was all I could think of under the circumstances, so I hastily pushed off through into my office and sat down. Sanctuary. Phew!

And for crying out loud what was all that about - 'and we'll change out of our site clothes?' I certainly wasn't in my site clothes. Being a Monday morning my shirt was actually clean and recalling her woolly jumper, tweed jacket and skirt it didn't seem to me that that sort of gear was ideal for drinking mugs of scalding tea and leaning on scaffolding discussing the race card at Doncaster either.

On my departure from her vicinity she had bustled off, presumably to do the coffee and 'bickies' which gave me a short breather. With a shake of the head I watched the door between our offices, I wasn't sure about all this at all. The nervous enthusiasm I could cope with - just - but there was something else a bit odd about her. I considered it further. She was not unattractive in a severe sort of way; fair hair cut in a centurion bob - I suppose it was that that produced the severity; pleasant enough face, make-up and businesslike clothes. That was it, her make-up, it was all wrong. Her skin was fair and her lipstick smudged and orangey. Her eye shadow was light green. I couldn't recall the colour of her eyes, but whatever they were light green eye shadow didn't do anything for them; and she had small globs of powder stuck in patches on her cheeks and nose. I supposed that in the army your make-up was not a major consideration when you're facing the might of Allah rumbling towards you out of the East in massed tanks across the dusty desert. But she had made an effort - that I did appreciate - and that was worth a lot these days.

That had been two months ago, since then we had got to know one another a little better. After two weeks of full frontal assaults on various habits of mine of which she did not approve, and of which there were many, she had retreated to out-flanking movements in the nicest possible way. But she was good at her job, there was no doubt about that. She was licking the whole office, not just my office, into shape.

I called through the open door that linked our two offices - two of the habits of which she didn't approve. 'I do wish you'd use the intercom, Mr Moon' and 'Everyone can see into your office, you know'. I had asked her what was wrong with that. Did she think that I was doing something naughty in there? She'd flushed, retired and the door had stayed open. "Margaret, can you book me on the BA flight to Washington on…" I looked at my programme. "…October third, Business Class, window seat, no smoking and returning on the 6th." As I would be over there in any case delivering our bid I might as well spend a couple of days lobbying within the corridors of power at the International Bank of Reconstruction and Development, which was the World Bank's official title.

She rose from her chair and came through - she would never call back - "What about hotels, Mr Moon?"

"Marcus," I said, "I do wish you'd call me Marcus. Mr Moon sounds so formal. Everyone else in the office calls me by my Christian name."

She smiled sweetly saying, "If you used the intercom, Mr Moon, it would be much easier for both of us and not waste your valuable time."

I could recognise a deal at 50 paces when I saw one and this had been brewing for some time. I conceded gracefully on this one.

"OK, Margaret, I promise to use the intercom in future, cross my heart."

"Shall I book you in at the Sheraton, Marcus, I see that you have stayed there before?" The deal had been struck.

"That will be fine," I smiled at her. "A room with a king-sized bed please."

Not a flicker showed in her expression but I knew it had registered. I studied her surreptitiously as she noted this down in her book, her make-up and tweeds were still as before but it looked to me as if she was letting her hair grow longer. Maybe she just hadn't had the time to get it cut, no matter.

"Thanks, Margaret," I said, as she returned to her desk.

I pondered my programme again, if I was to deliver the bid on the fourth, we had to have reached some agreement with Mazin Al Jabril before then. He was due in London shortly. I opened my briefcase and got out the notes I had made about him - just where were his weaknesses? I reread my list of adjectives applicable to him: ruthless, greedy, deceitful, unreliable, dangerous, cunning and sharp. It struck me suddenly that all of these adjectives related to one of them. The reason Mazin was all of these things, and many others, was because he was greedy. He wanted more and more money. It may be because wealth gave him power, or it may be he needed the money to fuel his extravagant lifestyle, but whatever the reason money was the thing, the only thing, that motivated him. So why had he had the nerve to come back to us? Not to do us any favours that was for sure. It must be because he thought, or rather he knew, he would be able to make money out of the arrangement, if it came off - and lots of money at that. The commission he was likely to get from us this time would be peanuts to him, so it was certainly not for that that he had phoned Hugo.

I thought back three years to the Egyptian Steel contract and tried to remember what he had done on that job, and, more to the point, what it was that he had wanted us to do.

What he had done was to get himself appointed as the local agent for some big Japanese and Italian heavy plant manufacturers. All foreign companies had to have local representation by law, as well as to assist them through the minefields of Egyptian bureaucracy, and somehow Mazin had been able to persuade two or three of the big boys to appoint him as their local man. What he had done then was to try to persuade us that we should specify their products in the contract documents for the construction of the plant. In this he had totally failed because, as we pointed out, the World Bank rules on bidding required everything to go out to open competition with the very rare exception of extremely specialist items where there was only one manufacturer. In the case of equipment for steel plants there were tens, if not hundreds of firms from all round the world who could bid, and thus we were not permitted to nominate or recommend any one firm in particular. What we had been able to do, at the request of the Bank and in association with them, was to draw up short lists of approved firms from which bids could be invited. Unfortunately - for him - none of Mazin's firms had been included, but he had obtained these lists just before bids were put out and gone scurrying round as many of the firms on them as he could, to see if he could get himself on board as their representative - without much success as far as I knew. So why would Sharjah Steel Plant be any different. The commercial laws were very similar to those in Egypt. Local representation was necessary, in fact a new local firm must be registered or an existing local firm used to represent the importer which had at least 51% of its shares held in local ownership. The World Bank rules on bidding had, if anything, been tightened since then so there was no margin for him there. No, I couldn't see what it was he was after. One thing I was certain about, however, was that there was something somewhere he had worked out to be to his advantage, and it must be big. He must know more than I did about this job, a factor which had me worried for a start.

Corks wine bar was a trendy pseudo Victorian establishment near the junction of Oakley Street and Kings Road. Lots of coated brass and mahogany veneer. I had secured a small cast-iron fretted table in one corner at quarter to six. It couldn't be said to be a quiet corner table, the place was packed with city workers of both sexes and the decibel level hurt the ears as they poured down the special offer Asti Spumante and Riojas. I preferred the Mâcon Lugny and was half way through the second glass when I saw her standing just inside the door looking around. I watched her for a moment, she brushed a stray wisp of blonde hair back from her forehead as her green eyes scanned the room and then she spotted me. Gratifying to know that she remembered what I looked like. I rose to greet her as she came over and seizing both her arms gave her a kiss on the cheek. She seemed slightly surprised by this but said nothing apart from responding 'Hello' to my 'Hi', and sat down.

"Would you like the white wine or something else?" I indicated the half full bottle on the table.

"No, a glass of that will be fine," she replied. As I poured the wine I could see she was watching me under long fair eyelashes.

"It's OK, I've had a shower and changed my clothes," I said. "Decomposing sweatshirts don't pull the girls like they used to. I've gone back to Giorgio Armani." She smiled faintly.

"You did smell a bit fusty." She took a small sip of the wine and waited. She seemed slightly hesitant, obviously she wanted me to open the proceedings so I did.

"Who's this guy that you told me needs looking after?" It was perhaps a bit too sudden for she looked mildly annoyed.

"Just some man I know, and I look after him because I like him."

"Like him?" I queried. "You don't love him then?"

She flushed a little and looked away. With a trace of anger in her voice she replied, "I didn't think we were meeting to talk about me, I thought you wanted to ask me something."

"I have," I said, "and you haven't answered it."

A spark flashed in her eyes and she put down her glass, "And I'm not going to, it's none of your business."

For one moment I thought she was going to get up and leave as she reached for her bag, so I said hastily, "I'm sorry, I didn't mean to pry, you're quite right - it is none of my business." Although I'm going to make it my business at the earliest opportunity, I decided. She withdrew a cigarette from a packet which she took from her bag and lit it with a thin gold lighter. I noticed that the hand holding the lighter trembled slightly.

"Do you smoke much?" I enquired as a casual conversation question.

She snapped back at me immediately. "No I do not, and you're questioning me again."

The green eyes flashed fire and I noticed a touch of confusion. Very interesting, but time to change the subject completely unless I really wanted to make her angry. I didn't, so I said carefully, "What I wanted to ask you was about Switzerland. Do you have anyone - a lawyer, accountant - anyone in fact who could get some information from the Registrar of Commerce in Geneva Canton. It's not a secret or anything, it is available records." She stubbed out her cigarette; she had only taken a couple of puffs without inhaling either, and reached for her bag again.

"I have jotted down the name and phone number of my ex boss on this piece of paper. I gave him a ring and said you would be getting in touch with him. He has promised to help if he can."

She handed me a slip of paper with the name Otto Hafner and a phone number written on it. The writing was clear and strong. Big loops, I noticed, and big loops are supposed to indicate a passionate nature. But slips of paper handed to me also seemed to indicate the ball had been volleyed neatly into my court thus depriving me of an excuse for finding out the truth of this.

I turned the slip over slowly in my fingers. "Thanks, Kate, it may turn out to be nothing but you never know. It was kind of you to go to the trouble."

The bait was dangled but rejected. She didn't ask what it was about but had another sip of her wine, picked up her bag and said abruptly, "I must go now." As she turned to leave I caught a glimpse of her eyes. They were glistening with tears. I cursed under my breath as I watched her back disappear through the crowd towards the door. "Well you made a right pig's ear of that, Moon," I muttered to myself. The one big chance I had to impress without diminutive Andy King-Knight ferreting around my midriff and noxious vapours wafting from unmentionable crevices, and I had blown it. Interrogating her like the KGB! The last two years of no serious female conversation had really dimmed my wits.

It took me 15 more minutes to finish the wine and during that time I mulled over our brief meeting. The mull concluded that she couldn't be that attached to this mysterious guy, she wasn't confident enough when talking about her relationship with him. It was just a small, self-indulgent consolation.

I phoned Hafner first thing next morning and, true to his promise, he phoned me back later in the day.

"Investment and Resource Holdings SA are registered in the Registre du Geneve, Canton de Geneve," he told me. "The sole signatory for the company is a Geneva lawyer, Dr Otto Weber. I can't tell you who the shareholders are because the company has issued only bearer shares to the value of 500,000 Swiss francs. As you know, the only permitted voters at the Annual General meeting are the person or persons who turn up at that meeting actually holding the share certificates. Likewise the signatory, Dr Weber, will only take instructions from the person or persons who demonstrate a controlling interest."

"Is there any way of finding out who holds the bearer shares?" I asked hopefully.

"None," he answered, "they could be passed from person to person at any time without anyone but the parties involved knowing."

"But do they have to file accounts listing their assets and profits?" I persisted.

"Yes, but they are confidential also and subject to Swiss Commercial Secrecy laws. Holders of the bearer shares will be given copies and receive dividends when they present their certificates."

"I see," I said. "Well, thanks anyway for your help."

He sensed the disappointment in my voice.

"Sorry it wasn't more use."

So that was that, a brick wall as far as Investment and Resource Holdings were concerned. I had no doubt that the holder, the only holder of the bearer shares was Mazin Al Jabril but there was no way of proving it - and even if we did, so what?

CHAPTER FIVE

For the next five days or so I worked on our proposals for the Sharjah Steel Plant bid. It was a fantastic project, they wanted the whole thing fully automated and to be the most advanced plant of its kind in the world. I assumed that one of the main reasons for this was to keep down the amount of imported labour into a small state which already suffered an imbalance of about four to one of expatriates to locals. The requirement to make it 'the most advanced plant in the world' was both specific and vague. I knew exactly what they intended by this from the Sharjan's point of view - they wanted the 'best' - but what made it vague was to define what constituted the most advance plant in the world - what was 'the best'! That, I had decided, was what would give us our edge. We had the experience and ability to pull together in our design the most advanced technology from all over the world and do it better than anyone. They naturally wanted the best, of course, for the cheapest possible price - both design fees and construction costs - a lot of hair tearing, blood spilling and the screams and wails of the tormented lay along the price road ahead, of that I had no doubt.

I had telephoned King-Knight's three times but each time Kate had either not been there or unavailable. She never returned my calls. Neither she nor Andy King-Knight had been to the pub either.

Hugo and I discussed Mazin's motive for contacting us, but until we saw him it was all speculation. Hugo felt that it revolved round the plant and equipment contracts. I was inclined to agree with him but I didn't see how he could do it. The total value of these contracts in the first phase would be of the order of $200 million and the civil engineering works contracts $150 million, and there were other, smaller phases to follow. The civils contracts for all the infrastructure, roads, port, scrap storage, power, buildings, stockyards and water supply would definitely go to one of the world's big civil engineering contractors who already operated in the Gulf. They all had their own string orchestras lined up already; they didn't need the Mazin Al Jabril's of this world to fiddle their causes. No, it must be the plant and equipment side, but how? How could he possibly work that to his advantage? All those contracts had to be put out to international tender, to approved manufacturers and suppliers - and not just approved by us but by engineers from the World Bank as well, it was a legal requirement.

"Which firms would you recommend be short-listed for the various plant equipment contracts?" asked Hugo and then treated his own question as a rhetorical one by saying, "I suppose it's far too early for that at this stage. We ourselves haven't got the design job yet so I don't suppose you will have given that aspect much thought?"

I pondered for a moment thinking of possible sub-contract suppliers but there were so many. "No, not really," I mused. "But all the big contracts, the ones where Mazin could really coin it in if he got involved, will be tendered by the Krupps, Arcelors, Kobe Steels, Mannesmanns, of this world. There are at least 20 and they will virtually cover everything."

"Well he's not going to get in with any of them for sure - if he could then he wouldn't need to come to us."

"Hugo," I said slowly, "let us not kid ourselves about Mazin Al Jabril. He is very smart, and totally ruthless. I don't think we should wait to see what he is up to and then try and counter it to our advantage if possible. That way, it seems to me, will lead to disaster, we could be far too late to do anything and I think we will have virtually no chance of getting our money back whatsoever. As you have talked me into agreeing that we take him on board let's at least try to do it on our terms, not his. I accept that that is easier said than done, but if we can agree that that is the way we approach him then maybe we can formulate an attacking strategy." Hugo indicated that he was listening and for me to continue.

"I believe we have got to ease him into what we want him to do, preferably with him thinking that he is making the running, rather than the other way about." I paused ruminatively for a moment as something else crossed my mind. "I also think that we should take some positive defensive precautions ourselves."

Hugo's eyes narrowed intently, "I agree with all you have just said - but like what?"

I sighed, "I don't know yet, it's just that it seems to be tactically safer to have something up our sleeve so he can't do us more harm."

Hugo laughed, "I suppose you're right but don't worry about it too much, Marcus, don't forget this is an IBRD job and he doesn't get paid till we get paid. That should keep him in line. If he harms us, he don't get the dough!"

"Hmm!" I acknowledged his point abstractedly. "But if it's all the same to you, Hugo, I am going to have a talk with Brian Mason about this."

"Sure," he agreed, "why not."

I made myself comfortable in the chair in front of Brian's desk - or as comfortable as one could get in the horsehair-stuffed Victorian bum batterer he called furniture - and folded my arms.

"Brian," I pronounced, "I need some advice. At the moment it is purely a hypothetical situation but it is very possible that it could turn into a real one before long, and it concerns an old friend of ours who has re-emerged from the primeval slime to haunt us yet again - Mazin Al Jabril."

Brian had been studying me impassively through his earnest brown eyes, but at the mention of the dreaded name his eyebrows shot up nearly to the roots of his hair.

"Good Lord!" he exclaimed, which for Brian was very expressive.

"Indeed, but not an apt description, however he has come up with what apparently is a good deal and Hugo thinks we should investigate it further."

I spent a few minutes filling him in on the Sharjah Steel project and then explained the circumstances about Mazin turning up.

"So what is this hypothetical situation you would like my advice about?" he asked when I had finished.

"Contact with Mazin is going to be dangerous at the best of times," I continued, "but Hugo feels that we could do ourselves more harm than good by turning him down, and, if we are alert enough, more good than harm by taking him on board. I must admit that I am not over enthusiastic about this to put it mildly but I tend to agree with Hugo for two reasons. The first is that Mazin might actually do us some good, not out of the kindness of his heart, but because by helping us he will be helping himself - in more ways than one! The second, and it is this about which I wish to pick your brains. If we take him on board it may, just may, give us a chance to somehow get back from him the money that he stole - the $2 million. If we chuck him and tell him to get stuffed then there is absolutely no chance of doing anything, so it is worth considering."

Brian nodded slowly. "Hmm, so...?"

"So Mazin is nobody's fool; he's bright, he's cunning and he's going to know that we are going to try to set him up somehow, and he will be on the lookout for it. But, and this is where I need your help, he's also bright enough to appreciate that whether or not he discovers how he is being set up, he must assume that that is what is going to happen. That being so he is bound to take counter measures to cover all eventualities."

Brian screwed up his eyes puzzling the significance. "I still don't see what you're driving at?"

"Put yourself in Mazin's shoes," I told him. "Imagine you are in his situation. He knows that we wouldn't trust him with one cent of our money, and he certainly is not going to let us get into a position where he has to trust us and rely on us to obtain his ill-gotten gains. He would be terrified that we would screw him rotten if he gave us the opportunity."

"And would you?"

"What do you think?" I contemplated the idea with relish, but realistically it was 'pie in the sky'. I wasn't that naive.

"So what would you do if you were Mazin?"

"Ah, I see now. Let me give it some thought."

Brian doodled on his pad for a couple of minutes and then said, "Well, if I were Mazin I'd try to manoeuvre us into a position where trust is irrelevant. I can only see two possible alternative ways he could do this at this precise moment. The first would be for Mazin to get hold of any money before it gets to us. That way he can legitimately take his slice of the action and we would have no redress as long as he paid over our fees. The second would be to get control over Bridge Holdings Limited. Then you can't set him up because he's in the driving seat and he can do what he likes with the company's money."

I was surprised at that. "But there's no way he can get control of Bridge Holdings Limited, Hugo and I own 25% between us, and the remaining 75% is held in trust in Jersey by one of Michael le Fevre's trust companies. They wouldn't - couldn't - hand those shares over without written agreement from us and all the other directors and ex directors/partners."

Brian corrected me. "That's not precisely accurate," he said in his ex banker's prim voice. "The design company in London, Consultant Design Group, is owned by Bridge Holdings Limited in Jersey, and it is the latter in which you and the trust hold shares. If he just got control of Consultant Design Group that would be more than enough to stymie you."

A puzzled frown crossed my brow. "But I don't see how he can do that either because all the shares in CDG are owned by BHL."

"Neither do I," admitted Brian, "but you said it was hypothetical so I gave you a hypothetical answer."

I considered that but it didn't seem to get me any further. I switched to another tack.

"Our accounts are available to the public these days, aren't they Brian, anybody can get hold of copies of them from Company House?"

He nodded.

I continued, "But for tax reasons although all the contracts are signed with Consultant Design Group and the fee income goes into that company, and it pays all the salaries, bills, costs, charges and expenses, the profits are actually accumulated in Bridge Holdings in Jersey through BHL levying management charges for the rent, furniture etcetera.

He agreed again, "Yes, that is so."

"So anybody inspecting our accounts will realise that Bridge Holdings Limited are the company making all the profit and, on paper, Consultant Design make nothing."

"Within limits," he said. "You and Hugo do take out some of the profit in your salaries on which you pay tax, but we do accumulate reserves in Jersey free of UK tax, and it does enable us to use those funds for overseas expansion should we wish to do so at some future date. Funds would only be taxed here were we to remit them back here."

He scratched an ear reflectively. "However, notwithstanding all this, I repeat, I don't see what you're driving at?"

"Neither do I at present," it was my turn to admit with a rueful grin.

I thanked him for his help and wandered back to my office mulling over the conversation. I disagreed with one thing Brian had said, I didn't think that there would be much point in Mazin trying to obtain control of Consultant Design Group. First of all I doubted if it was possible without us being alerted, and secondly there was a much better target if that was to be his plan.

Having been taught a severe lesson by our experiences on the Egyptian project, there was absolutely no chance of Mazin being given any power of attorney to come anywhere near getting his grasping hands on our fees from the World Bank before we did. He may be able to work some fiddle with other parties but there was very little we could do about that. The problem was that even if we could, it didn't provide a route to recovery of our $2 million.

Anyway the threat of withholding his commission would only serve to infuriate him and make life very difficult for us in Sharjah. It was peanuts to him in any case, he would be after much bigger rip-offs than the modest percentage he would get from us.

Greed! It all came down to greed. That was his weakness, if only we could exploit it. I still could not see a way but I felt that there was a germ of an idea lurking somewhere in what we had established today but, as yet, I couldn't pin it down.

As Hugo had said, Mazin would have to float a little further down the river.

Later that day I was trying to finish my letters when Margaret Braithwaite asked me if she might have a private word. As there was nobody else either in my office or hers it seemed a bit unnecessary to have included the word private. However I said "sure" and waited whilst she fidgeted a bit. To put her at ease I said, "Sit down Margaret," and pulled one of the battered chairs from the front of my desk. She sat and crossed her legs demurely. I noticed that although her pale coloured tights were a heavy gauge I could still see fairly muscular hairy calves through them. To support the muscular bit she was wearing what my mother would call 'sensible' shoes. Namely brown, flat-heeled walking shoes. Whilst studying her legs I was thinking, what the hell is all this about? A secretary and a 'private word' usually meant that they were a) pregnant, b) going to leave or c) pregnant and going to leave. In Margaret's case I doubted the pregnancy - although some guys I know do go for the muscular hairy ones - so she must be going to hand in her notice. I was disappointed. She really was good and although we had had our little battles, I didn't think they had been sufficient to make her unhappy enough to leave. We both became conscious at the same time that I was still staring at her legs, I felt myself colouring up whereas she gave a strange little smile. I pulled myself together hastily, I really must try and stop this staring.

"Look Margaret," I said anxiously, "if it's about all the guys in the design office standing up, saluting and shouting 'Heil Hitler' every time you go in there, they mean no harm. It's just high spirits."

"No, Marcus, it's not that," she replied with a shrug.

"Well, when the chief quantity surveyor stood outside your office window bawling 'come out and fight' he was pissed - you know that. He always gets pissed Friday lunch time."

"No," she said, "it's not that either."

"I did warn him, you know," I added. "I told him you had been trained to kill in hand-to-hand combat and could break his back with a flick of your wrist so I don't think he'll do it again."

She gave a weak smile. "That was very kind of you Marcus, but I assure you it's not that."

I gave up, I couldn't think of any other major provocations, excuse the pun, unless of course it was me she couldn't get on with.

"Is it me?" I asked as a last resort.

She looked puzzled, "Is what you? No, what I want to ask is a favour. My sister is due to have an operation towards the end of November and I wondered if it is alright, that is, if I may take a couple of weeks of my leave to help her out?"

I subsided with relief. "Of course you can, why didn't you say so sooner," I gasped.

"Thank you very much, I'll make it up some other time," she said with a smile, and marched briskly out through to her office. My intercom buzzed, it was her.

"Mr Elmes asked me to tell you he's gone home early, he has a City dinner tonight."

Ah, so that was the difference between a private word and a business word. I know now.

I phoned King-Knight's again on my private line: yes Kate Tennant was in, no, she couldn't talk to me - she was with a client! Right, that was it, it was time for action not phone calls. I closed my briefcase, made sure the electrical stuff was switched off - computer, shredder, ioniser - I was into positive ions, or was it negative ions at the moment, supposed to make you more 'active', and a fat lot of good they were doing for me with my love life at absolute zero. I didn't know whether the 20 quid invested in this ionising contraption was value for money or not but I was dying to find out. I switched off the lights, bade Margaret goodnight and headed for the car.

"Where are you going Marcus," she called after me anxiously.

"To buy a house," I called back.

I managed to find a parking place in King-Knight's private car park right up the boot of a flash BMW. A painted sign stuck on the wall above the car read 'Reserved for Mr A King-Knight'. Fine, so at least I knew who I was blocking in.

I walked into the front door and looked round. It was a narrow deep unit, it must have been a shop at one time and King-Knight's had converted it into a real estate office. The furniture was crisp, modern unit-plan with desks and terminals down each side of an aisle. It looked thriving and prosperous. Kate was sitting at a desk near the back reading through some papers. Before an anxious-looking receptionist could detain me and ask my business I had walked down to Kate's desk and plonked myself in the stainless steel and leather chair in front of it. She looked up with surprise, which turned to even greater surprise when she realised who it was.

"What do you want?" she hissed in a low voice, a touch of colour showing in her cheeks.

I beamed upon her. "Not a very welcoming greeting for a prospective client," I said cheerfully.

Her eyes narrowed a fraction. "Prospective client?" she queried.

"That's right." I glanced around ostentatiously, "This is an estate agent's isn't it, and I want to buy a house."

Her eyes widened in astonishment. "A house?" she said, "but you already have a flat." Ah! Ah! I thought, so she knows that, and I hadn't told her, interesting.

"Yes a house," I replied, "you do sell houses here I assume?"

Her manner changed and her face took on a closed look. "We do," she said, "I don't. You'll have to see either Mr King-Knight or Geoffrey, the man over there," she pointed down the office towards a grey-haired man speaking on the telephone.

"What do you do," I said persistently. She gave an exasperated snort, "If it's any business of yours, I'm a negotiator. I advise people about selling their houses, not buying." She resumed reading through the papers in front of her and I remained seated. When she couldn't stand it any longer she looked up and said, "Go away. Please! I've got work to do."

"I want to sell a flat," I said patiently.

She groaned, "Oh God, I give in." She reached for a form from a tray on the desk and picked up a pen. "You'd better give me some details."

"It's a cosy little one bed, large lounge-dining room, modern kitchen, bathroom, No 2A Palmerston Mansions, Prince of Wales Drive, Battersea and it has a nice dining table with candles, wine and a setting for two with a vacancy in one of the chairs."

She put down her pen. "And I suppose it has a cosy little king-sized bed with a vacancy on one side?"

I chewed my lip ruminatively; I had a growing feeling that this was not going quite as I had hoped. Further and more concrete evidence of this followed.

"Just leave me alone will you - please!"

I glanced round; a few heads were beginning to turn our way in the office. I turned back towards her and took hold of her hand which was still resting on the desk after she had put down her pen. She tried to pull away but I gripped tightly.

"Let go," she demanded fiercely.

"Look," I pleaded, "all I want to do is to take you out to dinner - as a thank you for helping me with Otto Hafner. He was very helpful by the way, sounded a nice person."

She shook her head adamantly. "No, I don't want to have dinner with you. Just leave it at that will you!"

"Well how about a drink then? I promise not to interrogate you again. We'll talk of other things – 'shoes and ships and sealing wax'," I quoted from Alice in Wonderland with a feeble grin, but that bit of wit and wisdom fell on stony ground as well. Solid rock more like.

Big sticky tears welled in her eyes. I let go of her hand, defeated. I knew she liked me, there had been that spark, that instant chemistry between two people that so rarely happens but when it does it must be followed up. So I had followed it up - and hit a brick wall. It hadn't been anger I saw in her eyes, although her voice and manner appeared angry, it had been distress.

"Er, is everything alright Kate?" The grey-haired man appeared at her shoulder regarding me with unconcealed hostility. He was not alone in that, I was getting the thumbs down from all and sundry in that office, I was about as popular as a pork butcher in a synagogue. There are times to stay and times to go, and the voting on this one was virtually unanimous that the latter would be the recommended course of action. I got to my feet, Kate was looking down and didn't move, so I eased down the office towards the door propelled by ten pairs of eyes.

Another massive bollocking was awaiting me in the car park from Andy King-Knight who was standing glancing anxiously at his gold Rolex and drumming his fingers on the bonnet of my car. It would have been the roof, I thought, but he couldn't reach the roof.

"Is this your car, Moon!?"

I could tell from the tone of his voice that he wasn't going to make me an offer for it.

"Sorry, Andy, I thought I'd only be a moment."

"I have a very important appointment I'll have you know and you've made me late," he continued angrily. I apologised again but there was no stopping him. He rabbited on for a further five minutes which I suppose made him even later. I wasn't in the mood to argue, I was still wondering how I'd managed to blow totally what should have been a fairly straightforward conversation between two rational - at least I thought we were - humans.

It had not been a 'be nice to Marcus Moon' afternoon.

CHAPTER SIX

"Mr Marcus, hello, how are you?"

I recognised the voice instantly, although it was three years since I last heard it.

"Hello Mazin, fine thanks," I replied cautiously, thinking no thanks to you, you thieving bastard.

"I am at Heathrow, I will be at the office in one hour." There was a click and the dialling tone. I put the phone down slowly. No 'are you free this morning?' or 'is it convenient to come?' He just assumed that because it was him the red carpet would be rolled out whenever he wanted it. It was a wonder he didn't want me to carry him on my back from the bloody airport followed by a train of coolies with his baggage. I hoped Hugo would be back before he arrived, I didn't think I was up to handling Mazin on my own. I suppose we'd have to make some sort of effort to be hospitable, Arabs tended to get very shirty if they were not made to feel welcome, whether they were actually welcome or not.

I checked with Janet that Hugo's office would be free all morning and asked her to get some filter coffee and freshly squeezed orange juice. Margaret I got to photocopy Mazin's original agency agreement - the one he altered and returned. There was going to be none of that this time. I read the photocopy very carefully making notes where there were weaknesses - and there were plenty, experience had shown that. Once we had agreed the heads of terms with him, our lawyers would be drawing up the final document. There would be none of the 'we all trust each other' and 'everybody is expected to act in good faith' approach this time. The new deal was going to be watertight, rock solid, nailed down and concreted in. I was just drafting out a few clauses when I heard Hugo enquire diplomatically of Margaret. "Is Marcus in?" It was patently obvious I was, the door was wide open and I was sitting in full view. This was Hugo's concession to the new military discipline - he was a little in awe of Margaret and didn't want to push his luck too far. I chuckled, waiting.

Sure enough she pressed the intercom: "Mr Elmes is here to see you."

I looked up and met his eye. "Tell him I'm not in," I intercomed back.

"Go right in, Mr Elmes," she said, "he's in one of his funny moods."

As Hugo ambled through with a grin I called round the door, "Margaret, what if I had been doing one of those unspeakable things you appear to think I do which required my door being closed?"

"Well you aren't," she retorted, "anyone can see that!"

I shrugged at Hugo, defeated by the illogical logic of this and motioned him towards a chair. "Take a seat Hugo, you've heard I suppose? He should be here any time now. What's the plan? Do we have a plan?"

Hugo crossed his legs and regarded me quizzically. "Now he's come floating past us in the river, let us wait and see what he says." He paused for a moment, "Do you think we should bring Brian in on this meeting, he is after all our financial wizard?"

I most definitely didn't, but would have to put it tactfully.

"It's a bit early for that I think, Hugo, after all this is a preliminary meeting just to feel out the position and I have kept

Brian informed regarding what has happened to date. I think he's gone out in any case."

Hugo nodded, "OK, let us 'play it by ear' then."

As we didn't have a plan there was not much option, so I agreed with him. We went back into Hugo's office to wait and we didn't have to wait long. The receptionist buzzed through to say that an oriental gentleman had passed through the outer office without introducing himself and was on his way towards us. Hugo leaped to his feet and scooted out the door. I could hear muffled greetings and apologies and Mazin appeared in the doorway with a slightly flustered Hugo in his wake.

"Mr Marcus, greetings. How nice to see you again after all these years. A void in my life has now been filled."

I bit my lip thinking that the void in his bank account had been filled long ago and at our expense, and returned his smile. "Hello Mazin, and how's the world been treating you?"

It looked to me as though the world had been treating him very well indeed, as one of Allah's chosen sons. His suit was still immaculate, dark blue with a faint pale stripe, his face a light brown, perhaps a little fatter but still handsome. He was my height, and when we shook hands his grip was firm and he looked me straight in the eye. You'd got to hand it to him - he certainly had cheek.

Having seated him at the coffee table, he chose the fresh orange to drink and Hugo and I had the filter coffee, we arranged ourselves opposite but in more of a triangular configuration than a direct confrontation.

"And how are things," he asked, without any real thrust to the question, it was just an opening platitude.

"Fine," replied Hugo non-committally. "We are very busy indeed. Our work, particularly for the World Bank and in the Middle East, has picked up enormously even though money is tight out there."

Mazin nodded. "So I heard," he murmured. "You are building a good reputation with the Arabs. They like British consultants, they feel they can trust British consultants," he continued. Bullshit, I thought, utter codswallop. The reputation, yes that was perhaps true, but 'like' and 'trust' - balls! They liked only those that put in the lowest bid and they trusted nobody. Still it was standard spiel, we'd heard it all before and would no doubt hear it all again. You just nodded and didn't believe a word of it, that was the standard response.

I nodded, smiled and said, "Well that is nice to know."

Hugo interjected before I could say more. "And how about you, Mazin, has the world been treating you well since we last met?" A look of sadness came into his dark eyes, his mouth turned down as he raised his hands heavenwards.

"Ah Mr Hugo, life is not easy these days, business is very quiet and money tight. It is the war you know, the war and its aftermath is costing millions, when will it all end?"

I couldn't resist asking, "So you're not into armaments then Mazin? I would have thought that with your connections you could have kept the whole Middle East going for years. American kit for the Kuwaitis, French stuff for the Iranians and Russian guns for the Iraqis. The bonanza to beat all bonanzas." He glared at me coldly and Hugo flashed a warning glance.

"Just joking, Mazin, just a joke," I explained. So he was a bit sensitive about that was he, maybe he'd tried and got his fingers burned - or maybe his name was on an Iranian hit list. An anonymous letter to the Iranian embassy? Then I remembered that, ever since the SAS blew shit out of it, the Iranians didn't have an embassy here, and in any case, a dead Mazin was no use to us. I backed off and changed the subject.

"So, would you like to tell us what you know about the Sharjah Steel Plant, Mazin, and where do you fit in?" Both Hugo and I sat back and waited whilst Mazin leant forward, eyes glittering.

"I tell you this, Mr Marcus, I can get you that job, that project is within my control. It is I who will say where the design contract is placed."

I raised an eyebrow, they all say this, the con artists throughout the world can always 'get you the job'. It is always within their control which implies that they can also give it to somebody else if you don't toe the line. This little speech is usually followed by some 'old Russian saying' or 'old Indian proverb' which is generally totally incomprehensible but meant to back the threat. I wasn't disappointed. He saw my raised eyebrow questioning his assertion and, raising a warning finger, intoned, "Do not forget the old Arab saying 'he who leads a donkey up the minaret can also lead him down'."

I persisted, "But how do we know that you can lead the donkey up the minaret?"

He gave a short laugh, "Has not Mr Hugo told you? My brother is the Minister of Industrial Development in Sharjah, it is he who decides which consultant is selected."

I pondered a little here; Hugo was leaving me to do this part of the talking as the Middle East was my territory. "But doesn't His Highness the Ruler have some say in this?" I asked. "And how many other brothers, cousins, sisters, uncles, sons, etc, are also pushing their corner?"

Mazin looked annoyed, he didn't like being questioned, particularly when the questions were awkward to answer, and he didn't like the idea that we could doubt his influence. "I am the eldest brother and I assure you that no one else in the family is connected to the bid."

"And what about His Highness?"

"The Ruler takes advice from his ministers, particularly in technical matters like this." He turned to Hugo, obviously pissed off with me. "Mr Hugo, do you want this job or don't you? I can easily go elsewhere." Hugo pacified him gently, assuring him that we most definitely did want the job and that our designs would be best and our prices the keenest. After five minutes of Hugo's best soft soap he seemed suitably mollified and relaxed a little, drinking some orange juice. Hugo then picked up an earlier point that he hadn't answered, deliberately I thought.

"And where would you fit in, Mazin?"

Mazin put his fingertips together and pretended to give consideration to the matter, as if up to now all he had been concentrating on was doing us a favour and for the first time it had entered all our minds simultaneously that there might be something in it for him.

"I think I could serve you best by acting as your representative. I would see myself handling all arrangements between us and the Government." He paused for some reaction but neither of us reacted. We knew there would be more to come. I liked the 'us' - it was a nice touch. He continued thoughtfully, "You would appoint me to represent you in all matters. Let us see, I would need a local office, fully fitted out with full communications of course..."

"Of course," I muttered, but he ignored that.

"...I would have to have a villa and, as your representative, it would need to be big enough to entertain high ranking people: ministers, sheikhs, even the Ruler himself. Plus the usual things: air fares, cars and my expenses paid during the contract." He paused again, but there was no reaction from us, we knew he hadn't got to the nitty gritty yet, that was still to come.

I thought that perhaps I had better say something at this point, and 'no way sunshine', although very appropriate, did not seem likely to encourage him to continue setting out his top negotiating position - which was what he was doing. That would come later. So I prompted him. "And that's the whole deal is it?" He gave me a haughty pitying look and turned to Hugo again.

"Then there is of course my percentage. What do you propose to offer me?" A clever move that - if we made an offer, that would be fixed as our lowest negotiating position and, by implication, we would have accepted all his previous requirements. Hugo would not fall for that.

"What are you asking for?" Hugo countered. This went on for a bit but eventually Mazin realised that he had got to open the bidding as we patently were not going to. Without a flicker of expression on his face he said smoothly, "I require 10% of your fee, paid in stages, within seven days of receipt of payments by you, plus $100,000 advance payment on signature of agreement."

I whistled under my breath and glanced at Hugo. The rogue's definitely got something hidden up his sleeve, I was convinced of it now, he's pitched his opening offer too low. A greedy rat like Mazin Al Jabril would normally be expected to start at at least 25% if he had the clout with the Sharjah authorities that he claimed he had.

"And what do you propose to do for us for all that," I asked quietly.

"Get the job, I've just told you that!" he snapped back.

"But what is the office for then, if we've already got the job?"

I knew very well what it was all for, it was to enable him to live a life of luxury and run all his businesses at our expense. He was taken aback slightly by my question, he obviously hadn't thought this through thoroughly.

"Are you stupid or something, I've told you that as well, it's to maintain close local liaison with the people that count," he rasped angrily.

OK, I thought, now we've got his negotiating position let's start to demolish it. I began with his office and villa.

"In order to manage this contract we shall have to set up a full project office in Sharjah to deal with all the government departments at the technical level: Highways, Power, Water, Ports, all those sort of things, and it will have to have full communications. If you wish, we can easily provide you with a room in that complex next to our project manager and you will be able to share his private bathroom."

I knew he wouldn't like that at all. The idea of sharing a lavatory seat with some hairy-arsed, sweaty site engineer would not appeal one iota to his fastidious nature. I continued before he could interrupt. "I also think that if there is company entertaining to be done, as is very likely, one of our senior technical experts should also be there in case any questions are asked. It would be both economical and sensible to use one of the conference suites at the Carlton or the Hyatt. Don't forget we have to be competitive in our bid so we must keep costs down."

Hugo nodded concurrence. "A much better idea, Marcus, then the hotel can handle all the catering."

I acknowledged his support and continued. "I also think that we would not be happy with an open cheque expense arrangement. Your expenses should be your affair, so you have the freedom to act as you wish, and not be confined to tight budgets set by our accountants. Of course if you want to be given a budget, and collect and submit your expense chits for approval, we could probably devise something."

He gave me a look of open distaste; the idea of collecting receipts and submitting his expenses for approval was not his scene. I continued. "If your expenses were included in your percentage, you would not have these restrictions and that would be much better."

All this was pretty routine foreplay, the testing out of each side's strengths and weaknesses in the negotiation; it was his percentage that really counted, that was the big money. The rest, if we had agreed to it, would just have been a major source of endless problems and arguments. We all knew that. So we were now coming to the crunch. This is where we were going to get the full repertoire. We would be into the abusive hysterics, a performance worthy of the Royal Academy of Dramatic Art, Shakespearean tragedies, threats of violence, imprisonment and torture, the curses of Allah and everything else he could think of under the sun. I knew it, Hugo knew it and Mazin knew it. Already he was sipping his orange juice to lubricate the vocal chords in readiness.

I turned to face him. "Hugo and I have given this some considerable thought," I began. "As you are aware this could be a half billion dollar project, which means our fees could be up to $20 million. You appreciate that these fees are not all for us - a large part will have to be paid to our sub-consultants, other specialists and outside technical experts. We accept, however, that in representing us you are also representing them, so we are prepared to agree to your percentage being calculated on the whole fee not just our part of it."

He nodded. This was also routine. I continued. "Now as far as you are concerned the amount of work you have to do for this job would be no different to, say, that for $100 million project so, bearing that in mind and being generous because we like and respect you..." There's a laugh, I thought. Well you've got to throw something like that in no matter how big a shit you think he is - and in this case it was pretty big - it all helps in the softening up process. "...we think one half of one per cent of our fee..." I held up my hand as his mouth opened... "which could" - I didn't say will or would - "...total $100,000, is reasonable."

I sat back and waited for the eruption, I was pleased that we had turned the heating off in the office because Mazin stood a good chance of producing enough calories in the next few minutes to compensate. Hugo scratched his nose nervously; this was all news to him. We had agreed between us what we would eventually settle at but how we got there he had left to me, so we both watched with interest.

Mazin's jaw began working furiously as he ground his teeth together, his face had grown redder and redder as I spoke and now the veins were standing proud on his neck and forehead. He crashed his glass down on to the table and leapt to his feet leaning over towards Hugo.

"I have not come all this way to be insulted," he bellowed, "I am a powerful man and can crush you like a fly." He smashed one fist into the palm of the other hand with a loud smack, "Like that! You treat me like an ignorant peasant, I make you pay. You people are nothing, zero without me to guide you on this project. I can get anybody - I don't need you, it is you that needs me. What you are offering is an insult, it is contemptible. Pouff, I snuff it out like a candle, I kick your offer into the gutter to lie with the filth of the dogs..." On he went, voice rising and falling, from purple-faced shouting to sinister sibilant hisses. It was world class fulminating by a master fulminator, and all the time his finger waggled a few inches from Hugo's nose.

Hugo didn't flinch one iota, he was made of sterner stuff but this performance was clearly a new experience for him.

We had a full 15 minutes of 'Jewish shysters', 'never work again in the Middle East', 'could forget any chance of getting this job', 'what did we think he was?' - (I could have answered that without thinking, but refrained - it was worth holding my tongue to experience a master of bullying tactics at his best in full abusive flow) - 'see us ruined' - conveniently overlooking the fact that he almost had - 'bring in the Japanese, Germans, Americans, in fact most of the United Nations' - 'blacken our name throughout the world', etc.

It was pretty good as it went, but typically of Mazin he had totally misjudged his target. If he had negotiated quietly he could have won Hugo round a little, but he had made the fatal mistake of assuming that because Hugo was a gentleman, presumably in contrast to his opinion of me, he was weak. But it was clearly obvious to me that all Mazin's ranting and raving had done was achieve the difficult feat of getting right up Hugo's nose - almost physically, but certainly metaphorically.

As Mazin paused to re-lubricate his tonsils, Hugo - with a tight jaw - started to rise from his chair saying, "I don't think I wish to hear any more of this. I am not prepared to put up with this sort of behaviour in my office from a man who stole $2 million from this firm and nearly drove us to the wall. I think we'd better terminate this discussion forthwith!"

I saw a look of shock pass over Mazin's face as he realized that he'd gone too far with the wrong person. Hugo was not used to negotiating with Arabs and had taken Mazin's diatribe personally rather than as a negotiating tactic. I rapidly stepped in to pour oil on troubled waters.

"I suppose, if we took your expenses into account, Mazin, we could up your percentage to 1%. Allowing for those, that could mean you would get around $200 000 - no advance payment. The deal is, you will get paid your share within seven days of us receiving the money in our bank account, and in the same currency that we are paid - that is likely to be US dollars."

A look of relief flashed across Mazin's taut features as he realized that the negotiations had not been terminated and were still open. Hugo sank back into his chair tight-lipped but silent.

The alarm faded from Mazin's eyes and he began to restate his case for more money in a reasoned way cutting out the hysterics.

Very interesting and illuminating, I thought, he clearly knows a lot more about this consultancy contract than we do, but why would he be so scared when he thought we were going to give him the elbow in the certain belief that we would have blown any chance we had of landing the contract as a result? I had no answer to that.

We haggled for another half hour, he came down to 5%, we talked ourselves up to one and a half; he came to four, then three. We finally settled on 2% and we would provide him with a separate office in Sharjah, with secretary, and full communications. No advance payment, and he would be paid within seven days of our receipt of our fees.

As our fees would be paid in increments over the length of the design and construction periods, this would provide him with a steady cash flow.

I said I would get our lawyers to draw up the agreement immediately. Mazin looked surprised at that but didn't demur, and we arranged to meet at 5 o'clock the following afternoon. Nothing further was said about our $2 million, but even though nothing was said, the direct accusation that he had stolen the money hung in the air and both sides knew that that was not the end of the matter.

As he was leaving Mazin could not resist sliding in a final shaft. Turning to me he asked, "Can you drive a Mercedes?" I nodded assent.

"Yes, why?"

He smiled. "My driver is away this weekend and I need somebody to drive me up to Cambridge and back." He didn't deign to offer a reason and the way it was put was a demand, requirement, instruction what you will, not merely an observation. Just in case I misunderstood this he added, "Be at my flat at 10.30 on Saturday morning, there's a good chap." He flicked a card on to Hugo's desk. "The new address is on that." He turned away leaving me nonplussed for a few seconds. I looked at Hugo and he gave a brief nod. OK, just this once, in the interest of good relations - a forlorn interest I felt - but you never knew, I might learn something to our advantage. Mazin knew I would drive him; he was still smiling.

Hugo showed him out with a brief and chilly handshake, he was still very nettled about being compared to 'a stinking pile of dung from a rabid pig'.

"One thing I've learned," I said to Hugo on his return, "I didn't think pigs could catch rabies!"

"That's not funny, Marcus," he responded frigidly, "that man gets my goat! The cheek of him, he nearly ruins us and then turns up here cool as you like and insults us like that. I suppose we have to deal with him?"

"We have, if we are to have any chance of getting our money back," I reminded him. "That wasn't meant to be personally insulting, it's just their way of trying to frighten us to a more amenable negotiating position."

"Well, I thought he was downright rude."

I gave a thin smile. "Confucius didn't say the bugger would be a nice, quiet person when he came floating past us down the river, did he? Anyway you're not the one who is going to have to spend most of Saturday in close confinement with him."

"Why did you agree to that anyway?"

"I thought you gave me the nod."

"No, I must have been easing my collar a little."

"Well no harm done, I may be able to learn something more from him. He can't sit silent all the way to Cambridge and back. By the way did you notice how desperately he wants this job with us?"

"No?"

101

I turned over the morning's events in my mind. I had got to know Mazin Al Jabril fairly well in the past and, although he could be rude, abrasive and inconsiderate, he could also turn on the charm. This morning's performance was not typical of him, it was much more that of a nervous man. He was usually more subtle and smooth in negotiations.

"Hugo, there is a lot more to this than meets the eye. Mazin was not comfortable. He was not his old, smooth, arrogant, confident self. It was too much of an act he put on rather than a proper Mazin-type negotiation. The sort of ritual that he thought we would expect him to go through."

Hugo grimaced wryly. "You could have fooled me," he murmured with a questioning look in his eye.

"Oh yes," I said, "do you remember when we negotiated his Egyptian contract? We haggled for two weeks over eighths of a percent and trivial details like his phone bills and taxi fares. He threw a few wobblies but nothing like today. There were other things wrong as well; for a start he pitched his opening bid far too low for an Al Jabril who believes he has our balls in a vice. Then he was terrified when you threatened to terminate the meeting and call the whole thing off. He didn't want that. Also the final deal was too easy and too quick. He could easily have strung us out for at least a couple of days and made us sweat. With the connections he claims to have, 2% is a pushover. There was no attempt to up the percentage after we had agreed his commission by throwing in such things as, 'of course my brother the Minister will also be requiring 2%'."

Hugo smoothed his hair, a sign that he was interested. "You could be right, but where does that get us?"

"I don't know, but it is a little something to hang our hat on. I'll try to find out more on Saturday."

Hugo nodded with a grin. "Yes and don't forget your hat."

"What hat?"

"Your chauffeur's peaked cap!"

I gave him the finger as I strolled out back to my office.

CHAPTER SEVEN

At 9.30 the following morning I presented myself, decked out in a City suit, to Major Margaret's approval, at the offices of Parker, Parker, Son and Parker. This bunch of venerable old hacks - 'but very well connected, Marcus' - represented our legal interests from shabby but expensive chambers in The Temple, one of the Inns of Court. I dealt with 'Son', or as he was known to the trade, 'young Mr Parker'. He was pushing 75 and well past his sell-by date so what the ancient, antique and decrepit Mr Parkers were like I couldn't imagine, Hugo dealt with them when we had long or complicated legal arrangements to sort out. For the quick stuff I was given the dynamic rising star in the Parker firmament, and 'Young Mr Parker' was not the sort of person you could ask about that sort of thing, he didn't encourage any familiarities. Come to think of it he didn't actually encourage much. Based on past experience his first reaction when presented with any proposition was to shake his head and, with wattles wobbling like a Christmas turkey three feet ahead of the axe, recite in sepulchral tones, "I strongly advise against it."

I sat uncomfortably on a hard Victorian horsehair-stuffed chair in his office and gazed around. Brown walls, worn brown carpet, brown furniture and dusty brown files. The environment alone convinced you that you were in deep shit before you opened your mouth. He studied me through narrowing cold pink rheumy eyes as I outlined our proposals for Mazin Al Jabril's agency agreement. A Scottish herring wedged in ice on a fishmonger's slab would have seemed more responsive. When I had finished he didn't move or speak and his eyes appeared to be closed. Christ, he's dead, I thought. I've spent the last ten minutes talking to a corpse. I wonder how Parker, Parker, Son and Parker will bill me for that?

To talking to Young Mr Parker, one hour or part of an hour	- £300
Allow 10% reduction for period when Young Mr Parker was no longer with us	- £030
Total Now Due	- £270

Plus VAT @17.5%
E&OE

I was just deciding whether to reach out to see if there was a pulse in the pale, blue-veined, skinny wrist that still lay extended across his blotter, or hit the door and demand to see a more lively member of their establishment when he spoke. I jerked convulsively as his thin, dry voice broke the silence.

"I don't like the sound of this at all, I must advise you that it is most unwise to proceed along the lines you have outlined."

I had to admit that on the lines I had outlined he was probably right, but then I couldn't tell him that the main purpose of this was to get Mazin on the hook so we could stitch him up, if possible, at some future date. No agreement, no Mazin, no revenge - it was as simple as that.

"Why?" I queried. "What do you see wrong with the proposals?"

He gestured at the heads of agreement I had passed to him.

"Far too woolly, far too loose, we should have been present at the discussions. Very unwise to have agreed matters as important as these without our advice." He blew his nose loudly on a large paisley handkerchief that he whipped out of his breast pocket with unexpected speed and then examined its contents. He was clearly more satisfied with whatever fall-out his nose had delivered than he was with my draft agreement. I got the message though. It was not that there was much wrong. After all, it was only a draft, and Mazin hadn't seen it, so no harm had been done. No, he felt nettled at being left out initially, a meeting at our office was worth £500 in fees and he felt done out of it. I explained that Mazin had only arrived the previous morning and that we hadn't had time to contact him otherwise we would have undoubtedly done so but because we had not had the benefit of his invaluable advice nothing had been agreed, it was only a draft, blah, blah, blah! Partially mollified, but still sore about the £500 he was light, he condescended to look again at the draft, constructively.

We discussed the points to be covered in turn and as the clock ticked on he warmed a little. By a hint of cajoling, promises, pressure and bloody mindedness I eventually persuaded him to agree to fax me a suitable agreement for Mazin Al Jabril formulated from the heads of agreement and detailed notes I had given him. There was no small talk or coffee, once the business was concluded he pressed a bell on his desk and then closed his eyes again. The beefy receptionist who had ushered me in turned up almost immediately to bounce me out, and within 30 seconds I was back in the street.

The fax arrived in the office about 3.30; it was quite short and we had it printed out in duplicate ready for signature within the hour. Mazin duly waltzed in an hour late at 6 o'clock quite unabashed, no apology, and unexpectedly accompanied by a thin sharp-faced westernised Arab in a black suit whom he introduced as his lawyer.

They both studied the agreement carefully, the lawyer donning a pair of half-moon glasses and making notes in Arabic on a pad.

Coffee was served, Mazin declined the orange juice. I think he had sussed out that we had given him Jaffa juice yesterday and Israeli products were anathema to him. I said nothing. The lawyer chap, whose name I didn't catch but it didn't seem important, looked alternately at Hugo and I over his half-moons. He had jet black eyes, expressionless eyes, the only other thing that could be said about them was that they matched his suit and fingernails.

"It says here that my client will be paid seven days after receipt of fees into your bank by you and in the same currency that you receive monies."

I nodded. "That is correct."

He frowned. "My client did not agree to that."

I raised an eyebrow; it was a peculiar point to question.

"Well whether he did or not that is what we told him, that is standard procedure..." and pushing it because I felt we had a strong negotiating position... "and that is what it must be."

The lawyer glanced at Mazin who shrugged and motioned him to continue. The lawyer turned back to me, "My client wishes to be paid in US dollars," he persisted.

I smiled at Mazin. "Mr Al Jabril knows that this is a World Bank financed job and that they work in US dollars. However, as we have not got the job yet, and therefore not signed a contract in which the currency is stipulated, we must cover ourselves. If Mr Al Jabril would like to wait until after we have signed our contract with the World Bank before we sign our agreement with him we will be delighted to include a specific currency in his contract."

Mazin gave his lawyer a sharp warning glance, there was no way he was going to risk being kicked into touch once we had got our deal signed up. The lawyer hummed and hawed a bit and then passed on.

"This agency contract is only for the one project, the Sharjah Steel Plant. My client would like it to be all embracing, covering all work you get in the United Arab Emirates."

I bet he would, I thought. We already had work in Abu Dhabi and Al Ain and were hoping for some in Dubai. There were many varied and good reasons why he should not have a sole agency, amongst them the fact that we had other agents already in other places, some of whom were very well connected and would not take kindly to be shunted sideways or sharing their commission with Mazin Al Jabril. In some cases the agent concerned had been 'suggested' by the client who had a coincidentally similar name. There was other follow-up work also in the pipeline through these people. I could explain all this and it would probably be accepted so I opened my mouth to do so, thought fuck it and said "No!"

Hugo's eyebrows shot up and Mazin flashed me a look of pure hatred. His lawyer blinked a bit and then said, "I would like to discuss this with my client privately." Hugo and I left the office, closing the door behind us.

"What are you doing Marcus?" he whispered anxiously. "You're pushing it, aren't you?"

"Let us see how much he wants this agency," I replied. "I think he's stretched over a barrel somewhere in this. If not then we can always climb down a little. No harm done."

Five minutes later the lawyer poked his head out of the door and beckoned us back in. Mazin was sitting there as impassive as an Easter Island stone. The lawyer adjusted his spectacles and after clearing his throat, gabbled, "In the interests of good relationships my client has agreed to accept the terms as drawn up. Perhaps you can call in an independent witness and we can sign and exchange the documents."

Producing his gold pen, Mazin signed both copies with a flourish, witnessed by the lawyer and Hugo signed for us, witnessed by Janet. We exchanged copies and the lawyer was about to put theirs into his briefcase when Mazin smartly removed it from his hand and tucked it into his own inside pocket. "I'll keep that," he pronounced, ignoring the lawyer's protesting gasp. "Leave us now," he told the lawyer, "we have other business to discuss."

Not so much as a 'thank you very much' or any other form of courteous separation for Mazin, once he had no further use for you, you were out on your ear like an empty milk bottle. The lawyer mumbled his goodbyes and pushed off un-remarked by anyone. He had only been brought along for show, I realised, he was never intended to make any positive contribution. It was just Mazin's way of countering my use of lawyers to draw up the agreement in the first place. A matter of face entirely. I remained seated and silent, it had come as news to me that we had other business to discuss, but no doubt all would be revealed in due course.

Whilst Hugo completed the briefest of courtesies in getting rid of the lawyer, I studied Mazin. There was a change in him now, he was much more confident, back to his arrogant demanding old self. Gone was the impassivity, his eyes were snapping round the room impatiently. He began tapping his fingers on the table and, when Hugo resumed his seat, launched straight into the attack. Addressing me he said, "Have you read the detailed brief issued by the World Bank?"

"Of course I have, Mazin," I replied. "I've studied it inside out, we need to do that in order to prepare our proposal, cost out our time and evaluate the construction costs."

"And what did you deduce was the most significant thing about the brief?" he questioned arrogantly.

I was not going to play these sort of bloody stupid games, if he wanted a run around he could run round himself, I had better things to do.

"You tell me, Mazin," I replied offhandedly, knowing full well that that was just what he was going to do.

"As you don't seem to have grasped it I will tell you," he sneered. "The Minister of Industrial Development in Sharjah requires this plant to be the most advanced steel plant of its kind in the world." He paused expecting comment.

"So?" I said nonchalantly.

"So what are you going to give them?" he demanded angrily.

The picture cleared a little for me. When he was not our agent he knew that there was no way that we would reveal our ideas to him when we were in competition with others. Now that we were tied together and our interests were mutual, I supposed he had a right to know - if he was to promote us with his brother. I also had a suspicion that somewhere in this was the kernel of his purpose in associating with us. I hesitated momentarily weighing up the pros and cons of giving him detailed information.

Hugo saw my hesitation and suggested, "You could show Mazin the layout drawing on which we have based the whole of our scheme. It will give him some idea of what we have in mind."

I nodded agreement. "OK, I'll get a copy from my office." I brought the rolled up site plan in and we spread it out on the coffee table holding the corners down with cups and saucers. I explained how it all worked. "The scrap and ferro alloys come into the port here, they are stocked mechanically and shipped automatically to the plant here, where they are weighed, batched and loaded into the furnaces here." I pointed to the various parts of the scheme. "The melted steel is cast into ingots here and again the ingots are cooled, transported, stored and loaded here, all automatically. The whole thing is computerised. These are the laboratories, these the offices, the power and gas come in here and the water-cooling is that complex there. The remainder is accommodation, rest and recreation facilities, hospital and general personnel."

Mazin followed it all intently. "What about the rolling mills?" he asked. "Where are they?"

"They will go in here in the next stage," I replied, indicating an area next to the ingot stockyards, "and again everything will be automatic - computer controlled."

He put his finger on the main building. "And all that area is for the furnaces?"

I nodded agreement.

"What sort of furnaces are you proposing?"

I smiled, it was a very good question, right to he heart of the scheme, there were no flies on Mazin Al Jabril that was for sure.

"I think that is where we have our edge," I advised him. "We are proposing to use newly developed 500 ton electric arc furnaces in this plant. They will have the largest capacity of any electric arc furnaces in the world and are just being brought into service by three firms, one each in Japan, Germany and here. They will be fully automated, economical on power and have a production rate 40% higher than anything else that is either planned or in operation, as far as we know, anywhere in the world."

Mazin straightened up still keeping his finger on the furnace building. "They seem to take up an awful lot of space," he commented. I agreed they were big and explained that they required plenty of clearance for mechanical handling and safety reasons. I wondered what he was leading up to; there was nothing

I could see in it for Mazin with any of the big three arc furnace manufacturers.

There was a silence for a minute then Mazin said offhandedly, "Have you considered using laser accelerated vacuum contained high frequency induction furnaces?"

I was astounded, totally taken aback. Firstly, that he even knew such things might conceivably exist, let alone be able to get their name absolutely correct. They did exist, it was true, but to my knowledge only as laboratory models in research departments and on a very small scale. Only one firm that I knew of had produced even a 20 ton working furnace of that type. And secondly, because this was clearly what he had been building up to and why he had taken all this trouble to associate with us again. It seemed to me a total non-starter and my heart sank. If that was the case and this was what he had in mind all along then I didn't see how we could set him up to get our money back.

My incredulity must have shown on my face because he gave a short laugh.

"Ha! So you haven't! The brief asks for the most advanced plant and you go for something years out of date - the Minister will not accept that."

I protested. "But nobody makes high frequency induction furnaces of that type - let alone 500 ton capacity ones."

"You should do your research, sonny," he sneered, looking at me down his nose, "that is what you are supposed to be paid for."

Hugo interjected sharply to give me a welcome breathing space, he could see I was rocked.

"Are you saying that such furnaces do exist? If so, how much do they cost and what are their performance statistics? Electric arc furnaces are quantifiable items. Supply and delivery is known. We know how they work, how they are loaded, tapped, powered, maintained, in fact all about them. Something of this kind of thing that you are talking about is an absolute unknown quantity! Nobody has any information about the required support facilities!"

That stopped Mazin in his tracks, he hadn't thought of that. "You mean you couldn't include these in your proposals because you don't know how they operate?"

"Exactly - nobody does on this scale."

Mazin pondered for a couple of minutes, his mind working at high speed. He was not the sort of person to let a little problem like practicalities thwart him.

"Right," he said, "this is what you'll do. You put in your proposals as before," he indicated the layout plan on the table, "with prices, programmes, everything; just as you would normally and using electric arc furnaces. I will ensure that you get the job and by then I will have obtained some more detailed information from the manufacturer of the induction furnaces on the back-up required. There will be nothing to stop us changing the scheme after you've got the job provided we can show it to be either cheaper, quicker to build or more economical to run - or any combination of these. The Minister will certainly agree to that."

It was kind of him to tell us what we would do, arrogant bastard, but I had to accept that what he said seemed reasonable and sensible, neither of which was characteristic of an Al Jabril deal, so there must be a dead rat buried in there somewhere. It was only when he was leaving having discussed a few more details that I smelt it.

"By the way, Mazin," I called as he made his way out, "who is the manufacturer of the laser accelerated vacuum contained high frequency induction furnace then?"

He surveyed me scornfully, proud of his superior knowledge.

"Pantocrator of Greece," he replied, "they are the only people in the world who make this equipment, and I am their appointed agent!"

Hugo and I sat down after he had gone and cracked a bottle of Sancerre. I waited till he had poured two glasses and then took mine to the comfortable chair in front of his desk.

"Are you thinking what I'm thinking, Marcus?" he asked, slowly sipping the cool liquid.

"I am indeed - we now know what it is he's after. He's tied up a sole agency with Pantocrator and he knows the World Bank's rules. This is specialised equipment and Pantocrator is the sole manufacturer. The World Bank will therefore permit a price to be negotiated with them instead of requiring competitive bids."

"Provided it can be shown that the installation of such furnaces saves time or money or both," Hugo added.

I turned the wine glass round in my fingers slowly. "Do you know what figure we have in our cost plan for the furnaces, Hugo, the total cost with all their special equipment that will all be a part of the same supply and install contract - $80 million!" I let that sink in and then added, "and Mazin as sole agent will be on at least 10% - maybe more - $8 million; which makes the $400,000 maximum he will get from us look like pin money."

"Jesus H Christ," gasped Hugo, "no wonder he was so keen to get his foot in the door."

I drank some wine and put the glass down on his desk and said with a slow smile, "And there's one other thing, Hugo, that will interest you. I had heard of a manufacturer who was developing this new kind of high frequency induction furnace. They have a working unit operating already, but it's quite small and they are

114

keeping very quiet about it so they can hit the market before their competitors get a sniff."

Hugo looked at me, "So you did know of Pantocrator," he said.

I continued smiling. "No, Hugo, the firm I know of is Costa da Silva of Sao Paulo in Brazil."

He looked at me quizzically. "You mean there are two firms?"

"Precisely!"

Twice during the day I had phoned King-Knight's, but the telephonist obviously knew now who I was and I got the stone wall.

"Well just tell her I'm sorry," I pleaded desperately, "say Marcus says he's sorry." In a frosty voice she said she'd pass the message on.

I left the office that evening still thinking over the Mazin Al Jabril situation, it was just after 8.30. I had plenty to think about. For the first time it looked as if we had an edge, although what we could do with it remained to be seen. I mentally tossed up whether to go down to the Frog or go home; I plumped for the pub and steered the car in that direction. It was a cold wet night and there were few people about the windy streets. I parked the MG close to the entrance and dashed for the door. The pub was warm and welcoming, but Andy King-Knight most certainly was not. He nailed me almost as I set foot across the threshold.

"What the hell's got into you, Marcus? Not only do you fuck up my meeting, I then learn you've been doing the same to my staff. Is there a state of war that I don't know about existing between CONDES and King-Knight's? And why don't you leave Kate

Tennant alone, she's got enough troubles on her plate without you adding to them for Christ's sake!"

I spun round from the bar halfway through ordering my pint. "What do you mean she's got enough troubles? What troubles has she got?"

He laughed scornfully, "Don't tell me you don't know," he sneered, "you've been trying to persuade her to dump him so you must know."

It appeared that today had been designated puzzle corner day for Mr Moon. First I had Mazin Al Jabril with his sodding silly games, and now Andy King-Knight with his magical mysteries. I had had enough.

I seized him by the collar and held him close, my nose two inches from his. "Dump who, Andrew?" I grated. He struggled indignantly but I think he realised I wasn't fooling.

"Dump Jonathan Grey," he spluttered angrily.

That name rang a dim distant bell but I couldn't recall why, it must have been something a long time past. No matter.

"And what's so special about Jonathan bloody Grey that he can't be dumped if she doesn't like him anymore?" I demanded.

He stopped struggling and looked at me with astonishment. "You don't know then, you really don't know?"

"For God's sake, Andrew, what don't I know that everybody seems to think I do know and about which I don't have a clue?"

His eyes searched my face seeking confirmation of the truth and seemed satisfied.

"The poor chaps dying of cancer, malignant melanoma," he said quietly: "He was given about six months to live, that was three months ago, and he's only 29."

I let go of his collar suddenly and his feet hit the floor with a thud. A cold chill gripped my whole body and I began to feel sick.

"She lives with him?" I asked in a low voice.

He nodded, smoothing down his rumpled suit. "Has done since she came back from Switzerland; they've been going out together, all told, for a couple of years. His cancer was only diagnosed relatively recently. They were away on holiday when this mole on his back suddenly started to grow and bleed but he decided not to do anything about it until they got home. Then something else came up, so it was a month or so before he went to the doctor. He was referred immediately to a specialist, but by then it was too late. The thing had spread. He's having radiotherapy and chemo or whatever, but it's not working. It's spread to vital organs and it's only a matter of time.

"They were going to get married this year and she wanted to go through with it, but he insisted that it be shelved. He doesn't want her to feel tied down."

I turned away shattered. Oh God, what had I done, and what had I said? She must have presumed that I knew about Jonathan and was trying to take advantage of the situation. She must think I'm a first-class shit. What could I do now? I didn't know. Shut up and keep away seemed to be the immediate answer but it was so negative and cowardly.

Andy put his hand on my shoulder.

"I'm sorry, Marcus, I thought you knew."

I just shook my head without speaking; it was dreadful.

I couldn't stay in the cheerful bonhomie of the Frog after that news, and so I left my drink half finished and went. I drove back to my flat in a daze without being conscious of any stage of the journey at all. I must write to her, I thought, it was all I could do. I began to try to compose a letter; it was not going to be an easy letter to write.

CHAPTER EIGHT

I chewed the end of my pen as, for the umpteenth time, I reread my short letter of regret and apology to Kate - it was not a Pullitzer prizewinner by a long chalk but it was the best I could do. Whereas I may have reread it umpteen times, I had rewritten it umpteen and squared, each time in long hand, the waste basket was half full of discarded efforts. With a sigh like a Victorian virgin I licked the flap, sealed up the envelope and then sat with my metaphorical finger up my metaphorical bum - I didn't know her address or that of Jonathan Grey. After some thought I decided to mark it Personal and Private in large letters and sent it, care of King-Knight's, to Kensington Church Street. It didn't look much as a carrier of last hopes, just a thin white envelope with spidery writing in black ink. Should I send flowers as well? No, that would be a bit creepy. The simple cri du coeur - if she recognised it as that - rather than a cheap attempt at ingratiating myself with her, was better. Well, I thought so.

Absently I handed it to The Major, still ruminating about the situation, and I only half rose to the bait when she upbraided me.

"You naughty boy! You've let your coffee go cold yet again. I'll have to make you another cup now!"

"Yeah, oh thanks ma'am, sorry about that," I murmured abstractedly. She responded with a kindly smile and strode out bearing the letter and the offending cold cup of coffee. I studied her back thoughtfully as she departed, she was definitely letting her hair grow, it looked both longer and more shiny. She actually didn't look too bad from the back, women in the services seem to wear those straight skirts that fit tight across the beam and stop short of muscular calves. Major Margaret had continued this fashion into civilian life, but I noticed that the skirt she was wearing today was tailored giving her a more flattering shape. A bit hefty but... I shook my head, good grief what am I thinking about, deprivation was clouding the judgement - there was no way that she was my type, but there would be many who wouldn't say no - half the letchers down at the Frog and Nightgown for a start.

I was just beginning to contemplate which of the little souls I could weld to hers; to tip toe holding hands along the pathways of life and give her a good rogering at the end, when Brian Mason heaved into sight beaming in the doorway like a dog with two dicks. He had the draft of our six-monthly management accounts which were due at the 30th September. The Major's relief programme was relegated to the back burner for the present whilst we went through the figures. They were good according to Brian, showing both increased turnover and increased profit. Miserable old Jenkins at the 'Bank that Moans like Hell' should be pleased - if anything ever pleased him. At least we were in credit, although the financing of the design work for Sharjah Steel would bite into that. I asked Brian to let me have a couple of the final copies when they became available.

On Saturday, filled with dread at the prospect of being closeted in close proximity to Mazin all day, I turned up at his flat at 11 o'clock, half an hour late, deliberately. I expected a tirade of sarcastic abuse but he was as nice as pie. He greeted me at the door, nonchalantly brushing his manservant to one side against the wall like a bead curtain, and ushered me into the magnificent sitting room which commanded a panoramic view over Hyde Park. Thrown carelessly on the rich parquet flooring were valuable Isfahan and Shiraz rugs. The inlaid tables bore silver ornaments from North Africa and Arabia, coffee pots, Kunjar daggers and filigree bowls. The armchairs were white hide and the light fittings crystal. There were no pictures on the walls but hung in their stead were finely scripted quotations in Arabic and Farsi, presumably from the Koran. He served the pale green spicy Arabic coffee in beautiful hand-painted eggshell china cups with a selection of biscuits - well he didn't, his manservant did, having recovered from being flattened against the wall, but Mazin was the one who offered it. Showing no signs of impatience he chatted conversationally until I had finished my coffee and declined a third refill by waggling the cup, and then suggested we made a start. We took a private lift down to his garage. The Mercedes 560SEL was waiting for us, spotless and gleaming. I baulked at opening his door for him so I left him to sort himself out and just climbed in the driver's side, but it didn't seem to matter. I wondered just how long he could last out under the strain of being pleasant. Half an hour was my bet. "Which way do you want to go Mazin? Any particular way?"

He shook his head saying easily, "I have to be at Trinity College at 2 o'clock I have an appointment with the bursar." I took that to mean I could choose the route as long as I got him there on time.

As I picked my way through the traffic leading up through St John's Wood and Swiss Cottage towards the A1 he told me that there were some ancient Arabic manuscripts in the Wren library at Trinity that he wished to examine. Apparently they were records of voyages made hundreds of years ago by navigators on the trade routes between Africa, the Arabian Peninsula and India. Allegedly these could have a considerable historical bearing on the disposition of tribes currently inhabiting the Northern Emirates, as Sharjah, Fujairah, Umm Al Quwain and Ras Al Khaimah were collectively known.

"I didn't know you were a student of history, Mazin?" I observed, thinking that such a scholarly pursuit appeared to be totally alien to the ruthless, rapacious, avaricious sod we all knew and loathed. The mask slipped for a moment as he sensed my cynicism.

"I'm not," he snapped, "but the Ruler of Sharjah is - and he wishes to know if these are genuine because if so, he might like to make an offer for them."

I stifled a laugh. I might have known that there was money in it. Mazin taking his 10% cut of history. However Mr Nice Guy returned, and if you ignored the egotistical slant of his conversation, he was quite entertaining. It was much easier to listen and drive than to hold a conversation, and the car handled a treat. By the time we turned off the A1 at Baldock on to the A505 he had me genuinely laughing with him at his stories - mainly about the gaffes of westerners - Americans in particular - when in Arabia, and how smart he had been. When he turned it on the charm oozed out of him like sweating gelignite.

"Tell me a little more about your firm, Marcus," he asked casually. "Now that you have become a company instead of a partnership does that help get business?"

I negotiated a tractor pulling a cartload of sugar beet and then cut my speed back to 80 before replying. "Oh yes I think it does," I said. "Partnerships are relatively secret things, they don't have to file accounts at Companies House, only the partners and the Inland Revenue see them. Whereas now we are a company, our accounts are available to the public. We have found that this gives our clients confidence because they can see that we are not men of straw. They can see our assets and turnover, what profits we make and what borrowings we have. It also helps with our bankers - fortunately." I added pointedly. Too right, I thought ruefully, if we had been a partnership there would have been no way the bank would have supported us after you, you bastard, had done the dirty on us. I smiled at him guilelessly. If the shot went home he ignored it and continued.

"And I suppose being a company makes control - decision making - easier?" he asked, equally blandly.

"Oh yes, yes indeed it does. As you are probably aware only Hugo and I are shareholding directors..." I knew he was aware of no such thing but it was as well to let him know where the power lay in case he tried to go behind our backs and influence the others. "...the rest of the people on the board are not shareholders although of course they are directors."

He pondered a moment and then with a winning smile observed questioningly, "Oh so you and Hugo own the firm?"

I shook my head. "No, we control the firm, and we control it here in the United Kingdom, hence we pay UK taxes, but the majority of the shares are owned by a Jersey trust."

"But don't they influence you then," he persisted. "If a trust owns the majority, doesn't it, or the trustees, exercise strong direction over the company's activities?"

I shook my head again. "No, it does not. The trustee is not an engineer, he's an accountant and the trust holds the shares for the purpose its name indicates, on trust for beneficiaries. The previous partners for instance, who retired because of age, are beneficiaries. We are left to run the business our way entirely."

He asked me a few more questions about our workload - which I told him was excellent and increasing - and the problems of recruiting suitably qualified staff. He told me that at one time he had run a large contracting business employing over 2,000 people out of Beirut but the civil war had put paid to that. He was very knowledgeable about the construction industry, as one would expect, and gave me quite a lot of information about the activities of some of our consultancy competitors in the Middle East and what they were doing. I informed him that I was taking our bid for Sharjah Steel to Washington myself on Tuesday to hand it into the International Bank for Reconstruction and Development on Wednesday before the deadline at 12 noon. He said in that case he would fly back to Sharjah the same day so that when the discussions took place between the World Bank and the Government of Sharjah he would be placed to make sure, as he put it, "that the correct decision was made".

I dropped him at the main gate of Trinity and arranged to pick him up at 4 o'clock. I could see him hesitate fractionally, he wanted me hanging about so that at whatever time he finished I would be on call, but there was obviously still enough sweetness left at the bottom of his honey jar so he just nodded and walked in.

Although the sun shone the wind was from the east, and it was a bit too chilly to sit on the banks of the Cam and watch the world go by, so I parked the Merc, on a yellow line - Mazin would get the ticket - and spent a very pleasant couple of hours strolling and thinking.

So what the hell was all that about" Is he trying to convince me that all along we had wronged him, misjudged his kindly intentions, and condemned him unjustly when all he was seeking was our benefit? Was it that beneath that sneering, arrogant exterior there lay a heart of gold, a human being kind to children and pensioners, but hard done to by the world for trying to make a crust? If so, I thought with a rueful grin, he's failed miserably but it was interesting.

When I returned to the car sure enough there was a parking ticket stuck under the windscreen wiper. I pushed it into the glove compartment amongst the half dozen others already there and drove off to our rendezvous. He kept me waiting for half an hour at the gate. Revenge for this morning or just Arab timekeeping? Who knows? And then promptly fell asleep in the car, remaining that way until we arrived outside his flat just after 6.30.

I promised to send a messenger over with a copy of our bid - a bit of a gamble I knew, but under the circumstances we thought we could trust him, and if he was going to promote our corner it would be as well that he knew exactly what it was he was promoting. Anyway he wouldn't get it until Monday night and there was not much our competitors could do between then and noon Wednesday to change their proposals and get them deposited in Washington, even if he leaked it. We shook hands and he said he would telephone from Sharjah if he had any news. It was all very matey, very civilised and totally out of character.

I wondered if he was pleased with his day. If he was as sharp as I thought he was, he would be - because on the previous Thursday night, lying in the steaming comfort of my bath, I had had an idea.

Whilst trying to sink one of the plastic ducks with a water pistol I had been turning over in my mind what we had learned about Mazin and the Sharjah contract.

He was desperate that we should get this project. Why?

Because he thought we would be easy to manipulate? Probably.

He was not overly concerned about the quantum of his deal with us, only that there was a binding deal signed appointing him our local representative. Why?

Obviously because he believed that he was going to make a heap of money out of the project in some other way.

But how was he going to achieve that?

By ensuring that we arranged matters with some other party or parties so that he would.

Who were they?

Well he had already given us a major lead about this with the introduction of the idea of using laser accelerated vacuum contained high frequency induction furnaces - LAVCHIFS. He had tied up an agency agreement with Pantocrator of Greece, presumably through his Swiss company Investment and Resource Holdings SA. Then he and his brother, the Minister, would ensure that Pantocrator got the $80 million plus sub-contract, which matched or exceeded the specifications, and were comparable in price to traditional furnaces. Therefore the World Bank would not require competitive bids only a negotiated price.

And who would front these negotiations?

That would be a CONDES responsibility.

And who would ensure that he was at the forefront of the proceedings? The evil genie himself, Mazin Al Jabril!

And Investment and Resource Holdings would net over $8 million commission!

Simple wasn't it? A lot of this was guesswork but, knowing Mazin's modus operandi from the past, I didn't think I was far out.

I squeezed the trigger on the water pistol and nailed a duck squarely in the eye. It rolled over and lay upside down in the water, 'Made in Brazil' clearly stamped on its bottom. Was this an omen I wondered? Could Costa da Silva screw all Mazin's well-laid plans up? They could if they were advanced enough, but how realistic would they be in competition? I didn't know.

The important thing about them was that Mazin didn't know anything about them. He didn't even know that they existed! He had already announced that Pantocrator were the only company in the world who made these furnaces, so he knew nothing of Costa da Silva.

Give a man, motivated solely by greed, a glimpse of gold on the horizon and he might not be as careful as he should be in his frantic pursuit of it. On this assumption I had formed my plan.

The idea that I was working on sprang from something Brian Mason had said when I'd asked him what he would do if he was in Mazin's shoes. He thought Mazin would be compelled to try to seize control of Bridge Holdings Limited, the company that owned CONDES, whether or not we had a plan to get our $2 million back. He couldn't afford to take the risk that in trying to do him down we might foul up his deal. He would have to get control over CONDES to protect his back, purely as a defensive measure to be able to counter anything we might try, and to ensure Pantocrator got the subcontract. He would assume that Hugo and I would not part with our shares and with the other 75% held by a trust, it would be virtually impossible for him to get hold of those - unless he could suborn the trustees. An unlikely scenario unless...

Unless, I was thinking, why don't we let him!

I ran through the idea mentally yet again. Risky? Perhaps, but what had we got to lose? Nothing, if we structured it correctly. Complicated? Definitely, it was going to take time to set up and would depend on many things including not a little luck. There was a lot of research to be done first.

A final blast from the water pistol took the little duck straight up the rear and it sank like a stone. Was that Mazin's or my idea I wondered?

Fortuitously, early on Friday morning Brian Mason heaved into sight wrapped around a smug look and bearing our draft six-monthly management accounts. I sat him down whilst Margaret cooked coffee.

After we had gone through the figures I broached my plan.

126

"I have been exercising my brains considerably about Mazin Al Jabril and the discussion you and I had a few days ago," I began.

"Go very far?" he asked cynically.

I ignored the sarcasm. "Well as a matter of fact I might have. You remember our discussion a few days back when I asked you to put yourself in Mazin's shoes and suggest how he could protect himself from our revenge?" He nodded.

"You said that taking control of Bridge Holdings would be one way."

"Yes it would, but there is no way he could do that. You and Hugo wouldn't give him your shares and the trustees certainly wouldn't hand over theirs."

"Can you think of any other certain way for Mazin to protect his back? You know that he has an agency deal with a Greek firm who look as though they are going to land a massive contract on the Sharjah project, and he is on for a slice of that? So he is going to make every effort to prevent us using that as a lever on him in some way."

"Kidnapping you would be another way," he said with a weak grin, "but I thought the purpose was for us to get our $2 million back. How would any of this achieve that?"

"Patience, Brian," I replied, thinking I hadn't considered kidnapping. "Maybe I'd better be on my guard driving Mazin to Cambridge!"

I continued thoughtfully. "What if we allowed him to take control of Bridge Holdings?"

I held up a hand to forestall his outburst. "Let me finish. Consider this. Why don't we arrange for Michael le Fevre to transfer the ownership of CONDES to a new Jersey company and let him get his hands on Bridge Holdings - which actually owns or makes very little - for a price of course? He would believe that

that would give him control over CONDES and prevent us from sabotaging his Greek deal."

Brian frowned, "For a price of..."

I finished it off for him "...$2 million!"

"But he won't do that without checking everything out thoroughly. He's not stupid. He'll want to make sure he's not going to load himself with debt and other liabilities, and he'll certainly smell a rat if we provide him with all the information to assist his coup!"

"That's the beauty of this. If we provide him with all the detailed information he would be immediately suspicious, but if we concealed it and somehow he managed to steal it from us then he'd believe it!"

A slow smile spread across Brian's pale face and he smoothed back his lank hair. "It needs working on, Marcus, but by Jove you could have a plan there. Let's look at it a bit further. What have we got? The Consultant Design Group accounts are available to the public so he can get those - although they are a year out of date. Bridge Holding's accounts he could get from Jersey. However our six-monthly management accounts for both companies are right up to date," he tapped the documents on my desk, "and they show an increasingly satisfactory situation up to 30th of September. Generally, apart from the big hiccup a couple of years ago, which he knows all about, the last few years show a pretty healthy growth."

He chewed a lip. "If we hive off CONDES from Bridge Holdings the next lot of accounts for Bridge are going to look very thin. All it will own is the lease on these premises and a large pile of scrap wood that we refer to as furniture."

"But he isn't going to know that, is he? These accounts..." I indicated the draft six-monthly figures "...still show an increasingly satisfactory position in Bridge Holdings up to 30th September.

If he were to get hold of these he would have no suspicion that things could have changed drastically in the few weeks after 1st October. He couldn't very well ask us could he!?"

Brian stroked his chin reflectively. "Very devious! The idea I like. It would serve him right, but how on earth are you going to work it?"

I shrugged, "I don't know yet. I'm seeing Mazin tomorrow, acting as his chauffeur to take him to Cambridge, perhaps I'll find out more."

"Watch out for the kidnapping," he said with a faint smile, adding, "Plan B is for you to be so objectionable that Mazin will pay us $2 million just to take you back off his hands."

"Oh thanks Brian! Just what I needed! But if I don't show up on Monday you can scrap Plan A!"

As he went out the door he turned, and with a flash of anger in his eyes, said, "Marcus, if there is anything I can do to help, anything at all, count me in. That man is...is...unsound. He deserves to be taught a lesson."

That took me aback a bit, Brian getting heavy. For a banker - well ex-banker, to use the damning adjective 'unsound' was virtually the same as being excommunicated by the Pope.

"Why thank you, Brian," I replied impassively, "you're a brick - a reckless fool - but a brick!" He gave a brief smile of embarrassment.

After he'd gone I had considered the matter further. What we had discussed was only an idea, it looked promising as such but obviously there was a lot of infilling to be done before it could even be considered as a workable plan. For instance was that what Mazin had in mind? If it was, why would he pay $2 million for Bridge Holdings - and why $2 million? I shook my head, there was a long way to go before this idea could be firmed up.

The first thing, however, was to discover whether or not he was thinking along those lines. Hence the advantage of the one to one with him on the trip to Cambridge.

I couldn't help having a feeling of smug satisfaction as I reflected on that trip. On the way there Mazin had slyly pumped me for information about the structure and ownership of, what he assumed, was CONDES; and, being naive, I had let him extract the detailed truth from me - well not quite the whole truth, I had led him to believe that there was just one trustee in Jersey.

So Brian was right. Mazin was looking at the possibility of going behind our backs with a sneaky attempt to seize control. A prickle of apprehension ran up my spine but the adrenalin was flowing. The game was on. If he wanted Bridge Holdings Limited it was going to cost him.

"Don't get pissed on the plane, I know you when there is a whiff of free alcohol in the offing," warned Hugo with mock severity - at least I hoped it was mock - as he shook my hand and wished me, and the bulky package I carried, God speed across the Atlantic. The Major, hovering about close by like a mother hen, checked that I had my passport, travellers cheques, credit cards and ticket - I was surprised that she didn't want to pin the latter to my knickers with a note for British Airways asking them to look after me.

She gave me a peck on the cheek - a bit unexpected that, I thought, as I surreptitiously wiped off the lipstick with spit and hanky as soon as I got out into the corridor. Even Brian called, "Good luck I'll keep my fingers crossed."

The taxi was due to collect me at 8.30 the next morning, so I wolfed down a microwaved lasagne and some apple pie and cream then hit the sack. I overslept by ten minutes, so after a quick bowl of muesli and a gulp of tea, I just had time to grab the post before bundling myself, briefcase and overnight bag into the waiting cab. I began to open the letters - bills mostly - on the way to Heathrow. Then I came across a small squarish envelope addressed to Marcus Moon in handwriting I didn't recognise but there was something familiar about it. It was postmarked SW11. I flipped open the loosely-stuck flap with my thumb and drew out one of those notelets which have flowers printed on them with space for a very short message. There was a message and it was very short: "Thanks for your kind letter, Kate." That was it. Six words that rekindled hope. So maybe I hadn't blown it after all. I tucked both note and envelope into my inside pocket. Yippee!!

The trip to Washington was uneventful, I delivered our bid to the IBRD before the deadline; spent a couple of days finding out what else they had in the pipeline and called into the Steelworks Project Division (Equipment Section) to make a few technical inquiries. Yes, they did know about laser accelerated vacuum contained high frequency induction furnaces, but not much. No, they wouldn't have any objection to their use, provided the manufacturer could prove that sufficient testing had been done to support the technical data claimed. And finally, no, they didn't know any manufacturer who had a commercial furnace of this type on the market. It wasn't my job to enlighten them, not whilst we were in competition, so I didn't pursue that matter further. What this also told me however was that nobody else had made a similar enquiry, so it looked as though, at least on the bids, we were all competing on a conventional basis.

It was a start.

CHAPTER NINE

It was fingers crossed time now as far as Sharjah Steel was concerned. There was nothing more we could do except wait and trust that Mazin Al Jabril would do whatever devious deeds he thought he could do to ensure that the contract came our way. Or, even if he didn't, I supposed we could still get the contract. After all we weren't novices at this, although I knew from my enquiries in Washington that the competition was pretty fierce.

There was one more thing I needed. On my return from Washington I drafted out a long fax message to Costa da Silva in Sao Paulo, Brazil, asking them for full technical details and marketing proposals for their new high frequency induction furnaces. They acknowledged and said that they would put the information together and air mail it to us as soon as they could.

I pondered that; it meant that perhaps they were not as advanced with their development as I had hoped.

Putting that to one side, I re-read the flowery notelet that lay on my desk. Six words dashed off in haste is not a lot to go on. Besides, what was I hoping for? On the basis that the glass is half full not half empty, I decided that to back off now that I knew she had a problem would be very negative and the least I could do was offer to give her a hand with Jon Grey if she needed one. With a rueful grin I reflected that it didn't seem to be a giant step forward on the path of my quest to reproduce my species however.

A faint bell rang at the back of my mind, I was sure I had seen his name somewhere before.

The Major had been hovering around since I had arrived in the office that morning but I hadn't taken much notice as I had other things to think about. I called out to her: "Margaret, will you please bring me the consultants' file on Herlihan and Partners please?"

She duly trundled in with a couple of blue files and placed them significantly on the desk. As you will appreciate, it is not easy to do something as mundane and unremarkable as putting two files on a desk with significance. The fact that she managed it, and it registered, caused me to glance up at her, and look again in a double take. She appeared different. She was different. It wasn't just the longer hair; she had changed her whole make-up. The weird orange lipstick had gone, and so had the green eye shadow and patchy powder. A much softer looking Margaret returned my startled look. A pale red lipstick and gentle blue eye shadow set off her fair skin and blue eyes. A faint dusting of powder covered her cheeks and nose, with a touch of blusher to highlight her cheeks. I couldn't help but comment.

"You've changed your make-up, Margaret. Very nice indeed. It makes you look ten years younger." I couldn't very well say it was a great improvement, but she seemed pleased that I had noticed.

"Thank you, kind sir," she simpered and went jauntily out. I couldn't help it but I was left with a fairly uneasy feeling. I'd felt happier when she was the way she was, I could handle that. One change here signified others there, and I preferred the status quo. You knew where you were with that. One never knew what these other things might lead to.

I put that aside with a sigh and opened the first file. There it was on the very first letter I came across: Jonathan Grey was an associate partner of Herlihan and Partners. A quick check through the recent letters in my out tray showed me that Jon Grey's name was not on the current Herlihan letterhead. I phoned Dan Herlihan who told me Jon had resigned three months previously because he had cancer. "A terrible tragedy," he said. "He's a super guy. We had him earmarked for a full partnership in a year or two and then he gets struck down suddenly with cancer. We still pay his salary but he's a virtual invalid, confined to home and bed most of the time. There's no hope apparently; the specialists haven't been able to do much other than slow it down a little."

I thanked him and replaced the receiver. That only made it worse. If the guy had been a shit of the first water, I might have felt differently. At least it solved part of my problem for me - I knew what to do now. I would help if I could, no strings attached - or so I told myself. I eyed the telephone and then decided that that was too impersonal. I would have to engineer a more genuine person-to-person approach.

Having parked the car as close to King-Knight's office as I could, which was about quarter of a mile away at 5 o'clock on a busy afternoon, I parked myself on the other side of Kensington Church Street opposite their office door. I could see Kate through the window working at her desk. Although it was mid-October there was a distinct nip in the air and I was without a coat, just in shirt and sweater. After ten minutes I had done all the shop windows in the immediate vicinity. You can only gaze upon apples, oranges and melons for so long, and funeral furniture and saddlery soon lose their attraction. I propped myself in a convenient doorway, sheltered from the wind, to wait patiently, lost in my own imagination. Mazin Al Jabril was pegged out in the arid bush, honey dripping from all his extremities with the fire ants just beginning to loosen up their mandibles, or whatever they inflict extreme agony with when... "Are you lonely like me?"

The pleading voice awoke me from my daydream with a start, to see myself confronted by a middle-aged man in a crumpled suit and dirty collarless shirt. He had the translucent puffy skin and fleshy loose lips of a brown noser. The watery eyes solicited concupiscence.

"No I am not," I snapped dismissively. "Piss off."

"Alright, alright, no need to get your knickers in a twist sweetie," he muttered as he shuffled away, disappointment written large across his face.

The scruffy puffy was followed shortly by a frizzy-haired African heavyweight who enquired if I 'wanted to go home with her for a good time'.

"No thanks, dearie," I said wearily, thinking of the old joke about 'who wants to go all the way to Nigeria for a shag'. She didn't seem put out; rejection for her must be commonplace. She prowled away in search of other prey leaving an aura of cheap scent and stale sweat hanging about my refuge. There was still no sign of movement from Kate, so to avoid the stink and loosen chilled joints I eased back on to the street and walked briskly up to the corner of the block and back again. I did this a few times throwing in a little jog here and there, to keep warm. This also attracted attention and funny looks and whispers, with mothers clutching their offspring to protective bosoms as I passed. Oh God, I thought, my flies are gaping, it must be that that was pulling the prowlers. Now it is not easy to check out this sort of thing in a busy street without inviting even more misunderstanding, or even enraged screams from mortified virgins and a collar-feeling from the hand of the law, particularly when one is already under suspicion and scrutiny. I hastily wheeled to face the nearest shop front and began to fumble for the zip. The greengrocer's face turned purple with fury as he beheld me hovering threateningly over his soft fruits and pineapple display, and he began to elbow his way frantically towards the door. I beat a rapid retreat to the next unit. 'A Blundell Funeral Directors. Service with Dignity', it proclaimed in gold letters across his window. He too was watching me suspiciously through the glass as I now confronted his display of funerary urns and other receptacles at navel level. I pushed on further to the newsagents; fortunately he had so much stuff in his window concealment was perfect. A swift check and a sigh of relief, all was correct. What was it about me then - maybe the pale mauve sweater was a bit...but I'd worn it before without attracting all this attention. I shrugged, and staying where I was facing the glass began to read the postcard ads exhibited in the window. 'Large chest for sale 44-32-36', 'Miss Stern controls naughty boys' and 'LOST - neutered black tom. One eye, one ear - goes by the name of Lucky'.

I nearly missed her. Out of the corner of my eye I caught a movement reflected in the window. She was well along the pavement going away from me before I could spring through a non-existent gap in the rush hour traffic, to a chorus of shouted opinions about my untraceable ancestry from drivers and cabbies. She heard my pounding footsteps and turned as I approached.

"Hello," I panted. "Pax, pax!" I held up my hands in a gesture of surrender. "Please listen to what I have to say before you go." I stopped, but she didn't move, so encouraged I ploughed on, "I'm sorry about before, it wasn't fair of me but I didn't know. I really didn't know about Jonathan, you must believe me?" I pleaded.

She gazed steadily at me with a faint smile on her lips. "Andy told me that," she said. "He told me you were totally shocked when you heard about Jonnie."

I nodded, "I was, and I'm sorry. So am I forgiven, can we start again?" I asked hopefully.

Her look grew more solemn. "Yes you are forgiven, of course, it was a bit flattering you know, to get some attention, but start again with what? You know my commitments, I don't want to start anything."

"No no," I said hastily, "I didn't meant that, I just wondered if I could help?" The proposition put like that sounded very lame, standing on a busy pavement with people pushing past us on either side determinedly homeward bound.

She scanned my face gravely; the green eyes a dark unfathomable green in the deepening dusk."And no commitments," she said, half statement, half question.

I shook my head. "Just friends."

A red Routemaster pulled up at the stop ahead of us and she glanced at it anxiously. "Look I've got to catch my bus. I'll think about it. Bye." She sprinted the short distance to the end of the queue.

"Give me a ring," I called out, as the bus began to move off. She smiled and nodded. I watched it disappear down the road, it was a No 14 heading towards Chelsea, so she must live not too far away and not out in the sticks. Wandering back to my car I didn't know whether to feel elated or depressed. At least I knew she didn't dislike me but that was a long way from actually liking me, and 'just friends' had been an undertaking really, a sort of unspoken contract that I wouldn't push for more intimate contact. A bit of a bugger in a way for a red-blooded man who was suffering from a severe shortage of 'oats'. I had hamstrung myself very neatly. I shrugged my shoulders philosophically, thinking that being philosophical is the only thing to be when there's no alternative.

The next morning I caught the 11.30 British Airways flight to Jersey. St Helier was warm and sunny, a perfect autumn day, it cheered me up. The taxi from the airport dropped me at Michael le Fevre's offices on La Motte Street. The building was modern and well built - it needed to be to hold up the hundreds of company nameplates that blanketed the entrance hall walls. I caught up on a few back numbers of Private Eye whilst I waited for him to finish a phone call. That rag must be required reading for a litigation lawyer, almost a clients directory for the legal profession. We shook hands and I accepted a black coffee. He laughed when I mentioned Private Eye.

"You'd be surprised," he chuckled, "but we usually act for the defence." His blue eyes twinkled shrewdly in his round brown face. It had been a good summer for sailing - and eating and drinking, judging by the increase in his girth since we last met.

"You wanted to discuss CONDES," he continued, "that is what you said on the phone, so I have pulled all the files out here ready." He indicated three slim blue binders on the side of his huge desk. They hardly merited the collective 'all' but I suppose it made a client feel a little more important.

I talked to him about CONDES and told him of our hopes and ideas for the Sharjah Steel project. He listened intently without comment. "Can you explain to me how Jersey trusts work?" I asked finally. "All I know is that the trustees have control but can they do what they want?"

He sat back in his chair, put the tips of his fingers together and looked up at the ceiling. I've noticed that doctors, lawyers and accountants are very prone to the ceiling stare syndrome. It's almost as if they expect the answers to your questions to be written there by 'the moving finger that writes and then moves on'. I looked up but couldn't see anything - maybe the moving finger writes in invisible ink or ultra violet only visible through special spectacles available to those professions. You get given a pair when you graduate, hidden inside the rolled scroll of your diploma. I was thinking this through so intently that I nearly missed what he was saying. Or rather had started to say and then stopped.

"Are you alright?" He was looking at me anxiously.

"Yes, why?"

"Your eyes seemed to glaze over as I began to answer your question." I assured him that it was just my look of concentration and asked him to continue. With a small frown he began again.

"Not exactly. There are two basic kinds of trusts, fixed interest trusts and discretionary trusts. For a fixed interest trust the trust deed actually specifies who the beneficiaries of the trust are, and this may include their descendants or anybody else that each beneficiary requires as his named successor. In the case of fixed interest trusts the trustees must act only in the interests of the beneficiaries and in the manner prescribed in the trust deed.

A discretionary trust is different, the individuals or companies that are the beneficiaries are not always named and the trustees, as the name indicates, are free to use their discretion. However it is possible for interested parties to indicate to the trustees how they would wish them to act and this is done by what are known as letters of wishes. I emphasise however that although trustees generally do behave responsibly and act in accordance with letters of wishes, there is no legal obligation for them to do so. The CONDES trust, as you are aware, is a discretionary trust." He paused and looked at me, awaiting the inevitable follow up questions. I obliged.

"How many trustees must a trust have, is there a set number or does it vary?"

"It varies. Any trust formed after 1984 must have more than one trustee unless only one is specified in the original trust deed."

I raised my eyebrows questioningly. "So we only need to have one trustee?"

Michael nodded. "Yes that's the minimum but again, as you know, at present you have three trustees: me, a lawyer in Sark and a lawyer in Guernsey. It is much safer that way. A Jersey company is different; it normally has at least two shareholders. If it tries to trade with less, the shareholder can be made personally liable for any debts the company may incur."

I pondered this awhile. "So there's no requirement for a trustee to be resident in Jersey?"

He agreed. "None."

"But if you are a beneficiary of a discretionary trust and you only have one trustee doesn't that leave you very vulnerable...?"

He smiled; he knew what I meant. "That is why we have always had more than one. But bear in mind even if a single trustee does misbehave, he could be held to be answerable to the beneficiaries if he turned crooked to their detriment."

He then explained how trust deeds were drawn up and trusts registered in Jersey and some of the finer points of their operations. We continued for a further hour before we had covered everything I wanted to know.

I declined his invitation to lunch, having arranged to see an old friend who ran a small consultancy firm in St Helier and have lunch with him. Michael le Fevre looked downcast at being turned down, I think eating a freshly grilled three-pound Jersey lobster washed down with a fine white Burgundy appealed much more if he had company. I promised 'next time!'

An hour later I ate a freshly grilled two-pound Jersey lobster and washed it down with a fine white burgundy at The Old Court House at St Aubin in the company of Cliff Rozell. We talked of the old days and I told him all about Mazin Al Jabril. He whistled when he had heard the full story. "Gee Marcus, I knew you went through a tough time but I didn't know why. I assumed some Arab client or government had defaulted. We had our problems here getting our money out of Libya but that was small stuff compared to you. I can understand partly what you must have gone through, so if we can help...?"

I thanked him for his offer and he thanked me for the lunch. I had some further business to do before catching the 5.30 plane back to the mainland so he dropped me off in the centre of St Helier having given me some advice on which estate agents were most helpful.

Dusty and dirty from scrambling about empty buildings, I caught my flight with five minutes to spare and as soon as the seat belt light was switched off ordered a large vodka and tonic to clear the dust from my throat. Consultancy is a funny business, I thought to myself. They only teach you the technical side at university, whereas consultancy - particularly overseas consultancy - embraced just about all aspects of life...and death. You had to be a lawyer, a banker - currencies, exchange control and fluctuations were a vital part of any overseas project, a social worker - solving staff and family problems from major upheavals like deaths, fortunately very rare, and divorce, fairly frequent on overseas postings - to such trivialities as one Gerald Morton who came into one of our overseas offices and complained that the jelly moulds provided in his fully-fitted-out company villa, were distorted. He was known from thence onwards as Jelly Mould Morton. Hugo called it the curtains syndrome. It was his theory that if, at interview for an overseas post, the guy asked what colour his curtains would be, reject him, no matter how well qualified and experienced he was, because he was guaranteed to be a perpetual pain in the arse. All in all I was pleased with my day, I now knew a lot more about the organisation and control of our business than I did before.

The phone call from Kate I had been waiting anxiously for came five days later. It came whilst I was out, and when I returned the call to King-Knight's she was out. We eventually made contact the following morning.

"I hate to ask you this," she said hesitantly, after the opening preliminaries, "but you did say you would help, and I'm stuck. Can you possibly give Jonathan a lift to the Royal Marsden tomorrow morning and bring him back. He's so weak after his radiotherapy that I do need help with him." There was a catch in her voice as she said this, it was almost as if she expected a refusal.

"Of course," I responded, "what time and where?"

The relief as she gave me the information was evident and I agreed to be at the flat in Redcliffe Square at 10 o'clock. It was only a ten minute drive to the Royal Marsden, London's main hospital for the treatment of cancer, so that would not be a problem. What was a problem was my old MG. It only had two seats, neither very comfortable. I buzzed Margaret on the intercom and asked her to look in the diary to see if I had anything on in the morning.

"You're free," she replied so I told her to blank it out from 9.30 to lunchtime just in case. I called Hugo on the intercom and asked if I could borrow his new BMW for the morning.

"Yes," he said, "but no snail trails on the upholstery!"

"Ha ha, very funny. This, my dear Hugo, is an errand of mercy not seduction."

"For you, Marcus, I thought they were one and the same," he chuckled. I cut him off before he had time to think of asking why I wanted his car.

Right, I thought, so we were back with at least a foot in the door but on reflection it did not present a pleasant picture. What did I want? Did I want him cured? In which case he would be major competition for the heart, mind and last but far from least, body of the delectable Kate. Did I want him dead? No, I couldn't wish that whatever the outcome. I supposed that the ideal would be for him to fall in love with his nurse at the hospital, be cured, and leave Kate and I to enjoy blissful sex in a little country cottage with roses round the door to the sound of bluebirds singing. An unlikely scenario you must admit, life didn't work like that, but you have to hang hope on some peg and that was the best I could do.

The next morning I parked the MG next to Hugo's BMW at 9 o'clock and went in to go through the post. Something made me check my stride at the door to Margaret's office. Was it the same woman or was it somebody different. Her hair had been restyled completely. Gone was the fringe and the bob, her hair was now swept back on either side and gripped into place. Gone also was the tweedy gear and jumpers she had worn ever since she started, that had been replaced by a white blouse and smart blue linen skirt. She even had silver bracelets on her wrist. The blouse was thin and through it I could see the back and straps of a pretty substantial bra, so no vest or slip. This really was a change, I wondered what had brought this about.

"Very smart, Margaret, you do look nice this morning." She jumped up startled and blushed furiously as she realised I had been studying her.

"I'm so pleased you like it," she stammered, still pink with embarrassment.

A faint warning bell began to ring at the back of my mind but I brushed it aside. It was out of character for her to be coy though, she was usually so self-confident. I gave her a smile and passed hastily through into my office. A couple of minutes later she appeared with my black coffee and a plate. On the plate stood a couple of Mr Kipling's French Fancies.

"A little treat, Marcus, just before you go out," she murmured, putting both plate and coffee down in front of me. She blushed again and quickly returned to her own office. Mr Kipling's French Fancies sat there in front of me ominously like two unexploded bombs. I weighed this up. No, there was nothing to it, there couldn't be; it was all part of the change to civilian life. A sort of retarded development of the growing up process, something she had missed out on earlier which had naturally caught up with her. Schoolgirls transformed from uniform, or at least some conformity, into trendy womanhood at 16 or 18, in Margaret it had been delayed a little - well a lot actually, about 30 years! That was all it was. Besides, I liked French Fancies so I ate them.

I double parked Hugo's car outside the flat in Redcliffe Square and rang the bell. The squawky voice on the entry phone said they'd be right down. Kate greeted me briefly and concentrated on helping Jonathan down the steps. I had never met him before. Andy had told me he was only 27; he looked 70. He was muffled up in a heavy topcoat with a tweed flat cap covering his head. His hand when I shook it was thin and brittle like a bird's foot and his face drawn and pale, yet his eyes burned brightly in their sunken sockets and flashed a brief humorous glint when I said, "Hi, Jonathan, we meet at last." He apologised for causing me trouble.

"I used to be able to get to the Marsden under my own steam but it's getting back now that's the problem. The treatment really knocks it out of you. It's kind of you to help."

"No trouble," I acknowledged, waiting till he was seated in the front passenger seat. Kate climbed in the back and I drove off.

We exchanged pleasantries but he sounded weary. Dan Herlihan had been to see him the day before and filled him in on what was happening in the consultancy world.

144

"I would love to work on Sharjah Steel," he said wistfully, a trace of enthusiasm tingeing his voice. "I like the Middle East - particularly now there are a lot more things to do there."

"Well kick this problem and you're on," I told him. "The mechanical and electrical services work won't start for three months so you've got time."

He smiled and nodded. I noticed that his gums had receded back from his teeth.

I found a meter just outside the Marsden and backed the car in. Hugo's pride and joy was involved, so great care was taken during this manoeuvre. Kate took Jonathan in, "We'll be about half-an-hour," she informed me.

Whilst I waited I took the post out of my case and went through it. No writs, no bills, no threatening letters, all practical business. Not a bad morning all in all. I had just finished when Kate re-appeared with a nurse helping Jonathan along the pavement towards the car. I leaped out to hold the door open. They almost had to lift him in. He didn't speak as we drove back, and I half-carried him up to the flat. He was very light, no more than seven or eight stones I would guess. Kate motioned me to lay him on the settee and she removed his coat and hat. His eyes were closed and I was surprised to see that great patches of bald skin showed all over his scalp. She put her hand on my arm, "He'll be OK now, it takes it out of him but he'll recover after a few hours' rest. I've left him some lunch - he doesn't eat much anyway - and I'll get him some supper when I come home from work."

'Home' I thought, with a stab of envy, looking round the room. It was a large room with a high ceiling; it faced onto the square. The furniture was solid but plain and worn. A dining table and six chairs abutted one wall and the three-piece-suite surrounding a rag rug was positioned facing a gas fire and a large television set with video recorder. The decor was soft pastels, and there were

145

many pictures and ornaments including some photographs in silver frames - of whom I couldn't see. It was a feminine room, a warm room. There were a lot of video tapes and DVDs scattered around, clearly Jonnie's main entertainment. Two doors led off this room, one to a small kitchen, the other was the door through which we had entered via a corridor. Kate had kept talking. "I must go to work now. Andy's very good about it but I have to pull my weight." She tutted and stooped to pick up a few videos. "Oh I must call in the video centre and change these, we get through them so quickly."

I studied her, there was a faint air of desperation in this monologue, she was still holding on to my arm.

"What's the matter, Kate," I said kindly. She looked at me startled and then pushed me towards the door.

"Bye Jonnie," she bent and kissed him, "see you later." He lifted a weak hand in acknowledgement.

"Cheers Jonathan," I said, "see you again." She closed the door behind us and led the way down the corridor towards the front door. There were three other doors leading off the corridor, the one behind me opened into a bathroom, I could see that because the door stood half open. The next door we passed was also half open revealing a double bed, unmade, and a jumble of clothes scattered around. All men's clothes as far as I could see. The third door was closed. Before I could say anything she stopped and turned to me.

"Did you mean that?" she asked tentatively.

I was puzzled. "Mean what?"

"When you said you'd see Jonnie again?"

I looked at her carefully - there was that hint of desperation in her eyes.

"What's the problem?" I asked her kindly. "If you've got a problem then tell me and maybe I can help."

She took a steadying breath. "He's dying, you realize that?" I nodded gravely. "He has no family here, his parents were both killed in a road accident five years ago and his only close relative is an elder brother who lives in Australia. We've tried to contact him at his last known address but he must have moved, there's been no response. They didn't get on anyway. Dan Herlihan has been a terrific help, but his office is in Kingston now so it's difficult for people to get here during the day. We have friends who come round some evenings but Jonnie is usually tired by then."

She paused with a faint smile. "So all he's got is me - and I have to work to keep this place going." She waved a hand around and then looked me in the eye.

"The problem is..." she paused momentarily, and then repeated: "The problem is, I can't drive. I've never bothered to learn." She paused to see if the implications of this registered with me.

"It's his treatment. Jonnie has to go for his treatment three times a week. It's his only hope; that is what he clings to. If one of Dan's boys can't come I have to phone for taxis. At busy times they are not reliable, sometimes they're on time, sometimes 10 to 20 minutes late, and on occasions they don't turn up at all. Getting him back from The Marsden is easier because we can usually pick one up on the street outside the hospital."

She took a deep breath.

"If you would be willing to help out now and then, I would really be grateful." A brief smile flickered across her face, "I might even buy you a drink!"

I laughed. "Look, it's not difficult for me, I'm only ten minutes' drive away from here and can easily spare an hour or so when called upon. If I can't do it, because I'm away or something, speak to Brian Mason at our office, I will brief him, and he will arrange for one of our guys to come in my place. That doesn't let you off the drink though!"

She smiled with relief and we moved toward the stairs. "I'll walk down with you."

I offered to drive her to King-Knight's but she declined saying I'd spent too much time on her behalf, and anyway there was a regular bus service from just across the Square that went direct.

As she pulled the front door closed behind her I noticed that it had an Ingersoll lock.

"Tell me, has Jonathan got a front door key?"

She nodded, "Yes, I gave him one sometime ago. I'll make sure he has it in his pocket."

"'At length I realise, he said, the bitterness of life'."

"Lewis Carroll," she said with a wan smile. "I can't recall where it's from."

"Don't forget, give me a ring anytime you're stuck for transport. Bye Kate."

"Bye Marcus - and thanks."

She walked away down the street with a fine stride and I watched her go with mixed feelings.

I returned to Hugo's car thinking that I couldn't remember where the quote was from either, but it must be her flat not Jonathan's.

CHAPTER TEN

Mazin had telephoned last Wednesday, he spoke to Hugo, telling us that the Ministry in Sharjah had recommended the World Bank to accept CONDES' bid – "even though it was not the lowest," he had added. He told Hugo that it was only due to his efforts that we had been accepted and without him we wouldn't have been in with a chance.

"What did you say, Hugo?" I asked silkily.

"Oil on troubled waters, Marcus, oil on troubled waters. No sense in rocking the boat at this time."

"It's all balls, you know that don't you? We must have had either the best price or the best technical offer, probably both, otherwise there's no way that either the IBRD or Sharjah would have accepted us. Anyway, accepting that's what Mazin said, let's wait till we get the official confirmation before we hit the Dom Perignon." We knew from past experience that a lot could change in a short time. There was bound to be some heavy lobbying, diplomatic pressure and, last but by no means least, massive bribes - 'commission', 'lubrication', call it what you will, on offer from unscrupulous Germans, Japanese, Italians, Indians and others, not necessarily in that order. We just had to hope that our massive unscrupulous briber, who was without doubt well up in the premier league in that field, and with the inside track, came through with the laurels. All the same, for this project we apparently were the current leaders in the gentlemanly art of international bidding, and the others would have to chop each other down before they could get to us - if they had time. They were an anxious few days but fortunately the time was short.

I had just got back into the office from taking Jonathan Grey for his treatment when The Major slid the fax on to my desk with a broad smile. I speed-read it, absorbing the important words like 'awarded the contract' 'sign the documents' 'negotiate the fees' - and 'as soon as possible' instantly. Then I re-read it slowly, lasciviously like a connoisseur rolling a fine wine round his tongue, savouring the key words like 'awarded the contract', 'sign the documents', 'US dollars' and 'fees'. My shout of joy echoed through the whole building, I kissed Margaret (a bit rash, that, but I got away before she could respond), capered down the corridor waving the fax, banged on Brian's door and danced into Hugo's office. He was talking to Janet so I kissed her and danced with him or was it vice versa? I don't remember.

"We've got it," I cried. "We've bloody well got the job!" Hugo eventually broke away from my hold and made a beeline for the drinks cabinet leaving me jumping about on my own.

Brian turned up puzzled by the racket but then joined in enthusiastically - for him - by smiling and repeating, "Well done! Well done indeed!"

"I've had this on ice since Mazin phoned," chuckled Hugo, as he stripped the foil and wire from the cork of a bottle of Moet et Chandon's best Dom P, 1966 - he must have been confident for that vintage. The rest of that day and evening slowly faded from living memory in a happy haze of increasing noise, inarticulate conversations, laughter and continuous brimming glasses.

I emerged into the land of the living-dead next morning stretched out on the couch in Hugo's office feeling very fragile. I assumed it was morning because it was dark, and my watch showed half-past five. It could have been afternoon, I suppose, it was November but if so which afternoon? Who cares anyhow! I struggled to my feet, somebody had removed my shoes, and switched on the main light. God, it was bright! I switched it off again and put the desk lamp on. It must be morning - the building was quiet, far too quiet for an afternoon. The shoes I found neatly tucked under the couch. Managing to fumble them on I heaved out into the corridor. Not a sound. Not a soul in sight. I looked back into Hugo's office - a movement which made the head swim violently. There were five empty champagne bottles standing on the desk. Jesus! Brian and Hugo must really have been putting it back. I wondered where they were. Carefully, keeping the neck rigid and the eyes fixed on the door ahead, I eased down towards the exit. I was contemplating the car or returning to Hugo's couch when by a stroke of sheer luck a prowling taxi showing its yellow light drifted into view. I hailed it and gave the Prince of Wales Drive address. He grumbled - they always do if they have to go south of the river - but grudgingly took me there moaning all the way, something I needed like a hole in the head - or as well as the hole in the head it felt like I'd got already. The meter showed £9. I felt in my pocket and gave him nine £1 coins. He goggled indignantly at them in the palm of his grubby hand as though he had just discovered religious stigmata.

"What about a tip then?" he whined.

"Never buy a Rolex from a man who's out of breath," I replied, and leaving him cursing my ancestry I unlocked the door. It was now a choice between bed or a shower. I drank a pint of milk from the fridge, undressed and stretched out on top of the bed still trying to make the decision. It was lunchtime when I awoke for the second time. I didn't feel too bad. After a shave, a shower and a slice of toast I felt better and tackled a mug of hot sweet tea.

Gee, so we had got Sharjah Steel, it was a big big job - the biggest we had ever handled. Maybe Mazin had helped, maybe not, in either case we were going to seek retribution. It wouldn't make any difference to that, but now the speculation had to stop and the action start. The starting gun had fired and the programme was rolling.

The fax from the World Bank required me to go to Sharjah as soon as possible to sign the financial contract and then go to Washington to agree the technical specifications. I would meet up with Mazin in Sharjah, at least he'd be useful for getting me into the right people and doing some interpreting. The Major could fax him the details of my flights and request him to meet me and fix me up in a decent hotel. That would piss him off, being used as a taxi driver and a booking clerk. That was his problem though, he could delegate it if he wanted to - and if he booked me in a dump like the Palm Tree then I'd tell him I was moving in with him, which would piss him off even more.

In the event I was wrong. When Margaret brought me his reply, whereas it wasn't exactly matey it was constructive. He had booked me into the Sheraton - fine, arranged for his driver to meet me - what I'd expected, fixed a meeting with the Minister - ditto, fixed a meeting with His Highness Sheikh Sultan, the Ruler of Sharjah - a surprise, and arranged for both of us to call in at Pantocrator in Athens on my way back to London - double surprise.

I scowled at this. The first surprise, the meeting with HH was going to cost us money. I could just picture the scene - "Ah Mr Marcus, welcome and greetings in Allah. We are deeply honoured that an international firm of your standing has agreed to work with us but you know we are a poor country struggling to survive in the developing world. You must help us, we expect our consultants to help us. This project will make you very famous, you will get lots more work because of it," etc, etc, the usual bullshit, concluding inevitably with a suggestion that we might like to review our fee proposals. That was the sort of suggestion you couldn't refuse. So already Mazin was going to cost us maybe a quarter of 1% - $1 million, not bad for somebody who was supposed to be looking after our interests, and we hadn't even signed up yet! You couldn't help but love him could you, but in truth I do exaggerate a little. We always allowed a negotiating margin in our fees because we knew we would have to make further concessions for contracts in the Arab world. There was a maximum 1% margin on Sharjah Steel and if I could get away with conceding only a quarter, or a half percent reduction I would be chuffed to death. HH the Ruler was only the last of the hurdles, there was a whole gamut of 'negotiations' to be played before the financial side would be finally agreed. The Ruler was the final step in the softening up process, the real heavies came in towards the middle with the rubber truncheons and the red hot pliers. The double surprise, the visit to Pantocrator, was a shrewd Al Jabril move. I didn't object to it, in fact it fitted in with our plans and it would be very useful to see first-hand what progress they had made with the development of the induction furnace. He was going to give me the heavy sell: he didn't know I was already sold.

The Mercedes 500SEL swung into a vacant parking lot outside the Ministry of Industry; Mazin and I climbed out of the cool air-conditioned interior into the 32° heat of mid-day November in Sharjah. The humidity was low and the sun, high on my back, felt marvellous. We walked up a short avenue flanked by dusty oleanders and hibiscus to the main entrance. The policeman on duty greeted Mazin, and after glancing at me decided to ferret in his left ear with his little finger for something more interesting to look at.

We passed through the double glass doors. I followed in Mazin's wake as he shouldered a path through the motley crew thronging the lobby towards the lifts. Indians in pressed shirts and flared trousers, Baluchi's with baggy trousers and waistcoats and Ethiopians and Yemenis with brown, blue and cream coloured robes wound round themselves and their heads, all were unceremoniously parted to make way for Mazin. It was like Moses crossing the Red Sea. The pieces of paper they clutched were waved angrily, but disdainfully ignored as we reached our destination. Hauling a couple of scruffy looking merchants out of the first lift car that presented itself, he entered with me still in his train. He pressed the button that closed the doors cutting off all further complaints and despatched us upwards in splendid isolation to his brother's realm.

Azmi Al Jabril was a surprise, a total contrast to his tall, elegant, aristocratic, snotty-looking relative. A round greasy ball of a man, with sweaty bald head, sweaty creased brown face, sweaty chins, and with no neck - even standing on his dignity - he failed to reach Mazin's shoulder.

"Your Excellency," said Mazin smoothly, "may I present Mr Marcus Moon, one of the senior directors of CONDES."

The greaseball rolled round the enormous desk and extended a plump, limp hand. I shook it briefly; it was soft and white with thick black hair on the backs of the podgy fingers sprouting between gold and jewelled rings. The Minister's voice was low and sibilant.

"Welcome, Mr Moon, welcome to our office." Sharp brown eyes appraised me shrewdly from the rolls of fat as he offered coffee or tea. I took the Arabic coffee, the thin hot green coffee made from cardamom seed.

As we sipped our drinks, courtesies were exchanged - you know the sort of thing: "Honoured to have such an international consultant to design our humble project... No, no, it is we who are honoured to be appointed to represent such a distinguished government under the direction of such wise people as His Highness and yourself... Delighted that the top man in person has come to sign the contract (I shot Mazin a sharp look at that but didn't correct the Minister)... No, it is we who are proud and pleased to be received by Your Excellency," and so on.

Once we got all that crap out of the way the real business would start. I wondered how they'd handle it, there wasn't too much time; both of us knew I had to be in Washington at the end of the week to sign the technical contracts. They only had a few days to beat me to a bloody pulp – metaphorically, of course, I hoped - before we agreed the fees which would go into the contracts.

The usual tactics were for the senior officials to press initially for some reduction and having secured it pass you on to the 'team'. The 'team' were the heavies. They would spend days bombarding you with their figures, making you produce alternatives, checking all your figures, picking away at small discrepancies trying to turn them into big ones, sweet talking you, threatening you, abusing you, reducing the work you were contracted to do and adding it all back in again later as a minor change for no extra fees. Then, when you thought you had finally got an agreement, you were trundled in front of the top man - His Highness the Ruler of Sharjah it would be in this case, and after a very warm friendly reception you would be asked, as a personal favour to him, to knock off some more.

This time, however, I had a little more power to my elbow. It was a World Bank financed project, the design work and specification was fixed by them and they would be paying the fees. It was clear also that HE the Minister was getting his cut as well because when we got down to the 'nitties', his heart clearly wasn't in it.

He started off falling down on more points than an Indian fakir. Before we got anywhere near talking about money he spent half-an-hour lecturing me on the progress Sharjah had made in its development, concluding with an emphatic requirement that this steel plant must be the most efficient, the most technically advanced and the most automated in world.

"We do not want a vast influx of coolies to work this plant Mr Moon, we already have a huge imbalance of locals to expatriates. It is essential that this is reduced not increased."

I nodded concurrence, thinking that he had put my case for not reducing the fees better than I could. Mazin obviously thought the same and said we would note His Excellency's wise requirements and would confirm that we would adhere to them. What he meant was that I would put all this in a letter and slam it into the Ministry of Industry's files, for the official record, as soon as possible - which I did first thing the following morning.

To save his face I let the Minister squeeze a quarter of 1% off our fees, that was good tactics, but I was buggered if the heavy mob were going to get even $1 more off. The remaining quarter percent I was saving for His Highness.

Mazin thought it prudent to be absent for the next three days' haggle. I had discussed my hard line tactics with him and whereas he thought I should be a bit more flexible he didn't object. I held the view that if the heavy mob failed to make progress the Minister would not be too dismayed because he could show that he personally had done his stuff and forced a reduction. He would give his team an almighty bollocking and in all probability fire a few of them for their failure but that was not my problem. The Ruler would also save face by persuading me to reduce further after the 'team' had failed. It was going to be a tough three days, or so I thought.

In the event I was wrong. After the first session the following morning I think their chief negotiator realised that his Minster had shot him in the foot with his now officially recorded and registered requirements, and that, coupled with my insistence that there was no room for manoeuvring on a World Bank project and therefore no point in a negotiation, put paid to whatever plans he may have had. I took the line that as far as I was concerned the purpose of these meetings was to clarify any outstanding points of detail and not to discuss changes in specification or money and I flatly refused to do either of these.

The upshot was that they did not have more than half a dozen points to be resolved, they were dealt with in half a day and I was wheeled into the presence of HH, sweating in best suit and tie, the evening of my third day in Sharjah. Mazin insisted on coming with me, so the two of us went through the formalities of being searched, waiting in the ornate mirrored waiting room with its heavy gilded furniture, huge chandeliers and fine Persian carpets and finally being ushered into the august presence. It all went as forecast; HH was very friendly and relaxed, we drank Arabic coffee, he drank orange juice, he talked about Sharjah and I about CONDES, and 20 minutes later, when Mazin and I were ushered out of the presence by the majordomo, I was $1 million in fees lighter. As we walked through the gates of the palace to the car I wanted to leap in the air and shout Yippee! But with Mazin looking down his nose in cold disdain, and bearing in mind that we may well have to negotiate with him on some other deal at some time in the future, I thought it prudent to keep deadpan. All in all though, it had been a very good three days for CONDES. In any other circumstances we would have been shorn of $4 million from our fees, no trouble at all, rather than the just $2 million I had conceded to Greaseball and H.H.

The next morning I signed the Sharjah contracts on behalf of CONDES, and with a copy safely tucked in my case flew with Mazin on the afternoon plane to Athens.

Mazin bent my ear continuously on the flight about how good Pantocrator were and how advanced they were with the new furnaces. The reception he had laid on was certainly impressive: a limo to meet us at the airport, a suite each at the Athens Hilton, champagne and caviar provided, limo out to the Pantocrator plant, met by the managing director - one Georgiou Antoniades, a gorilla of a man who looked as if he bent steel sections with his bare hands - lunch spread out in the boardroom with Greek delicacies and fine wines; we were offered the lot. It was blatant bribery. I was not at all sure whether it was morally ethical for me to accept this sort of treatment - but just in case it was, I got stuck into everything.

The Pantocrator plant was impressive, they had a big spread there, but it seemed to me that the buzz that should denote a heavy workload and a full order book was missing. What we were shown looked more like a staged presentation than a daily routine. Mazin so enthusiastically oversold everything that I decided he must have been an Egyptian postcard seller in his early days. When I mentioned this to him in passing he was not too pleased but at least it shut him up. In the research centre they showed me their prototype of the LAVCHIF, it was very fast and all their test results confirmed or exceeded its output forecasts with substantially lower running costs. I spent half a day going through the technical specifications and other data including the information from their computer modelling of the full-sized furnace. They convinced me that it was a winner and it was difficult to remain non-committal in the face of such enthusiasm.

In the evening we attended a dinner at Antoniades' house in our honour about which I recall very little except that it started off well and got even better. Like most dinners of that ilk it ends up as a competition to see who gets pissed last, the guests or the hosts - I don't know who won but I wouldn't bet on it being me. The company limo parked us at the airport loaded with documents next morning and we boarded the London flight. I didn't realise Mazin was coming back with me, but for some reason or other he seemed determined not to let me out of his sight and there was no way I could object, so we travelled together.

Just as we were crossing the Alps he turned to me guardedly, and with a frown creasing his forehead asked, "Do you really think I used to be a postcard seller?"

I snorted with laugher. "Get stuffed Mazin," I told him.

The following morning, being a Friday, I borrowed Hugo's car again to take Jon Grey for his treatment. One of the guys in the drawing office had stood in for me whilst I was away and he told me that Jon seemed to be a little better, and when I rang the bell it was he who let me in, not Kate. She wasn't there, he told me that she had to show one of King-Knight's clients round a property first thing that morning.

My disappointment must have shown for an instant because he gave a faint smile and said that she would be back when we returned from the Marsden. For some reason this twitched my conscience, it was the first time that I had actually considered what Jon Grey must think of all this. Me, helping out Kate, obviously on a friendly relationship with her, trying desperately not to make it too obvious that I wanted to make it even friendlier. He was not stupid, he must have realised the situation but it didn't seem to worry him or create any sense of insecurity in him. As I studied his face now, through the lines of pain there was a tranquillity about his features, an inner contentment, and I suddenly realised that he knew full well that he was going to die soon, and that he accepted the situation, and therefore did not consider me any threat to his future whatsoever. He clearly loved Kate and equally clearly knew that whilst he lived she was his and that was all he felt entitled to ask. After that he just wanted her to be happy. With something of a shock I also realised that it was me who was being 'interviewed' by him for the role of future happiness provider.

His eyes locked with mine and I knew that he had read my thoughts. We both smiled an unspoken agreement. I was no threat to him and he would support me thereafter. It turned us from a rather sensitive relationship fraught with spikes to good friends who had nothing to fear from the other.

I told him of the details of my trip to Sharjah and Greece, he was interested and alert. Even after his treatment, which usually knocked the stuffing out of him, he was able to walk to the car himself and climb in. There was a definite improvement. "It's only temporary," he told me with a sigh of resignation, "it may last a day or two or even a few weeks..." He left the sentence unfinished and turned to look out of the window so I couldn't see his face.

I didn't know what to say and so said nothing, concentrating on threading the car through the Friday morning Kings Road traffic.

Kate let us into the flat, supermarket carrier bags lay tumbled on the floor of the sitting-room just outside the kitchen door, she had obviously been doing the shopping for the weekend on her way back from King-Knight's.

We were both greeted warmly - she kissed us both on the cheek, Jon first then me.

"It's nice to have you back," she smiled at me. "Jon and I have missed you." She rested a hand on his shoulder and he nodded agreement.

"I'll make us some coffee." She turned anxiously, "You can stay for a cup?"

"Sure," I agreed, adding, "I'm afraid I will be away again next week and Peter Davy will be driving Jon."

I sensed Jonathan's disappointment and told them. "I have to go to Washington to sign up the rest of the Sharjah Steel contracts." I wondered whether to mention that I also intended to slip down to Brazil and check out Costa da Silva but decided against it. One of them might mention it casually to Pete Davy, or Dan Herlihan, or somebody, and it could just possibly get back to Mazin. Very unlikely but why take the chance. I hadn't even told the Major. I intended to book the flights myself when in the States and also phone Costa da Silva from Washington so they could fix me up with hotels and transport. The fewer people who knew about them and our interest in them the better, for the time being. I drank the coffee and the three of us talked mainly about recent DVDs, Jon was clearly feeling tired now but his eyes had a sparkle that had not been present on previous meetings. Kate noticed this and remarked on it.

"You two seem to be getting on well?"

"Why not, we are both engineers and as you know engineers are a very sociable bunch."

"Hmm, I'm not so sure about that," she said with a mock frown. I left them promising that I would be back a week on Monday and pushed off back to the office.

It was all a bit strange this relationship, it was fine for me to believe that Jonathan and I had got this sorted out between us. I supposed it was fine for him to believe it too, but what about Kate? I already had two sisters at home in York, I didn't need a third - but I only had myself to blame, it was me that had made that deal not her, she was free to move in closer if she wanted.

Maybe I was being unreasonable; after all I had been away and would be away again, what the hell could she do?

She couldn't really invite me out, or round to dinner, no it was just my imagination - play it by ear Moon, I thought - just give it time.

161

That was easier to say than to do though. This life of celibacy, with no immediate prospect of change, was beginning to penetrate from the subconscious through to the conscious. After all, at 33 the anxieties creep up and one begins to doubt that all the equipment is still in full working order. The urge for regular full road tests grows stronger by the deprived day. Once or twice I had even caught myself giving the Major the once over as a prospective test vehicle, and that had really worried me.

Margaret did look much better these days there was no mistaking that, and I gave her credit for recognising that if she wanted to be thought of as more than an ex-army drill sergeant in tweeds over baggy knickers with elastic round the legs, then a certain swallowing of pride was necessary and specialist advice had to be sought. That she had done, and the new clothes, hair and make-up reflected it.

The problem was that she wanted to try it out on somebody, and I had a very disturbing feeling that the 'somebody' was me.

When I arrived back at the office the post was ready on my desk and Margaret brought in the coffee. She walked round to my side before putting it down on the old beer mat that served to protect the scratched and worn surface from further depredations.

"There are one or two items that I think you should deal with urgently," she said. "I have marked them with stickers."

She leant across and turned over the post file cover to point out the yellow markers sticking out from the bundle of letters and drawings. As she did so her left hand rested casually on my shoulder.

I froze. It was like a burning brand lodged there. I went numb. I didn't hear a word she was saying and I couldn't - didn't - want to move in case it was interpreted as something. Acceptance? Rejection? I don't know, it just seemed better to stay still. After what seemed like half the morning but was probably ten seconds she said brightly, "So if you can deal with those first I will be able to collect the rest of the information and get it off in tonight's mail."

She removed her hand and stepped away, the numbness faded and normality returned.

"Can't they go on Monday when I'm away," I enquired, trying to keep my voice impersonal.

She wagged an admonishing finger at me, "You naughty boy, you've forgotten haven't you?"

"Forgotten what?" I hadn't a clue what she was talking about.

"My sister," she explained, and still seeing total incomprehension written across the Moon visage, shook her head resignedly and went on. "I asked you two months ago if it would be alright for me to have two weeks off, next week, whilst you are away in Washington, and the week after. My sister is recovering from an operation and I'm going to help out until she is back on her feet. You said it would be fine."

It all came back now - the Braithwaite shoulder fondle had driven all other thoughts from my mind.

"Oh yes, of course, fine," I said enthusiastically - a bit too enthusiastically it seemed, because a frown flickered across her face. She pursed her lips. "I've arranged for a temp to come in, a Miss Samantha Smith from the agency, but she won't have much to do. I've sorted everything out and left her precise instructions."

"Oh good, well done, thanks Margaret." She looked a bit woebegone so I added, "I'll miss you."

"Will you?" she murmured.

Oh shit, I shouldn't have. I'd done it again! I really would have to do something about finding her another target for both our sakes and find one for me too.

CHAPTER ELEVEN

After a little arm-twisting, Hugo and Brian agreed that I could fly BA 747 first-class to Washington, and so with a spring in my step and a song in my heart I hit the Bucks Fizz, courtesy of British Airways, as soon as I turned left through the plane door.

Washington was no problem, apart from a slight hangover, and I got all the remaining documents signed and dated - a mere formality, thus firing the starting pistol on the design programme for the Sharjah Steel Plant.

It was a big moment for us all. I faxed Hugo in London with the information to enable him to commence the build-up of our design team and then spent an uncomfortable few hours that evening as the enormity of what we had taken on hit me. I suppose if one is immediately actively involved in the frantic organisation of such a project, the transition from not really believing it is going to come off to its actually coming off is lost in the energetic excitement of commencement. Alone in a hotel room in a strange city all the doubts flood in. Could we really design a project of this size? Would the fees be paid on time or at all? What if the Middle East war flared up again? And last but not least, having allowed Mazin Al Jabril back into bed with us were we going to get screwed, stuffed and reamered right the way through and be left with nothing? The counter plan was full of unknowns as yet, optimistic and speculative assumptions, any one of which could blow it to smithereens if it proved negative or incorrect. I did not sleep well that night but the die was now cast, there was no alternative but to soldier on. Next morning dawned bright and sunny, a good omen for me. The VARIG agent got me a coach class seat on the daily flight to Rio de Janeiro which carried on to Sao Paulo. I telephoned Costa da Silva with my flight details from Washington and they said they would meet me. The film on the flight down to Brazil, I forgot what it was called, was dubbed in Portuguese subtitled in English - well American - and as the remainder of the passengers got restless when I raised the blind to watch the vast panorama of South America unfolding beneath us, I resigned myself to a couple of hours' peace and quiet in the darkness turning over my thoughts.

The Major had departed for her fortnight's visit to sustain her sister in Shropshire, leaving the place tidy to the point of perfection. Any further physical contact between us had been avoided - by me - apart from the standard two cheek touch with the fresh air kisses. It was patently clear that if I wanted to distract her from me then I had to stick her on to somebody else. I salved my conscience by telling myself that it was an inescapable fact of life that, if you are trying to divest yourself of potentially unwelcome attention, you first try to redirect it on to those people you know. People who, under the circum-stances, might deem it a misfortune to be numbered amongst your close friends if they discovered what you were doing! I made a list of them starting with Hugo - there was no reason to leave out the married ones these days. Brian Mason followed, and then a few of the senior engineers. That took care of any potential in the office but the social side took a little longer. I listed every single male contact I could think of in reasonably close geographical proximity to Major Margaret. I even weighed up one or two of the more dominant women I had come across, but reluctantly scratched them on the grounds that if the Major was that way inclined she'd have got herself sorted out in the Army long ago. I reviewed the runners and riders gloomily; the office was clearly a dead duck! If anybody had shown the slightest interest in her I would have known, and likewise would have worked out if she fancied any of them. The office list was comprehensive, there was nobody else; no magic chemistry seeking to bond two lonely atoms into a tight molecule existed within CONDES. The social side was an even more barren desert. True there gleamed amongst the names a couple of chauvinist cock-artists who could be relied upon not to say 'no' to a one night stand; one of them wouldn't say 'no' to an insouciant deformed pygmy, but that hardly encouraged a deep and meaningful relationship that would divert her attention from me permanently.

Glumly I sat there chewing a pencil, maybe I was on the wrong track, maybe it wasn't men per se but simply something to do that she was seeking. Something to occupy her time and on which she could devote her frustrated affections. A dog, a cat, a hobby? What about a hobby? Arm wrestling down at the local drill hall? Armour-plate welding courses at the tech. Well why not? I remembered reading in *Time Out* about a film made by some women's group entitled 'Barbara the Boilermaker' - why not 'Margaret the Machinist? And then it hit me. *Time Out*, that was it, advertise for her in the columns of the trendy magazines.

I scrabbled through my briefcase, I had bought a selection of these back at Heathrow to read on the plane. There it was, the Lonely Hearts section, designed, it said, for individuals wanting to meet other individuals on a 1:1 basis for a relationship. OK, I accept it didn't specifically say 'and for individuals who wanted other individuals to meet other individuals on a 1:1 basis for a relationship' but what the hell, they couldn't put everything in, could they?! Eliminating the gay and lesbian advertisements wiped out three quarters of the content, so I concentrated on the remainder. It makes you wonder, doesn't it, all those 'very special ladies' with 'stunning figures', 'ravishing good looks', 'intelligence' and 'style' who can't hook on to a man, and 'handsome, witty, 6 ft, business executives, (own flat)' who seemed unable to pull anyone off their own bat - but then I was hardly the current world leader in that respect was I!

I decided to tackle this in two ways: I would compose an advertisement for people to contact her and, if I could get a photo of her, I'd answer a few ads on her behalf - creatively of course.

First her ad, I drafted it out on my A4 pad. 'Exceptionally attractive lady, 49, military background, seeks caring intelligent professional man for continuing relationship'. I read it through sceptically. No, I didn't like that; it was flat and true! I crossed out a word here and there and made some changes. 'Exceptionally attractive lady, fortyish, well organised, humorous, sensuous, interesting, seeks caring, intelligent, well-built, professional man for continuing relationship'. That was better, I toyed with the idea of adding 'leading to marriage' but abandoned that. I didn't want them shying away too early. I gave the end of the pencil another pensive nibble. The 'well-built' also could be catastrophically misinterpreted by some conceited egoist who thought his willy should be in the Guinness Book of Records. I changed 'well built' to 'tall' and added 'please send photo'. That should cover that, now for a few replies.

I looked down the columns at the male adverts, most of the straight ones - 'tall, handsome, male, graduate/author/doctor/ accountant', were 'seeking large-busted, pretty, slim-waisted, girlfriend, 20-30, for travel and fun. Must have sense of humour'. I reckoned she'd need one!

The Major could not be into that, that was for sure - or was it? It could be worth a shot, if I couldn't line up something that I considered more 'suitable' - as my mother would say.

I made a note to get all the contact mags for a wider choice. Each reply would have to be tailored to suit but at least I had a plan now. Another idea sprang to mind - singles clubs. I noted that down as well to make some enquiries, there must be some in her area - the Citizens' Advice Bureau would help. I suddenly burst out laughing, another thought had just occurred to me. Maybe I could line up Mazin Al Jabril! By the time we had finished with him he might be willing to do anything, and that really would be a battle of the Titans before she finally knocked him into shape. It was tempting, but it was too close to home, so reluctantly I set it aside.

The next weighty problem, most definitely not connected with the last, was the Moon leg-over problem. No doubt Costa da Silva could be prevailed upon to lay on a bevy of Brazilian beauties to solve the problem - if they thought it would help clinch the deal in their favour, but I didn't fancy it, I wasn't that desperate. In any case it did not seem to be an entirely professional approach if CONDES' first request, when the loafers hit the Brazilian tarmac, was for a bedful of crumpet for one of their senior directors.

I racked my brains for a more suitable arrangement but there was absolutely zilch.

Belinda, normally front-runner as a test ride, was still out of the frame with pregnancy, and, apart from Kate, who was untouchable, there wasn't anybody else who I could see would be both willing and acceptable at short notice.

It was thus a somewhat subdued and introspective Moon that was met at Sao Paulo airport by a short, fair-haired, quick-eyed, energetic Brazilian going by the name of Dr Arnhold Herrera, technical director of Costa da Silva. He bustled me into his car and whizzed off to the hotel emitting a non-stop stream of facts and figures about his LAVCHIF. I got the whole picture on the three-mile ride into town, he could have turned round and delivered me back to the airport there and then if I could have remembered it all.

Everything turned out to be just as he had described. In technical development Costa's were at just about the same stage as Pantocrator. Although they didn't know how far advanced Pantocrator were, they did know that they were working along the same lines. It showed more for Costa's industrial espionage abilities than it did for the Greeks. Unless, of course, Georgiou Antoniades was being canny.

The weakness was that Costa da Silva were a much smaller company, their production resources were limited and the lead time they required to translate their research prototype into a production run was eight to nine months. Herrera made no attempt to conceal this but worked hard to persuade me that the construction programme of the Sharjah Plant could be arranged to accommodate what he thought Costa's could reasonably achieve in terms of start and completion dates, and we agreed to meet at CONDES' offices in London at the end of January to review the position.

That being arranged, he hurtled me off on a final quick tour round Sao Paulo - not very exciting, filled me with food and drink - better, but wouldn't fly 10,000 miles just to repeat it. He shook my hand vigorously, swearing undying friendship, and waved me through immigration.

I caught a British Airways flight direct from Rio to London, and slept most of the way, arriving just after 7 o'clock on Saturday morning.

It was after 9.30 on Monday by the time I parked the MG and hit the office door. I had temporarily forgotten that The Major was off for two weeks, to hone up her tank-busting skills with the Paras! No, I jest, I knew she had actually gone to visit her younger sister in Shrewsbury, to give her a hand whilst she was recovering from a 'woman's operation'. It was a mild shock therefore to behold this diminutive, dark-haired girl occupying the dragon's chair. Not as big a shock as I gave her, apparently; she recoiled like a startled fawn and blushed scarlet as I breezed through the door, with the result that we both ended up goggling at each other like two mating octopi. Being on familiar ground I recovered first. "You must be Samantha thingy from the agency." I couldn't remember if Margaret had told me her surname - it was a bit embarrassing. She nodded slightly, still pink and dumbstruck.

"I'm Marcus Moon." I offered her my hand, which she eyed tentatively as though it was a ring-necked cobra with a taste for virgins' blood before she briefly touched it, her eyes still examining me warily. You get somewhat nervous when people react like this in case you have got something horribly wrong with you - like a large hanging bogey. I discreetly carried out a bit of face tunnelling with my right index finger, under the pretext of scratching a tickle, but there didn't appear to be any untoward deposit in the area. Of course it could be a shaving cut that had smeared blood all over the place leaving me looking like Jack the Ripper before his evening bath.

"Excuse me one moment."

I turned and beat it back to the washroom where there was a mirror. The face that looked back at me seemed normal, or as normal as any face would look the weekend after flying 20,000 miles. The slightly bloodshot eyes behind the faintly puffy eyelids were no more than one might reasonably expect to see first thing on a Monday morning, or any morning for that matter. Well second thing that particular morning - I had dropped off some videos for Jon Grey first thing - that was why I was late. He hadn't had a foaming fit at my appearance. I returned to the office and re-entered meaning to get to the root of this problem. This time, however, it was different, this time she proffered a shy smile and held out her hand.

"Samantha Smith. I'm sorry for gaping like that," she apologised and then paused. "I was expecting someone much older," she explained, and then coloured up again with embarrassment. I tried to let her down gently.

"I will be in 20 years' time, but in the meantime what do I call you?" I said. This produced another wave of blushing; at this rate we would be able to save a fortune on the company's heating bills. Just couple her up to the boiler system, ask her questions about the size of her tits and she'd heat the whole office. That happy thought only served to draw my attention to them. Not bad, not bad at all, from what I could tell from the shape of her jumper, and nice legs as well. The blushing racked up another 10° centigrade as she realised she was being scanned and she instinctively reached to pull her skirt down over her knees.

"Well? Do I call you Sam Smith like the beer, Samantha like the Fox, Miss Smith like a dirty weekend, or Ms Smith like a dirty Dutch weekend - or what?"

Her eyes widened at the mention of dirty weekends but I put it down to shock not interest.

"Sam, most people call me just Sam," she stammered.

"Right. 'Just Sam', my name is Marcus, we don't go for the Mister crap in this firm. Provided you do your job it's all very informal you'll find. I think the Major - Margaret - has left you some notes..." She had, I had checked that before I went to Washington. I didn't want a repeat of the last time, when Belinda left some notes about me. This little delicate flower would have gone critical at the idea of having to work for an alleged raving sex maniac. No they were pretty mundane, typically Margaret, rather like the orderly room orders of the day. You know the sort of thing:

09.00 hrs. Open post, date stamp, record and place on desk. Don't speak - he's a bit sensitive early in the mornings.

09.30 hrs. Coffee - hot medium black sweet, one-and-a-half spoons of sugar.

10.00 hrs. Usually first appointment, etc etc.

She couldn't go far wrong with that but it didn't do a lot for my claims of informality - and I wasn't sure what she meant by 'sensitive'. I left 'Just Sam' to it and pushed on through to my pad. At least the agency hadn't sent me a dog like last time. She might be timid - she was timid - but she was also attractive. I found out later that Hugo had christened her 'Bambi' at first sight, and it fitted her to a tee.

Sam placed the post gently on my desk and faded out silently. She had taken the Major's written instructions literally, and didn't speak until 10 o'clock, except to murmur 'Good Morning' and give me any messages. Today the top item on the pile was a postcard from Margaret with a picture of the Iron Bridge across The Severn on the front, it reminded me that she would be back next Monday - her sister was 'doing well'. I couldn't for a moment recall what it was she was supposed to be doing well at, and then remembered the 'women's operation' - the boobs or plumbing? I'd no idea, but anyhow she was doing well at it whatever it was. This also brought me to realise that tomorrow would be Bambi's last day. In spite of drawing back like a frightened foal every time anybody spoke unexpectedly to her, and blushing furiously at every 'double entendre', expletive and lustful leer from the design office staff; even at compliments about her dress, hair, make-up or whatever; she had been very good. A willing worker, twice in the last three days she had voluntarily stayed late to complete sections for my civil engineering report on Sharjah Steel.

I nibbled a lip thoughtfully; perhaps I should take her to lunch or something as a small 'thank you'. She couldn't possibly be into red meat or game; bamboo shoots and brown rice perhaps? It would be more of a duty than a pleasure, but yes, I would do just that. I went through to her office.

"Sam, are you doing anything for lunch tomorrow?"

She looked up inquiringly, the automatic faint flush spreading in her cheeks. "Er, I'm not sure, why?"

I shrugged offhandedly and gave her an encouraging smile. I didn't want to be too forceful and frighten her off, on the other hand if she didn't want to come there was no point pressurising her too heavily with the result that we would both end up sitting silently resentful, staring across at each other like a pair of oversized bookends whilst we chewed our way through mounds of pulses, chlorophyll and roughage.

"I just thought it would be nice as a small thank you for all your help if I took you out to lunch."

The faint flush coloured deeper and spread down her neck; she met my eye and then looked down. She fumbled for a moment in her handbag and then produced a small, black, leather-bound diary. Turning on her swivel chair so that I couldn't see the pages, she flicked through quickly.

Disappointment crept into her voice, "Oh dear, I can't. The evenings are OK but I can't do lunch. I'm meeting my brother today and I've promised my mother I'd take her shopping in Peter Jones tomorrow." She shook her head slowly. "I can't really break it, she's been looking forward to it for weeks."

I did a quick mental cast forward, I was supposed to be playing squash tomorrow at 7.30 with Jamie Swallow. I could either bring it forward an hour or cancel it. He would be a bit sloughed if I cancelled, but he was a banker - they had to learn to get used to disappointments. Mind made up, I said, tentatively, "Well how about dinner tomorrow night then."

Her response was totally unexpected. She gave me a huge smile. "I would love it," she replied, "that really would be very nice."

"Oh, OK then. Er, I'll pick you up at 8.00 if that's OK with you?"

Fortunately she had already told me she had a flat in Fulham, just off Munster Road, so I knew I was not committing myself to a two hour trek to Cockfosters or Staines and back - twice. The arrangements were made. I was wrong in one assumption, she loved all kinds of food, so I asked her to book at Robert's in Fulham Road - traditional English with a twist. At least we'd get a good meal. That being settled I pushed off back to my desk with a little worm of doubt eating into my brain. It was nothing special, there was nothing I could put a finger on, but I couldn't help feeling that somewhere something had slipped slightly out of my control in the last few minutes. My essay into a casual lunch had somehow been converted into a fully-fledged evening out. No, it was nothing; she was genuinely pleased to be asked out. It did bugger up my Friday night though, but there you are, generous to a fault.

The MG slid up to a stop outside her flat at 8.10. There had been some water-main problem and traffic was all fouled up on Kings Road. I had meant to be early to have a look at her place, but in the event it was just another bow-fronted red brick terraced house with a minute front garden behind a low brick wall, the image of hundreds of similar houses on similar roads that make up the Fulham heartland. She had the top floor flat. I pressed the illuminated bell push beside 'S Smith' on the entry phone.

"Yes?"

Was I mistaken or was there a catch in the voice. It is hard to discern any vocal expression in the electronic squawk that these devices emit.

"It's Marcus," I said quietly, glancing over my shoulder nervously and wondering why one always does this with entry phones. One always imagines that if you say your name too loudly instant mugging will take place.

"I'll be right down," she said.

No muggers hove in sight and 30 seconds later the door opened.

She looked very attractive, a short jacket in some dark colour, maybe velvet, it was hard to see exactly what material in the street lights, worn over a high-necked, white blouse and the mandatory string of pearls for your qualified Sloane Ranger. South of the waist all I could distinguish was a dark skirt and smart leather court shoes. Her hair shone and her eyes sparkled. No they didn't, I looked again! Yes they did, but the reason they sparkled was that they were full of tears. They glistened.

"What on earth's the matter?" I took her arm gently to lead her to the car. She dabbed at her eyes with a wisp of cotton taken from her sleeve.

"I didn't think you were coming," she sniffed pathetically.

I gave a snort of ridicule. "Of course I was coming, I promised to come didn't I? I even got you to book the restaurant."

"You're late," she said.

"Only ten minutes - there was some snarl up in the traffic that's all."

I opened the car door for her and she got in. Now those with experience of low-slung cars can do this modestly, bottom in first, knees together and swing both legs in simultaneously. Those without - and she was one - put one leg in, then the bum, and end up legs apart and skirt up thighs trying to haul the spare leg inboard. She forgot her complaint trying to retain her modesty. I closed the door and went round to my side of the car. Marcus Moon you old dog you, you can really pull 'em. Bursting into tears because I'm a few minutes late. I didn't think it all meant that much to her. Still it was comforting to feel wanted again, one's company anxiously desired.

"And what is it like, Mr Moon, to be the prime object of weeping desire for the world's loveliest women?"

"Well of course there's a lot of them about, and there's only one of me, so I have to ration it very strictly. After all it is only right that it's shared out, it wouldn't be fair, would it, for any one 'lovely' to get more than any other?"

"Oy! Dozy! Are you going to stand there all night or are you going?"

The guy hanging out of the window of the Sierra was indicating to turn into the resident's parking slot that I was currently illegally occupying. He had a point.

"Oh sorry," I called, "just going."

I slid into the driver's seat and headed off down towards Fulham Broadway still feeling cheerfully chuffed.

The car rattles and bangs a bit on London roads and, with the wind and traffic noise coming through various holes and gaps, conversation in the Moon-mobile becomes limited. 'Bambi' was not exactly garrulous on a good day under sodium pentothal, and after a few inaudible whispers quit, realising that even Stentor would have difficulty making himself heard in my car.

It was only ten minutes to the restaurant and I slotted the car in behind a Bentley on the main road. Black knickers eh, I was thinking, they were a bit of a surprise. That maybe showed something else, but what that something was remained to be seen. The quick flash, however, did offer a very faint ray of hope for the future of the evening. One always likes to have some hint of lurking sensuality, and at least it was some indication that she might be interested in one subject that I was interested in.

"You're very deep in thought tonight," she observed timidly as we crossed the road. "Is it business?"

I coughed slightly. "Well sort of business - but not to worry. It's the start of the weekend, let's look at it like that and enjoy ourselves."

She looked even prettier in the bright light of the restaurant, a small heart-shaped face with dark eyes under the shiny black swept-back hair. Her skin was very smooth and quite pale. It coloured quickly as she met my gaze for a moment before lowering her eyes. I helped her off with her jacket and hung it on the back of her chair. I felt a twinge of disappointment, the black underwear theme was not carried upwards or her bra would have showed through the blouse. I ordered two Kir Royale and we studied the menu.

"They do a few very unusual dishes here, the baked brie with gooseberry sauce and the veal chasseur are delicious."

She closed her menu and placed it on the table. "Corn-on-the-cob to start and then you choose," she said, "whatever you have I'll have."

I smiled at her. "OK if you're happy with that but how hungry are you?"

"So, so, I don't each much anyway."

I ordered the baked brie to start with and then the veal chasseur for both of us. I thought that would do under the circumstances and she offered no objections to consuming infant cow. I also ordered a bottle of decent Chablis and some English mineral water.

The opening conversation was a bit one sided. I didn't want to make it an interrogation but when all one can extract are 'yes' and 'no' it's difficult. However the Kir Royale, followed by a second, loosened her up somewhat, and by the time the corn-on-the-cob and baked brie arrived I was well into her life story. She nibbled and sucked at her corn-on-the-cob with concentrated enthusiasm, her small white teeth picking off the juicy grains delicately. I watched her with interest. The veal chasseur arrived, two huge platefuls with all the supporting vegetables. For someone who professed not to eat very much she went into it like a power shovel and her plateful disappeared in very short order. I managed to keep her talking whilst I caught up.

She told me that she hailed from just outside Haslemere, her father was a vicar and her mother came from a wealthy family in her own right. 'Bambi' had done all the usual upper middle-class things: pony club, prep school, girls' public school - which she hated, and secretarial college - only the smartest of course. The mention of boyfriends turned her beetroot red but she avowed that she had no one in particular although she did know a few boys socially - more like brothers she added hastily. Beyond that I could not extract anything more of interest out of her - maybe there just wasn't anything. She ordered crème brûlé, but I declined a pudding; where she put it all, defeated me. The main thing was she seemed to be enjoying herself and emerging from her shell.

"Would you like some coffee?" I asked, as the waitress hovered after clearing the dishes and plates.

She hesitated a moment and colouring up again said, "I've got a better idea. You've taken me out and treated me to this lovely meal, the least I can do is offer you coffee back at the flat." I hesitated momentarily, thinking of Friday evening in the Frog, and then I thought, black knickers - and the way she had tackled that corn-on-the-cob. Marcus, mate, that bereft body of yours might, just might, pull a number tonight - and if there's a chance - for medical reasons only you understand, well...

With forced offhandedness I replied, "Well, if you are sure that's OK, it's fine by me."

She nodded. "Mmm."

I paid the bill and took her to the car; she linked her arm in mine as I towered over her.

"That really was a lovely meal in a lovely setting. You are clever to know all these places." She smiled up at me disarmingly.

Unlocking the front door of the house she ushered me through. I stood looking round as she fumbled at the door. The hall was decorated in pale yellow with a new beige carpet that extended up the stairs. When she turned I saw that she had put the security chain across.

"The people downstairs are away for a fortnight skiing in Verbier," she explained.

"Oh," I said non-committally. I followed her up the stairs to another door. She unlocked that and went through.

The top floor of the house had been converted into a one bedroom flat with a separate sitting room cum dining room, a small kitchen and a small bathroom, but clearly a lot of large brownies had changed hands. The kitchen was fitted out with expensive built-in units and had all the electrical gadgetry. The carpeted bathroom was tastefully tiled, floor to ceiling, with bath and shower as well as loo and washbasin. The bedroom had a queen-sized double bed sporting a small teddy bear, with bedspread, headboard, curtains and chair fabric all matched. The sitting room where I ended up, contained a comfortable-looking two seat settee, two other easy chairs, a tall corner cupboard, a small writing desk with an arrangement of bookshelves above it and a small dining table with four high-backed chairs. It was cramped but expensive. The colour television set had its own niche in the bookshelves over the desk. She went off to make the coffee whilst I browsed amongst her books. Jane Austen and Thomas Hardy figured, as did Jacqueline Susan and Danielle Steel. Joan and Jackie Collins were bunched in a section with Jilly Cooper and Julie Burchill. Julie Burchill! She was a bit hot for a little fawn like Bambi. She brought in a tray with two cups of coffee, a jug of milk and sugar in a bowl. "I would have offered you a brandy but I don't have any." She looked up at me embarrassed.

"Not to worry, I don't like it anyway."

I took a surreptitious glance at my watch whilst she cleared a place for the tray on the coffee table. It was still only 10 o'clock; I could still get down to the Frog and Nightgown if I was quick.

"How do you like your coffee..." she paused with a bashful giggle. "Of course I should know that by now, it's hot, black and sweet."

I watched as she spooned in the sugar and then brought it round to where I was standing. She didn't have to do that, she could easily have put it on the coffee table, it was just that by doing it she ended up standing four square in front of me and very close. Admittedly she occupied space in a much lower plane, I could easily see over the top of her head but when I bent to take the cup somehow her face turned temptingly upwards. The Frog and Nightgown vanished from my thoughts as quickly as black knickers re-entered them, and I kept bending towards her just as she kept reaching up. What happened to the coffee I don't know and didn't care because the kiss I got was quite definitely not the sort of kiss you get from your grandma. I felt one of her hands reach to hold the back of my head and the other slide inside my jacket. She was pressed so close that the only part of her I could grasp was her back so I grasped it - and then moved my hands up and down it. I knew now why no black bra had been visible through her blouse - she was, as they say, unfettered. Now those of you who are over 6 ft 2 and have passionately embraced somebody who is not more than 5 ft and peanut, will know that it is just not possible to do this for very long without both parties suffering major spinal damage. Nor is it possible to advance matters further. It is necessary - so I told her - temporarily detaching my lips - to equalise things, and the best way to do this, scientists have discovered, is in the horizontal position. By choice I am not a rug and carpet man myself, being a bit too thin to pad out the sharp bits when in close contact with a hard floor, and as a queen-sized bed lay within ten strides, I picked her up bodily, once again firmly locked to my face, by the simple expedient of putting both hands beneath her bottom and lifting. We collapsed on to the bed the same way. Little teddy gave his impersonation of a ground to air missile and we got down to business. After a lot of very interesting and exciting rolling around, both together and separately, we managed to undress each other. I had a problem with her tights - dreadful things for the amorous man. I could only reach down far enough to ease them to just below her knees whilst still in the kissing mode, so I put one foot between her legs on the waistband and straightened my leg sharply. The tights flew off both feet simultaneously and hit the dressing table. I suppose it was a good job they did, otherwise she would have been off my lips like a cork from a champagne bottle and across the room with them, feet first, into the moisturiser and nail varnish. The black knickers - I was right - got the same treatment. Not surprisedly, I got the impression that she expected me - the experienced man of the world, natch - to make the running, so I did. Caressing this, that and the other whilst murmuring things like 'my little fawn' and 'sweet little mouse' in her ear, if my mouth happened to be near that particular opening at that time. We made fabulous progress. She responded with tiny squeaks and gasps and the odd nibble here and there. Eventually, being the gentleman I am, and taking my weight on the elbows, we came, as they say, to the main event of the evening.

I will say one thing, she kept going and it was me that eventually rolled over pleading a rest. I held her in my arms with eyes closed trying to steady my breathing.

"So you think I'm your timid little mouse do you Marcus?" she murmured softly. "A poor frightened fawn who daren't say boo to a goose?"

I didn't like to point out that fawns couldn't say boo to geese anyway so I drowsily agreed with her and snuggled closer into the pillow.

"And the boys in the office nicknamed me Bambi didn't they?"

"Hugo did," I gave a sleepy chuckle. "He thought of it the instant he saw you."

"And did you agree with him?" she persisted.

I gave her kisses on her nose, eyes and forehead. "Mmm," I said.

"A big strong tough man like you."

"Mmm," I murmured again.

"Just a minute," she said, and slipping gently from my embrace padded across the room and out of the door closing it behind her. She's gone to the loo, I decided, and drifted into a happy doze.

It seemed like the next second there was a huge crash, which shot me bolt upright in the bed, the adrenalin surging panic stricken through the arteries. For an instant I thought the ceiling had collapsed or the wardrobe toppled over. It took me a moment to mark that the bedroom door was now open wide and it was the impact of the door slamming into the wall that had startled me awake.

"So you think I'm a mouse and you're a tough guy do you Marcus, well let us see just how tough you are!" Her voice now had an edge like a chipped glass and she was standing legs astride in the doorway silhouetted against the sitting-room lights.

"Jesus Christ, what the hell are you doing Samantha?" I gasped. "You scared the living daylights out of me."

"Come on, Marcus, if you think you're tough you do what I want now. We've done everything your way all evening, now we do it mine. You're not going to let a timid little mouse get the better of you are you?"

My eyes began to focus better and adjust to the light, she was still standing in the doorway but now I could see that she was wearing some kind of black body stocking and thigh length boots. What began to put the shits up me properly was that she was holding what looked suspiciously like a riding crop in her hand.

"Come on Marcus, come and be my naughty little pony - unless you're too scared that is!" There was more than a tinge of scorn in her voice as she threw down the challenge and this kindled a primitive but impulsive response in me. Well it was not really my scene but I supposed that there was some truth in what she said. I had had it all my way - although I couldn't recall her showing any reluctance - so maybe it was her turn, and if being a naughty little pony turned her on then who knows - the night was young and the whole weekend lay ahead. Now that I knew all the equipment had not atrophied from lack of use and was in fine fettle, the old self-confidence had returned. Anyway she was so small she couldn't do much damage - not as much as my pride would suffer if I chickened out.

It just shows how wrong you can be.

"OK then," I said, climbing out of bed, "what do you want me to do? Gallop round the room giving you a piggy back?"

She looked round the sitting room for a minute. "No," she said with a secret smile. "Not yet." She paused, tapping her left hand with what I could now clearly confirm was a rather evil-looking riding crop held in her right.

183

"No, first you must be disciplined before we go for a ride. I want you to come in here and bend over the desk." She pointed to the desk under the bookshelves.

I raised a warning finger, "Now hang on a minute, this is fun isn't it?"

"Scared?" she said contemptuously. Well I wasn't really, there was something quite erotic seeing her standing there trying to be dominating like that. It was just that experience had taught me the precept that venturing into the unknown always had an unforeseen outcome - but it could be exciting.

"OK," I warned her, "but just this once." She smiled. "If you don't try it you don't know whether or not you'll like it." I bent across the desk resting my head against the wall feeling a total pillock. It was the last painless thing I was to feel for a long, long time.

I remember a swishing sound and an agonising pain across the bottom as though somebody had laid a white-hot wire there. I jerked violently upright, and received a stunning blow on the head that felled me three quarters senseless across the desk enveloped in a shower of timber, plaster and books. There was simultaneously a smashing of glass and cracking of plastic, and then a blinding shaft of agony in my left foot. I could vaguely sense hot, sticky fluid trickling down my face but I couldn't move. In the far far distance a faint voice cried, "Oh my God!" and then I passed out. I must have been unconscious for 10 to 15 minutes because, when consciousness began to magnify the pain, the ambulance men were just lifting me onto the stretcher. Somebody had pulled on my boxer shorts and tied bandages round my throbbing head. My foot hurt like hell and I saw wet blood on my hands. I caught a brief glimpse of Samantha - now fully dressed I noticed abstractedly, as she dropped the rest of my clothes across my thighs.

"Are you alright, Marcus?" she asked, a pleading note in her voice. I could see now why she didn't have that many long term boyfriends, the local hospital only had 500 beds and I expected that they needed a few of those for other patients. I gave her a weak nod, which made the room spin violently, and then they carted me down the stairs to the blood wagon. They kept me under observation in Charing Cross Hospital for a couple of days to check for concussion. The back of my head looked like a monkey's bum. The hair had been shaved off and seven stitches inserted in the straight, deep cut where my head and the steel bracket supporting the bookshelves had been in a major disagreement. By contorting myself in front of two mirrors I could see that it looked as though a butcher's cleaver had neatly parted my skull. The X-ray of my foot showed two cracked bones and so the foot and ankle had been cased in an inflatable boot. Apart from that damage, a splitting headache and some very funny looks from the nurses, I was in good shape. I had no visitors because, fortunately, nobody knew where I was - except for Sam the Sadist, and she was nowhere to be seen. A bunch of flowers from 'Sorry!' turned up on Sunday morning so I had not been forgotten!

They discharged me on Sunday afternoon with a pair of National Health crutches and strict instructions to return them in three weeks when the boot could be replaced with a trainer.

In the taxi back to the flat I pondered. Serious pondering was required because this sort of damage could not be passed off as a shaving cut or falling out of bed. Questions were bound to be asked, and the answers had better be very convincing. I decided that the solution was to stick as close to the truth as embarrassment permitted.

The story would be that I was in an old school friend's flat, slightly pissed. They would believe that - well maybe not the 'slightly' bit!

I had stood up suddenly, not realising that I had been sitting underneath a shelf supporting the television, hit the bracket supporting the shelf and brought the whole lot down with the TV landing on my foot. This was roughly what I had told the hospital. The circumstances of the sudden standing would not be disclosed because if the truth ever came out, my so-called friends would wet themselves with laughter at my expense.

Well I would if it had happened to one of them!

CHAPTER TWELVE

Mazin Al Jabril sat in his deep leather executive chair at the carved oak desk in his study overlooking Hyde Park. He was leaning forward, one elbow propped on the desk; with his other hand he was gently tapping his teeth with a thin gold pen. Mazin was thinking and thinking hard.

It was all going well for him so far, his agency contract was in place with CONDES; his big agency contract to represent Pantocrator throughout the Middle East was signed - and what a deal that was. A hundred thousand dollars a year retainer to his Swiss company, plus 15% of the value of any orders for equipment he could get for them by fair means or foul. The furnace contract for Sharjah Steel alone would pull in over $10 million, and that was a virtual certainty. Ten million, he rolled the words round on his tongue savouring them like golden caviar. That would more than double the assets he already had stashed in Switzerland - and all tax-free as well. Taxes were for the financially incompetent, not for the big time international operator. Mazin did not pay taxes, mugs paid taxes. Nothing passed through Mazin's personal accounts apart from what, to him, was petty cash; it all went directly into Investment and Resources Holdings SA in Geneva. Any tax official seizing Mazin's accounts would learn nothing of his true worth. He smiled softly to himself. But if Mazin was a greedy man, he was also a shrewd, careful planner. Every angle was considered, every alternative examined, every loophole blocked. Bribery, threats, even violence on occasions had been used to secure him what he wanted. Undoubtedly bribery was the best method. It sucked a man in, enmeshed him inextricably, made him part of the activity, made him break the law and gave Mazin a hold over him from which he never escaped. When you've got them by the balls their hearts and minds soon follow was his favourite maxim.

But no bribery or threats were needed for the Sharjah Steel furnace contract - that was the beauty of it. True, his brother the Minister would expect a kick-back, a couple of million, less if he could screw him, but that was fine and that would give him a hold over his brother as well. The Ruler of Sharjah took exception to his Ministers skimming state funds off the top of the national budget; one or two unfortunates were currently rotting in jail for that right now, after a bribery scandal. Mazin smiled cynically to himself, his big soft brother, for whom the good life had blunted his cutting edge, insisting on being called 'Your Excellency' even by Mazin - a fat, ripe pumpkin these days, who would not relish contemplating the inside of a Sharjah jail one little bit.

All this had passed through Mazin's mind as he sat there, but now his concentration was fixed on tying the one loose end. The Pantocrator contract for Sharjah Steel should be a certainty but as yet it was not. Unfortunately the decision to make it a certainty could only be made by those two gullible English fools, Elmes and Moon, and lurking at the back of his mind there was a nagging uncertainty about those two. He had ripped them off ruthlessly on the Egyptian job, he knew it, and he was certain they knew it. Apart from Elmes' outburst, nothing had been said. It had all been very 'civilised'. He spat the exclamation out loud, "Huh, Englishmen!" Maybe they were scared to mention it in case it angered him, in case he did what he had threatened he could do and had had them struck off the list of bidders for the design contract. He laughed scornfully. They had fallen for that, he couldn't have done it anyway, they were too well known in steelworks design and the Minister, his brother, and the World Bank, had already approved them for the short list long before Mazin found out about it. That was why he had come hotfoot to London to get them signed up.

A scowl crossed his face, he didn't like the way he had been treated when offering his services. They hadn't been deferential enough, he didn't like that, they had insulted him by bargaining him down arrogantly. Mazin liked his bargaining to be one way - his way. He frowned pensively. But maybe, just maybe, they were not so stupid. Maybe they thought they were clever - cleverer than him. Maybe they planned to get their own back on him somehow. He thought about this for a long time, everything seemed to be well covered. He reviewed carefully the position to date. The World Bank had approved the use of the new type of high frequency induction furnaces, subject to certain technical conditions; Pantocrator were the only people to make these furnaces so they must get the order; CONDES were already incorporating the use of these into their design and 'Hop-along' Moon had been to Greece twice to collect all the technical data and see their working unit, so he was obviously happy. So what could they do to him? Sure they might not pay him the last instalment of his miserable agency fee - a mere $40,000 - puf! No, it couldn't go wrong, and yet it would be wise to take further precautions if at all possible, and there was one precaution that, if it could be taken, would tie the whole thing up rock-solid, 100%.

He stroked his chin thoughtfully. First of all collect all the information available then form your plan - that was another of his maxims. To make a start on that was easy. He selected a piece of paper from the blotter and wrote down three names. He then reached for the phone. The first call was to his lawyer, Ahmed Marzouk, a Jordanian who had qualified in both Arabic and English law and now practiced in Clarges Street. "Ahmed, get me a copy of the annual return of the CONDES Group together with their Memorandum and Articles, they could be listed under 'Consultant Design Group Limited'." He listened for a second. "Yes, they are a private company." He listened again then hissed quietly. "Now Ahmed now! I want them now! And Ahmed, if this leaks out to anyone I'll have you sliced up and fed to the pigs!" He pressed the cancel switch on the phone and crossed off the first name on the list. The next call was to his accountants, the senior partner.

"Desmond, can you get me copies of the last five years' accounts of a company called Consultant Design Group Limited trading as the CONDES Group. And Desmond this is to be kept strictly private and confidential, is that clear? Nobody must know about this except you and I, and, Desmond, if it leaks out I'll know where it came from." There was a long pause and Mazin's face grew darker and darker, then he exploded. "Ten days!" he shouted. "I want them now, Desmond, now; not in 'maybe ten days - if we're lucky'," he mocked. "Well send a man, send a whole team of men to Cardiff if you have to, but just get them!" He slammed down the phone infuriated by the sluggish response to his request and seethed quietly for a few minutes tapping his fingers on his knee. He then crossed off the second name.

The final call was to Arthurson, Smythe, Pegler and Booth, a big firm of City lawyers with international branches. This time he was all politeness and charm when they eventually put him through to their Channel Islands specialist. He asked for a brief summary setting out how Jersey trusts operated, and he asked for it to be sent round by courier as soon as it was ready. He then crossed off the third name.

The summary arrived the following day and, stung by Mazin's threats and rage, both Ahmed Marzouk and the accountants acted with unaccustomed alacrity. The lawyer went down to Companies House in Cardiff himself, the accountant sent a minion. Without realising it they boarded the same Inter City flyer both there and back. One firm could easily have done both jobs obtaining copies of the Annual Returns as well as the last five years' accounts but Mazin always compartmentalised his activities. That way nobody could assemble the whole picture except him. Need to know, that was what he believed, just what they needed to know to achieve what he demanded, nothing more.

The lawyer spent only ten minutes at Companies House and left with a copy of the Memorandum and Articles of Association of the company and the annual return, filed two months earlier, tucked into his briefcase. The last five years of accounts took longer but, for the payment of a modest fee, the accountant obtained copies of the microfilmed records of Consultant Design Group Limited going back for the last five years, including the most recent accounts filed with the annual return two months previously. Both the lawyer and the accountant made extra copies for their own files, you never knew when such information might come in useful, and then sent the documents round to Mazin Al Jabril's flat by immediate motorcycle courier.

To be exact, it was not his flat. Like all his assets it belonged to Investment and Resources Holdings SA. All the agency agreements, property, cars, gold and cash belonged to IRH. The Cessna Citation and the Riva boat had been hired. Mazin owned and controlled the company through his bearer shares but that had to be done via a Swiss lawyer who would only take and act upon instructions when the holder of the bearer shares appeared personally with the share certificate and issued those instructions. The lawyer would then carry them out to the letter - no more, no less, no questions. The bearer shares themselves were held to Mazin's order in a secure vault at Credit Suisse Geneva. Such an arrangement made Mazin fireproof. He could be sued, but as he personally owned nothing, such a course of action would be pointless. The company could be sued, but as nobody knew who owned the company, except Mazin, it would be impossible to prove the connection. It was a perfect set-up for the international crook, although he didn't look at it that way. The old saying 'When the going gets tough the tough get going' he had modified: 'When the tough get going the weak get stuffed', and he was proud that his arrangements provided a foolproof method for the stuffing process.

Both the annual return and the five years' accounts of Consultant Design Group made very interesting reading. He had started with the annual return which listed the directors; that showed him that the company was not mortgaged and most usefully, listed the shareholders - or, in the case of CDG, the single shareholder owning 100% of the shares. With increasing interest he noted down the name Bridge Holdings Limited with his gold pen on the pad. There was no further mention of Bridge Holdings other than to record that it was a Jersey company. He had a gut feeling about it. It could be the key to the final lock that would secure his position.

He reached for the phone. "Ahmed, go over to Jersey and get me the annual return and the last five years' accounts of a company called Bridge Holdings Limited. No! Today!" He listened for a few seconds and then cut in. "I don't know how you do it! You're supposed to be the fucking lawyer so just get over there and get them!" He slammed down the phone shaking his head in despair.

By Thursday he had all the information he needed. The documents from Jersey were very enlightening. The list of shareholders for Bridge Holdings Limited showed that Elmes owned 15%, Moon, 10% and a Jersey trust, the CONDES Trust, owned the balance of 75%. This confirmed what that fool Moon had told him on the drive up to Cambridge, but Moon hadn't said that the trust owned as much as 75% only that it had a majority. Seventy-five per cent was more than just a majority; it was a significant number. With a feeling of growing excitement he hastily turned to the Mem and Arts. According to the Memorandum of Association and Articles of Agreement, the legal documents by which the company must be operated, a 75% holding gave absolute and total control. Now that was very, very interesting, he considered. Over 50% of a company gave general control, but there were restrictions on most private companies that prohibited, for instance, the increasing of the share capital without agreement of 75% of the existing shareholders. Any body, or individual, who controlled 75% of Bridge could do what they liked with the company. Presumably they had arranged it this way for tax reasons, but as he was not wholly familiar with the complexity of general tax laws - apart from what was needed to evade them altogether, and British tax laws in particular - he could not work the reasoning out any further. It wasn't necessary anyway. He then turned to the last five years' accounts and began making notes on his pad with his gold pen as he worked his way through them. The first two years showed modest but healthy profits, increasing from £300,000 in the first year to £520,000 in the second. In the third year they had made a thundering loss, Mazin gave a thin smile when he read that, but in the last two years the profits had picked up, and picked up to such an extent that the accumulated loss had been eliminated altogether. It was clear that if one ignored the huge loss in the third year, the Group was expanding rapidly and was potentially very profitable. The projected profit for the present year could be nearly £1 million

- $1,600,000. That was real money he thought. His mind began to work overtime.

Originally the idea had been to devise a defensive plan. A plan to provide some means of protection to prevent Elmes and Moon getting their revenge on him, if that was what they were intending - although he still couldn't see how - and some counter hold over them would give him a bargaining lever. Now his plan was beginning to change. There was big money to be made here with careful planning and a slice or two of luck, but one always needed some luck, that was the will of Allah.

He went back to the figures jotted on his pad and reached for his calculator. Averaging out the profits for the last five years, ignoring the third year loss - he knew full well why that had occurred, he did some quick calculations. The Group as whole could be valued at £5-6 million, perhaps more, and it was a cash-rich business with no outstanding mortgages or loans and with money in the bank. Not much, but they didn't have an overdraft. CONDES' assets showed that there was none of its cash locked in huge items of plant, machinery or buildings, what money there was was tied up in the business. It was in brains and work already done but not yet paid for - almost as good as cash in the bank. It was a potential little gold mine as it stood at present - but that was by no means its full potential. Just designing projects for the fees and making ten, maybe 20% profit, was not Mazin's idea for the key to his paradise. He could see further than that altogether. No, what made his avaricious dark eyes gleam, and his palms itch, was the potentially real bonanza that absolute control over such a business could bring. Such a person would be able to manipulate specifications and bid documents so that a person's 'friends' of course, would pay handsomely for the inside track that Mazin could provide for them. There were millions to be made there. The Sharjah Steel project alone could be milked of £20-30 million, and then there were other large projects like the aluminium smelter for instance - the construction contracts for that had not been placed yet.

He re-read the annual return, he was under no illusions that what he was contemplating was going to be easy, or even that it was possible, but he was definitely going to attempt it by fair means or foul. There was no way he could afford to ignore such a potential windfall. However Mazin was also a cautious man and being a cautious man before attempting anything he wanted confirmation of his own conclusions. He punched out the numbers of his accountants and got the senior partner on the line.

"CONDES - I want a full and detailed report from you on this firm within seven days. I know you have kept copies of the accounts," he smiled to himself at that, "so that should not cause you any problems. I also want you to give me some idea of the value of the business assuming that the management charges it pays each year to its Jersey shareholder are retained in CONDES."

He listened for a short while to Desmond Bailey's response and then his face grew dark and he shouted in to the phone. "No, you idiot, you can't approach the company for more information, this is supposed to be confidential. And what is more if this does leak out I'll have your balls for breakfast, even though we Moslems don't eat pork, so just get on with it and make it quick." By Allah these cursed city people had no idea of business.

Still seething he phoned his lawyer. No preliminaries, straight in: "Ahmed, find out who the trustee is of a Jersey registered trust called The CONDES Trust."

The lawyer knew nothing at all about Jersey trusts but agreed to do as he was bidden. It was three days later, after he had hit a succession of brick walls, that he fearfully phoned Mazin back.

"Excellency, unfortunately the authorities are most uncooperative, it is not possible to find out the names of trustees of Jersey trusts. I have tried everything I know but it just is not possible."

Mazin cursed him for being an ignorant fool and told him that he wouldn't get his bill paid for his incompetence, then cut off his protests by putting down the phone. He thought long and hard about this hitch to his plans and then saw the solution. Obviously Elmes and Moon both knew who the trustee was. On the drive to Cambridge Moon had been stupid enough to tell him directly that there was only one trustee, at least he had said 'trustee' in the singular not 'trustees'. Well that made things much easier. One person was a much simpler proposition to negotiate with, and if necessary suborn, than three or more; and as Moon was so indiscreet, Moon would have to be persuaded to reveal the trustee's identity. The big problem would arise if the trustee was a partner in a big law firm or bank. That, however, would have to be left until the trustee was identified.

There was one other thing that must be checked somehow. The copy of the most recent accounts were for the year ending 31st March. It was now December, and a lot could have happened between March and December. Although everything seemed to be progressing satisfactorily on the surface there was no point in taking chances if they were not necessary. To find out the up-to-date situation in CONDES was going to take a great deal of ingenuity, if he was not to reveal his interest, but he would work on it - there was no desperate urgency.

To Mazin's disgust he had discovered years ago that in England everything shuts between Christmas and the New Year. Not that he was going to be in London working, he had his usual suite booked at The Grand at St Moritz for two weeks' skiing over that period. However, before he flew out to Zurich he was due to attend the pre-Christmas project meeting on Sharjah Steel at CONDES. He smiled grimly, they didn't like him coming to project meetings, he knew that, but it enabled him to keep a close eye on the detailed design and ensure that his interests were still kept to the fore.

So, two days after he had formulated his plan, he strode out of the entrance of the apartment block, the driver hurriedly docked his cigarette and rushed round to open the rear door of the Mercedes when his master hove into sight on the steps. It was a crisp cold morning and Mazin was well muffled in camelhair coat and chamois gloves. The weather, which had been unusually warm for December, had changed just in time and heavy falls of snow had recently been reported in the Alps. He was in a good mood as a consequence and was looking forward to his holiday. Not for the exercise and fresh air, he was only a mediocre skier, but as a poser he was Olympic class. Standing on the terraces of the smart restaurants at lunch time wearing his trendy gear and holding his 210cm skis - which he changed for his 170s when he had to ski - looking tall, bronzed and fit, he could really pull the ladies. Rubbing shoulders with minor royalty and celebrities of stage and screen in the cocktail bar of the Grand at night also stroked his massive ego to inflationary heights. He loved it - but if there was no snow, then there would be no show - hence his current pleasure.

He was, as usual, 15 minutes late for the meeting, but also, as usual, that arrogant puppy Moon had not waited for him and the meeting was therefore well under way when he was ushered in. Moon offered coffee and, noticing that he was still wearing his coat, suggested that he could put it in Moon's office. Mazin looked round for somebody to take it for him but the girl had gone and nobody else moved. Petulantly he stamped down the corridor to Moon's dog kennel. The dragon woman who normally guarded it, like Cerberus at the gates of Hades, was absent from her post so he passed through unchallenged to the inner sanctum.

He hung his coat on the coat stand and, being the nosy sod he was, quickly cast a glance over the papers lying in untidy heaps over Moon's desk. One particular document headed 'CONDES GROUP, Six-Monthly Management Accounts, 1st April to 30th September' caught his eye. By Allah, this was just what he needed, just the stroke of luck he wanted. He raised his eyes and, thanking heaven for bestowing it upon him, quickly folded the document and slipped it into his inside breast pocket. So much for ingenuity, he reflected with contempt. Checking to make sure nothing else was disturbed he eased back down the corridor to the meeting. Once he had satisfied himself that the designs were still being progressed incorporating the laser accelerated vacuum contained high frequency induction furnaces, or LAVCHIFS as they were now referred to, he made his excuses and left. This time the dragon was at her post and got his coat for him, even helping him put it on - there would have been no chance of any unauthorised access to Moon's office then. He thanked Allah again for his blessings.

The report from his accountants arrived the day before he left for Switzerland. A brief look through served to confirm his original ideas. They put a value on the whole firm of £4.86 million on a prices:earnings ratio of 8, but they warned him that there could have been changes between the 31st March and the current time. He smiled at that, the six-monthly management accounts showed that there had been changes but only for the better. Neither did the forecasts include Sharjah Steel, because the contract had not been signed by then, but the management accounts still estimated nearly £1 million profit for the full year. He rubbed his hands together in anticipation and threw all the documents, including the report on Jersey trusts, into his briefcase for further study in Switzerland.

I hadn't seen Mazin since the last Sharjah Steel project meeting two weeks previously but I had managed to survive the deprivation. He was due to turn up today for the next session. I had hoped to progress matters a little further at the last meeting, but the final six-monthly management accounts had been delayed because Brian went down with the flu. Today however, I had them. I looked round my desk and then laid them prominently on the side nearest the coat-stand. I called the Major in.

"Margaret, Mr Al Jabril will be attending the Sharjah Steel design meeting today, when he arrives will you make yourself scarce for a few minutes? I want him to be left alone and unobserved in my office."

She raised a questioning eyebrow, but I said, "Just do it, it's OK."

To make sure his attention was focused where I wanted it to be I laid the Aluminium Smelter finance file, and the World Bank project list prominently on the desk with the corners just touching, both left casually amongst the rest of the papers. If anyone opened either or both they would be moved. I also put a couple of those cheap bent wire coat hangers on the coat-stand. Satisfied I crutched out to chair the meeting.

Mazin, as usual, was late, and as usual, because he felt the cold weather, he was wearing his flash overcoat – 'camel-hair you know, especially tailored for me'. I told him to put it in my office where it could be hung up on a coat hanger and, after glaring round unsuccessfully for someone to take it from him, he reluctantly trudged off to dispose of it himself.

When he returned he looked satisfyingly bland and, as soon as we had dealt with the item on the agenda covering furnaces, he pushed off.

I could hardly wait. Eventually the meeting drew to a close and I legged down the corridor to my office setting world speed records for crutching. And there, as they say, there it was - gone! The bait had been taken. Nothing else had been touched. That confirmed it. He was only collecting information about CONDES. It was too much of a coincidence to believe that he had taken the six-monthly accounts merely out of a passing interest, the other stuff should have been much more interesting to a rip-off merchant like him.

Brian Mason had been out all morning, so I told him about it in the afternoon.

"We can't take the chance of him doing something we don't know about," I reasoned. "We've got to predispose him to do something where we know what he is up to because it's what we want him to do. You were right, I suspect that Mazin is going to try to get control of CONDES through Bridge Holdings. He doesn't know who owns the 75% controlling interest, only that the shares are held by a Jersey trust that has only one trustee."

Brian corrected me. "Three trustees!"

I conceded the point with a grin. "Yes, true at present, but I told Mazin that there was only one trustee. A man like Mazin will reason that one person is much easier to suborn than three! I'll bet a pound to a penny he'll try to find out who that trustee is!"

Brian scratched his chin thoughtfully. "So you think Mazin will try to bribe this single trustee into parting with the CONDES shares? He shook his head. "He won't expect to get them for nothing will he? What are they worth to him?"

I shrugged. "What do we want? We want our $2 million plus interest back. He would smell a rat if the trustee only asked for that. The trustee would have to put a commercial price on the shares and Mazin's tactics would be to screw him down with a bribe to the lowest acceptable market value. That way it looks to be a clean deal, both to Mazin and to the outside world. Although morally the trustee would appear to be a first-class shit from our point of view, he wouldn't have done anything illegal. It's a discretionary trust so he can act at his discretion."

I laughed. "Considering that Bridge Holdings Limited will actually be worth bugger all by then, far from selling us short the trustee will actually have pulled off a great deal, so we are hardly likely to sue him!"

Brian tugged at his ear. I had noticed, with Brian, that he always pulled or scratched some bit of his anatomy when thinking. Did this stimulate the flow of blood to the brain? I must give it a try sometime. Maybe tugging or scratching different bits stimulated different brain cells? I wondered if there was a book about it. Although if one scratched too much it could give the wrong impression to one's companions. Eczema, scabies or some other foul infestation that might be virulently infectious! I moved away from him a fraction. He was staring at me. "Are you still with us?" he snapped testily. "You went all glazed over for a while."

"Yes, sorry. Something just occurred to me," I apologized, refocusing my attention on the present.

Slightly nettled, Brian continued. "If Bridge Holdings Limited is to be made worthless what are you going to do about the Consultant Design Group shares? It still owns all those, and all our contracts, including Sharjah Steel, are with CDG."

"I've thought of that. Subject to Michael le Fevre's agreement, they would be transferred into a new company that he would set up for us.

"At this moment we are only speculating that Mazin is going to try to become involved, we don't know that he is. So whatever is done must be done before anything like that happens. That way we can never be accused of 'conning' anybody."

I thought of something else to tell him. "Incidentally you know the six-monthly management accounts you gave me this morning? Well, with any luck, Mazin is avidly absorbing them at this moment! He stole them from my office before the Sharjah project meeting!" I gave a chuckle as Brian raised a knowing eyebrow.

We discussed the plan again for a few more minutes and decided that we had better go and see Hugo and update him. If we were to proceed, it was going to mean laying out a reasonable chunk of the firm's cash in fees, rent etc etc, and that would need the unanimous approval of the directors.

However first, I had to phone Michael le Fevre in Jersey to make sure that I had got the thinking correct. There was no point going in with a half-baked plan with a big hole in it. Mazin would crucify us if I got it wrong.

I turned to Brian indicating his phone. "Can I use your phone to contact Michael le Fevre, that way you'll be au fait with what's going on?"

He nodded and pushed the instrument across his desk towards me.

I dialled le Fevre's private number direct; I didn't want the call going through either of our switchboards.

"Michael," I said after the usual greetings, "you recall our conversation a few weeks back about the CONDES Trust and the structure of our companies?" He said he did. "Well if we wished to restructure our group and, say, have 75% of Bridge Holdings Limited still owned by the CONDES Trust but replace the three existing trustees with one new trustee, can this be done easily?"

"Yes it can, but I would not advise it..."

I cut him off short. "Michael, just listen whilst I run through the whole thing and then tell me what you think.

"Can we also transfer all the shares in Consultant Design Group to a new company owned 75% by a new trust, both of which you would set up for us, with the same beneficiaries and the same three trustees we have at present? The other 25% to be owned by Hugo and me in the same ratio that we currently hold the BHL shares? Can you arrange that? Is it possible?"

There was a pause whilst he turned the proposal over in his mind. "Yes, we could do that. I don't see any problems there. I would have to have the agreement of all the beneficiaries, in writing to protect myself; but what is the purpose of all this? You don't save any tax, it's going to cost you money in fees and charges, and in effect everybody remains financially in exactly the same position as they are now."

Excellent!" I said. "That is just what I wanted to know."

He was silent for a moment. "Do you want me to draft out something now?"

I thought for a couple of seconds. "Yes please. If you could fax me the sort of agreement you need from the beneficiaries that would be a help. Don't do anything else yet, I'll give you all the details later if we decide to go ahead."

I put down the phone with a sigh of relief. Maybe, just maybe, the plan would come together.

Brian scribbled a few notes on his pad without commenting. I could see his mind ticking over, working out the implications. I reached for the phone again and punched out my friend Cliff Rozel's private number in Jersey. He knew all about our experiences with Mazin Al Jabril from our last meeting, so when I filled him in about the plan to stuff Mazin he couldn't wait to play a part.

"You really think he will pay over two million bucks for Bridge Holdings?"

"First of all, with any decent multiplier and, considering its profitability and growth, it's worth over twice that in pounds. The only bad year we've had was a couple of years ago and Mazin knows exactly why that happened so he will take that into consideration! Secondly, if he's going to make millions from Pantocrator, laying out funds now to secure his position is good tactics."

He turned that over in his mind for a few seconds. "Yeah, that makes sense to me. OK I've got the message, so what do you want from me?"

Cliff and I went way back to our college days and it was so refreshing when you told an old friend that you had a problem and their first reaction was 'How can I help'. Cliff was like that, no dithering about. I continued. "When we last had lunch together you recommended some local estate agents. From them I got the details of six vacant premises on short lets that would make small offices, and I found one that is ideal for our purpose. It's in Rue de Salines, St Helier, between the greengrocers and a firm of accountants. It's just what I want. A two storied single-fronted building, scruffy and dingy enough to indicate a degree of poverty but in a moderately respectable area. The outside can be left untouched, and, if the inside was given a lick of paint, it would be impeccably shabby without being over the top. One could move in virtually forthwith. What I am trying to achieve is a veneer of cheap respectability with a hint of desperation and a clear vulnerability to a good offer!"

It sounded like an advert for an aftershave lotion; I chuckled at the thought.

"What I would like from you, Cliff, if you can do it, is the loan of a girl and some furniture for a couple of months or so - if we decide to go ahead with the plan. She would continue to work for you; all I want is for her to be on the end of a phone in normal working hours and act as a receptionist occasionally. We will pay her salary, naturally, and something for the hire of the sticks. We will also subcontract a chunk of the Sharjah Steel project to your firm - say the design of the administration block, to compensate you for your trouble."

Day-to-day life in Jersey must be on the dull side at present, he could hardly contain his excitement. Did I want to pack the place with people; he could put his whole accounts section in there: did I want computers and faxes: he would put terminals here, there and everywhere? He personally would be prepared to show up if that was what I needed. I blinked a bit at all that. Jesus, I must have over-egged the pudding somewhat with the offer of the Sharjah Steel administration block, the truck drivers' latrine would have sufficed.

I calmed him down. "No! No! Slow down! I don't want to overdo it. Just a girl, perhaps with a computer and a filing cabinet, and a 'trustees' inner office. It would look a bit more professional without being ostentatious."

"Just let me know when, and it will be done," he said enthusiastically, and we signed off on that note.

I grinned at Brian. "I think he would have lined up the full marching band of the Grenadier Guards if I'd asked him to," I observed, sitting back as far as I could on the rock hard chair and folding my arms.

Hugo was equally enthusiastic when I outlined progress so far. He still bridled when he recalled Mazin comparing him to 'a stinking pile of dung from a rabid pig'. However being naturally cautious, or having experienced a few of my 'wizard wheezes' before, he made me go through the whole plan in detail before giving it the final nod.

After a lengthy analysis of our ideas we decided that it was prudent not to delay things. Setting up the trap would take some time and we didn't want to be caught short.

It was left to me to instruct Michael le Fevre to crack on with the change of ownership of Consultant Design Group and the reorganization of the trusts. Hugo would clear everything with the beneficiaries, and Brian, as company secretary, would liaise with le Fevre to prepare all the paperwork.

I would also contact the estate agents and arrange for a short-term lease on the office in Rue de Salines to be executed, and for Cliff to do his stuff. The lease would be in Cliff's name not ours, in case Mazin checked.

By then the clock on the office wall showed 5.05 so we decided that further action would have to wait until the next morning.

My first call in the morning was at the hospital outpatients department to have the boot removed from my foot. They seemed much more concerned that their crutches were undamaged rather than me. For one moment I thought they were going to X-ray them, or even give them a CAT scan, just to check that I hadn't abused the wretched things. I tested the ankle gingerly on the floor gradually loading it up with Moon. It was very stiff, but I found it would bear my weight without pain. I thanked the nurses for their attention but I don't think they heard me, they were gathered round the crutches still checking them out. Having forgotten to bring a shoe and sock for that foot, I limped and hopped out across the freezing car park to the car, and drove, cold foot, to the office.

Major Margaret tutted a bit at the sight of my bare foot, and after bringing in my coffee and today's 'treat', a Walnut Whirl, offered to nip out and buy me a pair of socks.

I phoned Michael le Fevre and instructed him to put the whole plan into operation.

"Do you want me to be the sole trustee of the CONDES trust then?" he ventured.

"No," I replied, "I think it better for all concerned if you are not involved with the CONDES trust." I explained that it would be safer if his firm was not connected in any way with the possible involvement of Mazin Al Jabril. I told him who the new trustee should be and he was quite happy about that.

I then phoned the estate agents and said we wanted to take a six-month let on the Rue de Salines offices. We haggled about the rent for a few minutes as a matter of form, but for the short let I conceded their asking figure. It wasn't much in the scheme of things. We exchanged addresses and details of solicitors, and I told them the lease would be in the name of Cliff Rozel but we would guarantee it, and they were quite happy with that. We wanted to occupy the premises from the first of January and they said they would instruct their client's lawyers to draw up the lease forthwith.

Ten days later I received the document in the post. We checked it ourselves, signed it, and returned it the same day with a cheque for six months' rent in advance. If Parker, Parker, Son and Parker had got their ancient hands on it we would still be arguing.

Hugo arranged for Michael le Fevre's 'Beneficiaries Indemnity' forms to be signed by ourselves and the other two beneficiaries; and Brian and Michael ensured that the shareholdings of the companies were duly restructured.

All would be ready on the first of January.

A Happy New Year, Mazin!

CHAPTER THIRTEEN

Jon Grey's remission had continued, the creeping insidious tentacles had been stayed in their tracks. 'Temporarily' was the unspoken word in everyone's mind, but 'permanently' was the hope - mine included. Driving back from the Marsden after his treatment he was quite perky.

"You seem to be improving, Jon," I ventured, wondering what he thought of the situation. He gave me a grin.

"Every day is another day lived, that's the way I look at it." He paused reflectively. "By the way Marcus, if you can spare a few minutes when we get back I'd be grateful for your opinion on something."

"Sure thing, what's the problem?"

"I'll tell you when we get home."

I slid the car to a standstill in a vacant resident's parking slot virtually outside his front door. He was able to get out of the low-slung car without assistance. He opened the door with his key and ushered me into the sitting room.

"Would you like some coffee?"

"I said I would make it, but he insisted so I didn't press the issue. I could hear him pottering about in the small kitchen whilst I looked through the latest videos he had. He came in bearing two mugs of black instant.

"Help yourself to milk and sugar."

"Just sugar for me."

I spooned in a couple from the bowl and then waited.

He held his mug in both hands watching the steam rising. Without looking up he said quietly, "I want to make a will."

I didn't know what to say, so said nothing hoping he would continue. He looked up then and stared me straight in the eye.

"I know I'm going to die soon and whilst it saddens me it doesn't frighten me. It's just that there is so much to do in this life, so many wonderful things, and I have done so little, that is the sad thing. Oh I hope for a cure, I hope the treatment works, that this remission continues. The people at the Marsden are brilliant but I can see the sorrow deep in their eyes when they encourage me, it is something nobody can hide when they know the truth."

I returned his gaze, there was absolutely no point in giving him any bullshit, he would have despised me for it.

"How can I help?" I said. He smiled gently and nodded.

"No flannel eh, Marcus, 'Que sera sera'!" He drew a deep breath.

"Right, to business then. I want to make a very simple will and a legal one, but I don't want to involve lawyers." He gave a rueful grin. "My last contact with lawyers was a tactful letter from some outfit in the City representing my esteemed brother. They said that they believed I was going to die soon and that if I bequeathed certain items outside the family - meaning my brother, there's nobody else - they would make trouble for me."

His grin broadened. "And we wouldn't want that, would we?" He shook his head.

"No, I want to keep lawyers out of it, produce a 'fait accompli'."

He paused reflectively. "There is a pamphlet I believe, and a standard form which can be used, could you obtain them for me from the Citizens Advice Bureau or wherever?"

"No problem," I told him, "but you will need two witnesses to your signature, neither of whom must be beneficiaries. If you like, Peter Davy, whom you know from my office, and I, will come over when you are ready and do the witnessing."

He smiled his thanks and then said, "I don't know whether this is going to help you or not, maybe not, but I've no alternative. Apart from my elder brother in Australia, who I have not seen or heard from directly for years, although clearly he knows I am ill hence his lawyer's letter, I have no close relatives - nobody that I am beholden to, and so I intended to bequeath all my worldly goods to Kate. She doesn't know this nor must she know, but I felt it only fair to tell you. It will mount to 30 or 40 grand plus some pieces of antiques and pictures."

I digested this slowly, I wasn't sure of the significance either but I was glad he'd told me. The elder brother was patently either a first-class arsehole or a nut, there could be no other explanation for instructing lawyers to send such a cold letter, and that had finally put paid to any chance he had of benefiting from Jon's will. As for the rest of it, so what, it just showed he was a nice guy.

I told him that I was going home to York for Christmas but that Dan Herlihan had fixed with one of his engineers to take him to the Marsden on Christmas Day and the next Wednesday. I gave him my present, a video history of the British Open Golf Championship, and he in turn gave me a small neatly wrapped package with a label which read, 'To Marcus, from Jon and Kate'. We wished each other a happy Christmas, and I drove back to the office feeling a bit of a shit because Kate's present I had had sent round to King-Knight's and Jon Grey must have wondered about that. Not that there was anything sinister in it but I had been in a rush and had dashed into a jewellers in Beauchamp Place and quickly picked out an item from their display trays. It was a small abstract gold pin brooch of no significant implications.

I didn't see either Jon or Kate again before Christmas although Kate telephoned me to thank me for cheering up Jon, and also for her present. At least I suppose it was a thank you.

"I don't know what you and Jonnie talk about," she said, "but he's always much brighter after your visits. And thank you for your present. It's a somewhat unusual present for someone to give to a friend wouldn't you say? It's not the sort of thing I expected."

"Oh well, yes but if you like it it was worth it," I mumbled, thinking, it wasn't all that unusual was it? An abstract brooch?

"I'd better not let my parents see it though, mother's very straight-laced."

Well that was up to her, I couldn't see my mother casting anyone out into the blizzard because of a gold pin but there you are. I just hoped she took after her father - and he was on the liberated side - otherwise my hopefully prospective future romance was not going to get off to an easy start.

"I haven't opened your present yet," I told her, "I'm saving it for Christmas Day."

"Well, it's quite decent I assure you," she added.

After we had wished each other a happy Christmas and arranged to meet at her flat with Jon for a drink when I got back from York, we signed off. The conversation left me slightly mystified but no doubt all would be revealed in due course.

Christmas at home went well, but four days of my sisters and their offspring racketing round my parents house wanting Uncle Marcus to play with their piles of presents was enough, particularly as they always beat me on the Scalectrix even though I stayed up half of Boxing Day night, when they were tucked up peacefully in bed, trying to suss out which was the fastest of the four cars. The head wound had healed quickly and, apart from a slightly piebald look where my head had been shaved preparatory to stitching, no outward sign of my brief encounter with shy Sam remained. I had had the rest of my hair cut short to match the newly-seeded areas to assist the restoration. The foot still ached at night if I had been standing or walking a lot during the day and squash was out of the question for another two to three weeks. At home they had questioned me about my injuries, so I had gradually let it be known that I had fallen down the stairs whilst pissed, and people thought that funny enough not to enquire too closely. Of Sam there had fortunately been no sight or sound.

The Major, however, had tutted vigorously when I crutched in on the Monday morning and had behaved like a mother hen ever since. Not only did I find it embarrassing, but other people in the firm were beginning to notice. The design office, never backward in sensing weaknesses and opportunities were, I learned to my chagrin, beginning to refer to us as 'the happy couple'. Immediate action was called for if this sort of thing was to be laid to rest once and for all.

As soon as I arrived at Palmerston Mansions on the Thursday evening I dug out the notes I had made on the flight down to Sao Paulo and began to redraft suitable advertisements for the Major's charms.

'Exceptionally attractive lady,' - I left out the 'fortyish' because anybody in their right mind would work out that that meant pushing 50, the use of the word 'lady' would cover the age problem - 'well organised, humorous, sensuous, interesting, seeks caring, intelligent, tall professional man for continuing relationship. Please send photo.' That covered the specification for the bids, now to reply to the offers. I thumbed through the few magazines I had collected, but the 'straight sex' solicitations were almost all from randy old buggers looking for not very particular, nubile, young, nymphomaniacs.

There was one possible amongst the dross. 'Professional man, mid-40s wishes to meet lady of similar status to explore ongoing relationship. Please send details.' There was a PO box number for replies. It didn't say much; I suppose that was what attracted my interest, no exaggerated claims about the size of his wedding tackle or fanciful descriptions of his appearance. I drafted a reply almost equally as vague but threw in 'wide ranging interests with sense of humour'. I thought that would cover everything from lepidopterology to bonking. Then I realized that with Christmas approaching it was not going to be a good time for advertising for a mate. Nobody was likely to buy you one for Christmas. I chewed the end of my pen for a moment. It would be better to wait until the New Year was over and the festivities forgotten. I re-read my draft, it wasn't quite right. A more sensible approach was necessary if I was serious about this. I threw the pen down and decided to leave it till January.

Mazin Al Jabril requests the pleasure
of the company of Mr Marcus Moon and guest
for cocktails at The Penthouse, Edgware Mansions
on Friday 14th January
6.30pm - 8.30pm
RSVP

"I've got one as well," I heard Hugo say as I turned the gold, embossed, stiff pasteboard round in my fingers.

I looked up; he was standing in the doorway of my office with a quizzical smile on his face.

"Are you going to go?" he continued.

"Sure, why not?" I replied. "I didn't realise my company sent him into ecstasy before, so why should I deprive him of one of the few pleasures he is able to get in his sheltered, poverty-stricken, miserable life?"

Hugo gave me a sharp look. "If you're going to go with that attitude I somehow don't think you'll fit in." He paused thoughtfully. "Mazin telephoned a few minutes ago just to make sure we would be coming. He wants to introduce us to some mid-European dowager princess - 'a close personal friend of mine whom you must meet', is how he put it."

I chuckled. "Really. I can hardly wait!"

Hugo shook his head. "Marcus don't be so cynical, maybe he just wants to be friendly. Anyway I'll telephone him to say we will be sending formal acceptances but that we both will be there. Emily will be coming with me, will you take anybody?"

I hadn't thought of that. I wondered if Kate would like to go. 6.30 to 8.30, it would give her a break and maybe, if Jon was still OK, she would go out for dinner afterwards.

I would ask her.

The telephonist at King-Knight's put me straight through to Kate so my stock must have risen at that company. Not much as it turned out.

"Oh Marcus, I would've loved to come but I can't." I didn't want to become the interrogator again so I waited and this time the explanation duly followed. "Andy is having a cocktail party here that evening for clients and friends of King-Knight's and I have to be in attendance all evening." That situation I could appreciate, but the miserable sod hadn't invited me as I observed forcefully to her.

She chuckled and pointed out that I wasn't a client, and Andy was still sore about me blocking his car in when he had an urgent appointment with his business psychologist. I pricked up my ears at that. Andy going to a funny farmer, there could be some mileage in this conversation yet.

"What does he go to a business psychologist for?"

"Perhaps I shouldn't have mentioned it," she mused thoughtfully, "but he feels that his lack of inches may be detrimental to his getting business. He thinks that he is at a disadvantage to the competition in dealing with prospective clients and goes for advice on providing a good service..."

"...from below the net," I added trying not to laugh.

She chuckled again. "Well I suppose so if you put it like that."

"Hmm," I responded, thinking that that was not exactly how I was going to put it the next time I met Andy King-Knight in the Frog. Not inviting me to his drinks party was one thing but he had been the one to really make hay about my cut head and fractured foot. 'Hop-along Moon the paralytic piss-artist'. God knows what he would have said if he'd known the truth! That, however, was not going to reprieve him, I had seen the very thing to settle his hash advertised in one of the seedier contact mags bought to assist the Major in finding eternal bliss, and I made a note on my pad to follow it up.

We exchanged a few more pleasantries and arranged to meet on the Friday morning when I turned up for the routine run taking Jon to The Marsden. When I put the phone down I felt comfortably cheerful, maybe a dinner or so was not too far fetched after all.

Although I was 20 minutes later than the advertised time the reception line for Mazin's party still straggled halfway down the hall of his apartment. I had had to show my invitation twice to security men to get even as far as the door. My coat was removed by the smooth-faced young Arab whom I recognised as the servant - or one of them - from my last visit, and I was ushered to the end of a line of sharp-suited Lebanese to await introduction to the 'presence'.

There turned out to be two 'presences' when I eventually reached the door: Mazin, turned out like a Savile Row dummy, and a very sun-tanned, wrinkled, old prune dripping with gold and jewels to whom, when it was my turn, Mazin said, "Princess, may I have the pleasure to present one of my oldest friends and business colleagues, Mr Marcus Moon."

I blinked at so fulsome an introduction, Christ if I was one of his oldest friends and business colleagues it didn't say much for the rest. Ninety-nine per cent of those present must hate him even more than I did. I sparkled up, it could be an interesting evening. I was so occupied with these thoughts that I missed the rest of his spiel but I did catch a 'Princess Sophie' and a 'von something-or-other Zollernhoe'. Not being too sure quite how to respond I shook the old bat's wrinkled bony claw, bowed a few inches stiffly from the waist, nodded to Mazin and headed for the nearest tray of pink champagne.

The guests were 80% men, mainly westernised Arab. I saw Hugo and Emily tucked into an animated group over by the window, lots of flashing gold fillings and nicely tanned skin. I wondered where Mazin had dug his princess up from, she didn't look like a skier or a bonker but you never can tell these days. The champagne was delicious, so I sank it all at one go and removed another glassful from the tray of a passing waiter. The next step in the Moon Party Procedure was to find someone interesting to talk to. At Mazin's party this could be difficult, we couldn't afford to make the acquaintance of another Mazin Al Jabril - the cash flow would never stand it. However I reckoned that con men didn't hunt in packs, they were solitary predators, and therefore most of the people there would be either potential 'marks' or current 'marks' in one way or another. That could also present a problem, it was only past 'marks' with whom I felt that I would have something in common, and I doubted if many of those would have been invited. Apart from Mazin, and Hugo and Em, there wasn't a soul I recognized, however, it was a progression of the Moon Party Procedure that, in that event, the thing to do was to pick out the girl with the biggest tits, on the basis that, even if she was boring to talk with, at least there was something around of interest.

I cast around carefully and homed in on a tubby blonde girl talking rather diffidently to a short fat guy standing behind a large flowered bow tie. I eased up alongside her and hovered. She became conscious of two eyeballs down the front of her dress and turned to follow the stalks back to their sockets. There she beheld me.

"Hello," I said cheerfully. "My name is Marcus Moon."

Her cold blue eyes scanned me slowly like a supermarket video camera surveying the frozen vegetable cabinet - and evincing as much interest.

"Really," she murmured, and turning back to the floral neckwear exchanged some remarks that I didn't catch that made them both laugh.

Hmm, I thought, so much for that Moon plan as it went down like a lead balloon, what next? I propped myself in a corner to survey the scene at leisure and contemplate. Something should happen sometime, Mazin had been ominously quiescent for too long and I was beginning to believe that my imagination had got the better of my judgement. So far Mazin had done nothing untoward, seeming perfectly content just to promote his corner with Pantocrator, and that was out of character.

I drank some more champagne, and was just wondering whether to make one last try at chatting up some of the unlikely looking women there, or to write the evening off as a dead loss and push off home, when I heard a nervous cough, like a new recruit for the army with the medical officer's hand under his balls. A soft voice said, "Mr Moon isn't it?"

Looking round I beheld a sharp-faced, dark-skinned man wearing a black suit like a professional coffin carrier. His face was vaguely familiar and wore a beseeching look.

"Yes, that's right, I know who I am but who are you?"

He didn't smile. "A thousand pardons, Mr Moon, I am Ahmed Marzouk - we met at your offices with Mr Al Jabril a few weeks ago."

The penny dropped, I glanced at his hands - black fingernails, he was Mazin's lawyer; I recalled him now.

"Ah yes, I remember. Are you enjoying the party?"

We exchanged small talk for a while about how wonderful Mazin was, and what a kind and generous host, and then he said offhandedly, "I wonder if you can give me some advice, Mr Moon. I have a client, a middle-eastern man of some wealth, who wishes to invest in this country..."

"Oh yes," I observed disinterestedly, "and how can I be of assistance?"

He grew even more earnest, "Mr Al Jabril mentioned that you have a connection in Jersey and my client would like to operate through Jersey. It pays him to deposit his funds there and borrow against them here. He avoids tax on his interest that way." He paused, presumably to allow me to absorb this wisdom. I nodded encouragingly.

"So I believe, I have heard from our trustee over there that overseas investors can do that."

Well, there was no point making it difficult for him was there, we might get interrupted before he could worm out of me the information he wanted. Relief flashed across his face as he seized the opening.

"Perhaps I could talk to this man then, he might be able to assist us also."

"By all means," I replied, "feel quite free to do so," and I made as if to walk away.

Well not too easy either, he had to do a little work for his master.

He clutched my arm hastily. "Excuse me, Mr Moon, but you haven't told me where I might get in touch with him?"

I gave a short laugh. "I'm sorry, forgetful of me. The firm is called Trustee Services Limited, they're in Rue de Salines in St Helier. I'm not sure of their exact address but I have the telephone number somewhere." I pulled out my diary, and he noted the name and number I gave him on a small note pad he produced from his breast pocket, thanked me and made his excuses.

I watched out of the corner of my eye as he pushed his way across the room to where Mazin held court but he didn't stop, he just passed by. However Mazin looked up at precisely the same moment, and glanced sharply in my direction. A prickle of apprehension ran up my spine; although his face was expressionless, there had been something in his eyes with that look, a gleam of triumph perhaps? Perhaps not, maybe I was getting neurotic about him.

I contented myself with the knowledge that Costa da Silva was coming to London at the beginning of next month and their latest progress reports had been encouraging.

Apart from head, hands and feet, I did not appear to have much in common with the rest of the gathering. For a start I was not a member of a dethroned east European minor royal family, a Lebanese building contractor, a British sleazy nightclub owner, a drug smuggler, arms dealer, white slaver or any other group of malefactors with whom Mazin Al Jabril was likely to be associated. I drifted across to say a quick hello to Hugo and

Emily, who clearly felt equally out of place as they were talking to each other, and then slid quietly towards the exit. I didn't think my departure would be mourned or even noticed.

I was just about to reach safety when I caught sight of long shiny chestnut hair moving backwards towards the same exit, obviously trying to extract its grower from the clutches of a large, fat greasy-looking City type who was grasping one hand. The hair managed the extraction, turned and headed in my direction. She caught my eye.

I froze. You know when you have one of those rare moments when the world seems to stop and everything around you pales into insignificance? Well I had one there and then. It was not that she was beautiful but she radiated an aura. Her mouth was too big, her blue-grey eyes too far apart, her chin too determined and her teeth very white but slightly uneven. Put together however, for me the whole effect was stunning. And she had a figure to go with it.

As she advanced I pointed with my thumb towards the door, she raised an eyebrow and then nodded. We arrived simultaneously at the portal, which left me with the opening gambit.

I threw out my carefully cultivated chat line, honed to a fine edge over many years and tried and tested in the Snug bar of the Frog and Nightgown.

"Hello!" I said.

For a moment I thought it was going to have the success it normally enjoyed - bugger all, but then she smiled and her face lit up.

There was something vaguely familiar about that smile but I couldn't place it. I was certain that we had never met before, she wasn't somebody you would forget in a hurry, she confounded me even more with her opening remark.

"You're Marcus Moon," she said, still smiling.

I was stunned. "How do you know that?" I gasped in surprise.

The smile grew even broader, the way her blue-grey eyes crinkled made my toes curl, so I was even more surprised when she said, "My cousin has talked about you, and I overheard Mr Al Jabril mention your name when he was pointing you out to some guy earlier this evening."

Now here was a conundrum, or two conundrums or was it conundra? Never mind it wasn't important, what was important was why would an unknown cousin talk about me, and who was Mazin pointing me out to, and, more important, why? A Palestinian hit man? No it couldn't be, this place was making me paranoid. Anyhow, first things first!

"So what did Mazin say?" I asked casually.

The grin grew wider. "If I remember correctly he said, 'You see that lanky son of a castrated camel over there, that is Moon so get on with it!'" She added, "He was talking to that shifty little man lurking behind those flowers."

She pointed out a bunch of gladioli across the room, behind which could be seen the unappetizing features of Ahmed Marzouk, Mazin's lawyer, and, I trusted, the bearer of glad tidings for him.

"Ah, I see," I responded, but slightly puzzled because Marzouk had met me before. I ignored that and continued, "And now how about the Marcus bit?"

She acknowledged the point with an inclination of her head. "My cousin is Kate Tennant," and she added, looking me in the eye, "and she told us how she had talked you into driving Jonathan for his treatment."

She cocked a quizzical eyebrow. "Are you keen on her then?"

She didn't beat about the bush with her questions, did she? And there were two blockbusters in what she had just said.

I was under the impression that it was me who had offered to help Kate with Jonathan, and before I bared my soul about my lusts and desires to anyone, particularly one as attractive as her - and single too - no ring of any kind on the left hand, I needed to know much more. I fended off the question by observing that I was only too pleased to help her with Jon in such a tragic situation, especially as Kate couldn't drive. A flicker of surprise crossed her face and she seemed about to say something and then checked herself.

I found myself anxious to get off the subject of Kate, and so I asked her what her connection was with Mazin in order to be invited to this shindig.

"I sold him the apartment," she said, adding "so I think he invited me along as 'eye candy' to boost his standing amongst this collection of poseurs and sycophants." This was said matter-of-factly, without any hint of conceit.

I warmed to her even more with this assessment of Mazin's guests. Then a thought occurred to me. "You don't work for King-Knight's like Kate do you?"

"Good Lord no! I work for Johnson Jacques, one of the big West End firms."

"So why are you sliding out early instead of networking? I would have thought that this was very fertile ground for buying and selling expensive property."

"Because I'm bored stiff with being pawed and patronised! And if it comes to that, why are you sliding off as well?"

"How do you know I am?"

"Because I've been watching you ever since I overheard Mazin pointing you out, and you clearly don't fit in."

I grinned. "I'll take that as a compliment," I said, then an idea sprang into my mind, well a lot of ideas did but this was a decent one! "Look, are you doing anything after this? If not why don't we have dinner somewhere? Do you like Italian? I know a super restaurant not too far from here. We can get a cab."

It all came out in a rush, not the smooth sophisticated invitation I had hoped to lay at her feet.

The blue-grey eyes gazed at me steadily for a moment. She appeared to reach a decision. "The answers to your questions in order are: nothing, OK and it's my favourite food! I'm Zoe Garrard by the way, my mother is Kate Tennant's aunt."

"I'm Marcus Moon and, if Mazin is to be believed, my father is a castrated camel."

"He's obviously not well up on reproduction," she observed with a chuckle.

"For which the world had to be forever grateful," I added feelingly.

We took a taxi to Como Lario, the smart Italian in Holbein Place. There we were ushered smoothly to a table in the window. I had never had one of those before but the proprietor was on top of his business, and knew a pretty girl in the window could pull in some passing trade - and if he wanted to put Zoe there then he had to put me there as well. He solved that problem by bringing a vase of flowers and putting it between me and the glass!

Whilst chewing bread sticks and sipping a cool Gavi di Gavi we chose from the menu. She ordered a salad followed by sardines, I lasagne and calve's liver in butter and sage.

"We're obviously compatible," she murmured ironically, munching a lettuce leaf as she gazed at my pile of steaming pasta. "Let's see what else we have in common!"

It turned out not much more, which made life interesting. With a mischievous smile she told me her father was an accountant and she was brought up in Newmarket. It turned out he was a successful turf accountant who measured life in odds of five to four against, whereas my father was the manager of a small branch bank in York, who measured life in eighths of a per cent. She liked ballet and tennis; I didn't! I told her the last time I had touched a tennis racquet I had won my match against this woman. I was one set down and four love down in the second set when her waters broke and she was carted off to hospital. Zoe laughed and said she didn't believe me.

The whole meal seemed to be spent talking and laughing, but about what I cannot recall. Two hours just slid by imperceptibly. Over coffee she asked me what my interest in Mazin was, or vice versa, that had secured my invitation to that 'exclusive' party, but I ducked the question merely telling her that we were jointly involved in a Middle Eastern design project.

"So why was he pointing you out to the slimy little toad?"

"He is Mazin's lawyer. He wants some information for a client of his about setting up a trust in Jersey."

"And did he get it?"

"Sure, why not. It was no skin off my nose. He may be able to do me a good turn one day." He may very well, I thought grimly, but not with any intention of doing so.

"So you sold Mazin the apartment, I bet he was not an easy man to do business with?"

"Funnily enough, from my point of view he wasn't too bad. I put him in touch with the owner. Another Middle Eastern gentleman, and they haggled the price out between them. The owner paid our fees, not Mazin. And by the way, he didn't buy the apartment; it was some Swiss holding company that is the new owner. I can't remember its name, Investment something or other, they own it although Mr Al Jabril signed the cheque."

She was quick to notice my increased interest. "Why, have I said something I shouldn't?"

"No, no, not at all." I passed it off with some comment about avoiding Capital Gains Tax when it came to be sold, but that was another interesting fact to confirm the way Mazin structured his affairs.

I found myself very drawn to this woman, she was warm, she was smart, she was fun and she was very attractive. I paid the bill although she offered to go halves.

"OK," she said, "then it's my turn next time."

We both burst out laughing again and I said, "We'd better exchange phone numbers and e-mail addresses in that case, to make sure there is a 'next time'."

It was all so natural, no embarrassment or awkwardness. It was as though we had known each other for years instead of only having met earlier that evening.

"I'll phone you next week - and thanks. Thanks for saving me from that awful party and even more thanks for a wonderful evening."

She gave me a quick kiss on the cheek and climbed into her taxi. It was such a heartfelt 'thanks' that I wondered about it.

I stood outside the restaurant for a full five minutes trying to believe my luck. Eventually, convinced it had not been a dream, I drifted off to find another cab along Pimlico Road.

Tuesday was a bad day. There was a fax from Costa da Silva awaiting my arrival at the office saying that they had encountered unforeseen problems in scaling up from their prototype to a full-sized furnace and could we delay the London meeting by one week, and also an urgent message saying would I telephone Miss Tennant at home. I rang the number of the flat in Redcliff Square immediately, and she answered the phone on the first ring. Her voice was full of anguish and despair. "Oh Marcus thank God you rang, it's Jonnie. He's desperately ill and there's blood all over the place. I've rung for an ambulance but I don't know what else to do." She was holding back the tears but the desperation was plain in her voice.

"I'll be right round," I said. "Has he cut himself?" I wasn't sure what the blood all over the place signified; he didn't seem the type of person to concede life by giving in to suicide.

"No, I think it's internal haemorrhaging, he is coughing up blood continuously. I've propped him up in bed but it won't stop."

"Hang in there, Katie, I'll be with you in five minutes!" I slammed down the phone and raced past the startled Major for my car. I arrived just at the same time as the ambulance.

"Cancer patient - internal haemorrhaging - to the Royal Marsden," I told them, as the two ambulancemen hauled out a stretcher and blankets and raced for the door. Kate, alerted by the siren, showed them through into the bedroom containing the big double bed, her face pale with shock.

"He was just fine until 20 minutes ago and then he just threw up great gouts of fresh blood. I got him back into bed but it won't stop." The paramedics were fast, they had Jonnie connected up to a drip and strapped onto the stretcher in two minutes. As they carried him past, his face deathly pale, his eyes opened briefly and he gave me a flicker of a smile and a nod.

"You go with him, Kate, and I'll do the necessary here," I told her. "I'll see you at the Marsden as soon as possible."

It was a cold raw day outside so I grabbed one of her coats from behind the door, pushed it into her hand and ushered her down the steps. One of the paramedics was radioing through the details to his base whilst the other held open the door waiting for Kate to climb in the back before following her in and closing the door. The ambulance took off like a rocket, siren howling, as it ripped out of the square towards the Fulham Road.

Jon Grey fought like hell for five days, but, in the end, his strength of will had no more reserves left to call upon and he died quietly, just slipping away unnoticed in the middle of the afternoon. Kate was with him reading a book and when she glanced up one minute he was breathing shallowly, the next minute he had stopped.

There were over 60 people at his funeral. Apart from Kate and I, Andy King-Knight and people from his office, Dan Herlihan and 15 guys from his team and all my guys who had helped with lifts at one time or another, friends of Jonnie's turned up from all over the place. He was cremated at Brompton cemetery, number four in the sad queue of hearses and mourners that awaited their turn in the cold sunlight of that January morning.

As he gabbled through the formalities with practiced impersonality, the resident vicar smoothly inserted Jonnie Grey's name and brief details of his short life into the service. Kate had jotted these down for him in the three lines available on the standard form, and within ten minutes it was all over, we were out the back door and the next coffin on its way in at the front.

As the final event in the closing of a young life it was a poor thing, an empty and barren final curtain. Affection, humanity, admiration and love were not reflected in the official ceremony, they existed only in the hearts and minds of the mourners. As we trooped out into the cold, bright sun it was clear that others felt as I, there was a vacuum, a feeling that the church, which held itself out as the official organ of love and charity, had failed to provide any measure of either for Jonnie when the chips were down.

Following Jon's death I had not been in touch with Zoe, but I expected to see her at the funeral. I was hoping to fix our next date with her when I saw her. However, to my disappointment, she wasn't there. In fact nearly all the people there were either friends of Jon or past workmates or both. He did not have any other close relatives other than his brother in Australia, or if he did nobody had told them. Puzzlingly there were no friends or relations of Kate either, apart from the people from King-Knight's.

I offered to drive her back to her flat but she said she already had transport but asked if I would take her to and from the crematorium the next day to collect Jon's ashes.

"So what now?" I asked as I carefully eased the MG into a parking slot in Redcliffe Square so as not to unbalance the urn on Kate's knee.

"I don't know," she sighed, "I can't think straight yet, I need time. There are lots of things to be done and I suppose Jonnie's affairs have to be sorted out somehow and somebody will have to do that." She sounded vague about the whole thing. I glanced across at her but her face was guileless. I wondered whether she knew that Jon had left her everything in his will, I debated mentally whether or not to bring up the subject and decided that I should.

"Jon left a will," I said carefully. "I know because he asked me about it and I was one of the witnesses to his signature. He left everything to you and you are the sole executor. That should make things easier for you."

She looked away so I couldn't see her face and was silent for a couple of seconds. "But what about his brother?" she enquired, turning towards me with a puzzled frown. "Surely he must have some say in the matter."

I shook my head slowly. "Not so," I said emphatically. "From what he told me his brother sounds like a first-class shit and Jon wanted nothing to do with him - as indeed he had nothing to do with Jon - particularly when he was ill."

She lapsed into silence obviously thinking all this over. "It doesn't seem right for me to get it all."

"Well that is what Jon wanted, and consequently you've got it. I think the best thing would be to find a friendly, not too lascivious, lawyer to help with the probate. Andy King-Knight should know plenty and they'll be less inclined to rip you off, and more inclined to be efficient if some of King-Knight's business is on one side of the scales."

She nodded pensively. I asked her if there was anything else I could do.

"It's all come as a shock to me, I still haven't come to terms with Jonnie's death. It happened so fast. I just need time, time to gather my thoughts..." Her voice trailed off. She put her hand on my arm, "I hope you understand Marcus, please don't think I'm being difficult but I just need to get away and think things over."

I left her to go into her flat whilst I climbed back into the MG, but she turned and came back. "There is just one other thing Marcus, and you did offer to help. Jonnie stated that he wanted his ashes to be scattered over the sea from the cliffs of his home town, Swanage, in Dorset, so could you take me there on Saturday to do this please?"

As I drove back to the office I had three things to occupy my thoughts. The first was if Kate knew nothing of Jon's will, how did she know that he had requested his ashes be scattered into the sea at Swanage? She hadn't said 'asked' as if he had asked her in conversation, she had said 'stated' as if written.

The second was to wonder how it was I had become a glorified chauffeur for her with no hint of any 'reward'.

And thirdly, why didn't I care?

It was a bright and breezy morning when we drove down to the Isle of Purbeck in the MG, with the bronze urn containing Jon's ashes tucked behind her seat. She told me Andy King-Knight had been very helpful and put her in touch with a bright solicitor who handled his own family's affairs. She had arranged to see this guy early the following week.

"Andy's been brilliant, letting me have time off to sort things out. He's even agreed to let me have unpaid leave to go and stay with friends in America. He thinks it will do me good to get away for a couple of weeks."

Oh does he, I thought, well maybe so. Perhaps it had not been such a bright move to suggest that she ask Andy King-Knight for help in finding a solicitor.

"Are you definitely going to the States then?" I asked.

She pursed her lips. "Yes, I think so. There are a few things to sort out first but they will only take a few days, and my friends can put me up anytime. Andy has booked me on the Wednesday's BA flight to Boston."

I was just waiting for the suggestion that I might give her a lift to the airport, then I remembered the Brazilians were coming over and would be in London at that time so I would have to excuse myself, but she forestalled me.

"It's OK Marcus, I've got transport all ready, Andy is going to take me."

Well that was a relief, I didn't have to feel guilty about it. The funny thing was I did have a feeling of guilt. Thinking about it, I realised it was because I'd felt relief that Andy was going to take her to the airport, not me.

Andy King-Knight had attended Jon's funeral but all through the service he had been twitchy, nervously glancing at his watch, shooting it out of his sleeve so those around could see the heavy gold bracelet. Being charitable, I assumed it was the only thing he could see without standing on tip-toe. He and I had exchanged frosty nods - or rather he gave me one in return for my warmer acknowledgement. I wondered why he had pushed off early, so I asked Kate.

"Andy doesn't like funerals," she replied. "He thinks they're morbid."

He doesn't like me either, I thought, following a fairly recent incident in the Frog and Nightgown. I had told the 'boys' about Andy's visits to a business psychologist because he felt his lack of inches was affecting his performance. This produced spluttered indignation from him. But not as much as he spluttered and indignated the following week when Pete Smallwood presented him with a pump-operated penis enlarger, and suggested that, if it didn't solve his immediate problem, he could climb into it and turn himself into a bigger prick than he was already. He was obviously still sore about that.

I mused to myself that Andy's name seemed to be cropping up quite frequently these days in Kate's conversation, and somehow my feelings were more of relief than jealousy. Her trip to the airport was a case in point. I was relieved, not disappointed, and I think she sensed my mood.

I glanced across at her, she was fiddling nervously with her handbag on her lap, and so to change the subject I said with a smile, "I see you're not wearing my pin."

She blushed faintly. "Well I daren't wear it in the office - it's a bit rude isn't it?"

She turned to study my face intently with her green eyes. I suddenly had a feeling of dismay. I could foresee a nasty hole opening up under me on this one if I wasn't careful. "What do you mean rude? It's an abstract chunky gold pin, I just thought you might like it." I put it to her.

"No it's not, it's very suggestive and I thought we'd agreed just to be friends! This is not the sort of thing friends give to each other." She extracted it from her hanbag and turned it over.

She had lost me here. Driving the MG it was impossible to get an eye full of it and so I just shook my head.

"If you really don't know what I'm talking about you can't have spent much time choosing it then - either that or you're fibbing," she challenged. "Which is it?"

There was not a lot to be said to that double-edged question and I was beginning to get irritated about the whole thing. I reached over and plucked the offending pin from her hand and gave it a quick scan. It still looked like an abstract gold casting to me, although there were some humps and hollows that looked as if they might have been sculpted rather than formed at random.

With a quick flick of the steering wheel I avoided placing a country vicar and his wife nearer to his God than perhaps they wished to be at this time of life, and re-set the MG back on my side of the road to give me time for another viewing. This time I saw the pin in a different light. You know how it is with some optical illusions, they suddenly leap out at you; well it was like that. The shapes suddenly sprang out in clear relief. My abstract pin was a casting of an intertwined, stark-naked, well-endowed couple having it off in a position that seemed to be physically impossible. She obviously saw my fleeting look of astonishment before I could put on the inscrutable face.

"Ah!" she exclaimed triumphantly. "So you did choose it in a hurry. I knew that's what you did otherwise you'd have been breaking the rules."

Oh, would I, I thought. So what! So that was why I was being given so much earache over this bloody pin. It was time to try to regain the initiative.

"Have you ever done it like that then?" I asked her with a grin.

This was not the right thing to say apparently. She flared up and snatched the pin back. "You've got a very dirty mind Marcus Moon - and you're not catching me out with a leading question like that."

She thrust the pin back into the dark recesses of her bag and sat tight-lipped and silent for the next few miles.

What was all that about, I wondered. A lot of fuss over nothing. It didn't seem that important to lose one's rag over. But did I care? Strangely I didn't. Instead I found myself not thinking about Kate, but going back to the e-mail I had received from Zoe that morning saying she had two tickets to the big *Trapperjacks* concert in The Albert Hall next Friday and would I like to go with her. She'd do dinner afterwards. That was definitely something to look forward to. I had replied immediately and suggested that we meet for a pre-concert drink at a little bar I knew just off Exhibition Road.

By the time we passed through Corfe Castle Kate seemed to have recovered her spirits and decided to let sleeping dogs lie. The pin was not mentioned again.

At Swanage I parked the car in a public car park and made a huge contribution to the local economy by buying a one-hour parking ticket for 20 pence. There was only one other vehicle besides ours but the driver was not visible. Swanage appeared to be managing quite well on 40 pence a day.

It was a bright blustery day with a westerly blowing straight up the English Channel putting a chop on the water, ruffling our hair and making us clutch each other for support as we thrust our way through a couple of fields and along the steep cliff path to the edge.

I should have foreseen the problem but didn't until it was too late. With a sad little murmur, almost to herself, of "Goodbye Jonnie," she whipped the lid off the urn and cast his ashes into the wind.

We drove back to London somewhat dusty and gritty in a more sombre mood, feeling a little guilty that Jon's last wish had been modified by nature and part of him was returning to the 'big smoke' in our hair. Kate was subdued and said very little, just content to watch the scenery pass so I concentrated on driving and thinking about Friday. I decided that I wouldn't mention that

233

I had met Zoe to her, I don't know why, but it was just a feeling that I had that Zoe was a card I should keep close to my chest.

When we arrived in Chelsea I weighed up whether or not to ask her to the Frog for a drink but decided against it. I dropped her, and the empty urn, off at her flat, wished her well for her visit to the States, parked my car in the office car park and went into the pub on my own for a swift pint. I didn't even get a kiss for my pains.

There was a message from Costa da Silva on Monday morning saying that they would be delaying their trip to London by yet another week to enable them to collect some extra data that they thought might be of benefit. This suited me down to the ground, I had plenty to do with my other projects and I had to see if I could get Major Margaret's intentions focused away from what I feared was the current situation. I was becoming her hair, make-up and dress consultant. Each morning seemed to start off with a sashay down the catwalk from her office into mine with my coffee, and it was clear that I was expected to pass congratulatory comment.

The Major's Christmas present to me had been a very nice Mont Blanc pen. Mine to her had been a box of scented soap and talcum powder, not cheap mind you, it came from Crabtree and Evelyn no less. The thought of filmy black crotchless knickers and a peek-a-boo bra did cross my mind - just joking!

So it was with a slight feeling of guilt that I was using that selfsame pen to have another go at drafting out her advertisement for the contact magazines. I had thought it better to get Christmas and the New Year well out of the way until the cold miserable February nights - might stimulate much more interest for a lonely soul to find a convivial companion to share a bed or whatever.

I couldn't improve on the wording from my Sao Paulo trip. 'Exceptionally attractive lady, well organized, humorous, sensuous, interesting, seeks tall, caring, intelligent, professional man for continuing relationship. Please send photo. Please reply to...?' Where? Most people gave a Post Office box number, or a reference number provided by the magazine, so that replies could be screened. On reflection I thought that would be safer than giving out her address. The thought of excited crowds of cock-happy professionals besieging her door, and clamouring for a chance to display their prowess brought a smile to my lips, but I couldn't do that to her. I was trying to help after all. I settled for asking the magazine to receive all replies and to forward them on to her.

Now the question was, which magazines? I scratched all the more obviously pornographic ones and that left just three runners: *Speed*, *Jack of Hearts* and *Thrust*.

The singles club idea needed more research, besides I couldn't think of a way to get her to go to one. I suppose I could forge an invitation but what would it say? 'You are invited to come and meet like-minded people at wherever for exciting social intercourse that will positively astound you.' Yes, I could see that going down a treat. It would hit the wastepaper basket one second after she had read it.

No, it was the contact magazines first. I printed out the advertisement and its accompanying letter on Brian Mason's computer - well you can't be too careful - and sent it off to all three magazines, with accompanying postal orders for £50 for a one-week insertion - no pun intended.

I calculated it would take a fortnight at least to produce some result - if there was to be a result.

Friday night was freezing cold with a biting east wind and a hint of snow in the air. Nevertheless I had been looking forward to this evening for the whole week whatever the weather might be. The little bar was cosy and warm and Zoe had already found a table for two by the time I arrived. She must have come straight from work. She was wearing a smart dark blue jacket and skirt with a grey blouse that matched her eyes. The collar was worn outside the jacket. She showed no jewellery apart from a small gold watch on a thin fabric strap. Her lambswool coat and pashmina scarf were piled on the other chair to reserve it. She had her hair tied back in a ponytail and gave me a soft kiss on the mouth in greeting. It was electric!

I got us both gin and tonics and we sat, elbows on the table, grinning at each other like two Cheshire cats.

"I hope you like *Trapperjacks,*" she said. "They are supposed to be one of the top bands these days."

"Are they indeed," I replied. "As far as I am concerned if we were going to see *Doctor Doom and the Deadbeats* I couldn't care as long as it was with you."

"So you're not a music lover then? You're coming along just for the meal? Typical man! Do you realize that I could have flogged these tickets for a fortune, they're clamouring for them out there. I had to sell my soul to get these. Well almost!" She pulled a severe frown which wrinkled her nose delightfully.

"Not just for the meal," I said with a grin.

"Oh ho! So what else do you think might be on offer - mistakenly, I might add, Mr Moon?" The frown changed into a wide-eyed astonished look and she clasped her hands across her chest in a maidenly gesture, but she couldn't hide the faint twitch of her mouth as she tried to suppress a smile.

"Well I am a world famous art lover, and, having enlightened you about that, you may want to show me your etchings, as they say!"

She gave a snort of derision. "You should be so lucky, sunshine. You are going to the concert, and you are going to enjoy it, otherwise my 'etchings', as you so delicately put it, will remain forever out of view. Anyway we'd better go or we'll miss the start."

She finished her gin and tonic, slung her scarf round her neck, grabbed her coat and my hand in that order and we bustled out into the night to join the crowds heading for the Albert Hall.

The information I had been waiting for from Costa da Silva arrived two days ago. It arrived attached to the persons of three Brazilians, Dr Arnold Herrera their technical director, their head of research - a tall serious boffin, and their production director - a practical man.

Full of enthusiasm for Sharjah Steel they had really gone to town to set out their stall. From the vast amount of research reports, technical assessments, production forecasts and cost analyses it was clear that they were at least equal with Pantocrator in technical development and on the construction and installation costings. Where they were weak was in production capacity. A much smaller company than the vast Pantocrator Group, they did not have the huge production resources necessary to manufacture, supply and install the furnaces for an $80 million equipment contract within the programme parameters we were considering. However, we still had the option to change the programme, and set the furnace installation to commence at a later date, but this would have a knock on effect which would add significantly to the cost of the remainder of the construction works - which was the larger part of the overall contract. I think the Brazilians realised then, in their heart of hearts, that this sub-contract was probably beyond them, but we parted after our two days of heavy discussions, on a very amicable basis with both sides agreeing to re-examine their scheduling. Mazin, of course, knew nothing of this, he still was not aware of Costa da Silva as a potential competitor to Pantocrator. I had made sure that he was out of the country when we met the Brazilians, there was no way did we want him bursting into the office whilst they were there. He would find out about them in due course but that most definitely would be at our time of choosing.

After they had departed, I propped both feet on the desk and re-read the latest missives from Washington and Sharjah. The Ministry of Industry in Sharjah wanted a very fast construction schedule and had persuaded the World Bank to pressurise us to accelerate the programme. They now wanted the furnace installation to commence exactly 46 weeks after the civil engineering work for the foundations started on site - and that start date was now fixed in tablets of stone as the 1st August.

I suspected that somewhere behind this lurked the hand of Mazin Al Jabril: he probably talked his brother into pushing for the faster construction period in order to get his backhander from Pantocrator earlier. That would not surprise me in the least, and no doubt the Sharjahns were willing tools in this. Politically they would be happier to get their steel plant producing as soon as possible.

At first sight this looked to be a disadvantage for our plan to use Costa da Silva as some sort of lever over Mazin.

Notwithstanding that they were going to re-examine their schedule, I think we both knew that they could not realistically meet the new tight programme. But of course Mazin didn't. He didn't know anything about Costa's.

The more I thought about it, the more I realised that if Mazin was behind the accelerated programme just to get his hands on the loot earlier, then the massive irony was that he had shot himself cleanly through the foot. This must have been done without any reference to Pantocrator, so the question was, could they meet the new programme? From my discussions with Antoniades about his concerns over the previous programme it would be extremely tight indeed.

All our arrangements were now in place for Plan A. The small office of Trust Services was established in Rue de Salines, furnished and staffed by one of Cliff Rozel's efficient secretaries, but so far there had been no contact from Mazin. If anybody did telephone, the girl was to say that the trustee would ring back. Likewise if anybody called off the street, she would say that the trustee was at a meeting on the mainland, take the caller's details, and say the trustee would get back to them. In either case she was to phone the trustee, give him the details and he would take the necessary action.

I was still confident that he would take the bait, although exactly what he would do was not certain. I thought it most unlikely that he would want to hold the Bridge Holdings shares in his own name; that would make him personally vulnerable, he would hold them in a company. What was the name of his Swiss operation? I reached for the file on Mazin and looked up my notes. Ah, there it was. Jamie Swallow had given it to me: Investment and Resource Holdings SA, and Kate's friend, Otto Hafner, had told me it was registered in Geneva and controlled by bearer shares.

Great balls of fire, I had nearly missed it! It was staring me in the face and I had overlooked it!

I did a quick recapitulation. The object of Plan A was to get our stolen money back from Mazin Al Jabril, and very satisfying and beneficial that would be. But there was a serious flaw in it. The certain outcome would be the creation of a very highly pissed-off

239

Arab with an influential brother, with both of whom we would be in very close contact for the next three years. An uncomfortable, not to say dangerous, situation.

Playing off Pantocrator against Costa's would be useful to keep Mazin in line for a few months, but that was only short term. As soon as Pantocrator signed the sub-contract to provide the furnaces we would have no leverage and no control over him. He was ruthless enough to do anything, and in three years, with a project as complex as this one, his devious mind would find plenty of opportunity to make trouble for us.

It wasn't the fact that he would be pissed-off that concerned me. He could be full to the gunwales with buckets of the stuff as far as I was concerned as long as we had an iron grasp of his bollocks.

And, by pressurizing us to reduce the design and construction programme, he had provided a way to ensure that.

He hadn't seen the revised program so I was certain he didn't appreciate the knock-on effect it would have on him. Therefore it was time to gee Mazin up a little. Put him under some pressure. Give him a metaphorical boot up the backside as we were all ready. I would fax him a copy of the accelerated program. He was bright enough to work out its significance to him without me having to spell it out, and that must galvanize him into action if he intended to do anything. I asked the Major to send copies both to his London flat and to Sharjah.

To my astonishment and relief this had an immediate effect. There was a tug on the bait early on the Monday morning. Carol, the girl Cliff had put into Trust Services, phoned around 10.30, highly excited. A Mr Al Jabril had telephoned a few moments earlier and wished to make an urgent appointment to see the trustee the following day. He had stressed that it was vital that he speak to the trustee. He had left a contact number which could be patched through to wherever he might be, and whatever time suited the trustee would be fine with him.

So, Mazin had made his move at last. We had worked him out correctly. Obviously he had calculated that the revised program had left him dangerously short of time to perform his dirty deeds and was now starting to panic. The anxious period of waiting was over and the prognosis looked promising.

Hugo was away for the day so I contacted the trustee and briefed him. He duly got the girl to phone Mazin and confirm an appointment for 11 o'clock on Tuesday 15th February at Trust Services' office in Jersey.

CHAPTER FOURTEEN

"So how do you see this working out, Marcus?"

Hugo set his long-stemmed wine glass down carefully on the polished mahogany surface of his dining table and looked across at me with one eyebrow cocked quizzically.

Emily Elmes, taking the hint, stood up and began to gather the plates and cutlery together. "I'll leave you two to talk business then." She gave me a pointed look. "It's about time you got yourself a girlfriend, Marcus, and then I'd have somebody to swap girl talk with whilst I'm doing the washing up," she added with a grin.

"I'm working on it, Em," I replied offhandedly.

She paused in her collecting and stacking, enquiring interest sparkling in her eyes.

"Tell me more? Tell me more? Who is she? Who is this paragon that can conceivably drag you away from my dear husband and the call of the office?"

Hugo interjected with mild asperity.

"Not now, Em, Marcus can give you all the lurid details of his conquests later. He's just about to reveal to me Plan A and it could be important."

He covered her hand with his. "Seriously, dear, it is a bit crucial so give us half-an-hour." She smiled affectionately at him and nodded acceptance. He turned back to me all alert. "Ok, fill me in, Marcus, what is the situation with Mazin Al Jabril?"

"Well, there's not much to report currently," I told him thoughtfully. "I decided that he needed a bit of a push so I got Margaret to fax him our revised programme for Sharjah Steel. As you know to try to save the extra cost of using LAVCHIFS, we have had to tighten everything up. This has cut down the amount of design time we have if we are to hit the new date of the end of June for signing the construction contracts. That doesn't present us with much of a problem but it does mean that whoever supplies the furnaces has to have them ready to be installed on site 50 weeks after that."

"So?"

"So 50 weeks is an extremely tight schedule for anyone to make these furnaces."

"So how is that going to help our plan and are you certain that it will?"

I sighed. It was true, nothing was certain; until Mazin took the bait there remained some areas of doubt and uncertainty, but I supposed that must always be the case - one could never be certain. However the basic principle, the cornerstone on which I had based my ideas, and yet been able to satisfy the parameter that we must not compromise our client, was, when I eventually arrived at it, remarkably simple. I began to outline to Hugo my thoughts, beginning at the beginning in order to establish their logical progression. I took a sip of the chilled Montrachet.

"As we know, Mazin came back to us really with one objective, he knew we stood the best chance of winning Sharjah Steel and he wanted to make sure that he was irreversibly and inextricably tied in early. He did this, not for the fee, but so that he could influence us to use a company with whom he had also tied up the sole agency, as a nominated subcontractor for the huge $80 million furnace contract, the biggest of all the equipment contracts."

Hugo smiled faintly. "Well he has certainly succeeded in that so far," he observed.

I concurred, "So far! But what he doesn't know of course is that there could be competition for him and his mates in Pantocrator. Realistically the idea of using the high frequency induction furnaces is a good one. Everybody agrees with that, the technical department at the World Bank are very impressed, the Ministry of Industry in Sharjah are chuffed that they are going to get what they wanted - the most advanced steel plant anywhere in the world - and we are getting the credit for being on the ball as leading consultants. So far so good, but Pantocrator's initial costings are producing figures considerably higher than those in our cost plan - between 10-15% higher, which I suspect could be mainly due to Mazin's cut being added to their true selling price."

Hugo interrupted me. "But is Costa da Silva a going proposition? Could they do the job in the time and have they got the technical resources to produce such high tech equipment?"

I scratched my head pondering his questions. "The answer to the last question is probably yes - they do have the technical ability but their resources are limited. This of course influences the answer to your first question, could they do the job in time? I honestly doubt it. We have three more days of meetings set up with them shortly but I suspect that their objective is to set out their stall to us for future business, they would not be broken-hearted if they didn't get Sharjah."

"But they are interested in Sharjah?"

"Oh yes, they are very interested - certainly interested enough to put the shits up Mazin if it came to the crunch." Hugo nodded contentedly and I continued.

"Now my plans centre round a basic principle. It would be wrong for us to set up Mazin Al Jabril if such an arrangement would be to the detriment of the project, either in technical excellence, programme or price." Hugo nodded emphatically.

"I agree, nice and satisfying although it might be to screw him, it could do us more harm than good in the long run."

I shook my head slowly, "I didn't say we weren't going to screw him, Hugo, I just said that we shouldn't prejudice the project in order to screw him. The objective, however, is not to fix Mazin, it is to get back the money he swindled from us. And get it back from him! Not from Pantocrator or Sharjah or anybody else - but from Mazin himself.

"And the second objective is to ensure that, after we have got our money back, Mazin, who will be very unhappy about this, is neutralized so he cannot do us and the project harm."

Hugo whistled in mild disbelief. "How can we do that?"

I grinned at him and drank some more wine - a little theatrical gesture to drag out the tension a bit more.

"We are not going to do anything, Hugo, that is the nice part, we do not have to go out of our way at all to set him up. Mazin is driven by one overriding force above all forces - that is the force of greed, he is a greedy man, one of nature's hogs. He wants to squeeze too much out of the deal. Instead of being satisfied with a reasonable commission, 2½% something in that order, he has gone right over the top because he thinks we have no alternative now and are fully committed to LAVCHIFS. He intends to rape this job and by so doing has created exactly the situation that is going to stuff him well and truly and, I hope, get our money back one way or another. You know the old saying Hugo, 'Pigs get fat, hogs get slaughtered'. We are going to slaughter him - or rather, and much much better - he is going to slaughter himself."

Now Hugo is not a man over whose eyes the wool can be pulled, he is an experienced professional engineer and I knew he would pick up one point in my dissertation that I had glossed over.

He was frowning and chewing his lip. This was no reflection on Emily Elme's delicious pheasant casserole and steamed treacle sponge, I was certain. I nibbled a piece of the blue cheddar whilst I waited for the straight line. "Marcus," he began somewhat hesitantly, "if, as you said, we will not do anything to prejudice the integrity of the project, I think you said either in technical excellence, programme or price, how can you reconcile that with the fact that we know Pantocrator are proposing to overcharge by 10-15% because they have had to add in Al Jabril's huge commission, and they think they can get away with it because we are bound to nominate them?"

"Hugo," I said, "you have, as usual, put your finger right on the button. Smack on the nail. If your love life is as precise as that, Emily must be a very contented lady."

Her voice floated in from the kitchen. "I heard that, Moon, and a fat chance when you keep him all hours at the office."

"Me, Emily?" I gasped, "I don't keep him, he leaves every night at 5.30. What he does between then and when he arrives home pissed and broke in the early hours - like you tell everybody - is nothing to do with me."

Her "How did you know?" coincided with Hugo's "Ha, bloody ha". However he continued undeflected. "So how can you reconcile the fact that the client is being grossly overcharged?"

He was right, I shouldn't joke at a time like this, he had every right to be concerned; it was he who had built CONDES from nothing long before I came on the scene.

I apologized, "I'm sorry, Hugo, but it is that very fact that will fix Mazin well and truly. I will explain.

"We have to cover that extra $8-12 million somewhere, the quantity surveyor has managed to trim about $3 million off the civils contract but all the rest is pretty tight. I don't want to eat into the contingency at this early stage so I am proposing to save that money another way - by shortening the construction programme. To do that it is necessary to reschedule the plant and equipment installation so that the furnaces go in early. We can save the extra money in reduced financial charges - interest etc, reduced preliminaries and an earlier commencement of production." The puzzled frown had not left Hugo's pleasant face.

"OK, Marcus, I can see that we do not compromise the project but I do not see how reprogramming is going to put Al Jabril in a position where he cannot cause us major grief in the future."

"I'm still working on that, but the plan I have will work provided..." I left it there but Hugo prompted me hard.

"Provided what, for Christ's sake? Come on!"

"You know me, Hugo, I don't like to speculate. I prefer to have something definite to report. All I will say is provided that Mazin Al Jabril is a rich man."

I wouldn't tell him any more in spite of his threats and pleadings, and eventually, after some grumblings and mutterings, he accepted the situation and indicated so by passing me the port which he had been hogging at his elbow until now.

On the economy flight the seats were narrow and packed tightly along both sides of the slim fuselage of the old Boeing. As was his custom Mazin waited disdainfully until the other passengers had finished their pushing, queuing, packing their coats and bags into the overhead racks, wrestling with their and each other's seat belts and generally milling in close bodily contact, before he condescended to stroll down the ramp on to the aircraft. The stewardess threw a scowl in his direction which changed rapidly into a professional 'full set of ivorys' smile as she took in the haughty, tanned face and tall figure looming above her in an elegant camelhair coat.

"Seat number 12A," said Mazin, "the window seat." She hesitated for a split second, custom normally called for only a painted smile and a briefly nodded 'Good Morning' to every third passenger. It did not require a full personal usherette service to the individual's seat, but Mazin had put her on the spot by remaining stationary and easing his shoulder between her and the pilot's cabin thus forcing her to turn down the plane. She had set off before she had worked it out and he followed.

By now the passengers in 12B and 12C were settled comfortably behind their Financial Times and Sun respectively, with seat belts fastened and hand luggage stowed under their feet. Leaving her to acquaint the two unfortunates with the unpleasant fact that they must up tents and move aside, Mazin stood there unconcernedly. After much struggling and heaving, the two bodies hung in the gangway clutching their now crumpled papers, spectacles and, in the case of the Financial Times reader, her large handbag, to their flustered bosoms. At that point Mazin leisurely began to take off his coat, making quite sure, as he handed it to the waiting stewardess, that those in the vicinity got a clear view of his solid gold Rolex, studded with diamonds round the dial, flashing on his tanned wrist. Thus having established himself - at least in his own mind - as a Very Important Person Not Accustomed to Travelling Economy with the Peasants - he eased into his seat, fastened his seat belt and wedged his arm proprietorially on the armrest between him and 12B, thus denying its use to the 'Sun' reader he had contemptuously dismissed as a travelling salesman. Suitably ensconced with one hand on his wallet, he closed his eyes and cut off any possibility of further communication with the remainder of the contents of BA2061 to Jersey.

The taxi dropped him in Rue de Salines just short of Number 22. He paid the driver off with a generous tip - you didn't know who was related to who in 'foreign' countries, and strolled slowly past the offices of Trust Services. It was not a very prepossessing building from the outside. Wedged tightly between a greengrocers and a firm of accountants, and built of weathered stone, it was a dingy two-storey pitched roof, single-fronted premise with faded peeling green paint on window frames and front door. Affixed to the door was a small brass plate which read 'Trust Services'.

His pulse quickened, this looked promising, no outward appearance of opulence, power or authority resided there. He pushed open the door and found himself in the narrow hallway of what obviously was once a house and now existed as offices. The door on the right - the old front room - was ajar, and through it he could see a youngish girl typing away intently on an electric typewriter. A typewriter, he noted, not a word processor. She looked up from her work and caught his eye.

"Can I help you?" she enquired with a smile.

Coolly Mazin looked round the office, he absorbed the old grey filing cabinets and the chipped wooden desk and cheap carpet. The decor was faded and stained with damp patches. Somebody, probably the girl, had put some fresh flowers in a vase to try to brighten the place up, they must have been from a greenhouse at this time of year he decided. He switched on to her the Al Jabril double dagger look between the eyes, it was time for business and things looked promising.

"My name is Al Jabril and I have an appointment at 11 o'clock precisely with the trustee."

She dropped her eyes, slightly shocked by his abrupt manner, and glanced at a desk diary. Mazin could see that there was no other entry for that day.

"Yes, Mr Al Jabril, the trustee is expecting you," she said brightly. "May I take your coat?"

Reassuring himself that, although shabby, the place was reasonably clean and dust free before handing his camelhair (£2500 from Harrods) coat over to her, he allowed himself to be led up a flight of wooden stairs to the room immediately above. The two other doors they passed on this short journey were closed but no sounds of activity leaked out. No telephones, typing, voices, anything that would indicate that a hive of industry had its home throbbing within these walls.

The girl knocked once on the door and immediately opened it allowing Mazin to pass her and move into the room. He was at full action stations, all his antennae tuned to maximum sensitivity already, sniffing out weaknesses and vulnerabilities. It was the instinct that the carnivores have, that immediate chemistry by which, when they meet, each knows who is the dominant and who the subservient. In humans it encompasses many factors all assimilated and assessed instantly. The decor of the room - in this case emulsion paint, the quality of the furniture - cheap - the thickness of the carpet - thin - the layout of the office - formal and defensive - and above all - the man behind the desk.

The man who rose to greet him was clearly nervous. It was not that he had any reason to be nervous, he had none - so far. It was just that any encounter with the new or the unfamiliar clearly made him nervous whatever the circumstances. He offered a brief handshake and indicated the shabby leather chair in front of the desk. Mazin's eyes swept over him in a single glance taking in the thin dark hair falling in a hank over the pale face. His suit - and Mazin was an expert on tailoring - was well pressed but old and clearly an off the peg multiple, his tie was polyester and tied in a large unfashionable knot between the gently frayed edges of a white collar. It was only the eyes that disconcerted

250

him slightly, for one moment they had seemed to be assessing him in precisely the same way, before they caught his glance and flicked elsewhere.

"May I offer you a coffee or perhaps tea?"

Mazin blinked; the trustee's voice was clear and precise.

"Coffee please, black, no sugar." Mazin smiled at him; it was a nice smile, a gentle smile, a smile that concealed the teeth, it was the smile of a dominant over the subservient.

The trustee gave instructions for the beverages to the girl still waiting at the door, and then sat back in his chair, his finger tips touching each other in front of his chest and a quizzical look on his face.

"You said on the telephone, Mr Al Jabril, that you were interested in establishing a Jersey trust. What, er, what precisely did you have in mind?"

Mazin pretended to look sheepish, he smiled again and spread his hands.

"A little subterfuge I'm afraid, please forgive me. My business with you does concern a trust, but it is extremely confidential, and the telephone..." he gestured towards the instrument leaving his sentence hanging unfinished.

The trustee nodded in understanding agreement. "Just so. But if you could be so kind as to enlighten me as to the real purpose of your visit then I may be able to help."

Mazin produced the slim crocodile skin wallet from his inside jacket pocket and slid an engraved visiting card across the desk towards the trustee. The man glanced at it and looked up questioningly. Mazin continued.

"Investment and Resource Holdings, the Swiss company whom I represent, is a large financial investment company with holdings in many countries." The exaggeration slipped easily off his tongue. "We have substantial cash resources available for investments and acquisitions and it is my job to seek these opportunities out and pursue them."

The trustee spread his hands in a gesture of appeal. "But how can I be of assistance?"

Mazin paused for a second, this sort of thing could not be rushed. He needed more background before he could decide on the method of approach although already he was excited at the possibilities revealed. However, caution always prevailed and more positive confirmation of his initial assessment was needed. Mazin gave him the smile again; the gently smiling jaws to welcome him in.

"First of all can you tell me a little more about Trust Services. Give me a brief rundown on the type of service you provide and the status of the clients for whom you act?" He leaned forward interestedly, as if expecting to receive the next set of tablets from Mount Sinai. The trustee flushed a little, his pale face showing a faint pink spot on each cheek, and he looked down, embarrassed.

"I, that is the firm, principally provide trust services to non-Jersey residents - both companies and individuals - primarily to enable them to, er, minimise, shall we say, their taxation liabilities." He then went on to explain the different types of trust that could be established and the differences between the settlors, the trustees and the beneficiaries. After outlining the Jersey tax position and the negotiable fee structure for establishing and operating trusts he ended rather lamely, with an enquiry to Mazin about which particular country's taxes he was interested in minimising. Mazin listened without interruption, all this he knew already from the report he had had from Arthurton, Smithson, Pegler and Booth. He also knew that it was just so much bullshit put out as a deliberate smokescreen to hide the fact that the trustee was avoiding answering Mazin's question directly. By avoiding the question of course, he had answered it, but Mazin was not going to let him off the hook as easily as that. He went for the throat.

"Yes, yes, I understand all that, but if my company is to put millions of pounds through Jersey we want to be absolutely sure that we are dealing with somebody of impeccable credentials, so if you will do as I asked and give me names of say half-a-dozen major companies for whom you act - in the strictest confidence of course - it will help me with the reassurance I need - for my directors," he added hastily. Mazin watched him carefully. Although the trustee squirmed awkwardly under the pressure there had been no mistaking the gleam of avarice that had flashed in his eyes when the word 'millions' was mentioned. He fought back.

"You must appreciate, Mr Al Jabril, that such information is totally confidential. I am not at liberty to reveal names of persons or companies for whom I act. The authorities here would not countenance such behaviour. I regret therefore I cannot give you such details but rest assured that we do act for some important people. Very important," he added portentously. The coffee arrived at that moment to save him from further interrogation and he took the opportunity, whilst the girl was serving it, to mop his face with his handkerchief.

Abruptly Mazin changed the subject. "Are you free for lunch today, I would like to continue our discussions further?"

The girl murmured that he already had an appointment for lunch but the trustee brushed that aside. "A social matter, ring him Carol and re-arrange it for another day." At Mazin's request the girl was asked to book a table for two at The Harbour at Gorey for 1 o'clock and forthwith disappeared to do as she was bidden.

Mazin sipped his coffee silently. Unless this guy was one of those 'do his duty come hell or high water incorruptible types, even if it killed them', the situation couldn't have been better - and from the look of greed that had shown momentarily on his face when big bucks were floated across the scene, it was unlikely that he was. The trustee drove them both to Gorey in his car, a battered old Rover 2000, and during the journey and over lunch revealed to Mazin, through discreet questioning, that he was having a struggle to pay for the private education of his three children. It transpired that he and his wife lived separately, she in a mortgaged house on the mainland - she thought Jersey claustrophobic - and he in a flat in St Aubin, and that she was spending money like water, although the business was 'a little on the quiet side at present' he was expecting a big upturn in the spring. By the time Mazin signed the credit card chit to settle the bill, he had the trustee's measure exactly. He had seen it all before, in the Middle East, in Europe, in America, all these little guys who wanted to live big and act big, but spent their whole lives slogging themselves to death whilst their families put on the big front instead. They all longed for the big time, the one deal that would make them, the deal that would turn them from small time operators to become the envy of all those around, and they would sell their souls for it, especially if it could be cloaked in a respectable disguise.

Normally Mazin would have sown a few more large numbers attached to expectations and then left him to sweat for a month or two. He would have taken him to the top of the mountain where he could see the sunshine all around and taste the financial wine, and then bounced him hard a few times until he was so softened up he would allow himself to be led by the nose into hell if required. Unfortunately time was short, so a more direct approach was necessary.

After settling the bill, Mazin suggested that instead of returning to the depressing offices of Trust Services they should have an informal talk in the hotel lounge. It was winter, there were no tourists or holidaymakers to interrupt, and Gorey lay peaceful in the late afternoon sun. The trustee ordered a small Armagnac, and Mazin some spring water. Giving him the smile yet again Mazin began carefully to weave his web.

"What we in Industrial and Resource Holdings are looking for is to acquire a small company that has the potential both to expand its services and its market."

The trustee frowned. "You mean a service company then, not a manufacturing company."

"Exactly! You are really on the ball!" Mazin smiled, he had already made him feel that a service company had been his idea and so he continued.

"A company or organisation that has high quality staff, an excellent reputation, a good track record but lacks the foundation of real capital to expand. We would inject such capital. A service company would give us a much higher return on our investment than a manufacturer, but of course you appreciate that."

"Of course, of course," the trustee sipped his Armagnac thoughtfully.

"And how would you go about investing in such a company if you found one?" he asked.

Mazin congratulated himself, already the guy was talking himself into the deal. The simple fact that he had substituted Mazin's more emotionally aggressive word 'acquire' for, to him, the smoothly acceptable 'investing' was evidence of that. That, and the fact that he had now knowingly and deliberately opened the trap in order to examine the bait to see if that was also smoothly acceptable. Mazin duly, and with full malice aforethought, made it so!

"We would pay full market price for the shares at valuation plus, say, 10% of the purchase price to the introducing agent as his commission. Of course we would not want merely a minority holding if we were to go ahead with such an investment. As our intention would be to inject further substantial amounts into the business we would have to have control over our money. You understand that?"

The trustee's eyes opened wide for a moment and then he said, "Let me get this clear, so whoever put up the proposition to you, brought the company to you, would get 10% of the price that you would pay for your shares? That is on top of the share price? In addition to it?"

Mazin nodded, "Oh yes, we would pay full value to the existing shareholder for the shares plus the 10%."

Mazin winced the moment he said it but the trustee apparently failed to register Mazin's slip, his use of the singular for the shareholder, he was apparently more concerned with the side issue - which from Mazin's point of view was the main issue.

"So if you paid, let us say, £1 million for the shares the agent would get £100,000?" Mazin nodded again.

"Indeed, it is a lot of money, I realise that, but there is a condition, a very strict condition, which is why we always pay our agents well." It was made to sound as though these sort of deals were just normal everyday business transactions to him. Mazin continued, fixing the trustee with his dark eyes. "We insist upon total secrecy. Absolute and total secrecy, that is fundamental."

The trustee frowned again, "That would not be easy, unless of course you hold the shares through nominees. Even then we are now obliged to disclose to the authorities the true interested parties who are behind any nominees."

Mazin choked for a moment, there was no way he was going to have anything owned by him in the hands of nominees - who knew what they might perpetrate behind his back - so that idea must be firmly stamped on before they started.

"No, no, that is not what I meant. The company, IRH, will hold the shares but nobody must know about the deal until it is completed. Not the authorities, not the directors, not the other shareholders - nobody."

The trustee's shoulders sagged visibly as this news sank in. "Oh dear," he muttered, "I thought I had just the company for you but I don't think what you ask is possible. I would really have to consult the directors, who incidentally are the other shareholders, it could not be avoided."

Mazin's heart jumped violently, this was it, he was nearly there, it had to be CONDES, the guy didn't have any other business of that size and type - he had already said so. Now was the time to play the double bluff. The ace card. The 'let's all come clean and put our cards face up on the table to show what honest and straightforward chaps we are' card.

"You're talking of CONDES aren't you?" said Mazin with a disarming smile, and holding up one hand he continued smoothly, "No, don't answer that yet, I appreciate your discretion, but let me put my cards face up on the table." He glanced around before leaning forward confidentially just to make sure that nobody else was in earshot - they weren't, and never had been, but it gave the impression that he was about to reveal a glimpse of the Holy Grail.

"This is absolutely confidential, top secret in fact. We have been studying CONDES for some time now and they are just the type of business that we are looking for to fit into our development plans. They are an excellent firm and very well run, but as you well know are very undercapitalised." He leaned further forward still and lowered his voice further. "In fact I would not be giving away any secrets if I told you that I know both Hugo Elmes and Marcus Moon personally. They are very good friends of mine, we get on well together."

The trustee gave a short laugh of astonishment and wagged a finger at Mazin in mock anger. "So that's why you came to me," he said, "you knew all the time that Trust Services effectively controls CONDES. You can only have got that information either from the annual returns or from the directors."

Mazin laughed back with him, "There's no fooling you is there, and the answer is both. Marcus told me that you hold shares in Bridge Holdings, which owns CONDES, and the annual return told me it was 75%. It is that holding we would like to buy."

"But what then is the objection to bringing the directors into the negotiations, if you know them and they you?"

Mazin shook his head rejecting the idea out of hand. "I only mentioned that to show that we will be able to work together in the event that we do acquire the shares, but my bosses in Switzerland don't know either Hugo or Marcus or vice versa, and it is they who insist on total secrecy. But do bear in mind that you will be doing them a huge favour, you realise that?"

The trustee raised his eyebrows questioningly so Mazin expounded. "They will get a very large cash sum each, via the trust, for the shares that the trust sells; they will still own 25% of a company that will receive massive injections of capital to finance a huge expansion programme and thus share in greatly increased profits, and they will be working with an old friend and colleague of many years. I have an accountant's valuation of the shares here with me, done by one of the top flight City firms, and based on the company's accounts for the last three years, and you will see that IRH will, from the valuation, have to pay £2 million for Trust Services' 75% shareholding, plus a further £200,000 to yourself for the introduction. It is one of those super deals where everybody can benefit."

Mazin held his breath, this was the big crunch, was the trustee going to be professional and stupid and insist that all must be revealed to all parties before any deal could be negotiated, or was he going to take the first step down the left-hand path?

The trustee said nothing and Mazin eased out his breath slowly.

The bait had been skilfully presented and the mark was interested. Having taken him up the mountain and shown him not just sunshine and wine, but honey and roses all round as well, it was now time to let him stew for a couple of weeks or so.

"That is our outline proposal, I know that as sole trustee you have absolute discretion in this matter if you so choose. If everything is at valuation and above board you can never be accused of selling the company short by the beneficiaries. You will have done them a great service in fact, but I warn you if one word of this leaks out to anybody, any single person, the deal is off. Only you and I know the details at present, so if it leaks, particularly to Elmes or Moon, it can only have come from you and you can forget your £200,000 forever. Think it over and I will see you sometime in the near future. Don't try to contact me, I will contact you. Have you got that clear?"

The trustee nodded anxiously, there were many questions he knew he should ask but he couldn't formulate them at the time.

Mazin reached over and shook his hand briefly, and with the same movement deftly removed his visiting card from the trustee's top pocket.

"I'll get a taxi straight to the airport - don't forget - not a word!" And with that he picked up his coat and hit the door into the cold winter air.

It was a fingernail chewing five hours, between 11 o'clock in the morning and 4 o'clock in the afternoon, until the trustee eventually phoned me. I'd been telling myself that no news was good news and, in truth, I was trying to convince myself that if it was a disaster I would have heard from the trustee much earlier.

Trying not to betray too much anxiety I asked tentatively, "How did it go?"

The trustee was almost beside himself with glee - and a good lunch I suspected.

"He's swallowed it hook, line and sinker, and do you know what?"

"No, what?" I responded patiently.

"He's offered me a bribe!"

A chill of apprehension gripped my heart, we had not discussed this possibility - my fault entirely. The trustee was as straight as a die and totally inexperienced of the ways of the financial ungodly from the Middle East.

"You didn't turn it down did you? Please say you didn't!"

I prayed silently to God that he hadn't done anything so stupid. Mazin would be very suspicious and cagey without a comforting web of corruption surrounding the deal.

The trustee snorted, "Good Lord of course not, he offered me personally £200,000 if I would sell the Bridge Holdings Limited shares to his company."

"Strewth!" I breathed, he was really going in heavy if he was prepared to lay out that sort of money. And there was one other little word in the trustee's last remark that caused me to prick up my ears.

"Did he say which company?" I enquired, keeping my fingers crossed.

"Some Swiss outfit. Investment and Resource Holdings I think it was. He didn't let me keep his card."

Jeronimo! I thought.

"So what is he, or his company, prepared to offer?"

The trustee ran me through the whole discussions in detail and it looked good. Mazin was talking serious money. Two million pounds for 75% was a good opening offer, although it was less than half of the true value of what he thought he was going to buy. Of course he knew that if he did control 75% that would make Hugo's and my stock worthless unless we danced to his tune.

He claimed he was a principal acting for a company in Switzerland and that the deal should be secret. I bet it should!

Still, all in all, it looked like it was a 'Be nice to Marcus Moon day'.

"So how was it left?" I asked.

"He is going to contact me again sometime in the near future when I have had time to absorb the full impact of £200,000 on my poverty-stricken wife and starving offspring in their heavily mortgaged terraced house in the back streets of beyond! And Marcus...?"

"Yes!"

"He's a terrible man, very clever, very smooth and very dangerous. Do not underestimate him."

"I know," I said. "I don't."

"And what is more, he says he's a very close friend of yours!" There was a burst of laughter as he put the phone down.

I sat back in my chair contemplating events. So it was all systems go now, we had to continue increasing the pressure, wind Mazin up and accelerate him faster than he would like along the wave crest to financial purgatory. The key was the tightened-up programme for Sharjah Steel. Pantocrator's technical team were due over here in the next couple of days so they could work on that. I needed to speak to the World Bank guys in Washington, and the final arrangements would have to be agreed with Georgiou Antoniades, Pantocrator's managing director. That would be the crunch, and to ensure that Georgiou did his stuff I would have to play the Costa da Silva card.

CHAPTER FIFTEEN

"Phew! So Al Jabril has floated £2 million across our bows, has he? Well that will cover our missing $2 million plus the interest."

Hugo steepled the fingers of both hands as he contemplated the notes the trustee had made of his meeting with the lascivious Arab.

"Plus a £200,000 kick-back to the trustee," I added, "and that is just his opening offer. When you consider that CONDES is worth only three times that, he really must want it desperately to pitch so high, particularly when we had gone to all that trouble to present such an image of seedy poverty. The old electric typewriter that Cliff dug out was a brilliant touch!"

"Are you going to accept it or try to push him higher? We don't want to frighten him off."

"He'll expect the trustee to try to up the price and be suspicious if he didn't, but he's experienced at these sort of negotiations and I doubt if he'll budge much. He obviously thinks he's got the measure of the trustee as a man to whom £200,000 is a fortune. He has left him to stew a bit so that his imagination can spend that money and afterwards he won't be able to contemplate life without it. Mazin thinks that the thought of losing it will reduce any strength on the trustee's side of any negotiation. That's how Mazin works."

"So is that it?"

"Mazin has signed nothing yet. All he has done is prepare the groundwork. If he thought Pantocrator was home and dry for the furnace contract he wouldn't need to lay out funds to take over CONDES. What we have to do now is sow some doubt in his mind, and that is what I am going to do at the next project meeting. Also you have forgotten Plan A Plus! That also starts today."

Hugo snorted irritably. "I haven't forgotten it because you never did tell me what it is! I hope you're not going to screw up Plan A by trying to be too clever?"

I grinned at him. "Let me assure you, Hugo, that there is no way Plan A Plus can screw up Plan A. I told you 'plus' does not involve us doing anything, with any luck Mazin will do it himself - if guided in the right direction."

"That's what worries me," Hugo grumbled, "I sometimes think that some of Mazin Al Jabril's influence has rubbed off on you!"

"Oh thou of little faith," I mocked him gently.

I met Hugo in the corridor whilst I was on my way to the boardroom for the Sharjah Steel project meeting. He was all dressed up in a smart grey broadcloth suit, institution tie and polished black shoes.

"Hi, Hugo, I thought you had a meeting in the city this morning?"

"Cancelled," he said. "They've changed it to tomorrow."

"It's the Sharjah Steel meeting this morning, do you want to sit in on it - it could be very interesting?"

He shook his head. "Al Jabril is already there, I caught a brief glimpse of him as I passed, and the answer is, no thanks!"

I grinned at his reticence, and reminded him, "This is 'M' day Hugo; the day the crocodile's jaws begin to gently close around the goolies of our Middle Eastern friend."

Hugo scanned me severely over the top of his half-moon spectacles.

"You haven't told me exactly what you are going to do. He's no fool you know, he'll not fall for any crack-brained scheme like the one you had for towing icebergs from the Antarctic to the Persian Gulf to provide them with vast amounts of fresh water."

It was a sore point and I bridled indignantly. "It certainly is not a crack-brained scheme as you well know, and for that matter neither was the iceberg plan!"

Hugo raised one eyebrow; he knew how to wind me up.

"Why don't we meet up afterwards and have a bit of lunch together and you can bring me up to date?"

I shrugged acceptance, "Fine."

I left him and wandered along to the boardroom.

For the first time ever Mazin Al Jabril was on time for a project meeting, he was sitting in the boardroom occupying my usual place at the head of the table when I entered.

"Morning, Mazin." I walked up the length of the room and stood beside him piling my papers and files on the table in front of him. We didn't shake hands.

"You going to chair the meeting then?"

He didn't smile and hesitated. For one heart-stopping moment I thought he was going to accept but then, with some reluctance he moved out of the chairman's chair with the arms, to a side chair without. It was almost as if he had been trying it for size.

I was pleased to catch him on his own for a few minutes before the rest of the design team turned up, it would save me several days of manoeuvring with him.

I turned to face him. "I wanted to have a private word with you, Mazin, we appear to have a bit of a problem I'm afraid, and it concerns Pantocrator. Perhaps you can give it some thought during the meeting."

I put on my serious, slightly bemused look, the one that I like to think gives the impression that although a problem exists I am doing my best to grapple with it. It involves screwing up the eyes and tightening the lips to a thin line. Brian Mason calls it the constipated dog look.

Mazin however was not concerned at that moment with whatever look I wore, his self-preservation sensors had picked up the two words 'problem' and 'Pantocrator', and to him that meant dollars flying out of the window.

"Problems, what problems?" he snapped. "I don't know of any problems."

I calmed him down. "Well it could be good news in one way - for you that is." No, I wasn't pushing him, I told myself, just guiding him a fraction so that he would see things constructively - I hoped.

"What is this problem then, and why didn't I know about this earlier?" He was still agitated but less so.

"The problem really stems from Pantocrator's quotation. As you know, because we have discussed it briefly before," (briefly because he refused to talk about it) "their price is above the budget figures for the furnaces..."

He interrupted me sharply. "Well, you'll just have to save money elsewhere. These furnaces are the best, the most modern and they are what Sharjah want, so if there's any problem it's your problem not mine."

Thank you, Lord, I murmured, thank you for helping me, it will not be forgotten.

I looked squarely at Mazin and said, "I agree." This took him aback, he expected an argument, he thought that these were the opening shots in a campaign to pressurise him to get Pantocrator to reduce their prices. What he didn't expect was a pushover and it made him nervous.

"What do you mean, you agree? Are you accepting Pantocrator's prices?"

I saw the danger here, he wouldn't expect me to concede that easily, so I allayed his suspicions by giving a short derisive laugh. "Good God, no, I think they're outrageous but they will be the subject of future negotiations. What I am concerned about more immediately is the matter you have just pointed out, and you're right. In order to fit in with the cost plan we must get the overall price down, and it is not necessary at present to get into heavy and protracted negotiations with Pantocrator when there is a simpler solution."

I was watching Mazin's eyes very closely and I saw the scorn that appeared as he digested what I had said. It was clear he was thinking what mugs we were if we thought we would have any negotiating position left if we managed to squeeze the whole project within the cost plan leaving Pantocrator's prices, including his huge backhander, at the present high levels. He nodded his head wisely in pretended agreement. "Very shrewd," he said, "yes, much better to do it that way. But how will you get the overall costs down?"

"No problem," I replied easily, "we have already agreed an accelerated programme with the World Bank proposed by the Ministry of Industry in Sharjah. The general cost savings on preliminaries, plus the big saving in finance charges that the new programme throws up just about offsets Pantocrator's extra costs."

"Brilliant," he laughed, scarcely being able to contain his delight and relief. I continued. "We've reprogrammed the whole method study for the job and it works. Our mutual clients are very impressed, it means that Sharjah will get into on stream production six months earlier."

I smiled at him and he smiled at me, two happy souls entwined in perfect harmony - it was the last time ever that we both smiled at each other simultaneously! I couldn't help but prolong the moment.

"Good, isn't it?"

"Excellent," he answered, and then he realised that, as yet, the mooted problem had not been laid before him. His smile dimmed. "But what is the problem then that you mentioned?"

I took a deep slow breath. "The problem, Mazin, is that to meet the new accelerated programme Pantocrator must start installation on site in exactly 64 weeks' time from today."

He didn't get it immediately.

"So?"

"So, that means, according to the tightest work schedule they can accommodate, they will have to commence manufacturing the furnaces two weeks from now. They have a 62 week fabrication programme and that is squeezing it as tight as they possibly can."

He still hadn't grasped it in total, although I think it was beginning to dawn on him that trouble might lurk somewhere. He frowned, "But they can start in two weeks, there's nothing to stop them. They will start as soon as they get the order and the 10% down payment."

I put on my serious, trying to be helpful look again, although I was in knots trying hard not to laugh, and I gently closed the smiling jaws. Shaking my head gravely from side to side I told him. "No can do, Mazin, no can do. Therein lies the problem. As you know none of the contracts are scheduled to be placed until the end of June - all the financing is geared to that date and it is just not available yet. I spoke to van Straten at IBRD, he's their top finance man on this job, and he takes the firm view that when they start is Pantocrator's problem. If they want the job then they must meet the programme. If they start in June, like everybody else, they will get their down payment and contract, but if they want to start earlier that is their decision and their responsibility. Their risk entirely. The bank will not make the money available to Sharjah earlier than June for this project. However, come June they will get their contract, so it's not so bad is it? After all, Mazin, you have assured me that they are the only ones who can make these furnaces so there is no difficulty is there!" He was badly shaken by this, I could see that; it had come right out of the blue, he had not foreseen it, and neither could he foresee the implications.

It was just as well that he couldn't foresee one of them otherwise he'd have gone into fiscal convulsions, the sort that could seriously damage your wallet, but I could!

It wasn't foresight either, it was the result of the recent meetings at design level with Pantocrator's technical team at which we'd piled on the pressure, and used every trick in the book to squeeze their programme down as tight as we could. This had culminated with a long telephone conversation between Georgiou Antoniades, Pantocrator's MD, and me, which started along the lines of 'never mind the money, Georgiou, we want those furnaces built and installed as fast as it is conceivably possible.' This had cheered him a little - it always does when they think they're getting a blank cheque. Consequent upon this I persuaded him to knock two more weeks off his work schedule and, although he wasn't too happy, he had eventually agreed to a 62-week programme including the tough penalty clauses for delay. However he was even less happy when he learned that he wasn't going to get a signed contract from the Ministry of Industry until the end of June, and that meant no 10% down payment until then either. And when he realised that he was going to have to fund about $10 million worth of work between now and June without guarantee, down payment or contract he verged on the downright suicidal. I got the full histrionics bawled out at full volume, the essence of which was - under no circumstances do they have that magnitude of financial resources themselves, and without a fatherless reproductive signed contract no fatherless reproductive bank is going to lend us the fatherless reproductive money. It cannot be done, it is not fatherless reproductive possible. This was just a brief summary of his observations, there were a lot of other Greek words and phrases interspersed amongst the English, Greek for things like 'sod me', 'Christ almighty' and 'here's a fuckin' how do ye do' - expressive phrases like that I suspected.

I let him bawl on for a while, and then pointed out that this unfortunate state of affairs had only come to pass because his quote was eight million fatherless reproductive dollars over the budget. That shut him up, he was doing some quick mental arithmetic but it got him nowhere. I knew Mazin would have screwed them to the bone in order to maximise his own take, there was no way they could cut even a fraction of $8 million from their true cost, and likewise he knew that there was no way he was going to persuade Mazin to reduce his huge slice. He knew it and I knew it.

I let a little silence hang in there so he could thoroughly re-acquaint himself about who was precisely responsible for his current situation, then I said, "I appreciate the problems, Georgiou, I really do, but the IBRD cannot make any funds available before June and thus there is no way Sharjah will sign any contract before then." I paused to let that sink in, then threw him the lifeline.

"There is one possible way that might solve the down payment problem in whole or in part but without a contract."

He had leaped at it, and I suppose I got the Greek for 'stuff the contract as long as we get the money'. I explained, "I'm sure Mr Al Jabril will help you out, he is a very wealthy man," - I hoped to hell that he was as rich as I was making him out to be, our - my - whole strategy depended upon it. I continued. "He should have no difficulty in advancing your company the funds to cover the 10% down payment. After all, Georgiou, the risk is negligible, his brother is the Minister, and I am sure that under the circumstances Mr Jabril would be happy to share the risk with you - it's only fair isn't it?"

I had to bite my lip to stop a chuckle entering my voice, Mazin would shit bones when he got the proposition; happiness would not be the first word that would spring to his mind at the thought of putting up several million dollars of unsecured money. It wouldn't be the full 10% I was certain of that, Mazin would negotiate Antoniades down to a lesser sum, but old Georgiou was a tough cookie in a strong position. Mazin stood to make as much if not more, out of this deal, than Pantocrator, so Georgiou was not going to let him off lightly. Even at 5% - $4 million - $4.4 million to be precise - we would have him by the balls, and surely he must have all of that. After all he had ripped us off for $2 million and we can't have been the only company that he'd turned over in a big way. One thing about Mazin, he didn't think small. Antoniades was non-committal about the idea but said he'd come back to us. It was no more than could be expected, but the fact that he didn't pursue his anguish showed that the idea had taken root. I applied a little more pressure. "If you want this business, Georgiou, you've got to hack the programme."

"What if we don't?" He flew his kite tentatively, so I shot it down with both barrels. I didn't want any half-hearted squeeze on Mazin.

"If you're telling me you can't do the business then we'll either switch back to electric arc furnaces, which, after all, is what we won the design contract with, or we'll go to Costa da Silva..."

I left the sentence hanging and held my breath. There was a long and very pregnant silence that had clearly shaken him rigid; his bluff had been called in spades. They needed this job, it would make them; apart from making a profit they would be renowned as the world leaders in plant for the steel industry and Antoniades knew it. He was a hard bastard, there was no way he would turn this down without a fight. He didn't, and back-peddled hastily.

I smiled across at Mazin thinking about this, I didn't imagine for one moment now that Antoniades would let him off the hook - a big, barbed, sharp hook that he didn't know he was on yet. He was nevertheless looking a bit pale and sweaty, even the vague possibility that the job could possibly slip from his greedy grasp made him feel nauseous.

"Give it a bit of thought, Mazin. I'll leave it to you to sort it out with Antoniades." I paused, I could hear voices through the door as the rest of the team moved up the corridor towards the boardroom, and then I said, "But I must know one way or the other by the 12th of next month - that is in two weeks time - and I must have written confirmation that Pantocrator have started work on their full manufacturing programme. Our inspectors will be sent out on that day to begin their checks."

As the others began to enter the room with nodded greetings and take their places round the table, he seemed to reach a decision. He eased back his cuff to let us all see the expensive watch - it was just after 11 o'clock - and got to his feet.

"Have you spoken to Antoniades about this?" he suddenly shot at me, his eyes narrowing suspiciously.

I shrugged, "Of course I have, we've had to liaise very closely with Pantocrator to establish both the programme and all their other technical requirements."

271

He gave an angry dismissive gesture, "Yes, yes, I understand all that, but does he know about not getting a contract?"

"Yes, he knows about that as well."

He grew angrier and snapped irritably, "So what did he say about it? Is he prepared to start work in two weeks?"

The rest of the team were by now assembled and listening with puzzled expressions to this exchange. I couldn't wind him up any more, much as I'd have liked to, so I gave it to him - well part of it.

"He wants to talk to you about it - but he knows that if he doesn't start work and proceed flat out then that's it. We scrap the LAVCHIFS and immediately go back to electric arcs. We have no choice in the matter."

He gave me a very sharp look, his nerve ends were telling him that all was not well and there was more to it than this, but what it was he couldn't fathom. He raised a threatening finger to me and to the rest of the team.

"Don't begin making any changes to this project. The Minister of Industry, and the Ruler himself, Sheikh Sultan, have approved these furnaces. This is just a minor matter of no significance and will be sorted immediately."

He turned to me. "I'm going back to my flat to speak with Antoniades. Don't forget, no changes."

"Of course not," I murmured as he swept out of the door.

Mazin stalked through the door of the CONDES offices and gestured angrily for his driver. Hastily pushing his copy of the Sun out of sight under the seat, the driver manoeuvred the Mercedes out of the tight parking slot and drew up five yards away where his master was standing impatiently. In rushing round to open the door he managed to stand on Mazin's toe. They both looked down horrified, Mazin because his hand-made Lobb calfskin now had a large scuff mark on the shiny toecap, the driver because of the bollocking that would inevitably follow.

"You stupid clumsy clown, these shoes cost over £400! That will be deducted from your bonus this year." The driver secretly cheered up at that, he hadn't known he was getting a bonus till then, and ushering his master into the rear seat, climbed into the front wondering what else he could do to discover his future benefits. Not much as it turned out - Mazin fired him as soon as he had been driven back to the flat.

Sitting contemplating in the back of the car, the feeling grew that all was not well. Moon had been far too confident, too much in charge of the situation, and Mazin didn't like that, he liked his associates nervous and apprehensive of the future. He thought of what he would say to Antoniades. He could have made the call from CONDES' offices but a sixth sense warned him that it might not be advisable to telephone where he could be overheard - particularly by somebody like Moon.

He got straight through on Antoniades' private line. The conversation was protracted, one-sided and to the point. Antoniades told him that there was absolutely no possibility of Pantocrator starting work in two weeks' time without a substantial injection of funds. He followed that up by adding that without a signed contract, or even a letter of intent, their banks would not put up one drachma. Mazin pointed out that the contract was a certainty, there was absolutely no risk, his brother was the Minister etc etc, and thereby neatly dug himself the deep pit into which the waiting Antoniades promptly pushed him.

"In that case, Mr Al Jabril, why don't you advance us the funds?" There was a stunned silence as the import of Antoniades' statement slammed home.

"Me? Why me? I'm not a bank; I'm just an individual. I don't have that sort of money," he gasped, appalled at even the idea of having to shell out some of his precious ill-gotten gains. Antoniades pressed him harder; there was no other source of money available. Mazin pleaded impossibility, impracticality, poverty and every other lie he could think of but Antoniades was inflexible.

"No funds, no job. We don't start!"

Mazin tried threats, promises, everything under the sun.

"No funds, no job. We don't start!"

Eventually in sheer desperation Mazin said he would fly to Greece that day.

He banged down the telephone and glowered at the file he had on CONDES on his desk. They must have a hand in this somewhere. That fool Moon had been too self-possessed, too confident, but what exactly were they up to? He shouted to his manservant to book him on the next flight to Athens - "Any airline! Just get me there today!" - and then reviewed the whole position. Where was the danger? Pantocrator had been approved as nominated sub contractors by both the IBRD and the Ministry of Industry; CONDES could not change back to electric arc or any other kind of furnace without his brother's approval, the overall cost was back within the budget limits and, provided Pantocrator met the programme, the job was theirs. The only risk would be if the whole project was to be cancelled.

The IBRD had allocated the funds in their next three years' budgets so the money was secure, the Ruler of Sharjah himself had personally approved the whole scheme and he would lose face dramatically if he cancelled it - the IBRD and the United States, its chief backer, would not stand for that sort of treatment.

He could not see any flaw in his reasoning. A Gulf wide war might cause problems, but the Americans would not allow that to happen, they were too concerned about their oil supplies.

A local coup in Sharjah would be problematical, but the last one of those had been many years ago and massive precautions had been taken since then to ensure that it would not happen again. Besides there wasn't any political unrest in Sharjah, not a murmur of it. All the same he didn't like it, he did not like it one little bit. This situation was not in his planning. He sucked air through his teeth as he pondered the position. If, just if, it was Elmes and Moon behind it with some cunning plan then it would be as well to safeguard that flank. He brightened considerably, it was not just a question of safeguarding a flank - it was a positive way of making a fortune as well. A double benefit. He made a decision, that matter would have to be given the most urgent priority now and there was very little time in which to get it tied up.

The manservant knocked and came into the study. "You are booked on Olympic taking off at 2.40, Heathrow Terminal Two, master. Your ticket with an open return is available for collection at the Olympic desk."

"Pack me an overnight bag and get a move on!"

The manservant bowed and eased out. Mazin looked at his watch, 12.15, that gave him about half-an-hour. He took out his pocket book and looked up the telephone number of Trust Services in Jersey. A girl, he supposed it was the receptionist, answered the phone. The trustee unfortunately was out, could she take a message? No, she didn't know what time he'd be back but she could get a message to him if it was urgent. No, Mr Al Jabril couldn't telephone him, he was in an important meeting elsewhere and had given instructions not to be interrupted. Mazin ground his teeth in frustration but could not penetrate her security. Eventually he settled for telling her to get the trustee to ring him within the next half-hour or she'd likely be out of a job tomorrow.

Annoyed because he had been thwarted, he telephoned the Swiss lawyer who ran IRH. He got straight through to Geneva but that was all he got.

"Mazin Al Jabril, Dr Weber. I want an up-to-date figure of IRH's total cash deposits?"

The lawyer's voice was cold and precise.

"I regret that I cannot provide any information of that nature about any business, which may or may not be clients of this firm, over the telephone."

"But it's me, Dr Weber, Mazin Al Jabril, surely you recognise my voice. I need this information urgently. It is vital."

"If it is you, Mr Al Jabril, then you will recollect that you gave explicit written instructions not to reveal any information to any person whatsoever over the telephone and, if it is not you, Mr Al Jabril, you will recollect why you gave such instructions."

The humour was not intentional nor did Mazin appreciate it, there was a devastating finality about the illogical logic that forbade any further pressure on the lawyer, Mazin knew it would be useless. Gritting his teeth in frustration he told the lawyer that he could be expected in Geneva in the next two or three days and to make damned certain that he, the lawyer, was there in person and that he had all the information at his fingertips. In his precise unruffled voice he replied, "Indeed I shall look forward to your visit, Mr Al Jabril."

Mazin slammed the phone down cursing and began to do a few calculations from the information he had available in code in his pocket book. It looked as if he could lay hands on somewhere between $4.5 to $5 million cash and could probably raise a further $3 million or so quickly, on short term back-to-back loans secured against previously valued assets. He scowled, it was going to be barely enough, particularly if that bastard Antoniades dug his heels in, and for quick money the banks would load the interest rate. They would know he couldn't afford the time to negotiate more favourable terms and so they would screw him. He swore violently, if only he'd known about this earlier he could have given himself much more flexibility, but by God what ever rate the bank charged him he would pass on to Pantocrator plus 3% - and charge it on the whole loan including his own money. Antoniades could like it or stick it - that was one lever he did have to pull. Maybe he could insist on securing the loan against Pantocrator's assets, but time became the problem then. It would be possible for the lawyers to draw up a loan agreement with a blanket covering of Pantocrator's assets without valuations, but if, as with most industrial companies, they were hocked up to the eyeballs already, the banks would have locked up a first charge over all the assets in any case and this would make his security virtually worthless. Still it was worth a try, and to concede this point may enable him to wind up another quarter or half percent on the interest rate, or reduce his exposure on the loan. He was just considering if there was any other possible way for Pantocrator to get the funding without having to risk his money when the phone rang.

It was the trustee from Trust Services returning his call. Mazin wasted no time.

"I refer to the arrangements we discussed at your offices on the 15th of this month; my principals in Switzerland have considered the matter and wish to proceed on the lines we proposed."

He drew a long breath. "There is just one point, whereas the agent's fee is acceptable they feel, having studied the company and its financial record more closely, that it is over-priced at £2 million for a 75% holding. The accounts show a certain volatility and that concerns them. The trough in 1996-97 has worried them and they feel that a figure of £1.5 million is a more equitable price."

He gripped the phone tightly, it was a risk and he knew it. An Arab or even a Western businessman would easily recognise that as the opening shot in a negotiation. However accountants and lawyers, particularly small fry, sometimes took such a proposal as a final fixed figure and either agreed it, or rejected it out of hand terminating the deal on the spot. Mazin was one of those people who couldn't resist trying to lever that bit extra out of a deal, he calculated that he had a two-to-one chance of winning this and no chance of losing. Either the trustee would accept - bearing in mind the 'commission' he was going to get - and Mazin would save £500,000, or he would negotiate in which case the final figure would be somewhere between £1.5 and £2 million and there would still be a saving. With the bribe he was getting there was absolutely no chance whatever of him rejecting the deal out of hand and terminating discussions on the spot. Mazin knew precisely the power of money to corrupt. There would be a lot of indignant spluttering, accusations or double-dealing, squawks of outrage and fulminations of umbrage, but all that would be water off a duck's back to Mazin. Pacifying noises would be made and the trustee would eventually agree a deal. That was Mazin's theory.

"In that case you can stick it up your arse," said the trustee quietly, and put the phone down.

Mazin heard the click and the dialling tone at the same time as the words impacted on his brain.

"Hello!!" he shouted, "Hello! Hello! Hello!"

"A cripple on a bleeding crutch!" he screamed frantically, hammering at the telephone but of course it was to no avail.

The manservant peered timidly round the door thinking he'd been called, "Yes, Excellency?"

"Get out! he howled. "Get out, you incompetent pile of pig shit! Get out of my sight! Get out! Get out of my sight or I'll kill you!"

The frustration had boiled over into temporary insanity; he was terrifying in his rage and the manservant fled to the front door and beyond fearing for his very life.

A minute cell of reason prevented him from smashing the phone to smithereens but he smashed every other item on his desk.

Silver photograph frames bearing photographs, mostly of him greeting Middle Eastern potentates, were hurled across the room to crash into the panelling, a Georgian silver inkstand ended its long life embedded in the innards of his television, having passed through the front of the tube at 90 miles an hour, the clock calendar was stamped through the next century into eternity, everything else was swept onto the floor.

Mazin sank into a chair panting with effort, his tubes bulging to bursting. Gradually his breathing slowed and the red mist faded from his eyes. He slowly got a grip of himself and reason replaced rage. He had to get that deal with Trust Services back on the rails - he just had to. The whole scene had started to run away out of control and it had all happened so unbelievably quickly. At 11 o'clock this morning everything had been going as smooth as silk. Pantocrator was a dead cert, the trustee was on the hook and IRH had assets and cash amounting to eight million safe and secure dollars stashed away in an unbreachable Swiss bank vault. It was - he looked at the diamond studded gold Rolex - it was now 1 o'clock and all four accursed wheels were falling off!

Blood and sand, his plane to Athens left in an hour and 40 minutes! He screamed for his manservant.

"Ahmed! Ahmed! Where the devil are you, you little bastard. I'll strangle you with my bare hands if you don't get in here double quick!" There was no reply. Ahmed was half a mile away steaming past The Dorchester and still going strong, with only oxygen-starved muscles slowing him down.

With the blood pressure rising into the red again Mazin searched the flat. He didn't find the manservant but he did find a packed bag in the entrance hall. He glared at the telephone for a moment wondering whether to risk another call to Jersey but decided that there wasn't time. It would be finally fatal now if he tried to rush anything, rats would be smelled and the whole thing could blow wide open, he would have to take a chance and Mazin hated taking chances. He stood at the door of the apartment block bawling for his driver. The Mercedes was there parked askew on a double yellow line, but of the driver there was no sign. That worthy, having thrown the keys into the adjacent flowerbed and let all four tyres down, was down at the nearest Job Centre re-planning his future. A, by now, almost deranged Mazin, cursing and swearing, was left with no alternative but to hunt for a passing cab. The taxi driver, bribed with an extra £10, got him to Heathrow in 35 minutes and he made the plane by the skin of his teeth.

He fumed and plotted throughout the 3½-hour flight, declining savagely all offers of food and drink, but it got him nowhere positive. That Moon and Elmes were behind these troubles somewhere, he was convinced, but the evidence for this assumption was totally non-existent. The doubts however persisted and grew. He had to cover himself now, it was no longer a question of buying control of CONDES to make a future fortune - it had become a question of saving his neck. The total effort of all the years of cheating, lying, boot-licking, browbeating, wheeling and dealing was going to be at stake if he could not see any other way for Pantocrator to get the down payment in the time. That swine Moon meant what he said about reverting to electric arc furnaces, he'd do it just to spite him and stop him getting his commission, and then lay the blame firmly for the change at Mazin's door with both the client and the IBRD. He was being painted into a corner and he didn't like the feel of that one little bit. He brightened a little, look on the positive side, he said to himself, when Pantocrator do this job you will make nearly $12 million from Sharjah Steel alone, plus whatever else could be got out of CONDES. Twelve million dollars, he rolled it around his tongue. And with the $8 million or so he had already stashed away he would be set for life. Rich and powerful.

I stuck my head around Hugo's door and told him the project meeting had finished. He acknowledged that with a wave of his hand, pushed some papers back into a file and stood up.

"I've booked a table for us at Como Lario," he said, "I hope you're in the mood for Italian."

I smiled, I had happy memories of Como Lario.

We got a private table in the back area and ordered two glasses of Barolo.

"Right," said Hugo briskly, settling himself into his chair, "give me the full picture."

I took a deep breath. "I'll start at the beginning to ensure that I've got the reasoning correct, interrupt me if you think I'm off beam.

"You and I know that Mazin Al Jabril stole $2 million from us about three years ago. We want that money back plus three years' interest.

"Mazin has come along somehow attached to this huge Sharjah Steel contract, funded by the World Bank, to which we have been appointed consultants.

"Mazin thinks he has found a sure fire way of ripping off a very large sum of money from the World Bank by using the loophole in the Bank's bidding procedures that permits a contract to be negotiated, without competition, with somebody who has something that is unique. He believes Pantocrator of Greece is the only company in the world who make a special kind of extremely high-speed furnace, and he has got himself appointed their agent.

"His brother is the Minister of Industry in Sharjah and it therefore appears to be to our advantage to appoint Mazin as our local representative, which we did before we knew about Pantocrator.

"However, we know, and Pantocrator know, that there is another company, Costa da Silva in Brazil, who also can make this type of furnace, but they are still in the prototype stage and could not come anywhere near matching Pantocrator's programme.

"Watched like a hawk by Mazin we have incorporated the LAVCHIFS into our design and used Pantocrator's quotation in our cost plan. This, we believe, includes over $8 million for you-know-who."

I looked across at Hugo, he was following me intently, his eyes screwed up and his lips in a tight line. I continued.

"Mazin is no fool, and we believe that he is fully aware that somewhere along the line we will attempt to get our money back from him.

"Now this is the crux of the matter. The only time he is vulnerable is before the contract documents are submitted, by us, to the World Bank. After that nothing can be changed, and, if Pantocrator are included and their quotation is in the cost plan, he is home and dry! So the only time we can make our move is between now and submission.

"However, there is so much money at risk for him, should we thwart his scheme, that he has to cover that vulnerability if he can, and the only sure way to do this is to gain absolute control of this firm so that no adverse decisions, adverse to him that is, can be made without his permission. And the only way he can gain control is to buy a controlling interest."

I paused for a sip of wine, Hugo was still following me intently. I continued.

"We, on our side, have worked this out and the plan was to move all the assets out of our holding company, Bridge Holdings

Limited, so that it owns and controls nothing, and allow him to buy it for at least what he owes us, plus interest.

"However, although he has taken some preliminary steps to protect himself along the lines we anticipated, he has not committed himself to anything. He hasn't needed to, up to today all has been going well for him: Pantocrator are included and his big rake-off has been covered by tightening up the programme to cut the overall costs back to the budget."

Hugo nodded, "Yes, I follow all that but where do Costa's fit in?"

"I'm coming to that," I murmured. "We want Mazin to buy Bridge Holdings but if he thinks that Pantocrator are certain to get the sub-contract then he doesn't have to."

"So?"

"So he needs a little push. Well, as big a push as we can give him actually! At present the situation is that if Pantocrator are out, Mazin doesn't lose anything, it is just that he doesn't gain anything. However, if we can structure the situation so that he has actually got funds irrevocably tied up in Pantocrator getting the job, and they don't, then he loses money. His incentive to prevent this is much greater. This morning's discussion was to move him along that road. So he's off to see Antoniades to work out how to keep Pantocrator in the frame."

I gave Hugo a smile and waited for the straight line. He saw the missing piece immediately.

"So what?"

"So, if Pantocrator want to stay in the frame, then to meet the tightened up programme - tightened up because of Mazin's greed - they have to start fabrication in two weeks' time and they won't get their signed contract and first payment until the end of June!"

"You mean they'll have to do three months work speculatively, funding it themselves without even a letter of intent?"

Hugo frowned. "Antoniades would never take that risk. And you said he knows about Costa da Silva as well? Never! Nobody in their right mind would do that..."

"Unless," I murmured, "unless he persuaded a very rich Mazin Al Jabril to fund it or else Pantocrator would pull out."

The glass of wine that was about to reach Hugo's lips stopped dead in mid-air.

"You cunning devil! Jesus, that will really put Al Jabril up at the sharp end. What is that likely to cost him up front?"

"We estimate there is about $10 million worth of work, but I think Antoniades could manage quite easily on half that if you take out profit and Mazin's 'commission'. I think he will be looking for 3-4 million from Mazin."

Hugo whistled, then another thought occurred to him. "Does Al Jabril know about Costa?"

"Good Lord no, not yet. The idea is to tell him once he has given Pantocrator his money!"

"But won't Antoniades tell him? That would blow your plan wide open."

Shaking my head I disagreed. "No, I don't think so. First of all why should he tell Mazin? Antoniades knew all about Costa da Silva long before I mentioned them. He must have known because he knew exactly what I was talking about without question when I dropped their name. It is because he knows about Costa that there is no way he is going to use Pantocrator's money for a speculative start.

"That Pantocrator would be doing this work at their own risk has been spelled out to them quite clearly in writing. Nobody can say they have been misled by us.

"Now that he knows that Mazin is well heeled he has every incentive to get out the thumb screws. He now has an alternative that not only solves his problem and eliminates this risk, but will give him personal satisfaction also.

"At the point Mazin hands his money over to Pantocrator, then I hope and pray by keeping everything we've got crossed, he has to secure both it and his future commission by taking control of Bridge Holdings."

Now Hugo is a kindly man and I could see that something was still troubling him. He wanted our money back as much as I did. After that I believed he still had, at the back of his mind, the idea that once a wrong has been righted all would be sweetness and light. Harmony would reign and, whereas it would not quite be tiptoeing through the tulips together, we would march forward arm in arm with Mazin, to tackle the future. Although Mazin had roughed him up once, since then it had been me who dealt with the Arab on a day-to-day basis. I think Hugo was not capable of conceiving that a man of Mazin Al Jabril's unprincipled vindictiveness could exist.

"I asked you where Costa da Silva fitted in and you said 'not yet'. We know that Pantocrator are going to get this job if we use LAVCHIFS, because we know that they are the only people who can do it. So why don't we just say to Al Jabril, 'There is another company who also make LAVCHIFS and unless you pay back that money that you stole from us we will recommend either that bids be invited for the LAVCHIFS or we revert back to electric arc furnaces'?"

I conceded that, on the face of it, he had a good point. "That is fine and we can certainly try it. However we know we are stuck with LAVCHIFS because they are the best for the client. The problem is that that reasoning only has force up to the point when we have to finalise the contract documents. At that point the decision has to be made whether to go for bids or nominate Pantocrator. The outcome would be the same either way because Costa can't do the job, although Mazin doesn't know that.

"But if he calls our bluff or, more likely just procrastinates to buy time, then we are lost. Knowing Mazin, the chances are heavily against him paying up on that basis so we must have a fall back position - and that is what we have set up.

"However I'll give your proposal a go, there's no harm can be done by doing so - except we could end up with a very pissed-off Mazin for the rest of the contract."

"Ah, yes," said Hugo, "but you have a plan for that? 'Plan A Plus' I believe, but you won't tell me what it is?"

I didn't want him to think I was holding out on him, it was just that it was such a flyer that I didn't want to raise his hopes unnecessarily. "It's not that. It's just that there is no certainty about it. If it comes off - all well and good. If it doesn't there will be absolutely no harm done and we will not be any worse off."

He gave me a penetrating look but didn't pursue it further. I felt somehow that he was not totally convinced.

After our lunch I returned to the office. Major Margaret was waiting for me all of a tizzy. Hopping about from one foot to the other and clutching a piece of paper to her ample bosom. At first I assumed it was a highly excitable and erotic response to the advertisements in the contact magazines, and she wanted the afternoon off to give it a go before the feeling wore off.

It transpired that wasn't the cause of her excitement, much to my disappointment, but the trustee had phoned to say that Mazin had rung the office and would I phone back urgently.

So something must be on the move at last.

I got straight through to him. "What's happened?" I asked excitedly. "Has Mazin made contact?"

"He phoned a couple of hours ago, I've been trying to get hold of you since then!"

"OK," I replied, impatient for the news, "well bring me up to date now."

"He wanted to do the deal, but at £1.5 million. Gave me some bullshit about the accounts showing volatility."

"Good, good," I said. "That's a nice high figure for him to open negotiations with. So what did you pitch in at? Three million? Three-and-a-half?"

There was a pregnant pause on the other end of the line, then, "Er, no, not exactly, I told him to stick it and put the phone down."

Now I've never been trained in boggling, I can honestly swear that secret boggling sessions have never been undertaken by me nor have I read any manuals on it. But the boggle I executed when he told me that he had cut Mazin off at the knees without a crutch, would have won the chocolate mouse at any international boggling competition.

"You what?" I choked, seeing all my carefully laid plans disappearing in one well chosen but quite specific phrase.

"I told him to stick it up his arse! Did I do wrong? I thought he was trying to cheat on what we had previously agreed and I don't want to deal with that sort of person."

"But he is a fucking cheat!" I howled. "That's the whole point of setting this up."

There was no point in blowing a fuse, it wouldn't get us anywhere, so I took a few deep breaths and patiently explained the rules.

"What he was doing was the standard negotiating ploy, he would claim that you had established your maximum figure at 2 million at your previous meeting but that he hadn't agreed to that. He has come back with a counter offer of 1.5 million expecting to settle somewhere between the two. Hopefully, in his case, closer to his 1.5 than your 2. You have just sawn him off at the knees before negotiations could commence."

The funny side of it struck me and I started to laugh, he'd have to come back I realised, he couldn't possibly leave it there, but that would have rocked him right back on his heels. He wouldn't quite know how to handle that; I could just imagine his face. Maybe we could use the situation to jack our price up - I'd think about it.

The plane's wheels bounced and spun in puffs of smoke as they hit the runway. Mazin unclipped his seat belt, grabbed his hand luggage from the overhead compartment and then stood fuming for five minutes, with his head wedged at an uncomfortable angle, whilst an old lady struggled to reach up for her battered old handbag, blocking the aisle to the exit. Eventually he lost patience, elbowed her out of the way and gained the ramp.

Not being a citizen of the EU or a Greek he had to join the long queue of miscellaneous foreigners at Immigration, most of whom either had not filled in immigration forms, or if they had, had done so incorrectly, and wait whilst these sorted themselves out. Eventually he made it through Customs with only a cursory glance and gained the outside air.

There was no car to meet him at Athens airport; he remembered with an oath that he had forgotten to phone Antoniades with his flight details, so he took a taxi to Pantocrator's plant. Antoniades was expecting him and had waited in his office.

"Have you found the funding?" Mazin enquired hopefully, as the Guccis first sank into the carpet.

Antoniades shook his massive head. "No chance, no bank here will touch it. An untried system, no contract, no letter of intent, no assets to back another loan of such magnitude - Path!" He spread his huge hands dismissively. Georgiou Antoniades was as tough as he looked. He was only 5 ft 6 tall but built like a bull. Powerful shoulders supported a head that looked as though it had been cast from slag. Great beetling brows topped craggy features into which were set the deep dark shrewd little eyes that glittered at Mazin.

Those few words drew the battle lines and Mazin metaphorically girded his loins as tightly as he could for the negotiation that lay ahead. Antoniades had got two weeks to thrash out a deal, Mazin had only two days, three at the most if he was to make Geneva and Jersey and tie that end up.

By lunchtime on the third day still no deal had been struck. Antoniades had punched, bored and reamered him well and truly, reducing Mazin to playing his final card. After pleading, with eyes full of crocodile tears, that $4 million was all he could possibly scrape up in the whole wide world even if he tore the rings from the fingers of his grey-haired crippled grandmother - Allah preserve her - he pulled his final bluff. He walked out, an apparently broken man, and headed for the airport hoping like hell that Antoniades needed this contract as much as Mazin believed he did. Antoniades played it right to the limit, testing Mazin's sphincter to the full, before fetching him back from the check-in counter and resumed negotiations. He finally accepted Mazin's offer to put up $4 million as an unsecured loan to Pantocrator at 2% over base rate, only repayable seven days after Pantocrator received their down payment on the Sharjah Steel contract. Mazin was also required to put his $4 million up by certified bank draft, drawn on a recognised international bank, within seven days from 12.00 that day. Pantocrator's lawyers drew up the deed that afternoon and both parties signed it in front of witnesses. Antoniades clapped him heartily on the back as the copies of the loan agreement were exchanged.

"Hey Mazin don't take it so bad, we're all going to make money. There is an old Greek saying 'When the tough get going the weak get stuffed' - eh?"

Mazin choked violently, he had no doubt in his mind who it was who was getting stuffed. He managed to force out a weak smile pretending that they both believed it was the client who was going to be stuffed and nodded.

You wait, you cocky Greek bastard, he was thinking, you wait till you're on site and I have control of CONDES.

I'll screw your balls off and make you eat them on this job. By God you'll sweat for this when I'm in charge.

Mazin left as soon as he could and caught the first available flight to Geneva. It had really been brown trouser day for Mazin Al Jabril, although he had at least secured seven days' grace before he had to stump up the cash, it had been at a fearful price. He gave a defiant grim smile to himself; if it suited his purpose he could still renege on the deal and would have no hesitation in doing so. A Greek contract operable under Greek jurisdiction held no fears for him. If he wanted to welsh, he could still pull out at any time within the next week and screw the Greeks. It was the only small satisfaction he had to offset the two per cent over base rate interest he had been forced down to, not the four he had wanted. Much worse was the clause Antoniades had insisted upon which meant that if no contract was signed by Pantocrator for Sharjah Steel he would never get his money back. It would be gone forever, secured for eternity in a lot of useless unfinished pieces of laser accelerated vacuum contained high induction frequency furnaces, rusting futilely away in a scrapyard in southern Greece. The thought terrified him.

There was better news awaiting him when he arrived at Dr Otto Weber's stuffy office in Geneva the following morning. Mazin had gone through his usual routine of opening his safe deposit box in Credit Suisse, taking out the bearer bond that established his ownership of Investment and Resource Holdings SA, taking the waiting cab on to Rue Gerard-Muzy and presenting both himself and the bearer bond to Advocat Doktor Weber. The lawyer was more interested in the bond than Mazin, he examined it carefully before returning it.

"Very well, Mr Al Jabril, I have the information you requested."

He slid a folded sheet of paper across his wide desk towards Mazin who, trying to appear casual, left it lying there and nonchalantly flicked it open with one finger.

Most of his cash was on 7-day deposit, with $1 million approximately on 28 day. There would be small penalties for withdrawing early from these accounts. He totted up the figures, $5,162,417.28. The lawyer interrupted. "The company's property assets have recently been revalued and the bank holding the deeds will lend 75% of valuation immediately. Repayment on demand, of course, but unofficially at six months. They would renew then, subject to a certified revaluation."

"I'll bet they would," scoffed Mazin. He added up the valuations of the various properties the company owned. It came to a further $5,750,000. Estate agents are not as precise as bankers, he thought cynically. Seventy-five per cent of that came to about $4,300,000 he calculated in his head.

That made nearly $9.5 million. He gave a snort of pleasure, at least he had conned that greasy shit Antoniades into believing that $4 million was all he had. There was the purchase of Bridge Holdings to be allowed for. He pulled at his lip thoughtfully; it looked like he would have to allow for the full £2 million plus that swine of a trustee's rake off of £200,000. He picked up his pen, £2.2 million at 1.6 to the pound; that made just over $3.5 million. By Allah that was tight, it only left $2 million to play with.

He gave instructions to the lawyer to collect all the funds into Credit Suisse and procure a draft made out to Pantocrator for the $4 million. After some further thought, with time being of the essence, he decided to gamble that the actual sight of the money, or its equivalent being dangled in front of his eyes, would be quite sufficient to persuade the trustee to grab the original deal with both hands. Reaching for his pen again he wrote two further instructions to the lawyer, the first to procure a bank draft made payable to Trust Services for the sum of $3,200,000 - approximately £2 million - and the second to procure a draft for cash to the tune of $320,000 - approximately £200,000. If they wanted it in pounds they could pay the bank's extortionate commission on the exchange themselves.

Dr Weber promised he would have these drafts by 10 o'clock on Monday morning.

Mazin went spare. "Monday!" he shouted, "I don't want them on Monday, I want them here now! Today! As soon as possible! Phone the banks this instant!" He jabbed a furious demanding finger at Weber's telephone, his face red with rage. The impassive old lawyer, shocked by such unseemly behaviour, shook his head gravely.

"I'm sorry, sir, but it is past noon now, trading has ended for the day. I can undertake the arrangements for all the money loans and transfers, but it is not possible to get the drafts until the banks officially open on Monday."

Mazin raged and fumed but, realising that it was useless to argue further, contented himself with the threat that the drafts 'better had be ready by 10 o'clock', and he took himself off in a temper to his suite at the President Hotel on Quai Wilson. Once ensconced in privacy in his rooms, he dialled Trustee Services in Jersey.

The trustee was in a meeting but would phone him back shortly.

Mazin waited impatiently marching up and down and flicking his fingers. Half an hour later the phone rang sharply catching him by surprise.

"Yes?"

"Is that Mr Al Jabril?" It was a girl's voice, but it was a different voice to the one that had replied to his earlier call. Nobody else knew he was here so he took a chance and admitted his identity.

"It is."

"It's Trust Services here, I have the trustee for you."

He heaved a small sigh of relief.

"Good afternoon, sir, very kind of you to call back." Mazin's voice oozed honey, it was definitely time for the velvet glove after Monday's fiasco.

"I am currently in Geneva, as you will be aware, and have been discussing our little misunderstanding with my principals. They didn't mean to infer that the original proposal was withdrawn, merely that there might have been room for a little movement." It was a last despairing try and it was left hanging there like a cracked cup in an AIDS hospital.

Mazin was forced to continue. "But, in view of all the circumstances, I have been authorised to continue with the original arrangements, and to that end I would be grateful if we could meet at your offices on Monday?" There was a silence and Mazin could hear pages being turned over. He hid a quiet sneer, if the trustee's diary was anything like as empty as it was on his previous visit there should be no problem.

"Yes," said the trustee in his precise voice, "at what time?"

This threw Mazin, he hadn't worked out how to get to Jersey from Geneva yet, but it was bound to be late afternoon if he had to collect the drafts at 10 o'clock.

"Late afternoon - I'll ring your secretary on Monday morning with the time. It will depend upon the flights."

"I shall look forward to our meeting, Mr Al Jabril," the trustee said dryly, and disconnected.

Mazin heaved an enormous sigh of relief, it looked as if the deal was back on the rails, but the swine had not budged on the price. What sort of a businessman was he, this amateur who insisted on keeping to a deal?

CHAPTER SIXTEEN

Since Mazin exited our humble abode on Monday it had been ominously quiet. I had telephoned his flat on Wednesday but the manservant was too terrified to say anything other than gabble that he'd gone away. Where? He wouldn't tell me. When would he be back? Nothing. How long would he be away? Zilch. So all I gathered from my very one-sided telephone conversation - if a monologue could be referred to as such - was that Mazin wasn't there and had probably departed these shores. I hoped he was in Greece locking horns with the Minotaur

Whilst Britain wept, my curiosity did not remain unsatisfied for long. Antoniades phoned me around 11.30, I was just planning what to say to 'Frank the Bank' at today's lunch - I was paying - we were 'big mates' now, Frank Jenkins and me, it was 'Frank' and 'Marcus' these days, I was no longer rated beneath Jesse James as far as banking was concerned. Antoniades' call, however, put all immediate thoughts of banking to one side, this was important.

"Hello Mr Moon," this came through the earpiece at about 100 decibels, one got the impression he believed that the telephone wire was a narrow tube and a powerful input was absolutely necessary to force speech from Athens as far as London.

Holding the earpiece at a safe distance, I didn't want to put him on the loudspeaker - the whole office would hear, I said cautiously, "Hi Georgiou, how's it going?"

I could hear the cocky exuberance in his voice as he replied, "I am pleased to tell you, Mr Moon, that we appear to have overcome our temporary financial difficulties."

Antoniades was keeping me on the hop! I wanted the full details, I wanted to know if Mazin was on the hook but couldn't ask outright - we were not supposed to be involved. He'd get round to it sooner or later - I hoped, it was vitally important to CONDES to know what had transpired, just how important Antoniades had no idea. I played along for the time being, it didn't do to become beholden. "I am pleased to hear that, Georgiou, so you will be commencing manufacture a week on Monday?" A note of caution entered his voice.

"I confidently expect to."

Now 'confidently expect to' was not the same as 'Yes', and I hadn't the inclination to play guessing games with so much at stake, so I gave it to him smack between the eyes.

"Mr Antoniades, I want concrete proof that work will start a week on Monday. If I do not get it I have no option but to inform the World Bank that LAVCHIFS are out, Pantocrator are out and arc furnaces are back in." That took the boom out of his drum. He spluttered and protested for a minute, and then opened up fully and told me the whole story about the loan deal he had negotiated with Mazin Al Jabril. He told me that the agreement had been signed and witnessed and registered that morning at the Ministry of Finance.

"But have you got the money, Georgiou?" That was the four million dollar question.

He hesitated, and, reducing his volume 50%, told me, "He has until noon next Thursday to produce a certified bank draft drawn on an international bank. We had to give him time to make the arrangements, nobody can pull $4 million out of the sky instantly."

I supposed not, but it made me nervous. I asked the other question that had formed in my mind as he had outlined his discussions with Mazin. "But $4 million is only half of the normal 10% down-payment, how can you sustain your manufacturing costs between now and the end of June on that?"

There was a short embarrassed silence whilst he decided whether or not to come clean. Whether he did I don't know but what he said reassured me.

"Mr Al Jabril has to put up his $4 million first, unconditionally, before anything happens. That will cover costs for seven to eight weeks at least. I think that then we may be able to cover the balance of costs from our own resources, but I assure you, Mr Moon, that after we have received Mr Al Jabril's injection of funds there will definitely not be a problem about funding."

I bet there wouldn't, I thought, not under those circumstances! I could just imagine negotiations that had taken place between Antoniades and Al Jabril. Both sides pleading abject and total poverty, both sides lying through their teeth and, from the chuckle that lurked in Antoniades voice as he assured me that now Mazin was on the hook then funding the balance for the early manufacturing would not present a problem, I reckoned Mazin had been well and truly screwed into putting up as much as $4 million. If the chips had been laid right down I also reckoned that, once Pantocrator knew that they had been nominated, they might have risked funding the start-up themselves. However, once Antoniades found out from me that Mazin was loaded, the eyeball-to-eyeball confrontation was inevitable and Mazin had blinked first.

I thanked him for keeping me informed and asked that he let me know as soon as Mazin handed over his draft. After putting down the phone I leaned back in my chair, propped my feet on the desk and contemplated. For the first time, a trickle of optimistic adrenalin slid into the bloodstream. Sure, things could still fall apart, but somehow I didn't think they would. The big danger was that Mazin would learn about Costa da Silva before he put up his bank draft. I thought about that again and felt satisfied. We kept them a closely-guarded secret here, and obviously there was no way Antoniades was going to let the cat out of the bag before he got Mazin's money. No, it looked as though Plan A was out of the traps and running, but they were going to be an anxious next seven days until the jaws closed irreversibly over Mazin's cash.

I asked one of the senior engineers to go to Greece to carry out the inspections of the work from Pantocrator's start date and then pushed off down the corridor to give the glad tidings to my senior director. I noticed that the Major was ominously, and unusually, silent as I passed through her domain and, come to think of it, had been like that all morning. However, I was feeling too chuffed to do anything about it now, I would tackle her later - it was probably 'the change' or something.

I stuck my head round Hugo's door.

"I've just had a call from Antoniades." He looked puzzled.

"Antoniades?"

"Yes, you remember the MD of Pantocrator, bawls like a bull."

"Has he?"

"Not has - does! And he tells me that Mazin has agreed to put up $4 million advance payment to enable Pantocrator to start work before they sign their contract."

"Half of that money was ours," Hugo said savagely, uncharacteristically missing the point - but as I hadn't explained the point to him previously I suppose I had some sympathy with his initial reaction.

"Not was Hugo - is," I corrected him. "This triggers off Plan A and as soon as Pantocrator have got Mazin's bread under lock and key, we are going to line him up fair and square and then hit him with the nasties." I watched Hugo's face slowly change from mild irritation, through incredulity to cautious exultation.

"If you mean what I think you mean, you mean that once he has committed his money to Pantocrator you will tell him about Costa da Silva?" I nodded, and continued watching as his exultation fell away. His face grew serious and concerned.

"That's all very well to give him a nasty shock, but there are two weaknesses in our plan which I am sure will not have escaped you. I trust you won't mind if I run over them for the sake of clarification?" The mild sarcasm I deflected easily with one of my most encouraging smiles.

"Go ahead," I invited disarmingly.

He studied me suspiciously. "You're a devious devil at times, Marcus Moon, but OK I'll play the straight man and feed you your lines. First, we know Costa da Silva can't do the job so Pantocrator will end up with it come what may, and Al Jabril will still get his rake off. Secondly, I do not see therefore at what point in all of this $2 million, plus interest, miraculously appears in the CONDES' credit column."

"Fair comments," I replied. "But the second point is contingent on the first point to a large extent so I'll answer your first point. What you said is not in fact correct, Costa da Silva can do the job, it is just that they can't do it as fast as Pantocrator. But who knows that - only us! Costa don't know, because they don't know Pantocrator's programme; Pantocrator don't know because they don't know even if Costa have been approached, let alone what their programme might be. Finally, if it came to a competitive bid situation, who knows what the World Bank would go for - the cheapest price? The fastest programme? Or even political considerations might dictate giving the project to Costa to reduce Brazil's international debt? So it is by no means certain that

Pantocrator will end up with the job - unless we actually nominate them as the only sub-contractor who can make these furnaces, and meet both the price and programme parameters. Brazil's debt is no concern of ours and forms no part of our brief.

"The decision therefore still lies with us, and the idea is that we suggest to Mazin that if he would be so kind as to repay the loan of $2 million we made him in 1997, plus interest at 3% over UK base rate, he would earn our undying gratitude. We also suggest that the money arrives in our bank two days before a certain date, which, coincidentally, happens to be the date on which all the design, the specifications and our reports are finalised for the Sharjah Stage One submission to the World Bank. Mazin knows that whatever is frozen on that date will be incorporated in the final design of the project. Once that submission hits the World Bank's desk there can be no going back. If we have recommended either bids for the LAVCHIFS, or even bids for electric arc furnaces, then that is what will happen. They won't over-rule us and scrap competitive bids, if that is what we have specifically recommended."

Hugo held up his hands in mock despair.

"OK, OK, I concede. The logic seems sound - and I must add that I like it, I really like it!" He chuckled to himself, "I love the loan repayment idea, it makes me feel much better."

"When does the execution take place?" he asked after a minute.

I considered my notepad and chewed the end of my pen. "He's got to produce the draft to Pantocrator by noon next Thursday, which means, I think, that he will have to take the bank draft himself, he wouldn't take the chance of anybody else handling it. We have the big CONDES Sharjah Steel project meeting the following Monday - the 13th - to finalise everything for Stage 1 ready for the printers on the Friday - that is the 17th. I think that on Monday morning, just before the project meeting, is the time to bring a little sorrow into his life. That will give him just two days to get the money. Also two days leaves him virtually no time to check Costa da Silva out. Whether he comes through or not he will know that we still have two days to change our recommendations. I doubt very much that he will repay us; in my opinion he is much more likely to seize absolute control by buying Bridge."

Hugo reached for his desk diary and blanked out the whole of the morning of Monday the 13th. "I wouldn't miss it for the world," he murmured with a grim smile, more to himself than me.

I wandered thoughtfully back towards my office through the Major's territory to be aware that she had fallen in behind me on my progress through my door.

"A word, if I may, Marcus," she said tightly as I sat down. Clutched in her hand she brandished a sheaf of miscellaneous sized and coloured sheets of paper. Oh shit, I knew instantly what they were and swore under my breath for forgetting to prepare my cover story for what was inevitably going to happen.

"Do you know what these are?" she asked aggressively.

I shook my head. "Job applications?" I suggested.

"No they are not!" she snapped. "They are a collection of the most disgusting utterances, from what I can only think are depraved perverts, that I have ever set eyes on!" I wondered briefly what other disgusting utterances she had set eyes on previously to be able to make the comparison, but sensibly refrained from asking as she continued, warming to her theme.

"Somebody, and, I suspect, somebody in this firm, has been advertising my...er, my..." (he faltered slightly - it could have been deliberate so I kept silent.) "...services, in contact magazines," she continued after the pause, "and I am very, very annoyed about it!" She plonked the offending bundle of correspondence on my desk and stood, arms akimbo, glaring at the world in general and, I suspected, me in particular. Now this situation had opened a whole lot of possibilities and it was going to be difficult to pick the right response without increasing her suspicions let alone allaying them.

What I actually wanted to know was if there were any good offers included amongst the dross, but as I wasn't supposed to know any details, other than what she had just told me, that line could not be followed - at least as a direct question. I also was dying to read all the replies just to see what response the carefully worded ads had elicited that so incensed her.

There was also the question of the identity of her suspect, and it was a toss-up between pursuing that line or asking her what 'services' she was offering that she didn't want advertised. One look at her flushed, angry face ruled any flippancy out of the question, calming noises were the order of the day, not pokes in the eye with a sharp stick.

"It's probably just someone in the drawing-office with a misguided sense of humour, I shouldn't worry about it Margaret," I said soothingly.

"Worry!" she exclaimed indignantly. "Worry, I'm not worried, I just want to get my hands on whoever is responsible, for five minutes, and I'll show you who'd be worried then."

I eyed those big hands apprehensively, I'd seen those knocking shit out of Brian Mason's computer and it was becoming easy to believe my own propaganda about her abilities in unarmed combat.

"Er well, I suggest that you leave these with me Margaret," I said encouragingly, "and I will look into it with the design office manager."

She hesitated momentarily, a flicker of doubt in her eyes at this unforeseen suggestion, and then said, "Very well, Marcus,

I'll leave it with you but I'll just keep a couple of these for the time being."

She reached over and whipped two handwritten letters from the top of the pile before I could read anything on them. I noticed that they were both neatly written and one appeared to have a photograph pinned to it. There was something slightly devious about this move and she looked away quickly as I shot her a quizzical glance.

"Is there anything else?"

"No," she replied, "but don't forget you're having lunch with Mr Jenkins today."

She retired to her den with the two letters clutched tightly at the side away from me having neatly changed the subject. I chewed a thoughtful lip as I locked the remaining letters away in a drawer for future analysis at a more convenient time. Maybe, just maybe...?

Lunch with Frank Jenkins was a duty not a pleasure, at least it was for me. Nobody would describe him as a bundle of fun at the best of times. He certainly was not one of those souls who would die of laughter, but for a small, thin man he could wield a knife and fork with the best of them - particularly if somebody else was footing the bill - as I would be today.

That was the dark side of the day. After him would come the sunshine. Zoe and I were going out to supper - very casual - at the house of one of her friends in Putney. Friday had become our regular evening for doing something together and, if work permitted, we both tried to make lunch each Tuesday. Tonight she was picking me up in her VW Golf at 7.30. Drinks and supper 7.45 to 11.30ish, back to her flat by 12.00, and back to Palmerston Mansions late Saturday morning for a clean shirt! Life was good!

I sat there for a few minutes wrapped in a happy daydream, until Margaret poked her head round the door and reminded me,

"You're booked at 'Sarti's' at 1 o'clock, and you've got to collect Mr Jenkins first. You'll be late if you don't leave now."

Was that a smile on her face? If it was it was a sudden mood change from the angry lady who had fulminated in my office earlier. Sadly there was no time for further investigation so I grabbed my jacket and pushed off for my lunch with 'Frank the Bank' feeling chirpier than I had done for days.

Over lunch, whilst Frank Jenkins droned on about limited recourse finance and back-to-back loan margins, I was thinking over my last talk with the trustee. If Mazin had opened the door to a renegotiation we should stick our foot in first.

When I arrived back at the office the trustee was waiting for me in Reception with a grin on his face. My heart leapt. He gave me the thumbs up. "Al Jabril had made contact again, we've arranged to meet in Jersey late Monday afternoon."

"Phew, thank God for that, I was getting nervous," I admitted. "What about price? Did you discuss money?" I asked, hoping against hope that they hadn't.

He shook his head. "Nope, he flannelled around a bit trying to extract himself from the pit he had dug, and referred to the original deal, but actual amounts were not mentioned."

"Right," I said decisively, "this is what we'll do. When you meet on Monday tell him the price has gone up to £2¼ million for buggering you about, and let him negotiate you down - but not below two mill. It's essential that we keep him on the hop now so that he doesn't have time to think, because he's no mug, but if we can get him running every which way but straight, and keep him off balance, he will panic and maybe miss something that might normally set off his alarm bells. String him out a bit longer until we know for sure that he's impaled on the Pantocrator hook, and then, when he's really panicking, we nail him."

"You mean I sell the shares and collect the money?"

I looked at him steadily, now was the moment of truth. This was Plan A Plus. My own piece of forward thinking to try to ensure a life strife-free from Mazin Al Jabril for the next few years. Neither Hugo nor Brian Mason knew the details of 'Plus'. Hugo, because his sense of fair play would compel him to think that it was too severe, too over-the-top; and Brian, because I thought he would consider it 'not cricket' and possibly illegal. 'Not the sort of thing a chap should do'. I took a deep breath.

"Not just that," I said calmly, "there is more to it than that. The position as I see it is that Mazin has told you that he is acting for a Swiss company who want to buy the 75% of shares the CONDES Trust holds in Bridge Holdings Limited."

He nodded.

"How do you know that that is true? As trustee you couldn't reasonably sell a huge block of shares for a large sum of money to some stranger that wandered in off the street claiming he represented some unknown foreign outfit - even if he produced the money. You are bound to satisfy yourself that the purchaser is bona fide, and you're bound to get the written permission of the directors of BHL to approve the sale - The Memorandum of Agreement and Articles of Association of the company say so. The latter is no problem, Hugo and I will give you that today in writing, but you must also be satisfied about the purchaser." I raised a questioning eyebrow. "Normally how would you do that?"

He screwed up his face pensively.

"Well, I suppose one should ask for certified copies of the board minute of the purchaser's board of directors approving that the purchase be done, and require to see the certified power of attorney for whoever was acting for the purchaser, to do it."

"OK, fine. Well wait until he has pen poised to sign and then ask him to produce them! Say, 'Can't do the deal without them'!"

He looked stunned. But if he hasn't got them he'll have to go all the way back to Switzerland to collect all that paperwork - and it will take days."

"Or he'll have to do something else that will satisfy you - and the authorities," I added, as if as an afterthought.

He frowned. "Like what?"

I smiled. "Like producing bearer shares showing that he actually controls the company - which he does incidentally."

"OK, so he produces them, then we do the deal?"

I smiled again, this was not easy but we were getting there.

"No, you give him the BHL share certificate and take his certified bank draft, but the Jersey authorities will wish to satisfy themselves that the transaction is properly executed and the purchase is bona fide."

He frowned even more. "What Jersey authorities? I didn't know that the Jersey authorities came into this."

"Do you know that they don't?"

"Well, not for certain."

"Neither does Mazin. So when you tell him that you have to produce the evidence, either certified board minutes sealed by the company and notarised by a notary public plus his Power of Attorney; or the equivalent of these, in this case the bearer shares, to the Jersey authorities to enable them to register the share transfer and change of ownership, he will have to believe you!

"He won't like it one little bit but there's nothing else he can do if he wants to be the owner of Bridge Holdings Limited."

"Won't he dispute this and check up?"

"He won't have time to dispute it! Look, the timing is crucial. He is coming to see you late Monday afternoon. You tell him you want more money, so he has to go back to Geneva to get it. He has to be in Athens before noon on Thursday to give Pantocrator their draft, so he can't get to Jersey again before Friday. On Friday, when he turns up to do the deal, you tell him you need either certified notarised board minutes or bearer shares; he can't get the latter till Monday because of the weekend. He dare not miss the Sharjah project meeting about the furnaces at our offices on the Monday morning - when we will hit him with the Costa da Silva bombshell. So he will have to fly to Geneva in the afternoon, in a panic, to pick up the bearer shares on Tuesday morning. Hence the earliest he can present you with the bearer shares is Tuesday afternoon."

"And then what...?"

The trustee was nearly there.

"Then you fold up your tent and steal away in the middle of the night, boarding the night ferry to Portsmouth, with his bearer shares, and the bank drafts, clutched tightly in your hot sticky hand!"

The Arabic allusion tickled my sense of humour and I couldn't help but smile at the shock registering on the trustee's face.

There was a long pause as stunned astonishment was slowly replaced by practical realization.

"Jesus Christ! Christ almighty, Marcus, he'll go mad when he finds out! Total bananas!"

I gave a happy smile. "Yes, won't he! And whose going to tell him? We'd better draw lots to pick the winner!"

The trustee sat back in his chair whilst he thought it over. "Do you really think it will work?"

"Why not? By then Mazin will be whizzing about from pillar to post not knowing whether it's Monday, raining or breakfast time. He will have a deadline to be at the Sharjah Steel finalisation meeting in this office at lunchtime on Wednesday, which he cannot miss, otherwise his Pantocrator deal, and his $4 million, go down the chute. Yes, it'll work if you can pull it off."

The trustee shook his head in amazement and then started to laugh. At that point I knew he could and would do it.

CHAPTER SEVENTEEN

Although the flight from Geneva was delayed for an hour, 'due to the late arrival of the incoming aircraft' causing Mazin palpitations, in the event he had reasonable time to catch the connecting flight to Jersey. The afternoon flight was not full and he had a row of three seats to himself. No sweaty plebeians to discomfort him. The plane touched down at 4.25, and by 4.50 he was outside the shabby offices of Trust Services. Just about to barge in in his usual blustering way, he paused for an instant, caution ringing alarm bells in his brain. This was the big deal, the once in a lifetime chance to make it into the real big-time, there was no point in antagonising that asshole of a trustee until he had got what he wanted. And he had to get it, those fools in CONDES were up to something, of that he was certain and it had to do with the Pantocrator affair. Moon had definitely been too smug, too confident at their last meeting, and if life had taught Mazin anything it was that nobody, but nobody, was going to just lie down and take it, after being so obviously and cold-bloodedly separated from $2 million. They must be planning something. The chill breath of fear prickled his neck, and, whether they knew it or not, now was when he was most vulnerable. He drew a deep breath to get the oxygen into the brain, thinking that that situation would change dramatically in the course of the next few minutes.

He pushed the door open and, exuding the confidence he did not feel, walked in. They were expecting him, the young girl in the office on the right was on her feet as soon as she recognised him. He handed over his camelhair coat and watched whilst she carefully put it on a hanger and hung it from a hook behind the door. She said, "The trustee is expecting you, Mr Al Jabril," and set off up the wooden stairs. He followed.

The trustee greeted him with a brief handshake and motioned him to the battered leather chair in front of the desk.

He asked Mazin if he'd like a coffee or tea, and, when it was declined, dismissed the girl with a brief smile and a "Thank you, Carol."

Mazin studied him carefully, he looked much the same as before, same pale face, same lank dark hair, same old suit even the same striped tie. His shirt was different, today it was pale blue with no sign of fraying.

There was something else different also, something much more disturbing than the fact that the trustee had two shirts. At their last meeting his senses had detected that subtle scent of fear that is present when predator and prey encountered each other in confined spaces. The trustee had been subordinate, almost ineffectual; he'd needed propping up and reassurance, he'd been timid and hesitant. Greedy, yes, but then that sort of person was always more susceptible to temptation than the strong. The weak and ineffectual generally have never had much, and blame most of their misfortunes on those who have. Mazin knew how to play on this cleverly and, by giving the consciences of the 'have nots' an out, it became easy to manipulate that bitterness to be used against the 'haves'. To his increasing concern, he became aware that this time the trustee's demeanour was different. He might look the same insignificant person in the same shabby office, but this time he met Mazin's stare eyeball to eyeball with remarkably astute eyes, and eventually, in order not to provoke a confrontation before he had done his deal, it was Mazin who dropped his gaze first, covering his defeat by speaking.

"I apologise for the slight misunderstanding over the phone last week but I can now confirm that my principals definitely wish to proceed with the acquisition of the CONDES Trust's shares on the basis we agreed at our last meeting."

The trustee had still not lowered his gaze and now sat back in his chair examining Mazin carefully. He spoke in his precise clear voice.

"So that there is no misunderstanding, let me set out your proposition again, Mr Al Jabril. The company you represent, Investment and Resource Holdings SA of Geneva, wish to buy from the CONDES Trust the 75% of the share capital that it holds in Bridge Holdings Limited?"

Mazin nodded, "Yes precisely, for £2 million as we agreed."

"And you have fully satisfied yourselves regarding this company? You will be prepared to sign a disclaimer confirming that that is so, and that at no time have you relied upon any information whatsoever provided by me personally, or Trust Services Limited, or that you have even asked us for any information about this company?"

Mazin sneered mentally at that, it was a typical lawyer or accountant's ploy to make sure that their noses were clean if ever the shit hit the fan. He nodded again dismissively, "Of course."

The trustee continued, still giving Mazin the double eye whammy, "And there is one final thing, Mr Al Jabril, that I must bring to your attention. So far we have only had discussions, I have not agreed anything."

Mazin jerked upright, a spasm of alarm flashing through his mind. "And what is that supposed to mean?" Adding pointedly, "I thought it was agreed that you would receive £200,000 for the assistance you have given. Assistance which you now require me to deny in writing that you have provided," he sneered.

The trustee interrupted. "What it means, Mr Al Jabril, is that the deal is still negotiable - as you so clearly demonstrated in your telephone call. The shares are for sale, that I confirm, but I think I would not be doing my duty as a trustee if I were not to get the best price possible."

"And just what do you think that is?" snarled Mazin dangerously, torn between total blind panic and sheer cold-blooded murder. At least the shares were available, that was something. The trustee must have sensed the thread because he eased off the pressure and leant forward to pick up his pen. "I have done a few calculations myself," he said quietly, "and I think that £2.5 million is the correct figure."

Mazin had to grit his teeth tightly to restrain his explosion, he knew it would only be counter productive to rant and rage; this guy, for all his nondescript appearance, was showing steel. The abrupt termination of his phone call still dominated his thoughts, he didn't want - couldn't risk - a repeat of that.

Some cold reason was necessary here. Mazin pulled himself together and feeling in his inside pocket drew out his crocodile skin wallet.

"I have here two certified bank drafts drawn on Credit Suisse, one for..." he read the amount on the draft "...$3,200,000, and one made payable to cash for $320,000."

"Equating to £2 million and £200,000," commented the trustee impassively.

"Yes," replied Mazin, and laid them flat temptingly on the desk in front of the trustee.

"Well, you'll just have to get some more - for both," the trustee observed, with a faint twitch of the lips. "Because the price is £2.5 million and I think my fee is too low at 10%, 15% would be more appropriate, don't you think?" Mazin goggled like a freshly rogered bullfrog, temporarily stunned out of his mind. This little shit was now trying to turn him, Mazin Al Jabril, over.

"You, what?" he managed to gargle out, as the blood suffused his neck and face. "No, I don't think it would be more fucking appropriate. I don't even think £2.5 million is appropriate as you put it, I think it's absolute daylight robbery."

"OK," said the trustee agreeably. "Let's accept that it's daylight robbery but nevertheless that is the figure - in pounds," he added. Mazin swallowed hard, at least the deal was still on, the haggle now was between £2.5 million and $3,200,000, it should not be beyond his negotiating powers in dealing with this nondescript to settle closer to the latter figure. If he conceded the trustee a slightly increased percentage for himself to start with, he would be less inclined to push too hard for his client in the big bucks field.

They negotiated for a further half hour, the trustee finally agreed to accept payment in dollars plus a further $250,000 for the shares and a fee of 12% of the total deal. Mazin confirmed he would arrange it and they agreed to meet again at 9.30 the following morning.

After repairing to Longueville Manor and up to his suite he telephoned Dr Otto Weber at his office. Fortunately Weber was still working. Although he got the same negative reaction about taking instructions over the phone, Mazin eventually persuaded the lawyer that nothing would be prejudiced if he just made the arrangements for further bank drafts for a $250,000 for the shares, and $94,000 for the trustee. The instruction would be confirmed in writing by Mazin, before he collected both the Pantocrator draft and the new ones, during his forthcoming Wednesday visit to Geneva on his way to Athens. Dr Weber thought it over for a few moments and accepted that this was possible. Mazin replaced the telephone and sank into the deep armchair. He was nearly there now unless that asshole of a trustee changed his mind. He reviewed the position to see if there was even the remotest possibility of a crack. Starting with the money - he always started with the money, it was an incontestable fact of life, no matter how willing the flesh - no money, no project. For Sharjah Steel the money was available, it was set in tablets of stone in the IBRD's budgets. It had been approved by all the committees and finally by the Director General himself. It was therefore 100% committed. He examined the other end, the Sharjah end, the construction of the steel plant could be cancelled but the only person with the authority to make that decision was the Minister - his brother. A cruel smile flickered across his lips - there was not likely to be a problem there. The file he kept on his brother's darker activities would ensure that his big, soft westernised brother would spend at least ten years rotting behind bars in a Sharjah jail if he didn't toe the line. Only a major war could disrupt the project, and he didn't believe the Americans would allow such a thing to happen at that end of the Gulf. It would not be in their interests.

He then went on to analyse his part in it. The consultants, CONDES, controlled the project; they made all the major decisions, the decisions important to Mazin involving hundreds of millions of dollars. Admittedly they were overseen by both the World Bank and the Ministry of Industry in Sharjah, but that would not present any difficulties to a man of Mazin's skill. With total control of CONDES, and manipulated skilfully, it would be a gold mine. His pulse quickened at the thought of the opportunities that would be presented. Both he and his accountants had checked out Bridge Holdings Limited, the CONDES Group holding company, and it was worth over twice what he was paying, it was still a bargain in spite of that miserable little turd of a trustee winding up the price. He had even got the last management accounts, which only served to confirm the value. Nobody apart from him and the trustee knew he wanted to buy the company, and the trustee had only known that for a couple of weeks or so. Nobody else had a clue. He rubbed his hands together, a shrewd operator could make a real killing out of this before anybody caught on.

And Pantocrator; any slight risk there would be totally removed when he controlled CONDES. Pantocrator would be nominated, and Mazin would screw that bastard Antoniades into the ground financially. He could wind up with another $3-4 million there alone.

He smiled with quiet satisfaction, he had the whole thing tied up tighter than a eunuch's balls. If those cretins Moon and Elmes thought they had something tricky going there to turn him - Mazin Al Jabril - over, they were going to get a paralysing and devastating surprise. He could hardly wait to sock it to them, arrogant swine, and if they didn't like it they could either lump it or go. It was a happy thought, he mulled it over undecided whether it would be better to fire them regardless, they could be nothing but a constant source of trouble if they remained in executive positions. No, he had a better idea, Moon would definitely get the bullet, straight out on his ear, Elmes - well maybe it would be better for the business if he remained, perhaps for a couple of years in some figurehead position like chairman, but with no executive authority whatsoever. For himself, the title of chief executive would suit, it had the ring of authority commensurate with his anticipated new status.

He fell asleep that evening designing his own personal CONDES stationery. Something that was on hand-laid notepaper headed, 'From the office of the Chief Executive', with, underneath printed in gold, 'Mazin Al Jabril'. He slept soundly.

His meeting the following morning with the trustee was fairly brief, Mazin confirmed that the extra drafts were being prepared. The trustee said, 'OK, deal now agreed', and they shook hands on it, which made Mazin smile inwardly - these westerners, would they never learn. The trustee undertook to prepare the share transfer documents, the new share certificate and the disclaimer. Mazin confirmed he would be back in Jersey by the same afternoon flight in three days' time, on Friday. He took with him the two certified drafts although the trustee suggested they could be locked in his safe for security. Does he think I was born yesterday, reflected Mazin wearily, as he walleted the two slips of paper and took his leave. The only late morning flight to the UK was a flight to Southampton. He caught that, and took the train from Southampton to Waterloo arriving at his flat mid-afternoon.

After instructing his manservant to book him to Athens via Geneva the next day, he phoned the exclusive escort agency he and other rich Arabs used and asked them to send round two blonde girls in half-an-hour, they already had his special requirements.

After a foam jacuzzi, and an energetic night which left both girls bruised, bleeding and richer by £1000, he felt a new man and caught the early plane to Geneva enjoying a buoyant optimism.

Thursday morning found him breakfasting in his suite at the Athens Hilton. The cheerfulness had slowly evaporated as the time to hand over an irrevocable draft for $4 million with no collateral drew closer. Nagging doubts grew larger and closed in upon him, maybe he would be better hanging on to his $4 million together with the money to purchase CONDES, and live out his life in the comparative luxury that that would provide. It would be the easy way - the no risk, no aggravation - way, but what would happen if he did. Elmes and Moon – pah! - they didn't count, he had already beaten those two, they were losers. He thought then of his brother, the high and mighty Minister. 'His Excellency', would crap on him from a great height if he pulled out now. That would be really bad news, and his brother carried clout, not only with the family but throughout Arabia. The word would go round the majlis' and private rooms of the Middle East that Mazin Al Jabril couldn't hack it when the big chips were down. Today they might hate him but by Allah they respected and in some cases even feared him. If he pulled out now Antoniades would spread it through the Mediterranean like wildfire that he was a no-account bullshitter who fell off the pot when called upon to piss. The respect he had would vanish - he would be a no no. Nobody would touch him for a decent deal ever again, they would always be frightened he would crap out when things got crucial.

'When the tough get going, the weak get stuffed'. That had been his maxim, but that was what he did to other people, now that sod Antoniades had used it against him. Him! Him weak? But that's what they'd say about him if he didn't go through with this deal.

That was what Mazin really believed in his heart of hearts, and that was why he went along and handed the draft to Antoniades before 12 noon, taking the receipt and flicking it into his slip briefcase with a contemptuous nonchalant gesture as though it was a mere bagatelle to a man of financial stature.

He didn't realise that nobody in the Middle East - or elsewhere for that matter - gave a monkey's toss about Mazin Al Jabril or his tricky deals. Those that knew him, and that included his brother, thought of him as a cheapskate, a wheeler-dealer spiv; and, in spite of his flashy suits and his veneer of sophistication, they wouldn't have given him even a sniff of any decent sized operation unless they had no alternative.

Antoniades despatched the draft by courier to the bank immediately and instructed the man to telephone the instant it hit the deposit account. When the confirmatory call came through he nodded briefly, put the phone down and gave Mazin a smile.

It was the first time Mazin had seen Antoniades smile, he didn't want to see Antoniades smile at him again. It was the sort of smile that Vlad the Impaler might have given on contemplating the Eiffel Tower.

"We can now begin, Mr Al Jabril. It is a great day for both of us, perhaps a small celebration to toast our joint endeavour?" He paused, one finger raised. "Before that, however, we must confirm to CONDES that all is in place and manufacture will commence Monday as programmed."

He rapidly dictated the letter in Greek and gave instructions for both the Greek, together with the English translation, to be faxed to CONDES in London immediately. He then ordered the ouzo and water.

Mazin - being a Moslem, albeit non-practising - was not a heavy alcohol drinker. Antoniades - being a Greek industrialist - was. It was no contest. Four hours later, more stoned than an Arabian adulteress, they dumped the unconscious agent on to his bed in the Hilton and left him, with a copy of the Pantocrator letter to CONDES stuffed into his jacket pocket, to sleep it off.

Ouzo is wicked stuff and, for those not used to it, it can do things to the constitution that one could really do without. Mazin did with! Vomiting, splitting headache, no sleep, diarrhoea, sweating, stomach cramps, he suffered the lot, until by the time dawn broke over the Acropolis, a sight he was not able to appreciate, he was willing to settle for death rather than continue.

The hotel doctor was summoned, a man very experienced in two fields of medicine, venereal diseases and booze, and, with no sympathy whatsoever, gave him a jab in the arse, a box of pills and some blocker to swallow. He charged him $100 for the privilege, got roundly cursed for his pains and departed with a happy smile. At least the treatment enabled Mazin to move. He checked his wallet in a blind panic, thank God the other drafts were there.

A shower removed the sweat and vomit but he was still feeling like death when the cab dropped him at Hellenikon Airport for the 9.25 flight to London. It was the worst flight he had ever had in his life. Turbulence over the Alps didn't help, and eventually he just locked himself in the lavatory and stayed there, refusing to come out even when the plane landed at Heathrow. The remonstrations of the crew sloughed off him as he grabbed his bag and shouldered his way through the passengers and up the ramp. He had three hours before the Jersey flight was due to be called so he checked in at the Heathrow Hotel and gave strict instructions that he was to be woken at 2.30 precisely before collapsing on to the bed.

Feeling better, but still fragile, he was shown up the stairs to the trustee's office as usual. This time he accepted strong black coffee. The trustee surveyed him dispassionately but quizzically. "A touch of flu, I think," muttered Mazin.

"I'm sorry," sympathised the trustee, "there seems to be a lot of it about."

Mazin was not in the mood for idle chat, he could feel the nausea building up again.

"Have you got all the documents for me to sign. I have here the drafts all drawn on Credit Suisse."

He laid them on the desk in front of him like a three card trick.

The trustee went to the old safe in the corner of the room and removed a plastic folder. The top document in the folder was an imposing printed sheet with a large red seal in the bottom right-hand corner - the share certificate. A piece of paper that seemed so relatively small and yet meant so much. Mazin resisted the temptation to grab it. The trustee slid all the documents out of the folder and separated them. He showed them to Mazin.

"This is the share transfer document which confirms the transfer of 75,000 ordinary shares of £1 each from Trustee Services Limited to Investment and Resource Holdings SA for the consideration money of £2,156,000 at Monday's rate. It needs to be signed here and here."

Mazin loosened his thin gold pen in readiness and reached over for the document. The trustee put his hand on it.

"Now if you will let me have the notarised copy of the minutes of the IRH board meeting confirming the offer, plus a copy of your authority to act on the company's behalf, we can get the formalities completed in five minutes?"

Mazin froze, his expression hanging there like a crucified saint.

"What fucking minutes?" he croaked eventually.

The trustee looked puzzled. "I need the minutes authorising the purchase. How else do I know who is buying these shares? I have to register the purchaser with the authorities and I need proof!" The nausea swept over Mazin, of course he should have realised that, these bureaucratic bastard Brits always had to have pieces of paper for everything. He gave it one last try.

"But you know who I am, and anyway as long as you - the company - get the money what the hell does it matter who buys the shares?"

The trustee was inflexible. "I'm sorry, Mr Al Jabril, but apart from what you personally have told me, which is entirely unsubstantiated, I don't know anything. I must have the proper authorisations from you otherwise I cannot register the transfer. It's as simple as that!" Mazin groaned inwardly, it was by no means 'as simple as that'. It was unbelievably complicated.

"What exactly do you need?" he asked wearily.

"Two things," said the trustee precisely. "One, a copy of the minutes of the board meeting of IRH which authorises the company to make an offer to Trustee Services Limited for the shares in question and specifying the price. And two, authority from the directors of the company appointing you to act on their behalf in this transaction. Both documents," he added, "should be notarised by a notary public and certified by the local Chamber of Commerce - Geneva I believe, in this case."

Mazin groaned audibly this time, there was no way he could get this done in a month of Sundays. Weber didn't know anything about what he was doing and had made it quite clear that he wouldn't accept instructions over the telephone. It would mean going to Geneva again, sorting it all out with Weber, drawing up some minutes, getting all the directors together and carting the lot down to some notary for him to witness their signatures and from thence to the Geneva Chamber of Commerce. The Chamber of Commerce could take days to authenticate the notary's stamp and signature. And one little error and he'd have to go through the whole lot again. Waves of sickness swept over him and he gasped, "Where's the toilet?"

The trustee pointed him down the short passage to a room at the top of the stairs and he shot in, bolting the door. He sat there on the lid holding his head in both hands, desperately swallowing like fury to hold down the bile. Sweat formed on his brow and his head throbbed. He was not a happy Mazin at that moment. There must be a simpler way than all that performance, there just had to be - and then he had it. He didn't like it, not one little bit, in fact it could be risky, but there just was not sufficient time to collect all the garbage that the officious little turd wanted. It would mean breaking his cherished rule of anonymity but it could be the way out.

After five minutes of heavy swallowing, and a sip of water from the tap, he felt recovered enough to emerge. The trustee was solicitous. "My word you have got a dose of something nasty there, Mr Al Jabril. Would you like an aspirin?"

Mazin accepted and swallowed a couple, they might help the head.

He turned to the trustee and forcing a weak smile blurted out, "If I could prove to you that it was me that controlled the company would you be prepared to accept instructions from me then?"

The trustee raised his eyebrows. "But you have told me that your principals in Switzerland control the company. How can you control it also?"

Squirming with embarrassment Mazin confessed that it had all been a convenient fabrication to conceal his own interests. He was sure the trustee would understand, operating in Jersey as he did, that such things happened to international business in order to avoid jealous rivals and unwanted interest from enquiring tax authorities.

Nodding gently the trustee enquired, "Very well, accepting that, how are you going to prove to me, and to the authorities, that you control IRH?"

Mazin drew in a deep breath, held his nose and jumped into the deep-end. "I hold all the shares as bearer shares," he confessed.

"I see," mused the trustee thoughtfully. "Well I suppose if you were to present the bearer shares to me that would be sufficient authority to enable the share transfer to take place. Yes, I think that would be acceptable."

Mazin folded up with relief, that would not present any problem at all, and Weber would not need to learn anything about the deal until it was done. He was just congratulating himself on tying it all up when the trustee's dry voice cut in.

"There is one other matter, Mr Al Jabril, a matter of arithmetic."

Mazin nodded, listening with half an ear, he was planning his trip to Geneva and back to collect the bearer shares. "And what might that be?" he asked disinterestedly."

The trustee gave a dry cough. "It is the agency commission?"

Mazin looked up sharply. "What about it? We agreed 12% and that's what you've got - give or take a few cents."

Shaking his head sadly the trustee corrected him. "No, Mr Al Jabril, what we agreed was 12% of the total deal, and the total deal includes my fee. That means I should receive..." He did a quick calculation... "$470,450." He pointed to the cash draft lying on the desk, "Not $414,000."

Mazin groaned as another stomach cramp seized his intestines. What was happening to him? It should all have been so straightforward, or as straightforward as normal with his warped business methods. He put up token resistance, but for once in his life he could not bring any convincing power to his bargaining, he just wanted to lie down.

"Alright! I'll bring another accursed bank draft when I return with the bearer shares," he ground out bitterly. By the Prophet's bones he'd be glad to be out of this morass, it seemed ever deeper and time was rapidly running out.

He gritted his teeth, he just had to stay with it for another few days. Today was Friday, neither bankers nor lawyers worked over the weekend so that was dead time. He must be at the big CONDES meeting on Monday; that was the meeting that should finally confirm Pantocrator as nominated sub-contractor for the furnaces. He dare not miss that. If he flew to Geneva on Monday afternoon, picked up the bearer shares from Credit Suisse as soon as they opened Tuesday morning, collected the new draft from Weber and caught the earliest possible flight back to London he could just make Jersey by late afternoon again. By Allah, it was tight. He swore violently to himself. Somebody was going to pay for all this hassle sooner or later, there was not much he could do to the weedy little sod smirking in front of him, but by the Prophet, Moon and Antoniades were going to pay, and pay dearly. Maybe he wouldn't fire Moon, maybe he could publicly humiliate him first, then fire him. Antoniades, he would screw into the ground later. He would work on the idea, it would brighten up what looked like being a dull evening.

He turned to the trustee. "I'll be back on Tuesday at the same time. I'll telephone if there's any change."

He swept up all the bank drafts from the desk and tucked them away. The trustee locked the share transfer documents in the safe.

With the briefest of nods Mazin gingerly walked out of the office to find the nearest hotel bed.

CHAPTER EIGHTEEN

"My word, Margaret, you do look nice this morning." It was a risky thing to say but it was true, she was done up like a dog's dinner this fine sunny March Monday morning, for what reason I didn't know but no doubt all would be revealed in due course. I felt a stab of conscience as I looked at her and took in her nicely coiffured hair, smooth make-up, twin set and single rope of pearls. For all she was pushing 50 she looked very attractive. A qualm assailed me as my previous fears resurrected themselves, but she coloured up and looked sheepish, embarrassed even, not the sort of reaction of one who has set out her stall to attract a customer – particularly if the customer was intended to be me. No, this display was clearly not intended for me, the embarrassed look was semi-apologetic - very perplexing.

"Thank you kind sir," she replied with an attempt at Elizabethan humour, but I could see she was warily judging my reactions.

I didn't quite know what to make of this so to cover my temporary confusion I gabbled, "Oh, by the way the design office manager is still looking into the business of those letters, but so far no real results - but he has his suspicions."

To my surprise she dismissed the subject. "It's not of any consequence now," she replied, "just some practical joker I expect. Boys will be boys I suppose, and at least it shows that some members of this firm have a lively wit. It doesn't matter, Marcus, there's no point making a song and dance about it."

I carefully refrained from pointing out that the 'strangling with bare hands' was not singing or dancing, nor was it my proposal in the first place and contented myself with a mystified, "Oh! OK then," before sliding through into my den to try to absorb the significance of these events.

'Now what?' I puzzled. She had said 'it didn't matter now'. The inflection in her voice as she said 'now' clearly meant now that something else had happened. I wondered what it was. Well, there was only one way to find out. I went back into her office, she was singing a little tune as she fed a new disk into the computer but turned at my entry.

"What did you mean by 'now' Margaret?" I asked her gently. "What has happened to brighten up our lives over the last few days?"

She immediately coloured up again. "Oh it's nothing, Marcus, it's probably just me being a silly woman." She turned back to her disk feeding, but I was not going to be put off as easily as that. A 'silly woman' was not a description that would readily apply to Major Margaret Braithwaite WRAC. Besides, there was the singing, she had never even hummed in the office before, let alone launched into extracts from West Side Story.

"Come on Margaret, you can tell me - something is making you cheerful. What's the good news?"

She heaved a sigh and turned round.

"Alright, I'll tell you. I've met a man."

"So?"

"Well, I like him and I think he likes me."

"I'm delighted for you, Margaret, when did this come about?"
She looked embarrassed again.

"Last week," she said. "His was one of the only nice letters in that bunch from depraved perverts that wrote to me. Richard and I are having dinner tonight. He's taking me to the Savoy."

She looked down nervously as she told me this as though she expected me to object. I swallowed hard, this was a bit tricky, it looked as if my plan might have worked and quicker than expected. When in doubt be non-committal, that was my thinking.

"Well I hope you and Richard have a lovely evening," I said with a tight smile, and pushed off back to the seclusion of my own office. At least she was no longer after the blood of the unknown ad inserter. I would have to keep a close eye on the situation but the pressure was off to find the perpetrator of that dastardly deed - I could relax in that respect.

In other matters, however, today was going to be all action, and the Major's love affair would have to sort itself out, for today was the day Hugo and I had been looking forward to for three long, hard years. Today was the real start of Mazin's come-uppance.

Antoniades' letter - both the Greek and English versions lay in front of me on my desk. With them lay a second translation from a local language bureau - I wasn't going to be caught like that again. I compared the two, they were virtually identical. So Mazin had been separated from 4 million of his dollars finally and irrevocably, he and his money had at last been parted and there was no way Georgiou was going to hand that lot back. He was now cracking on with at least a $4 million contract whatever happened! I slipped the letters back into the Pantocrator General file and pushed it to one side. I pulled the Costa da Silva files to me but did not open them, I was wondering exactly how to play this.

The Major put my coffee down with a couple of chocolate-coated oatmeals. I glanced up at her and she smiled back. There was still something in her eyes, but it was now as if she was apologetic rather than affectionate. A touch of guilt tweaking her conscience perhaps, because Richard had supplanted me as front runner in whatever race she had laid out in her mind for which she was first prize. It was a tricky situation, the last thing I needed was for her to think that I was going to compete, just in case friend Richard scratched and went home leaving me the only runner and automatic recipient of the gold cup. No sir, Richard could have her all to himself, unchallenged, and with my full blessing and support, but no woman likes to believe that, do they? However it was bad tactics to feign a broken heart, just as it would be even worse to send them a double bed and crack open a bottle of Moet's finest to publicly celebrate escape from a close shave. The best course was to go straight down the middle, pretend nothing had ever existed - which as far as I was concerned it hadn't - and therefore nothing had changed.

"Thanks, Margaret," I acknowledged, and then checked her. "By the way will you telephone all the Sharjah Steel design team and tell them that the time of the project meeting today has been changed from 10.30 to 11.30? All except Mr Al Jabril that is." She nodded and made to leave but I added, "And when Mr Al Jabril gets here will you tell reception to show him straight up to Hugo's office, not the boardroom."

It was important to get Mazin on his own, and before rather than after the project meeting. Apart from Dan Herlihan, none of the others had been involved with Mazin Al Jabril before and the less they knew about the past, or the future, the better. We certainly could not give him the 'coup de grace' in front of an audience without a full explanation, so I decided that the deed must be done before we got into the question of ratifying - or not - the sub-contractor for the LAVCHIFS.

My watch said 9.20, Mazin would probably be on time again to make doubly sure his interests were being protected, so we had just over an hour to wait. I cast a desultory eye over the mail but my mind wasn't on it, the nervous tension was too great. I rehearsed the alternative openings for the confrontation; we could punch him gently into oblivion - 'I'm terribly afraid we have a bit of disturbing news, Mazin...' Or we could shoot him four square between the eyes with a knockout bolt: 'Right, you bastard, this is where you get yours...'

I thought back to those awful years when survival hung daily by a thread, the way the bank had humiliated us - Hugo in particular - he had aged ten years in the first fortnight after we discovered Mazin had screwed us. I thought of the faces of the staff we had had to lay off, the shock that showed on their faces when people, who thought they had an established future, had it suddenly chopped from under them.

I thought of the cheap hotels, the bucket shop airline tickets on unreliable aircraft, the business friends we hadn't been able to pay - some of whom had gone to the wall, and I thought of my own life.

No, there was no way Mazin was going to get the quick bullet, I wanted to watch his face as it slowly dawned on him that far from being in the driving seat he was caught in a vice by the balls, and there was no way out except to do as he was told.

Margaret stuck her head round the door, "The meeting's been re-scheduled for 11.30, everybody knows." She noticed my face with surprise, the grim feelings must have been showing through for she retired without a further comment.

I picked up the sets of Pantocrator and Costa da Silva files and drawings and took them down the corridor to Hugo's office. He too looked grim and apprehensive. He opened out immediately. "I'm not so sure about this Marcus, what if it should get out? What would the World Bank think - and what would all our other clients think?" he ventured uneasily.

"Hugo, why should it get out? I won't say anything, except that Mazin has repaid the money he borrowed, you won't say anything, and for sure he won't say a dicky bird. Wild horses wouldn't drag it out of him!" I could see that he was still disquieted and needed reassuring. I smiled at him, he was such a nice man, even the idea of roasting an out and out trickster like Mazin Al Jabril over red-hot coals upset him. It just made me even more determined to sort the sod out for taking advantage of Hugo's trust.

"Look, Hugo, just think of the last three years, just think what we have been through - and our staff and friends - and all as a result of Mazin's greed."

He smiled at me and looked at me over his half moons. "I have been doing just that," he said, "and when you think deeply about it, overall they were good years. They taught us not to take things for granted, that nothing worthwhile comes easily, that really hard work has its reward. And we've had some fun as well, haven't we?"

Of course he was right, he usually was, but the point was that Mazin hadn't ripped us off for our benefit. If we'd gone to the wall it wouldn't have meant so much as a grain of sand to him - he had got the money, that was all he cared about.

"Besides, Hugo," I said carefully, "we know what he is up to again. The man is an out and out bastard who uses people and then discards them like empty cartons for somebody else to sweep up in the trash. He's a crocodile and you're either astride his back or he'll tear you apart and eat you. You know as well as I do what he is doing, and he's doing it entirely off his own bat; we haven't pushed him into it in any way, we have just taken precautions to protect ourselves. It's our money we are getting back, don't forget that. It's ours not his - or anybody else's."

He studied me impassively for a few seconds and then a slow smile spread across his face.

"You're right, it is our money, and he jolly well deserves some grief for all the suffering he has caused our staff and friends."

He grew serious again and frowned. "He really is the limit Marcus, I didn't think people could do things like that. How can a man behave in that way? Why does he do it?"

"Greed," I told him. "For Mazin Al Jabril 'self' comes before anything else. He's sick really. The accumulation of wealth is an insidious disease, he can't help himself - not that he's tried very hard!"

There was a tap on the office door and Janet entered.

"Mr Al Jabril is here," she announced.

She could have saved her breath because her announcement only preceded, by a split second, Mazin's appearance in the doorway like a genie from a bottle.

"Get out of my way, girl," he snarled, shunting her roughly to one side as he stormed through.

"What's going on around here, why is the meeting delayed and why wasn't I informed immediately?"

This piece of Al Jabril courtesy was addressed primarily to Hugo and accompanied by a lot of arm waving and air-sawing. I glanced from Mazin's suffused haughty face to Hugo. He was sitting there tight-lipped with shock at Mazin's rudeness. Any lingering feelings of charity and 'live and let live' he may have still harboured for the arrogant Arab were totally extinguished at that point. I opened my mouth to illuminate the first step in the plan to take Mazin up the scaffold, but Hugo forestalled me leaving me as obsolete as a coronation mug.

"How dare you burst in here like that, Al Jabril," he blazed, "and how dare you speak to one of my staff in that way. You will apologise to her instantly otherwise our business can be considered as terminated from this moment!"

I don't know who was more thunderstruck by this, Mazin or me. Hugo had not only lit up the whole scaffold at one go with his incandescence, he had swung back the axe to chop Mazin's head off instanter.

A variety of expressions flitted across Mazin's face: fury, defiance and ultimately sly cunning. I watched him carefully. He clearly didn't like it - not one little bit, but he wasn't sure too of his ground at this unexpected development. So, much as it riled him, he decided that concession was the better part of pride. He was a clever devil, you had to give him that. No unmarried mother he to be cast out into the unknown of the driving snow without a map.

Turning to the astonished Janet, still standing with her hand clasped to her mouth as though inserting an oversized gob stopper, he turned on the charm.

"Dear lady, please forgive my rudeness. We are all working under such high pressure these days that sometimes we forget the common courtesies. I do most sincerely apologise if I offended you in any way." And, taking the hand that was not held to her face he kissed the back of it. She looked at Hugo seeking advice, he inclined his head towards the door so she detached her hand nervously from Mazin's and slid quietly out, closing the door behind her.

Hugo was seated behind his desk and I was standing beside one of the two visitors' chairs in front of it. I motioned Mazin towards the other one. "Have a seat, Mazin, and we'll tell you why the project meeting has been postponed." He looked at me warily and I looked back po-faced. Hugo was still simmering reproachfully. I waited for Mazin to sit before beginning.

"As you are aware from the programme, we have a critical path node point on Friday the 17th, that date is the absolute deadline date for freezing all technical information to have it ready to go to the printers. The printers require two weeks to print and bind the document and we submit to the World Bank on the 31st March." I paused as his eyes narrowed but uncharacteristically he didn't interrupt.

"So by Friday we must have made the firm decision on who..."

"Whom," interjected Hugo abstractedly.

"On which..." I continued giving him a sharp look "...company will undertake the furnace subcontract."

Mazin got the point instantly and blew a fuse. He could contain himself no longer, this together with his previous rancour burst out in a torrent of fury and indignation.

"I haven't come here for a damned lesson in the English language, I couldn't give a shit whether it's 'whom' 'which' or 'what', all I am telling you two is that it is Pantocrator, and that is final!" He yelled, a shower of spittle enveloping both of us. He glared around and saw on Hugo's desk the Pantocrator file with Antoniades fax message prominently on top. He jabbed at it violently with his finger. "You've had the confirmation you demanded, you know that they have started work and will meet the programme. There is no more to be said, that is that, the decision is made, and my brother, the Minister, is not going to like this sort of performance when I tell him." Little flecks of foam showed at the corner of his mouth. "The firm decision was taken months ago, fixed, final and irrevocable, so I won't have any more of this nonsense!" He glared at both of us, as if daring us to challenge it, and then sank back down into his chair. We waited in silence whilst he composed himself. The silence itself was more ominous than any spoken word would have been. It was Mazin who eventually broke it.

"What's all this about? I hope for your sakes it's important, because I'm a busy man so don't waste my time!"

I smiled at him gently. "I don't think you'll find it a waste of time, Mazin, and at the risk of repeating myself I will reiterate that by Friday next we must have made a firm decision about which company undertakes the furnace subcontract."

"We have," he bawled, "Pantocrator!"

"Mmm," I murmured, "but that was when we believed that they were unique, that nobody else could make these special furnaces. Unfortunately - for you that is, Mazin," I bestowed another kindly smile upon his flushed face... "unfortunately they are not. There is another steel company who make LAVCHIFS to almost the same specification."

"I don't believe it," he burst out angrily, "you're winding me up."

Picking up Costa's files from the cupboard behind me I placed them in front of him. "See for yourself." He eyed them like a man with a ticking parcel, and then methodically began to turn the pages over. We waited patiently as he worked his way through the pile, his face turning ashen as the truth slowly but irresistibly dawned upon him.

I gave him a poke with the toasting fork.

"It's all there, Mazin - the prices, the specification, the programme, the lot."

It wasn't! I had removed Costa's programme, it may have blown it if he'd seen that, but he was too stunned to notice the omission. For the first time in our acquaintance he was dumbstruck. Whatever he had been expecting it certainly wasn't that.

"But you have instructed Pantocrator to begin manufacturing, you can't go back on that," he countered desperately. "It would not be professional!" Coming from him that took some swallowing but we managed it.

"No we haven't," I told him categorically. "We made it perfectly clear to Pantocrator, in writing, that if they went ahead with the manufacture before contracts were placed it was entirely at their own risk."

"They'll get it anyhow," he sneered, more trying to convince himself than us.

"Not necessarily," I told him. "We already have Pantocrator's price, which we believe has a large agency fee included in it. The Brazilians could well be much cheaper without that, in a competitive bid."

The awful truth of this hit him hard.

He sat there for several minutes thinking, his mind recovering quickly and the gears beginning to mesh again.

I thought it time to tighten the screw some more.

"I understand you have put up some initial funding to Pantocrator, Mazin. A foolish thing to have done, you know, if you'd asked us we wouldn't have recommended it, you could lose it all." It did no harm to let him know quite specifically that we knew the score. It would save a lot of beating about the bush in the end.

I fully expected him to go into his act, and rant and rave and swear and curse, those being his usual tactics when thwarted, but instead a mask of impassivity settled on his face, but not before I noticed the cunning gleam in his eye.

He was going to try to get out of this somehow, but first of all he'd try to find out what the deal was.

Oh he knew that there was a deal to be done, that was patently obvious to him, otherwise we would have revealed all publicly at the project meeting, not at a little private tête-à-tête between the three of us tucked away cosily in Hugo's office. What he had to do now was find out what exactly the deal was. The Arabs hated to open the negotiations; they always tried to make you propose your minimum or maximum figure before revealing theirs. This time, however, it was different, he didn't have a maximum or minimum, he didn't even know vaguely what he was going to be hit with. I was very tempted to start him off at $6 million just to see him shit himself, but Hugo would not approve - apart from the principle, it was his chair and carpet that might suffer.

Mazin opened his mouth to ask but I got in first.

"So what do you think we should do, Mazin?" He knew it wasn't going to be that easy but he tried.

"You should continue to behave as a professional firm and honour your binding undertakings to Pantocrator," he responded.

"And why would we want to do that?" I asked gently.

That was when it was confirmed to him that his balls were caught in a vice, but his next remark showed that he didn't realise at all what it was that we were after. It was beyond his comprehension that we just wanted to recover the money he had stolen from us. He assumed that we were after a large part of his backhander from Pantocrator, and he started off by offering us 10% of his cut. Hugo couldn't believe his ears and I fell about laughing.

"Bloody hell, Mazin, after what you did to us, do you think for one moment that we'd trust you to hand over even one cent of your commission to us once you had got your sticky hands on it! You must be crazy man!"

He flared up like an immolated Buddhist at that.

"Well for the sake of God what do you want?" He glared at both of us, anger glittering in his eyes, the mask had slipped for a moment. Hugo decided to put him out of his misery.

"We want our $2 million back - plus interest at 12% compound say."

Mazin looked incredulous. "Is that a..." He tried to stop himself but he was too late. Hugo picked him up.

"Yes that is all, that is exactly what we want."

"Unless you are prepared to offer more without obligation," I added. He clearly thought we were mad, he was expecting a much higher figure. I sighed inwardly, maybe I should have...but no, it was better this way. I wanted him well and truly in the trap, and if he thought we were fools, so much the better.

He visibly relaxed. "Well that is accepted then, I will pay you $2 million, plus interest, as soon as I get my commission from Pantocrator."

I gave another snort of laughter. "Get stuffed, Mazin! Gee whiz, you're priceless! No, I'll tell you what the deal is exactly. It is very simple, it's called 'money up front'. You produce a certified banker's draft for $2,800,000 by 12 noon on Wednesday at this office and Pantocrator get nominated. If you don't produce it, then we will report to the World Bank that competitive bids should be invited for the LAVCHIFS, and we'll fix it so Costa da Silva get the contract." We probably couldn't do that, but it was the way Mazin would think, so he accepted the threat as real.

He recoiled at that. "But what guarantees do I have that, if I hand the money over on Wednesday, you will fulfil your part of the bargain and confirm Pantocrator's nomination?" he remonstrated.

"You cheeky sod," I exclaimed indignantly. You'll get no guarantees from us, it's our bloody money in the first place, you will have to trust us this time. Besides, you have no alternative Mazin," I added evilly.

If looks could kill I would have been dispatched on the spot. He gave me a look of pure hatred but strangely didn't attempt to argue further. Nor did he fulminate and rage. There was something frighteningly calculating about the way he just sat silently glaring, it was as if he was locked into some inner thoughts that gave him strength. Eventually he rose to his feet still glaring and said tightly,

"Do not even think about changing anything. Pantocrator are to be nominated. I will see you both on Wednesday."

With that he departed without further ado, totally ignoring my inquiry as to whether he was going to stay for the meeting.

Hugo took off his spectacles and massaged his nose, this sort of aggravation distressed him.

"What do you make of that, Marcus?" he asked, slightly bemused by the whole performance.

I pondered awhile before replying.

"I think we've got him. He is absolutely flummoxed. We agreed that we would give him a chance to repay us and we have done so. We have played it straight all the way through. He has a choice between doing the right thing now, and repaying us, or not."

I took a deep breath. "But he's not going to do it though, Hugo, you realize that? There is no way he is going to repay our money. I spoke to the trustee this morning; Mazin has already arranged to see him tomorrow afternoon to clinch the deal to buy Bridge Holdings Limited behind our backs. There is absolutely no chance that he will turn up here on Wednesday and repay us. We should have no sympathy for him whatsoever. He is a nasty, extremely unpleasant crook."

I stood up and walked to the window, looking at the river, whilst Hugo digested this. I continued, "It's a good job that we were prepared to spend some time and money preparing a defensive strategy otherwise we would not have had a snowflake in hell's chance of seeing one cent of our stolen money again."

I gave him an encouraging smile. "Also, I am pleased to tell you, that it looks as if Plan A Plus, the extra ingredient that will safeguard our future, may just work. The trustee has laid the groundwork beautifully, so keep your fingers crossed!"

Hugo shook his head. "This is getting a bit beyond me. Are we secure? What if he investigates Costa da Silva and finds that they can't meet all the parameters?"

Tapping their bulky file I told him. "He hasn't got time to start checking Costa out or anything like that - at least not in the detail necessary to evaluate whether or not we were bluffing. If he phones them, they will only confirm what we have told him - that they have developed a vacuum contained high induction furnace and they would love to get the Sharjah Steel contract. No he's cornered, the Wednesday meeting will be interesting to say the least!"

"Well I hope you're right."

So did I!

After a few moments' reflection, screwing up his face in thought as if trying to get a bad taste out of his mouth, Hugo gave me one of his mischievous grins and said, "Changing the subject, Marcus, what's got into Miss Braithwaite these days? She beamed at me this morning, she looks ten years younger and was singing in her office when I went past." His grin grew even broader. "It's not you is it? You haven't been...?" He raised his eyebrows questioningly.

"No it bloody isn't!" I responded angrily. "And no I haven't. If you really want to know, she's found herself a man, but for heaven's sake don't say anything, it's all a bit delicate at the moment and the last thing I need is for that boat to be rocked!"

"I just wondered because you've seemed much more chipper these days, and people tend to put two and two together..."

"And make five!" I added with feeling. "No, you're barking up the wrong tree. I have a girlfriend but it is definitely not the Major. You'll get to meet her in due course I promise."

I recalled the various replies Margaret had received to my advertisement. I must admit it was successful. Apart from the two, presumably serious and reasonably respectable letters she'd abstracted from the bunch, the rest were from an amazing collection of perverts, cock-artists, fetishists and the downright desperate. She certainly had had a wide range to pick from. I daren't tell anybody about that, not even Hugo, so he must have wondered what had brought the smile to my face as I gathered up the files and drifted out of his office to the Sharjah project meeting.

Mazin went beserk, he screamed at the new chauffeur for not opening the car door quickly enough, and hurled Ahmed, his manservant, to one side crashing him against the wall as he swept through the door of the flat. He seized a hapless umbrella, which happened to be to hand in a rack in the hall, and laid about him at random in an uncontrollable paroxysm of violent red rage, smashing glassware, statues, ornaments, ripping the paintings and finally trying to tear one of the Isfahan rugs to shreds with his bare hands. The manservant hit his usual escape route, down Lancaster Gate and up Leinster Terrace, legs going like a road-runner, whilst Mazin rolled and thrashed about on the floor, tearing at the rug with feet, nails and teeth, foaming at the mouth and threatening any moment to burst a gut. The rug had withstood many centuries of tartar treatment and was thus totally impervious to the manicured hands and capped teeth of Mazin Al Jabril. Eventually he ran out of steam, fingernails and dental cement, and lay there, sides heaving, surrounded by shattered debris and ceramic caps, cut and bleeding where he had come into forceful contact with the results of his demolition work. The spectators, watching with fascinated interest at the wide open front door, moved back hastily as he scrambled to his feet and then dispersed rapidly as he advanced towards them wild-eyed and frothy. He kicked the door closed with a slam that shook the building and stormed into his study.

How dare they, how dare those ignorant motherfuckers threaten him. It was insufferable and almost unbelievable that they had had the gall to challenge and cheat him. By God's blood they would pay for this, he would make sure of that. It was a good job that he had been clever enough to anticipate something of this kind happening, although the seriousness of it had stunned him totally when he had seen it. But it was still serious - he had to tie up the deal with the trustee now; that was imperative. He gradually calmed down, took a shower to wash off the blood, examined his mouth, now short of two caps and two gold crowns, manicured his split nails into some semblance of shape and stuck plaster over the cuts and grazes. All the time he was thinking, racking his brains to evaluate his position and check every angle.

He put on a silk robe and returned to the study. The first thing was to check if those two piles of camel shit were bluffing. The Costa da Silva information looked genuine enough but that meant nothing these days. Documents could easily be forged with modern photocopying equipment.

He put a call through to the Brazilian Embassy Commercial Section. Yes, Costa Da Silva did manufacture equipment for steel plants, yes they were a reputable outfit, no the Commercial Section didn't know anything about LAVCHIFS, and yes they would give him Costa's telephone number in Sao Paulo.

He looked at his watch. It was still early morning in Sao Paulo and he would have to wait another hour before he could contact them.

Notwithstanding that, the important thing was to get control over CONDES; once he had that, Elmes and Moon would be wiped out. He would be the owner, the chief executive and the sole arbiter of who got the LAVCHIFS sub contract. It was a pity that all he would be able to do to them was to publicly humiliate them and then fire them. He wanted them ruined, tortured and killed. It was some small satisfaction that he was going to take their firm from them for less than half its true value, but they would still get money from the deal and that galled him. He ground what was left of his teeth in frustration. He pulled himself together, and made two phone calls, the second to his dentist for urgent treatment.

He then called for his manservant but to no avail, Ahmed was nearing Westbourne Grove still going like a train. Cursing him violently, he looked up the number of Swiss Air himself, and then confirmed a booking on their late afternoon flight to Geneva. Cursing again he packed his overnight bag with clothes for two days, collected the fall-out from his teeth and then waited impatiently until the start of business in Brazil. Mazin spoke to Herrera, claiming he was from the Ministry of Industry in Sharjah, 'just checking one or two details'. Herrera confirmed they did indeed manufacture LAVCHIFS, they were interested in the Sharjah Steel project and that their furnaces could meet the outputs specified, but said cautiously, that any other details he could not provide over the telephone without some official request in writing from an authorised body. Mazin pressed him but he was adamant. So those sons of dung-eating pigs in CONDES weren't bluffing, well he didn't think they were, but it added an additional complication when he got control of CONDES, however that could be overcome. He might even squeeze something extra out of this by suggesting to Costa da Silva that he could assist them to get the contract - provided they paid him for his services up front of course - and then dumping them. That cheered him a little.

There was one more call to make - to Weber in Geneva. He told Weber to book him in for one night at The President Hotel and persuaded him to make arrangements for yet another cash draft from Credit Suisse. Although it rankled, Mazin still managed to squeeze out a thin smile - for this draft was not for the $2,800,000 those assholes Elmes and Moon thought they were going to get, this draft was for the trivial sum of $56,454 that that little shyster trustee had demanded as extra for doing bugger all.

The chauffeur, having missed the internal histrionics, although puzzled by the speed at which a wide-eyed Ahmed had flashed passed him, was still waiting patiently along the road. As soon as he saw Mazin appear outside the block, carrying a small case, he eased the car up the 20 metres or so until the rear door was exactly opposite his master and leapt out to open it.

He was told to take Mazin round to the dentist, and from thence to Heathrow. On the way he wondered why Mazin had kept his mouth tightly pinched whilst giving these instructions, and the usual torrent of abuse had been absent.

Feeling a bit nervous about the next two days, but generally cheerful and confident, I decided to call in at The Frog and Nightgown for a pint on the way home. Andy King-Knight was there on his own; I hadn't seen him since Jon Grey's funeral but that void in my life hadn't traumatized me sufficiently not to touch him up for a pint. Astonishingly for a guy who was famous for being the first out the taxi and last in the pub, he seemed pleased to do so. And then came the reason. He couldn't wait to tell me that he and Kate had been e-mailing each other and speaking on the phone regularly. He studied my face intently as he delivered this intelligence, and his face fell when I clapped him on the shoulder - hard - and wished him well. "Don't forget, Andy," I said as I picked him off the floor, "the old saying about short men and tall girls..."

341

But before I could give him the punch line the door burst open and half dozen other friends surged in surrounding us and demanding to know who was 'in the chair'.

"Him," I indicated Andy and watched as he blanched at the prospect of buying another six pints of Ruddles Best Bitter.

I left them to it after one more round, and drove home. The rush-hour traffic was worse than usual that Monday evening and an accident on Albert Bridge Road, my usual route to Palmerston Mansions, had caused all traffic to be diverted across Battersea Bridge. The consequent dead stop and crawl left me not much to do but think. It was strange, I had felt nothing when Andy gloated over his contacts with Kate. She was of no interest to me these days. In my mind she was a one-dimensional personality. I was just reflecting on this when my mobile rang and Zoe's name flashed up on the screen.

"Hi! What's with the posh houses today then?"

She chuckled. "Not a lot on a cold March Monday. I was wondering if you are free to have lunch tomorrow with a young lady who desperately desires your witty and charming personality and a touch of your boney knees?"

"Ah! So it's the knees that pulls the girls is it? I knew it was something about my body, I must flash them around more often and see what happens."

"You'd better not, or 'what happens' might not be to your liking, Mr Moon! Anyway, are you free?"

"As you would expect, for a person like myself in great demand, I am not - but I will cancel all my very important engagements with titled people etc etc and see you at 1 o'clock - Como Lario?"

"Como Lario at one it is! I'll make the reservation," she replied.

That was something much better to look forward to than a couple of bacon sandwiches, and an evening watching people on television pretending to be delighted after some TV berks had redecorated their house whilst they were away. Turning a comfortable, cosy, suburban semi into a bamboo jungle with purple ceilings and walls festooned with hideous batiks.

She was there first again, and at a window table with a bottle of Gavi de Gavi already opened.

"Have a good morning?" she asked as we kissed and sat down.

"Quiet," I replied. "Well, quiet after yesterday,"

"Why what happened yesterday?"

"Oh, it was a big day yesterday," I told her. "You remember Mazin Al Jabril?" She nodded. "We have a business deal with him in the Middle East - Sharjah actually - and he stands to make a lot of money out of it if we specify a Greek firm, for whom he acts as agent, as a main supplier of equipment for the contract."

"Is that legal?" she enquired with a puzzled frown.

"Yes, it's perfectly legal; provided they are the only people who made that particular type of equipment." I paused wondering whether or not to tell her the whole story. "And they are really. There's a South American company who do the same sort of thing but, if the truth be known, they are two years behind the Greeks. They could compete but not yet. However we have told Mazin that they are a serious competitor so that he will believe his huge commission is in danger. To prevent that he is intending to go behind our backs and take over our company so that he can control its decisions," I grinned, "and pay £2 million for it! He thinks it is worth twice that at least!"

She looked shocked. "But that sounds monstrous. Can you prevent it?"

I grinned even more. "We don't want to stop him. He doesn't know that the company he is buying is worthless. All the valuable contracts and assets have been moved out of it months ago."

She was silent for a couple of minutes and when she spoke her eyes had narrowed and there was an edge to her voice.

"So you are swindling him out of £2 million! Why are you doing this? It's not the sort of thing I would expect from you or your firm Marcus!"

I was taken aback by the intensity of her obvious anger, and realized that I had been carried away by my own conceit and not explained things properly.

"No, no! It's not like that at all! I should have given you the full story from the beginning."

I then told her about Egyptian Steel, and how Mazin had stolen $2 million from us three years ago; the trouble it had caused us and how we'd asked him to repay it. In fact I gave her the full nine yards so that she had the complete picture.

After I had finished she looked very pensive and eventually said, "I didn't know that."

"Is there any reason why you should?" I enquired, without thinking too much about it.

"No, no, I suppose not," she replied hastily, forking a heap of Caesar Salad into her mouth.

My liver and bacon arrived which put paid to further serious conversation.

Whilst munching on a nice crispy piece of bacon I had an idea, which drove all other thoughts from my head. As all the documents for Sharjah Steel would be sent to the printers on Friday, this left me with the first quiet weekend I had had for months. "Are you doing anything this weekend?" I asked tentatively.

"What have you got in mind?" she said.

"Hot sun," I replied. "Lovely hot sun on our backs. Why don't we push off to Portugal on Friday afternoon. Spend the weekend lazing on sun-kissed beaches sipping cool white wine, and return Sunday night or Monday morning?"

She hesitated. "That sounds a super idea, but I'll have to check. Can I phone you?"

"Sure. In the meantime I'll make some enquiries about flights and hotels."

After we had finished our meal we both had to get back to work. She caught a cab to Johnson Jacques in Cavendish Square, and I walked back to the office planning the trip to the Algarve and to check the weather forecast.

Zoe Garrard was wrapped in deep thought in the taxi on her journey back and, barely acknowledging the rest of her team, went into her office and closed the door. She had a lot to think about.

Indeed she'd had a lot to think about ever since Mazin Al Jabril had suggested that she could earn £5000 if she came to his party last January. All she had to do, he told her, was to make friends with somebody and then report any interesting information that she could extract from that somebody that involved him - Mazin Al Jabril. It turned out that the 'somebody' was Marcus, and he had been pointed out to her at Mazin's party when Mazin described him to her as 'that lanky son of a castrated camel'.

It had seemed like a bit of profitable fun initially but, as contact continued, it wasn't so funny. In fact it had become very disturbing. However, there hadn't been anything that she could have reported had she wanted to, and she had decided that the whole thing was an exaggerated piece of nonsense. It was just Mazin puffing up his inflated ego still further - until now.

He had called her yesterday afternoon. His voice sounded muffled, as though his mouth was full of cotton wool, but there was a note of desperation in it that caught her attention. He had said that there was something going on with Moon, and if she expected to get a sniff of her £5000 she'd better get her finger out and find out what it was. She was to telephone him immediately on his mobile, no matter where he was, or what time it was as soon as she knew something. In spite of his rudeness she had felt a twinge of pity for him, and so she had phoned Marcus to fix today's lunch.

There was no doubt in her mind now that Mazin Al Jabril had every reason to be worried. If what Marcus had told her took place, Mazin was going to be done up like a kipper. It would be a brilliant sting that had been set up.

She thought the whole thing over once again, and then reached for the phone.

Mazin took a taxi from the airport to the President Hotel in Geneva; spent a restless night with toothache and miscellaneous bruises on various parts of his person; skipped breakfast and was at the door of Credit Suisse on the dot of opening time. He stowed the bearer share certificate safely in his briefcase and walked the 100 metres or so to Dr Weber's office. Weber went through the same procedure each time. Mazin had to present the bearer share certificate, Weber studied it carefully and when he was satisfied handed it back to Mazin and business could commence. Today it took no more than 30 seconds. Weber asked no questions. Mazin requested the additional bank draft; Weber went to his large safe and extracted it; Mazin signed a receipt; and with a brief nod, exited the office.

By 4.45 he was standing at the door of Trust Services in St Helier. The timing had been cut very fine, high cross winds at Jersey airport had made the Jersey flight touch and go, but eventually it went, much to Mazin's relief. He had a face refilled

346

with teeth and, strapped in a money belt round his waist, five bank drafts and one bearer share certificate for 499,999 shares of one Swiss Franc each in Investment and Resource Holdings SA. A Swiss registered company with a half million Swiss Franc share capital.

"You have now the drafts and the authority?"

Mazin struggled to unfasten the belt and extract the documents. The trustee examined them carefully.

"That all seems to be in order, the transfer can take place."

He opened the safe and produced his plastic folder. The first document he handed to Mazin was the indemnity. It made it absolutely clear that Mazin had made all necessary enquiries, satisfied himself fully about all aspects of his purchase, not relied upon any information provided by the company or its directors, Trust Services or the trustee and had entered into the acquisition entirely of his own free will. Mazin thought it was pathetic, a real 'cover your arse' document for the trustee, he signed it with contempt. After reading the share transfer document he signed that also, but this time with a flourish. The girl witnessed both signatures. He noted in passing that the share transfer had already been signed on behalf of the company and sealed with the company's seal. The trustee watched him impassively, and, when he had finished, the trustee spread out all the documents lying on the desk whilst Mazin was stowing away his pen. "Your company is now the owner of 75% of the voting stock of Bridge Holdings Limited," he pronounced, and pushed the red-sealed share certificate across to Mazin. "I presume you will wish to call an Extraordinary General Meeting immediately to establish your control and to activate your future policies. Do you wish me to send out notices?"

Mazin picked up the share certificate and looked at it. Riches beyond his dreams - and revenge for the humiliation of yesterday. It was a stupendous feeling of power. And it meant power, he was now the virtual sole owner of a large reputable firm with enormous influence, there would be hundreds of things to cash in on, contractors and suppliers would grovel to him, bankers and politicians would treat him as their equal and he could cream off millions. But first he had to dispose of Moon. Elmes, he still wasn't quite sure about, and Antoniades was going to suffer the tortures of the damned unless he toed the line.

"Ahem!" The trustee's polite cough snapped him out of his reverie. "Do you wish me to send out notices?"

Mazin looked at him coldly. "Do whatever you have to do to get me in total executive control of this company at the earliest possible time."

The trustee's earnest pale face gazed steadily back at him. "Well, Mr Al Jabril, effectively that is now, but there are the formalities. Nobody could do anything in the company now without your consent otherwise they would be laying themselves wide open to the severest penalties. I will of course inform Mr Elmes and Mr Moon forthwith of your involvement."

Mazin stopped him dead, there was no way he was going to have his moment of pleasure spoiled prematurely.

"No you won't," he snapped, "you will fax them at precisely 12.05 tomorrow. Is that clear? Nothing is to be revealed about my ownership until then."

The trustee nodded acceptance. "As you wish," and continued.

"That concludes our business then," he said, "all that remains is for me to register the transfer with the Commercial Offices of the States here." He began to gather up all the remaining documents, and with a jolt of alarm Mazin saw his bearer share certificate beginning to disappear into the trustee's folder.

"I want that back," snapped Mazin sharply, reaching across the desk to grab it. The trustee held on to it and moved it fractionally out of reach.

"Of course, but I need it first to effect the registration of the new share ownership."

Alarm turned to cold fear as the trustee's words sank in. Mazin glared at him angrily. "You didn't say anything about this before," he snarled. "I want it back now."

A faint flicker of anger showed in the trustee's cheeks. "I beg your pardon, Mr Al Jabril, but I told you quite clearly at our last meeting that you had to prove to both myself and the authorities that you controlled IRH. How am I to do the latter without producing this certificate?" he added waspishly. "And I must tell you that without such proof they will refuse to register the transfer, in which case it will be null and void."

Mazin froze. The cold fear in his heart turned to ice-cold terror at the thought of being separated from his bearer shares by this unknown little creep. He must remain calm outwardly at all costs, it would be fatal to show even a flicker of fear because that would reveal the depths of his vulnerability. Swallowing hard to lubricate the half-strangled vocal chords, he managed to ask with commendable equanimity, "You're not going to send that by post are you?"

The trustee shook his head vigorously.

"Oh no, no, no! It is only the State's authorities here that need to see it. Twenty-four hours that is all it takes. I can deposit the documents by hand first thing tomorrow morning and may even be able to collect the registration before close of business at 5 pm."

"Why don't you take a photocopy, surely we can get one certified and notarised this afternoon?" It was all Mazin could think of, one last hope, but that was dashed.

"I'm afraid not. I told you that they normally require certified minutes of the board meeting authorising the purchase, plus a certified power of attorney for the person actually executing the transaction to so do it. You have produced neither. When I spoke to the Chief Commercial Officer, he said that for bearer shares they must see the original."

Mazin did not like this at all, even letting control slip out of his hands for 24 hours terrified him. The option of staying an extra day in Jersey and accompanying the trustee to the State's offices with the bearer shares was denied him. He had to catch the early plane to London if he was to make the final Sharjah Steel meeting and ensure Pantocrator's nomination, otherwise those bastards would throw the furnaces contract open to competition. He saw that he had no alternative but to trust the trustee with his precious certificate.

Well if he was going to be terrified so was the little administrative shit. Mazin's eyes hardened to flints and he leant forward riveting the trustee with his stare.

"Now listen to me and listen good. The money behind this is not mine. It belongs to some very, nasty people. If you so much as breathe one word of this - schlick," and he drew a finger across his throat.

"Black September operates out of Beirut and Libya, they do not like to leave those places except to execute..." He stressed the word "...executive missions, and anybody who double-crosses them dies an extremely painful death. Do I make myself clear?"

The trustee gulped twice.

"Are you saying that this is terrorist money then?" he croaked. Mazin smiled significantly but his eyes stayed hard.

"I'm saying nothing - but bear it in mind. Also..." Mazin reached across the desk quickly and seized the bank drafts for cash, representing the trustee's commission, that he had set on one side. "...I will keep these as security just to ensure that you don't try to be clever. I will be back tomorrow afternoon, and when I get my bearer shares back you get these." He held them up temptingly in front of the trustee's eyes.

The trustee protested plaintively. "But that wasn't the deal. The deal was I get my commission when you get control. I want my money now. Investment and Resource Holdings has got the Bridge Holdings Limited shares. I demand that you give me my commission!"

"Tomorrow," said Mazin conclusively. "When I get my shares back," and he tucked the drafts away in his wallet putting an end to the discussion - if it had even been one.

Next morning he caught the 9.30 plane to Heathrow and was back in his flat by 11.00. Ahmed opened the door apprehensively, but relaxed when he assessed his master's mood. The hallway looked bare but had been cleared of debris. Mazin told the manservant that he wanted the car available to go to CONDES at 11.40 precisely, and then took a quick shower, put on a cream silk shirt, blue and red striped tie and a fine hounds-tooth check cashmere two-piece suit by Grieves and Hawkes of Savile Row. If you were the big wheel in a firm of consulting engineers you needed to look the part. He tucked a matching silk kerchief into his breast pocket, gave himself a final squirt of Georgio Armani and, with the share certificate safe in his slim briefcase, set off for what he knew was going to be one of the most pleasurable experiences of his life.

"Do you think he'll turn up?" enquired Hugo nervously, "it's 11.50 now."

I reassured him. "Hugo, stop worrying. He's got to turn up sooner or later."

We were both dressed for the occasion, Hugo with his charcoal-grey double-breasted and Old Carthusian tie, me in dark blue pinstripe and Harrods Christmas sale neckwear. We knew we were going to lose the sartorial stakes, but that was insignificant to the total stuffing of Mazin Al Jabril that was going to take place.

At 11.58 a flustered Janet appeared with a bemused look on her face. "Mr Al Jabril is here." She hesitated and then blurted out, "He walked straight past and told me to tell you that he expected to see you both in the boardroom immediately."

Hugo gave her a calming smile. "Fine, Janet, we'll be right along."

We looked at each other's faces impassively and moved out.

Mazin was sitting bolt upright in the armchair at the head of the table like a Savile Row Buddha. His cold arrogant expression betrayed no emotion, both his hands were flat on the table in front of him. Hugo said quietly, "You're sitting in my chair, Mazin, would you please move to the other one on the right?"

He made no move to comply but a scornful smile flickered on his lips. It didn't spread to his flat dark eyes, as expressionless as two wet pebbles on a sandy beach. I had a try.

"Have you brought the draft, it is now 12.02, you're over the deadline." That ought to wind him up. It certainly made him move, but not out of the chair. He reached down and took his briefcase from the floor and placed it on the table. Slowly, with his eyes still fixed on both of us standing by the door, he slid open the zip and pulled out an official looking piece of paper.

"Perhaps you should see this," he murmured, beckoning us down towards him. We went, one either side of the table and sat down. He slowly turned it over so that we could read it.

"What is that?" he said, mastery tingeing his voice.

"It's a share certificate," I said astutely.

He could contain himself no longer. "It's your bloody death warrant!" he shouted, triumph echoing round the room. "It is the one single item that gives me total control of you and you..." he stabbed a finger at Hugo and me, "...this firm, Sharjah Steel, everything. I am the one who is in charge now, I own you lock, stock and barrel, you're mine, you will do exactly as I say."

He turned on me savagely. "And you, you long streak of piss, you're fired! You can pack your things and go. Get out, you've got 15 minutes to clear your office and do not come near this place again. You pathetic pile of manure, you thought you were so clever to try to stitch up Mazin Al Jabril but you didn't stand a chance. Two point eight million dollars! Pah! You couldn't even negotiate a handful of sand from a Bedou. Well you're done for, taken over, wiped out." He paused to draw breath, eyes wild and staring, spittle running down his chin, all his pent-up malice and hatred radiating from him.

Hugo put his hand on the table and turned the share certificate so he could read it more easily.

"He's right, Marcus, this gives a Swiss company called Investment and Resource Holdings SA, which I presume is his, 75% of the stock in Bridge Holdings Limited."

I looked at Hugo and he looked at me, then we walked back to the chairs and sat, one on either side of him, and put our heads in our hands.

CHAPTER NINTEEN

The strange thing about that moment was that I had no feeling of exultation: no elation, no eager anticipation of the come-uppance that was going to fall upon Mazin's head from a great height; and, when he looked up, from the expression on Hugo's face, neither did he.

I glanced at Mazin, who was still glaring triumphantly at me, and an overwhelming sadness entered my soul. I was sad that this cocky, conceited creature had reduced us to such devious practices in order to safeguard our business, our good name and our self-respect. He was sitting there so arrogant and self-confident without the faintest idea of what was coming up. His insults and rudeness had meant nothing; they were a pathetic reflection of a pathetic man. He had had no qualms whatsoever about stealing from us, using us, and ultimately intending to ruin us for his own selfish gratification, and that was going to cause his downfall.

I was sad that I could not muster one atom of sympathy for him, or find a single redeeming feature in his behaviour.

This is not how I had expected it to be now that the occasion, to which I had been looking forward, had arrived. I wished that none of it had been necessary and consequently my dislike of Mazin Al Jabril intensified.

This must have shown, because Hugo had opened his mouth to speak, and then, noticing the expressions passing across my face, stayed silent.

Mazin, in his inimitable way, assumed that we were both too shell-shocked to react and couldn't resist turning the knife.

"So get out, Moon! You've already used up 5 of the 15 minutes I gave you and my patience is wearing thin."

He put both hands firmly on the table, arms stretched out: a proprietorial gesture.

That did it for me, that was the last straw. Looking at Hugo I shook my head and started to smile.

"Didn't I tell you he was a right royal bastard, Hugo! A top class, 24-carat, fully paid-up shit of the first water - and stupid into the bargain!"

And turning to look Mazin straight in the eye, I said, "By God, Mazin, but you really are the most evil, greedy person it has ever been our misfortune to encounter."

Hugo also leaned on the table and fixed Mazin with a steely look.

"Let's get this crystal clear, Al Jabril. Are you telling us that you have not brought with you a bank draft to repay the money that you stole from us, and that you have no intention of ever paying it back?"

Mazin snorted with disbelief at what he perceived as Hugo's naivety.

"Are you thick, Elmes? Haven't you got it yet? I control CONDES now; it is mine. I do not need to repay myself anything, whether or not it is due."

This was so outrageous that both of us looked at each other and started to laugh. The tension was shattered and a slight hysteria took over. We managed to stop for a moment, but every time we looked at Mazin sitting there, with a perplexed expression on his brown, handsome face, sitting there like a king in a gold hat, we started to laugh again.

Mazin eyed us warily, I think he thought he'd pushed us over the edge and we'd both gone mad. He eased his chair back surreptitiously out of reach. A small frown gathered on his face. This was not exactly the response he had expected to his brilliantly planned bombshell at all, and it made him nervous. These weird Brits were unpredictable, very difficult to deal with. He regarded us angrily, that it must be temporary insanity was all he could think of. Two normal people, suffering the shattering blow he had just delivered, should not be falling about laughing. They should be begging on their knees, pleading for mercy, crushed and stunned by the awful shock. He was going to put an immediate stop to this, the way Elmes was heaving and twitching, a man of his age, his heart could fail at any moment and Mazin needed him to tide the firm over for the immediate future.

"What's so damned funny? You'll be laughing on the other side of your faces before I've finished with you...!"

Hugo took a deep breath and brought himself back under control.

"He wants to know what's funny, Marcus. You tell him, it was your plan." He switched his attention back to Mazin. "You're not going to enjoy this, Al Jabril, not one little bit - but I am. I can promise you that from, what was it - 'a stinking pile of dung from a rabid pig'?"

I think that was the moment when Mazin realized that something had gone terribly wrong. It all came to him suddenly that he had laid out over $7 million so far, and all he had received in return was the piece of paper which lay in front of him bearing a deep red, embossed seal which glared back at him like a large, malevolent, unblinking eye. He touched it briefly seeking reassurance but obtained none. I saw the blood begin to drain from his face and beads of cold sweat form on his high forehead. The contempt and fury in his eyes faded to be replaced by a glassy wariness that stemmed from an inner dread. His gaze became fixed on me like a mesmerized rabbit and he sat - waiting. For what he did not know, couldn't guess; but, with a ghastly sinking sensation in the pit of his stomach, he knew that he was about to be stuffed.

"You recall, no doubt, appropriating $2 million of ours from the Egyptian Steel contract. Yes of course you do!" I gave him a smile. "Well, we didn't like that. It caused us and our colleagues major financial troubles. When you turned up again we decided to ask you to pay it back - at the right time, to give you a chance to redeem yourself. But knowing what a nasty, greedy man you are..." I gave him another smile, "we knew you would have some lucrative side deal going, and, sooner or later, you would try and shaft us. We calculated that the only sure way you could do this was by going behind our backs and taking control of Bridge Holdings Limited."

A spark of hope flickered in his eyes. "Well I have," he snapped.

"Yes, indeed, ownership and control has passed from us into other hands, but not yours."

"What are you talking about? There is the share certificate! What more do you want?" He picked it up and waved it in my face.

"We'll come back to that in a minute, but I think the first thing is to say we are puzzled as to why you would go to all the trouble of shelling out all that money for a worthless company? Naturally it was much appreciated by Hugo and I, because it restores our finances to what they should have been if you hadn't stolen our money, but I'm sure that that wasn't your main reason."

His spark of hope died and his eyes opened wide. "What do you mean 'worthless'?" he asked roughly.

"Worthless! It has no assets, no cash and all the contracts are with Consultant Design Services - the company Hugo and I run here."

Mazin snorted, "But Bridge Holdings owns Consultant Design!"

I shook my head. "It used to, but we changed that a couple of months ago. It doesn't own it any longer."

There was a long period of silence whilst he absorbed this. His quick mind analysed the situation rapidly. If it was true he was down just over £2 million, or $3.5 million, as far as CONDES was concerned, but what about Pantocrator? That was the big one. Were they bluffing or not? It was bowel-gripping time. There was one vital thing he needed to know. His heart raced as he considered how to phrase the question.

"What about Sharjah Steel? I am still your agent for that, there is a signed contract. And what about the project?"

I glanced across at Hugo wondering whether or not to wind Mazin up further but Hugo's face was like stone so I carried on. I knew what he meant.

"Oh! You mean what about Pantocrator?"

He nodded, trying to be off-hand but the sweat trickled down his face.

"No problem there," I said cheerfully. "Pantocrator were always going to be nominated. Costa da Silva can't do the job. They couldn't get anywhere near matching them for quality or speed. We have already written Pantocrator into the documents and this cannot be changed. The first batch went to the printers this morning."

Mazin took a deep breath as he realized he had been out manoeuvred, but now all was not lost and hope flared up suddenly. They had missed a crucial trick. His $4 million was safe now, and his commission from Pantocrator, and he had a lever.

"You fools!" he shouted. "There's nothing you can do now, and, by the Prophet's beard, if you don't pay me back for your useless company, I will make your damned lives a misery on that project. My brother is the Minister so you know I can!"

It was sad really, Mazin was like a man who kept walking into a door and he'd just walked hard into another one. With my eyes riveted on his, I called Janet on the intercom to ask her if she would tell Brian Mason to come into the meeting.

He walked through the door in his well pressed but old, and clearly off the peg, blue suit, white shirt and chainstore tie. His pale face looked a little tense but he gave Mazin a courteous enough nod.

"We meet again, Mr Al Jabril," he said pleasantly, and sat down next to Hugo.

"You know the trustee of course, Mazin," I observed dryly.

Brian was right with his forecast, he did go mad! Sitting there in the chairman's chair at the head of the table he first went sheet white beneath his tan and dumbstruck. That was only a transitory situation, and then, as the colour flooded back into his ultra-violet irradiated face and his quick mind began to receive oxygen again, he went totally bananas.

"I'll sue you for every fucking cent you have ever owned, I'll have you through every court in the land for this," he screamed. "I'll reduce you to zero, break you into little bits and grind you to dust..." He paused to draw breath so Hugo interrupted.

"And on what basis do you think you can do that?" he asked quietly. Mazin glared at him savagely.

"You tricked me, you have deliberately misled me, you let me buy a company which you knew was virtually worthless because you had moved all the valuable assets out of it. That is fraud!"

Hugo shook his head slowly. "We didn't do that did we Marcus? We decided to re-organise the business a long time before you came on the scene. We didn't know you were going to try to buy it behind our backs. If you'd asked us we'd have told you."

I chipped in here, "In any case, Mazin, you've signed an indemnity confirming that you had entered into the deal entirely of your own free will, made all necessary inquries, satisfied yourself fully, and not relied upon any information provided by the company, its directors, Trust Services or the trustee. As far as we are concerned you have agreed in writing that you knew exactly what you were getting - if it now turns out to be different to what you thought - tough shit!"

His face now grew purple, as a sideshow he would have given a chameleon a run for its money.

I smiled at him placidly. "Besides you have another small problem don't you? It isn't you that owns Bridge Holdings, is it? I pointed to the share certificate lying in front of him. "If you will look carefully at it you will note that the owner is Investment and Resources Holdings SA of Geneva."

It could be said without fear of contradiction that what had apparently started out well was, now, not one of Mazin's better days as the awful implication of what could follow if his bearer shares were born by somebody else, dawned upon him. And follow it did!

I continued. "In fact, as I understand it, IRH owns the apartment you live in: it was IRH that loaned Pantocrator $4 million: Pantocrator's agency deal is with IRH: and, for that matter, our agency deal is also with IRH. So whoever controls IRH controls that lot."

"I control IRH," he snapped angrily, but his eyes flicked nervously in Brian's direction as he said it.

"And how do you do that?" Hugo enquired before I could. Well it was only fair that others should have some satisfaction without me hogging the limelight.

"I hold all the issued shares," he ground out, but there was a touch of fear in his eyes.

"As a point of fact," said Hugo, "I believe that they are bearer shares, and that at this moment you do not hold them."

Mazin flushed angrily. "Stop this nonsense!" he shouted, pointing at Brian Mason. "He has deposited them with the Commercial Office of the States of Jersey to register the BHL share transfer and I will have them back this afternoon!"

Turning to Brian again he stabbed a furious finger at him and shouted, "He is supposed to be a trustee - in a position of trust. He has taken my bearer shares; he has acted illegally as a trustee in selling a company without permission." His voice rose an octave or two. "In the name of God, he told me himself that it was illegal to sell the shares without permission - and that cancels the contract as far as I am concerned. The cheating dog asked for, and took, bribes for doing it and that must be against the law as well!"

He paused to take in air and wind up his elastic tighter. "I'm going to sue him for every penny he's got. I'll have him in court, and you as well," he screamed, embracing Hugo and me as well with a wave of his arms, spittle spraying in all directions and little flecks of foam appearing at the corners of his mouth.

Have you noticed that in life those who love to dish it out to others are, invariably, the ones who like it least when it is done back to them?

Mazin hit both the red and violet of the spectrum. He loved putting the boot in when on top, showing no mercy - charity was as foreign to him as gardening. But now he was on the receiving end there was no, "It's a fair cop guv - can we do a deal'. No, he still thought he could bully and bluster his way out of it.

Brian, who was clearly relishing Mazin getting his come-uppance, was totally unfazed by this performance, he put his fingertips together and, in his very precise way, replied, "Taking your points in order, Mr Al Jabril, what bearer shares would they be to which you are referring? Do you have a receipt, or any proof that you ever had any bearer shares that belonged to you in the first place? And, if you ever did have some, why would they be deposited with the Jersey authorities? There is no requirement for such a course of action. Secondly, I did get permission to sell the shares. I have written permission from both the directors and the beneficiaries to sell the shares to Investment and Resource Holdings SA, dated before the sale, and notarised." He ferreted in his briefcase and flicked a document across the table towards Mazin. "And thirdly, I recall you offering a bribe but you will recall it wasn't accepted. You still have the drafts, made out to 'cash', in your possession."

"So there you are, Mazin," I told him cheerfully. "Look on the bright side, you haven't lost everything after all. You still have - what is it Brian? - $470,000 left. You can buy a semi-detached in Bognor Regis for that, and still have a few dollars left to keep you in your old age!"

I thought Mazin was going to split at the seams, but with a huge effort he kept control. He knew now that he had been tricked and that his bearer shares were in our hands.

"I'll tell Antoniades about this," he rasped, gritting his teeth, "and he'll repay the loan and pay the commission to me if I tell him to."

"Not a very sensible thing to do that, is it? Once Antoniades knows that Pantocrator have been nominated then he doesn't need you - and a dispute over who owns what would be just the excuse he needed to avoid paying anybody. Anyway there are binding legal agreements, enforceable in law, between IRH and Pantocrator. He's not going to pay you on your say so, and risk IRH suing him for another $10 million is he?"

I turned to Hugo and Brian and observed. "You know it might be worthwhile somebody going over to Geneva to see Dr Otto

Weber to find out just what Investment and Resource Holdings does own?"

The mention of Dr Weber's name was the crunch point for Mazin. The fact that we knew of him collapsed any remaining resistance he had. His shoulders slumped and he suddenly looked ten years older. He was beaten and he knew it. There was no way out of the trap he had constructed for others and walked right into it himself. The old saying 'He who diggeth a pit shall fall therein' couldn't have been more apt. The bearer shares had finished him. Moon knew, or had guessed that IRH owned everything he had, and he knew Weber would act precisely in accordance with the law and take instructions only from whomsoever presented the certificate in person.

"Alright, what do you want?" he groaned out savagely.

Hugo was a gentleman and therefore kind to animals. He considered him levelly and measured his reply.

Me, I would have said, 'Want! Want! We don't want anything except for you to disappear and never darken our door again'. I think I could have kept him on the run for a long time yet.

I hadn't told Mazin about Zoe, and how she'd phoned me to tell me about his £5000 proposal that she spy on me. That had backfired on him as well! I told her that he'd never pay up anyway, and she could put it to the test by phoning him and telling him she'd learned, from me, that we were pinning all our hopes on him repaying us by bringing a bank draft to today's meeting. He'd told her that her information was useless, and she could whistle if she thought he was going to cough up five grand for that - or words to that effect. I chuckled at the thought, and chuckled again at the other thought that she was coming to Portugal with me for the weekend.

I suddenly realised that I was the focus of everyone's attention; obviously chuckling was not appropriate for the occasion.

"Sorry," I apologised to Hugo, "it was just a thought. Carry on."

"That's very kind of you," he said testily, before turning back to Mazin.

"Fortunately for you, Al Jabril, we are not thieves like someone not a million miles from where I sit. We have drafted out a deal that returns to us all the money you stole - plus interest: compensates us, and others, for the hardship you have caused; reduces your extortionate commission from Pantocrator to an acceptable level: and acknowledges that you stole money that didn't belong to you. You, of course, will sign it and your signature will be witnessed by two independent persons. All that will keep you out of our hair, and mischief, until this project is completed. There will be no argument about this and eventually you will get back what is yours.

"I can't say it's been a pleasure doing business with you because it hasn't, but today does make up for a lot. May I bid you farewell and suggest that you attend these offices next Monday at 10.30 to formalise things."

"Tuesday," I chipped in. "I can't do Monday."

"Right. Tuesday, Mr Al Jabril."

With that Hugo and Brian gathered up their things and walked out.

I was a little slower and collected my few bits of paper into a small pile. Mazin looked as if he'd been hit by a train. I don't think he could believe what had happened to him. I reached over and whipped the Bridge Holdings Limited share certificate from under his nose, and added it to my pile. He made no protest, just stood up, collected his coat and headed out of the door without another word.

At Mazin's appearance through the office entrance the chauffeur hastily pinched out his cigarette, wafted away the residual smoke and rushed round the car to open the door. He needn't have bothered. The zombie-like state that Mazin was in rendered him impervious to what was happening in the outside world. The chauffeur couldn't believe the transformation that had happened to his master in so short a time. He had entered the building brisk and smart, all cocky and strutty, arrogance and confidence oozing from every pore; and exited it crushed and crumpled up like an old cigarette packet, looking ten years older, his face grey under its tan and shoulders bowed as if under a great burden.

He managed to catch the mumbled instruction of, "Back to the apartment," before Mazin collapsed into the soft leather seat at the back of the Mercedes.

By the time they reached Edgware Mansions Mazin had managed to pull himself together, his sharp brain was starting to tick over again measuring up all the angles.

He threw his coat at Ahmed and told him to bring thick black Turkish coffee, "and get a move on," whilst he went to his desk and took out his telephone book. His first reaction was to telephone Ahmed Marzouk, his lawyer, and he reached for the phone. Then a spark of caution flickered in his brain staying his hand. If he told Marzouk what had happened to him then another person would know that he had been well and truly stitched up by CONDES. Marzouk was a Jordanian Arab, and Mazin was under no illusions that their relationship to date had been one of sweetness and light, it wouldn't be long before Marzouk told somebody else in the Arab community of Mazin's travails, and before you could say Allah Akbar the story would be all round the Middle East.

That would be fatal. He would never be taken seriously again. He would be a laughing stock, and his brother, the high and mighty Minister, would exult in his discomfort. No, if he wanted legal advice, it had to be obtained from somebody who didn't know him or anything about him, and had no Arab contacts. That was going to be difficult, it would require some careful thought, and he only had until Tuesday before he would be forced to sign that accursed document admitting that he was a crook and a thief.

He glanced round the beautifully furnished apartment seeking divine inspiration and it came, but not in the form he was hoping for. It suddenly dawned on him that it was no longer his apartment. That swine Moon had made it quite clear that they knew that the apartment, and its contents, were not owned by him but by Investment and Resource Holdings. A spasm of terror gripped his bowels, they would throw him out into the street, Moon had hinted as much, and take all his beautiful furniture and artefacts for themselves.

Anger flared up in his heart. Well for a start he could thwart that idea. He got a momentary flash of pleasure as he thought how he could frustrate their gloating over his treasures. He would send all the valuable items to his brother in Sharjah for safe keeping, and the sooner he did it the better in case Moon, Elmes, or that tricky little bastard of a trustee, what was his name - Mason - moved in. He reached for the phone book again and thumbed through quickly to 'Packers and Removals (Overseas)'. Selecting a firm at random he began to phone and get quotes for so much a crate, packed and shipped from London to Sharjah. When he was satisfied he had a competitive price he gave instructions to the selected firm for them to come round immediately to begin. He promised that if they brought the contract with them, and covered the insurance, he would sign up and pay them their deposit. That done he sat back with at least a small feeling of satisfaction that he had managed to score a point however small.

He looked round his lovely apartment again and depression flooded over him. He couldn't help savouring all the rich tapestries and wall hangings embroidered with gold thread; the finest silk carpets from Shiraz and Isfahan scattered on the floors, with the tiniest hand-tied knots that could only be done by the fingers of 6 year old children; the cabinets with their contents of gleaming silver swords and daggers with filigree handles from Saudi Arabia and Oman; the Indian tables inlaid with fine marble and gold and the original oil paintings of Arab horsemen in full dress, thundering in clouds of dust across the stony desert. Doubts began to surface about the wisdom of sending these to his brother. His brother had always envied Mazin's possessions, and more so when he had stayed at the apartment, but he was the only safe haven out of the clutches of Moon and Elmes that he could think of at such short notice.

He brushed aside these doubts, there were much more important things to concentrate on if he was to survive. The first thing was to get those bank drafts for cash into his private London account. Then he must go to Geneva to see if he could prevail upon Dr Weber to give him access to IRH's assets. He thought about going on to Athens to see Antoniades but realized that that swine Moon was right. If Antoniades sniffed a weakness he would try to cancel the agency deal and hang on to the $4 million.

All this would have to be handled very carefully and discreetly, Elmes and Moon wouldn't expect him to roll over and lie down, they would expect some wriggling but, if they found out what he was up to and he failed, they might change their minds, and, despite what Elmes had said about returning to him what was his, that was only if he toed the line.

He cast desperately about for other options. His bluff to the trustee about Arab terrorist funds and the dire consequences of reneging on him had been called in spades so there was no mileage left there - or was there? He contemplated the idea of kidnapping someone and holding them to ransom until he got his bearer shares back. But who? One of Elme's children or his wife? Or Moon? Moon was a much more attractive idea, the idea of having Moon in his power and all the nasty tortures he could inflict upon him cheered him up a little; but then he realised that he would be the prime suspect for any kidnap, and the idea of spending 20 years in an English pokey damped his enthusiasm for that course of action.

He drummed his fingers on the desk, this line of thought threw up something else that he had neglected. He realized that if there was a weakness in CONDES it was Elmes. Elmes was a typical English gentleman, a person where honour and trust still meant everything - and to Mazin that was a weakness. Moon was clever. If Moon had thought up this plan, as Elmes had indicated, then Mazin begrudgingly, had to acknowledge that fact. The other fellow, Mason, was no fool either. He had completely taken in Mazin, when posing as a trustee. No, if he was going to work on somebody it must be Elmes. Calling him a stinking pile of dung from a rabid pig had not been the best of starts, he acknowledged that, but an appeal to Elme's British sense of fair play could work.

"Ahmed! You lazy dog, get yourself in here now." And when the quivering servant appeared, Mazin told him to book the first flight to Geneva tomorrow morning, returning the same afternoon. Also to get the car round to the entrance immediately. He then phoned Dr Weber's office and made an appointment to see the lawyer for 11.30 the following day. He refused to say what it was for, only that it was a personal matter.

Checking that he had the bank drafts secure in his slim crocodile skin briefcase, he headed for the door.

In the meantime, after Mazin had departed our space, Hugo, Brian and I started to work on the sort of agreement we intended that he should sign. Hugo had given him an indication of the terms but, although Mazin was given the impression otherwise, we hadn't actually given it much thought, preferring to await the outcome of the meeting.

"I think that you gave him the gist of it, Hugo, so let's start by drafting out clauses that cover those points. He accepts that he stole the money in the first place. That nails him if we were to go to the police about it. He agrees to repay all the money he stole plus interest compounded at, say, 15%. He agrees financial compensation - of what?" I looked at them questioningly.

Brian said, "I think that should include all the additional expenses we, and the others, incurred in having to refinance everything with the banks; all our legal and accountant's fees; all the time everybody spent on sorting out the mess at full charge-out rates: my salary and overheads that you had to pay to the bank and a lump sum to cover miscellaneous office costs."

"So how much is that?" Hugo enquired.

Brian picked up his calculator and made a few calculations. "I reckon that comes to the best part of £250,000 or $400,000."

Hugo made an addition on his pad. "With the interest, that comes to $3,450,000. And what has he paid for Bridge Holdings Limited?"

"£2,156,000, which equates to approximately $3,450,000!" said Brian.

"Eureka! So we got it right then, with our estimate!" smiled Hugo. "We owe him nothing and he owes us nothing. We can concentrate on the job and keeping him out of our hair. He paused for a second. "Now we know we've got everything back we could ease up on him a bit. Surely what he gets from Pantocrator is not our business?"

"Hugo," I said grimly, "It is CONDES who have nominated Pantocrator; we have appointed what would be seen as Mazin's company as our agent: and that company is ripping off the World Bank to the tune of millions of dollars. What do you think the World Bank would deduce from that if they found out?"

He looked shocked. "But we're not getting a penny!"

"There are nasty, suspicious people out there, Hugo, who might not believe it. If they didn't, we could write off any more World Bank work forever." I continued. "The bank will accept that a reasonable commission is paid, because they are worldly wise enough to know that that is how business is done in the Middle East, but not Mazin's extortionate rate."

Hugo conceded the point and agreed that Mazin should undertake to limit his commission to 3%, and that we would cut Pantocrator's figure accordingly in the contract documents.

"Is there anything else?" I asked, and when they shook their heads I said, "Well in that case, after Janet or Margaret has typed out the draft, I'll fax it over to Parker, Parker, Son and Parker, our solicitors, for them to cast an eye over it and draw up a watertight agreement. I'll go over and see them myself tomorrow to make sure they get on with it."

It was not an encounter that I looked forward to with eager anticipation as I paid off the taxi in The Temple and entered the gloomy portals of their offices. Young Mr Parker was dealing with it, and I was told to await the summons into his presence. In the meantime I was seated on the same horsehair stuffed Victorian bum-numbing chair as I had had the last time I was in those premises. Nothing had changed. There was the same brown carpet, brown walls, brown furniture, and dusty brown files. The same beefy receptionist, with the Buster Brown haircut, 5 o'clock shadow and tweeds, glared at me from behind her desk. I jumped in the air as a buzzer sounded behind my left ear. "Young Mr Parker will see you now," she rasped, and then turned back to shuffling yet more brown files.

Young Mr Parker hadn't changed either, in fact I don't think he had moved, except perhaps to be dusted every now and then. At least this time he appeared to be alive. He was studying my fax with his cold pink rheumy eyes. A claw-like hand motioned me to a chair, the twin of the one in the reception.

"It's a bit one-sided," he observed in his thin dry voice.

Of course it's bloody one-sided, I thought, that's the whole idea, and it's not supposed to be 'a bit one-sided', it's supposed to be 100% one-sided - in our favour.

"Yes!" I said. "But as you will appreciate we are dealing, here with a crook who has no scruples whatsoever, and if there was the slightest chink in this agreement he would be through it and away like a ferret up a pump. We wouldn't want that to happen!"

He got the message instantly and his gaze narrowed as he thought about his professional indemnity insurance premiums.

"I see," he murmured. "Well we mustn't allow that to happen, must we?"

I waited whilst he tapped his fingers on the desk and then appeared to reach a decision. He reached into a file and extracted a few sheets of paper.

"I've drafted something out on the lines I think you need." He pushed them across the desk towards me, leaving a trail of dust.

I read them through carefully. It was all there, everything we had requested but put into lawyers' speak. I re-read it, it was very good; simple but to the point. I had to hand it to him, dry and slow he may appear but he knew his stuff. This would stitch Mazin up so tight that he'd be lucky to breathe without whistling.

"Excellent," I said, as I handed it back. "Can you let us have the engrossment by Monday evening please?

He nodded and pressed a button on his desk. Buster Brown, now acting as chucker-out showed up, and I hit the pavement at the run.

Friday dawned a bright, sunny, crisp morning, the sun sparkling on the windows of the apartments on Cheyne Walk as I drove across Albert Bridge on to the Embankment. I swung the MG into a space between the wall and the rubbish skip. Unusually for me I was the first car in the office car park. I didn't beat the Major in however, she was pottering round her office humming quietly to herself and doing a bit of filing. She looked up with a start when I called, "Good Morning Margaret! Lovely day today! Are you doing anything this weekend?"

It was only meant as a courtesy question as I wandered past her to my bolthole, but it brought a flood of colour to her cheeks and she turned hastily away.

"Nothing special," she replied off-handedly. "As you are away on Monday I thought we...I might spend it in the country somewhere."

The flush returned again in spades. She was as bad as 'Just Sam' for generating heat. I was intrigued, had my little subterfuge started to bear fruit? There must be something interesting behind this. The question was; did I want to know what it was? Too bloody right I did! I hadn't gone to all that trouble for nothing! Margaret knew I was off to Portugal for... well I don't know if she knew exactly what for, but I did! So what was she up to? Had Richard come up trumps? I looked at her. Nice make-up that softened her jaw line, hair done professionally, smart blouse and skirt showing off her figure and jewellery that I hadn't seen before. A gold bracelet and gold earrings. She was aware of my scrutiny and that I was drawing conclusions so, calling on her army training that attack is the best form of defence, she snapped, "You're not the only one who can have some fun at the weekend. Richard and I are going to Stratford. He's booked to see Richard III at the Royal Shakespeare Theatre!"

"Well I hope you have a wonderful time and the weather holds for you," I told her, and then drifted through to my chair, thinking that things seemed to be cooking nicely all round. A bit of pre-marital Shakespeare might work wonders.

The remainder of the Sharjah Steel documents went off to the printers on Friday morning with Pantocrator's price reduced by the deduction we had made from Mazin's commission. There being nothing more that required doing urgently, I went home at lunch-time to pack for the weekend.

I wondered what Mazin was up to. It was a sure fire bet that he would contact Dr Weber but, as Brian had been to Geneva on Wednesday afternoon, he would be wasting his time. Brian had reported that Dr Weber had asked no questions. On presentation of the bearer shares, he had accepted Brian's right to give instructions with regard to Investment and Resource Holdings SA, and merely asked Brian what his instructions were. Brian had asked for a schedule of all IRH's assets, and requested that this be faxed to CONDES by Monday lunchtime.

One other thing had come up. Dr Weber had told him that as his fees hadn't been paid for over a year, he would be obliged if they could be settled now; and he had produced his bill. The implication was: no fees, no schedule. Brian had to make a quick decision, and immediately scribbled on the bill Weber's authority to withdraw that amount from IRH's bank account. That would help to keep Weber sweet.

Mazin's flight from Heathrow was delayed for three hours by a lightning strike of French air-traffic controllers, so it was 1.30 by the time the cab deposited a hot, flustered and very pissed-off Arab outside Weber's grey stone offices. The receptionist told him Dr Weber had gone to a Chamber of Commerce lunch and would not be back that afternoon.

Gritting his teeth he asked if there was anybody else who he could see, or could she give him Weber's mobile phone number.

"No!" she said, in accordance with her instructions from Dr Weber before he departed.

Mazin persisted. "It's vital I see somebody, I've been robbed."

"Well go to the police," she responded, "we don't do criminal law here."

"You don't understand," he ground out, "it's to do with Investment and Resource Holdings."

The receptionist froze rigid with shock. "I do not discuss with strangers anything about anything in this firm. If you wish to make an appointment please telephone, otherwise good day to you," she snapped and turned away to her computer.

Mazin was left standing there glaring at her back with his thumb up his bum and his mind in neutral. His only hope vanished because of the French. Silently he cursed them, the Swiss, the English, the Scots and anybody else he could think of, before finally accepting defeat and trudging out of the door to find a cab to take him back to the airport.

We met at Victoria Station at 5.25 on Friday afternoon. Zoe looked wonderful and seemed very relaxed and cheerful. She gave me a big kiss and a hug. "I've never been away on a dirty weekend before," she said with an impish grin. "It's my first, so what do we do? An experienced seducer like you will have to guide me into the ways of wickedness."

"Well," I said, looking down the station, "the first thing we have to do is run like hell before the train leaves without us, and when I get my breath back I'll fill in the rest for you!"

We sprinted down the platform, and to an angry shout from the guard, just managed to drag open a door on the Gatwick Express and pile in with our bags.

Collapsing with laughter we found ourselves a couple of seats side by side, and settled down for the half-hour run to the airport.

The British Airways flight to Faro was on time and, having cleared immigration and customs without any trouble, I picked up the rental car and we set off for the Dona Filipa Hotel.

It was late when we finally hit the door of our suite and dumped the bags. Neither of us had touched the meal on the plane and we were ravenous.

I phoned room service. Zoe ordered a crab salad and grilled sardines; I asked for gambas and a baked fish of some kind, two bottles of Crystal champagne and some bottled water.

That task being completed we grinned at each other knowingly. "We'd better wait till the food comes," she said, raising a warning finger, "we wouldn't want to cause the waiter any embarrassment. Let's go and have a quick wander round."

I can tell you that it's very difficult to eat gambas and drink champagne pressed against a warm nubile body in the shower, and I'm sure, if you asked her, Zoe would tell you the same about crab salad - but it was fun.

The sun shone on us the whole weekend, both literally and emotionally. I hadn't enjoyed myself like that ever. We lazed on the beach: swam in the sea; rode horses - I fell off - and got teased mercilessly for it; went water skiing - she fell off - and got teased similarly by me. We ate grilled fish and hot bread with our fingers in beach cafes; drank litres of the crisp local white wine; nibbled the area's marzipan specialities; danced in the light of the moon, and made love, morning, noon and night.

We parted outside Victoria Station just before lunchtime on Monday, having arranged to meet on Wednesday evening. She headed back to her flat but I went straight to the office. I wanted to get an update - if there was one - on the Al Jabril saga.

The Major was at her desk humming happily to herself with a sparkle in her eye. She coloured up violently when I breezed in. Ah Hah! So her weekend had gone well, Richard must have done his stuff - whatever it was! I decided not to mention it. If she wanted to bring it up - fine, but I thought it tactful to say nothing.

"Hi, Margaret, have a good bonk?" was what I wanted to know, but "Hi Margaret, what a lovely morning," was what came out, fortunately!

"Yes indeed, it really looks as though spring is on its way," she trilled happily. "Did you enjoy Portugal?"

I grinned. I suppose 'Did you enjoy Portugal' and 'what a lovely morning' were just the same as 'did you have a good bonk'! And the answer was a resounding yes in my case, and, from the colour of her face, the same went for her.

"I did indeed. Some wonderful architecture and scenery, beautiful hills and valleys," I replied, trying to keep a fairly straight face as I headed into my office.

"Brian wanted to see you as soon as you came in," she called after me, "shall I tell him you're here?"

He beat her to it and came in waving a fax from Dr Weber. "It's all here; everything that Al Jabril has is owned by Investment and Resource Holdings SA," he exclaimed excitedly. "It looks like we've hit the jackpot!"

I took it from him and scanned it. Apart from his agency deal with Pantocrator, he had two other big agencies, one with an Italian contracting company and one with a Japanese liquefied petroleum gas importer. However those were of no interest to us, it was the cash and property that I wanted to learn about. There was his loan agreement for $4 million with Pantocrator, $1 million cash on 28-day deposit with automatic roll-over; property worth $5.75 million, of which his London apartment was over $3 million, and at least another $1 million in various bank accounts. There were also various works of art, antiques and other bric-a-brac nearly all of which were in his London pad. No value was put on these.

"Has Hugo seen this?" I asked Brian.

He nodded, "I showed it to him as soon as it arrived from Weber."

"Let's go and see him then. We may have to make some changes in Mazin's draft agreement. Parker, Parker, Son and Parker are supposed to be sending the final document round by courier later this afternoon so, if we are to change anything, the sooner the better."

In the event we decided not to change anything, just to leave it simple, covering only the repayment of our money with interest and compensation and his acknowledgement that he stole it in the first place. We removed any reference to Pantocrator to avoid any claim that there could be any connection between this agreement and the holder of the bearer shares in IRH.

All that was left was to await the entry of the demon king tomorrow.

CHAPTER TWENTY

It was a very subdued Mazin Al Jabril who turned up in our conference room at 10.30, the barging, bounce and bluster he usually exhibited were all the more conspicuous by their absence.

Hugo, Brian and I were waiting for him as he trudged in playing the 'old soldier with the war wound' - or shell shock perhaps. It was brilliant; I couldn't help a touch of admiration for his act. It really tugged at the heartstrings.

Three copies of Parker, Parker, Son and Parker's engrossed agreement were spread out on the conference table awaiting his signature. Major Margaret, still blooming like a dahlia just opened to the summer sun, and a young lawyer from Parker's office very nervous and twitchy in her shadow, hovered in the wings ready to do the witnessing.

We assumed that he would turn up with his lawyer, the black finger-nailed Ahmed Marzouk, but he came solo. I guessed that he thought the fewer people who knew about his stuffing and nailing to the floor the better - especially in the Arab world. That was fine by me. I couldn't see any advantage in spreading the word - unless he stepped out of line.

Hugo greeted him with a courteous, "Good Morning Al Jabril," and motioned him to a chair opposite Brian and me. He sat down warily. He was still turned out like a tailor's dummy. Plain grey

Gieves and Hawkes single-breasted suit, Turnbull and Asser striped shirt, Herbie Frogg tie and highly polished black shoes from Lobb, but there was a crushed air about him, a wariness. A question flickered briefly in his eyes as he noted the three copies of the agreement spread out on the table.

Brian helped him out. "One for you, one for us, and one for our lawyers, to be held in a vault by them in case...!"

"In case of what?" growled Mazin.

"In case of eventualities," I snapped. "We're not stupid, Mazin, although you appear to think so. Just because we play it straight doesn't mean we don't realise what you are up to. We know you went to Geneva last Thursday. No doubt since then you have been turning every which way to try to worm your way out of signing this agreement - and the fact that you are here shows you have failed so far. But, knowing you, you will continue to try and wheedle your way out of it, notwithstanding the fact that you will have signed it."

I paused for a second, holding his gaze.

"Therefore let me paint a picture for you so that there is no misunderstanding. From now on, we, that is the whole firm and our families, are holding you personally responsible for any misadventure that may befall any of us at any time. If Brian is stung by a bee we will assume it has been trained by you to attack. You might think that, through your dubious Middle East contacts, a bit of violence or kidnapping would bring us to our knees, or a convenient fire in our offices would destroy our copy of the agreement. Well the third copy is to prevent that. Parkers will store it in a secure vault, and, at the first sign of trouble, they have been instructed to publish it far and wide, and hand a copy to the Director of Public Prosecutions."

I saw Hugo blink at that but he stayed silent, because that wasn't quite true, we didn't actually want Mazin clapped in jail for a bee sting but, if he was to get the message, he wasn't to know that!

Looking a bit green around the gills because we had read his mind, he decided that now was the time to play his last card. It was quite clever really, seeking to obtain confirmation, in front of witnesses, that we did hold his bearer shares, he growled offhandedly.

"What about my bearer shares?"

Brian replied lifting an eyebrow quizzically. "What bearer shares are those?"

"Weber knows that I held those shares, he can testify to that."

Brain said coolly, "He now knows that you don't, but he doesn't know whether you sold them, gave them away or traded them for something else, so what would his testimony be worth?"

I gave a tight smile and watched his eyes. I thought he would flare up again and denounce Brian, accusing him of cheating, fraud and whatever but astonishingly he did no such thing. He reached over and picked up a copy of the agreement and began to read it.

We watched him in silence, waiting. He latched onto the interesting point immediately and addressed Hugo.

"It says here that you are prepared to consider any reasonable request that I might make to ease any financial burden that I may face. What does that mean?"

Hugo looked at me and I just shrugged. We had discussed this. Angry as we were at Mazin's thievery and deceit, our objects were to recover our money, get a fair price for Sharjah Steel for our client and prevent Mazin from screwing us in the future. Hugo made the telling point that, tempting as though it was for a little revenge, we didn't need to hamstring him, or ruin what other devious business deals he may have set up, as long as we maintained a firm grip around his throat. I deferred to Hugo's pragmatic approach that we should ease up on him a little. Hugo said, "Well, Al Jabril, for instance if you were to suggest that it might be beneficial to stay in your apartment, and keep all the furniture and artefacts, we might well support that suggestion. It wouldn't do for people to think that CONDES' agent was a man of straw would it?"

We goggled in astonishment at his reaction to this. From pale green he went through bright pink to regal purple. The veins stood out on his neck like leeches and his eyes bulged like bull's-eye glass in a cake shop window. He couldn't speak for several moments. We watched this metamorphosis in amazement. We didn't know then that he had sent all his precious furniture, paintings, sculptures and other treasures to his brother in Sharjah, and he was now realizing that there was no chance whatsoever of his covetous brother returning them. The IKEA, MFI and Homebase replacements that he had sent Ahmed out to buy were what he would have to live with from henceforth.

He managed to drag himself back under control. "What about my agency fee?" he ground out.

"IRH's agency fee," Hugo reminded him. "Well I think if you requested an income along those lines from IRH we would support it and they may be sympathetic."

"And Pantocrator," he spat.

"Ah yes," mused Hugo, tugging gently at one ear. "As we told you, there have been some changes to those arrangements. We have faxed Pantocrator telling them that IRH has agreed to reduce its commission to 3% and they must reduce their price by an equal amount. Antoniades has faxed back confirming this, and the reduced price has been incorporated in the contract documents." He beamed at Mazin. "Still, from IRH's point of view 3% of $80 million is $2.4 million - a fair return don't you think?"

He obviously didn't. His facial colour went back through the spectrum from purple through pink to green again. He swallowed heavily as he realized that even when he was paid his commission in full he was not going to make any money out of Sharjah Steel at all.

In fact he would lose money and the irony of it struck me at the same time. Mazin had paid out $3,450,000 for Bridge Holdings Limited and would only get $2,400,000 from Pantocrator, plus the $400,000 from us as his agency fee. Out of that he would have to pay his brother, the Minister, a big slice. I wondered if the Minister knew what Mazin's original percentage was. If so, Mazin was in deep shit right up to his eyeballs. I couldn't help a chuckle escaping as I thought of Mazin trying to explain to his sceptical brother, why his share had been dramatically reduced.

This little interplay had escaped Hugo, he was just winding up to his final serious peroration and my chuckle was not deemed appropriate to the occasion. He gave me a slight frown before continuing. Looking straight at Mazin he said quietly, "We have told you, Al Jabril, that we are not thieves. Everything that is yours will be returned to you in due course. All your other nefarious deals are your own affair but the monies will be collected into IRH and accumulated there unless you request a distribution. I suggest that you address your requests to Dr Weber in writing. I imagine that there are other people whom you have to pay off, like your brother, and Dr Weber will consult with the appropriate authority to arrange for money to be made available for that purpose. All this, of course, provided we always have your fullest cooperation!"

I was watching Mazin closely, and whereas this still held him in thrall, I could see that his mind was racing to calculate what he could get away with. It was not significant to us anyway, it was his money, so whether he got 20% this way, or 50%, we still had the whip hand.

Hugo pushed all three copies of the agreement across the table towards Mazin and beckoned Major Margaret and the legal eagle to come forward. "Please sign where the crosses are, and put your full name, address and passport number underneath, where indicated."

There was a moment's hesitation as Mazin realised that this was it. This was the irrevocable step to bondage. If he didn't sign he would be ruined - a pauper and a laughing stock. If he did sign - well there was a chance of something. So he took out his golden fountain pen and, with a flourish, signed and completed all three copies. The witnesses did their bit and each party received their copy.

"What now?" he asked with a sneer, as he slid his pen back into an inside pocket.

"Well, that completes the business, so now, we go away, and we'll be in touch in due course - if we need you," said Hugo rising to his feet and pushing his chair back. He didn't offer his hand to Mazin. Brian and I followed suit, and all three of us, with the two witnesses, walked out of the room back to Hugo's office where a cold glass of champagne awaited us, leaving Mazin to make his own way out.

I didn't see him again for three months. In fact, it was the beginning of July when he telephoned and suggested that we had lunch. I knew what he wanted, he wanted to know if Pantocrator had signed their contract, and more importantly, got their large down payment so that his $4 million could be repaid.

A lot of water had passed under the bridge since he last departed our environs. I can't honestly say that we had missed him. The detail design work on Sharjah Steel had kept to the programme; Pantocrator's fabrication schedule was being met; the World Bank had received some very competitive bids from international contractors; our fees were being paid regularly, and Jenkins at the bank was delighted with the cash flow. All in all, things were going unusually smoothly at work without us having to perpetually look over our shoulders to see what the devious Al Jabril was conjuring up.

Major Margaret and Richard were still going strong, she had even trundled him along to the firm's summer party. He seemed a decent enough chap, a bit on the timid side and two stones overweight, but I suppose that was all right. You can't have two commanding officers and already she was knocking him into shape. 'Richard, come here and meet my boss, Marcus! Richard, my glass is empty! Richard, don't drink too much, you're driving!' He just smiled and trotted off to do her bidding, seemingly quite happy and content to have his life organized for him.

I had sold my flat in Palmerston Mansions, added the money to my long delayed share-out from the money Mazin had paid Trust Services for Bridge Holdings Limited and in turn added that to the money Zoe got for the sale of her flat, and we had moved into our own, mortgage-free, four bedroomed terraced house in Chelsea. We were just in the process of having some alterations done, putting in new bathrooms and a new kitchen before finally furnishing it.

Andy King-Knight, although he was still a pompous prat, had done us proud in finding quick sales for our properties and a good bargain for our new house. Kate had returned from America a couple of months ago and she and Andy had just announced their engagement. In fact, this evening Zoe and I were just off to the engagement party. As she drove to the Hurlingham Club, where the party was to be held, I considered yet again how I could have blown the whole Mazin set-up by talking too much. I leaned over and gave her a kiss. She didn't have a clue what for, but I did.

The Marcus Moon series...

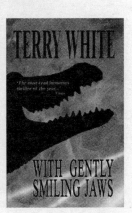

D'Arcy Lyell carefully measured a dose of Oral Fresh into a glass and rinsed out his mouth. Taking the flower-painted tin from the bathroom cabinet he dusted his balls with Lady Penelope Redolence's Rose-Scented Talcum Powder then carefully eased into his mother's favourite dress. He noted that the fit wasn't as tight these days since he had lost weight, and the zip slid easily up the side. Moving into the large drawing room he took the black velvet opera cloak from where it lay across the back of the chaise longue and knotted it around his shoulders. After a glance in the mirror to check that all was as he wanted it, he stepped through the open French window.

I read about it in the *Daily Mail* the following day; page four was full of lurid shots of him being scraped off the pavement by the paramedics – well, you don't bounce much from six floors up when you follow Icarus to eternity, even wearing an opera cloak. Apparently Ricky had been arrested on suspicion of murder, but the press had no doubt it was suicide.

My first reaction was how would Charlie take this? She had no affection for Lyell these days, but she would feel some responsibility, it was inevitable; she was that sort of person. I would have to handle this very carefully. I felt a pang of remorse that he had got himself into this state but annoyed that his action would upset her.

A selfish bastard to the end, was my uncharitable thought as I slung my bag into the passenger seat of the old MG and hit the starter. And how had this come about, I reflected as I set a course through the morning traffic to the office.

READ ON... GET YOUR COPY TODAY!

Available from Amazon.co.uk, Amazon.com, eBook for Kindle and via all good bookshops

ALSO AVAILABLE FROM INDEPENPRESS...

Blind Trust
Red Széll
£7.99
978-1-78003-160-6

Also available in large print
£12.88
978-1-78003-204-7

As featured on BBC Radio 4

On the face of it, househusband Joe Wynde has it all - apart from his sight. Robbed of 90% of his vision by a degenerative eye disorder, Joe's goals, are simple: to raise his two sassy daughters properly while avoiding close physical contact with street furniture and bored banker's wives.

Compared to the lifestyles of his wealthy neighbours this may seem unglamorous, but with financial crisis rocking the City, some of them are going to discover just how exposed they are.

When Joe is falsely accused of driving a fellow stay-at-home dad to suicide, he turns to unrequited old flame Miranda Lethbridge for support. A journalist with a keen nose for local gossip, she smells a conspiracy, which draws them into a web of illicit affairs and blackmail amidst London's wealthy elite.

A racket others will protect at all costs.

Blind Trust is a slow-burning thriller providing a unique insight into the world of those deprived of their major sense, while casting a wry glance at the nature of wealth.

Red Széll spent his youth devouring green Penguins. Graduating into a recession, he began working life in a hospital mortuary, saved hard and escaped to London to pursue his dream of journalistic greatness. Before failing eyesight halted his progress he had scaled the dizzying foothills to the post of Debutantes' Correspondent for The Evening Standard. A boring decade of sending oil and tunnelling engineers to dodgy parts of the globe followed. Salvation came in 2000 when he 'gave up work' to become a househusband.

Blind Trust is his first novel.

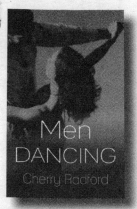

ABOUT THE AUTHOR

Terry White worked in the UK and the Middle East for many years as a Consultant Civil Engineer.

He has experienced the whole gamut of doing business in those areas. His books feature oil sheikhs and oligarchs; con men and capitalists; friends and lovers.

Very funny and perceptive, they take a scathing look at the procedures, practices and people involved where vast sums of money are a driving force. They are a must read!

Although still a Yorkshireman at heart, Terry now lives on the lovely island of Guernsey.

www.terrywhitebooks.co.uk